MW00791450

Too Good to Be True

KRISTEN ASHLEY

ROCK CHICK
PRESS

This book is a work of fiction. Any reference to historical events, real people, or real places are used fictitiously. Other names, characters, places, and incidents are products of the author's imagination. Any resemblance to actual events, locales, or persons, living or dead, is coincidental.

Copyright© 2023 by Kristen Ashley

All rights reserved, including the right to reproduce this book or portions thereof in any form whatsoever. In accordance with the U.S. Copyright Act of 1976, the scanning, uploading, and electronic sharing of any part of this book without the permission of the publisher is unlawful piracy and theft of the author's intellectual property. Thank you for your support of the author's rights. If you would like to use material from this book (other than for review purposes), prior written permission must be obtained. Please address Rock Chick Press, 4340 East Indian School Road, Suite 21-413, Phoenix, Arizona, 85016, USA.

Cover Image: Pixel Mischief Design

A MURDER MYSTERY ROMANCE

Too Good to be True

One

DUNCROFT

"This makes me nervous," Lou declared.

I didn't know how to reply because I found what she said odd.

Though, thinking about it, perhaps not too odd.

Portia wasn't Lou's biggest fan, she hadn't been since the very beginning. Even I was surprised my little sister asked Lou to spend this week in the country at the family home of Portia's boyfriend.

Me? Yes.

The older sister. The only sibling. It made sense.

Portia and I had our times of strife (a lot of them), but like she always had her father's devotion, she always wanted her big sister's approval.

When Lou came along, she took some of the former, which was why Portia had never accepted Lou as part of our family. Dad had spoiled Portia, and when he took some attention from his youngest in order to shower Lou with his brand of love, Portia wasn't happy.

As for my approval, it wasn't often forthcoming, mainly because Portia didn't often make decisions I approved of.

I wasn't the stuffy older sister.

Portia was the mischievous younger one.

According to me.

Also according to me, that description was being nice.

In other words, Portia could often be a pain in my ass.

Lou's invitation to this week in the countryside? The much-younger third wife of our now deceased father? A wife Portia had butted heads with for the last decade?

That made no sense at all.

Due to this, Lou feeling nervous wasn't odd...as such.

However, she'd been a member of our family for a long time. She'd sat vigil at Dad's deathbed right alongside Portia and me. And Portia knew I wouldn't be thrilled if she cut Lou out of something as important as a meet-the-family with a man who Portia had been seeing for some months now, her longest-ever boyfriend.

So, Lou's assertion was also odd.

I glanced from navigating the narrow, winding road edged in thick hedgerows to the passenger seat where Lou was sitting, and I saw she wasn't just nervous. And it was important to note, former supermodel Louella Fernsby-Ryan didn't often get nervous, or if she did, she knew how to hide it.

No, now she looked—there was no other way to put it—*terrified*.

Any normal person might be, considering all we were heading into.

That said, Lou wasn't a normal person. She'd been hobnobbing with the rich and famous for the last twenty plus years. She was beautiful. She was confident. She'd been incredibly successful in her chosen career.

But we were to spend the next ten days at Duncroft House, the country seat of the Alcotts. That being Earl Alcott, Richard, his wife, the Countess, Jane, and Daniel, their youngest son, Portia's new beau.

Then there was Ian, their oldest, the heir to the title, who Portia told me promised to make several appearances that week, but she and Daniel were hoping he'd spend the whole week and make it a real family affair.

Yes.

And then there was Ian Alcott.

Hmm.

These folks were old-school aristocracy, and unlike many of their ilk who had lost no status but a lot of capital and assets across the centuries, they were old-school, big-time *money*.

New American big-time money didn't rub against old aristocratic money very well. It never had. And I had quite a bit of experience knowing that our progressive age hadn't changed that.

This all didn't include Duncroft House itself.

A well-known jewel in England's heritage crown. Perhaps not Buckingham, Windsor, Sandringham or Kensington caliber, but not far off.

It was supposed to be extraordinary.

And it had a notorious past.

"It's going to be okay," I told Lou.

"I don't think so," she mumbled to the window.

"Portia's grown up a lot since Dad died," I pointed out.

"Mm," Lou hummed noncommittally. As she would.

Yes, Portia had matured.

This might have had something to do with the fact that Lou and I both managed her trust. Although Portia had (even I had to admit) an insulting monthly allowance of two thousand pounds neither Lou nor I could touch, the rest of her substantial inheritance was doled out at our discretion.

Though, that discretion had instruction from Dad, and if Portia didn't stay gainfully employed, she didn't get a penny above that two grand until she managed that feat. Further, if Portia remained in a job for less than twelve months, there were strict limits set on what money was forthcoming, again, until she'd accomplished what Dad demanded. Last, if Portia got into trouble with the police, with drugs or alcohol, or with unsavory characters or dubious projects, that money was frozen.

And if this behavior didn't cease by the time Portia hit age thirty-five, Lou's and my trusts were each augmented by half of Portia's, and she received no more. Not even the two thousand.

However, if she managed to keep her shit together for five straight years, the entire trust would be at her disposal without oversight.

At first, Portia took this not as Dad intended, his way to prompt her to shape up, but instead as Dad's beyond-the-grave assertion that he loved Lou more than her.

But recently, she'd been pulling herself together.

Portia getting it together was not due to efforts from Lou. Lou wanted Portia to like her, always had from the first time we met her (that included me, but I was less of a challenge). Now, Lou was the soft touch when Portia asked for money.

No. Portia was learning to toe the line due to me being o-v-e-r *over* her antics.

Dad had given her that two thousand so she wouldn't starve because he knew I'd be a hard-ass.

And hard-ass I was.

So Portia finally seemed to be pulling it together.

And now there was Daniel Alcott.

"Have you met the Alcotts?" I asked Lou.

"I know Richard," she said in a weirdly hesitant voice.

I glanced at her again. "Well?"

"Sorry?"

"Do you know him well?"

"Not really. Met in passing at a party or a dinner here or there."

She said this, but it sounded like a question, like I could confirm she'd met Earl Alcott at a party or dinner here or there.

I didn't inquire further about that.

"Not Jane?" I asked.

"No," she murmured. "I've never met 'The Countess.'"

Yes.

"The Countess," capitalized and in quotes because this was how she was known in the media.

Jane Alcott was quite the mysterious character. Ethereally gorgeous, if the rare photo of her was anything to go by, and highly reclusive. Even when she was younger. Therefore, obviously, with beauty, a title and money, she was an object of fascination, which could explain why she was reclusive.

It was not the same with Richard. Or Daniel.

And definitely not Ian.

They weren't reclusive, and as for the two sons, they didn't shy away from the media at all.

I couldn't say Ian sought it like Daniel seemed to, but it sure sought Ian.

"Have you heard about the house?" I went on, hoping to shake her out of her mood.

"Everyone's heard about the house," she answered.

"What have you heard?"

"It's haunted." I knew she'd turned my way when she asked, "Have you heard that?"

"Yes," I said. "People tend to die there."

"It's been around for hundreds of years," she reminded me. "There was a fortress there during William the Conqueror's time, so a dwelling has been there for over a millennium. It's bound to have had a death or two."

A death or two?

"When Portia told us things were serious with Daniel and asked us to this week at Duncroft, I looked it up," I informed her. "Some pretender to the throne was tortured and killed in the castle that sat there in the thirteenth century. The torture was medieval, Lou, literally and brutally. Then they threw him in a pit and starved him to death. Apparently, the new house is built over that pit, and his bones are still there."

"Why a week?"

From the subject I was talking about, I was confused by her question. "Pardon?"

"Why not invite us for a weekend? Or if she wanted more time for us to get to know Daniel and his family, a long weekend? Or, really, starting off with us all going to dinner in London? That would be easier for everybody. Why are we here from Friday to the next Sunday? That's a long time, it's a lot to ask, it's a lot of pressure for everyone, and it's strange."

"It's Portia."

I heard Lou sigh.

Yes. The time suck. The drama.

All Portia.

"Then there was that earl's daughter in the fifteenth century who wasn't thrilled with the man her father chose for her to marry," I continued with my theme to take us from Portia's larks, which I found annoying and Lou had a lot more patience for, but they had to wear thin for her too. "So, on the eve of her wedding, she poisoned her fiancé, and not to leave them out, also poisoned her father, her mother *and* her husband-to-be's father and mother. Not exactly the Red Wedding, but the story goes that the poison she chose made them expel everything from blood and bile to unmentionables from both ends until they died. I'd call that worse than the Red Wedding...by a lot."

"It's pretty gross," Lou agreed.

"There was also that countess and her lover. I forget his name."

"Cuthbert."

I nearly smiled. Of course she knew about the fortress, the castle and Cuthbert. She'd looked it up too.

"Cuthbert," I repeated. "Found *in flagrante delicto* with the countess by the earl. They were quite into what they were doing, didn't know he'd come upon them. He had time to get hold of a dagger, and then he gutted old Cuthbert in his cuckold's bed while his wife watched in horror, before he turned the dagger on her."

"Poor Cuthbert."

"And poor Lady Joan," I added. "Her blood pooled with Cuthbert's as she bled to death beside him in that bed."

"Yes," Lou replied. "Poor Lady Joan."

"Four people have hung themselves in that house," I carried on. "At least two have died in duels in the forest surrounding it, though there could be more. After that practice was outlawed, it still went on. And then there's what happened to Dorothy Clifton in the twenties."

Lore had it that Duncroft was possessed of more than one ghost.

Dorothy Clifton, it was said, was the angriest spirit of the lot.

I could tell Lou was warming to my theme when she spoke.

Then again, I suspected she would. She was always trying to get me to cuddle up with popcorn and ice cream and watch things like *Get Out* and *The Shining* and *It*. She loved that kind of thing.

I hated it. That would be *hated* it, with a passion.

It took a while for me to love her, but eventually I did. I wasn't as ugly about it in the beginning as Portia, but Dad marrying someone I could be friends with in the manner we were actually contemporaries was not fun.

Then we became friends, and things changed.

"What I don't understand is, why the secrecy?" she asked. "From what I know, never, not once have they opened the house to the public. By invitation only. And those invitations have been scarce. Every generation, rabid privacy. It's really unusual in a heritage home in England like Duncroft."

"I know, right?"

"It's like they're hiding something."

It totally was.

"I guess we're going to find out," she noted. "Ten days there, plenty of time to see a ghost."

"Yes," I replied. "Plenty of time. Plenty of time to uncover secrets too."

"Yes," she whispered, again sounding off, and I almost didn't hear it when she finished, "Secrets."

I didn't push further on that either, though I thought it was weird, regardless of the fact I knew Lou had secrets.

We all did.

I didn't dig for hers, mostly so she would return the favor.

As for what we were soon to face, I'd caved in watching *Get Out* and *The Shining*, because they were classics and I liked films. And I would admit I thought they were both really good. I put my foot down on such as *It* and *The Ring* (and others).

But I wasn't concerned about Duncroft's supposed ghosts because I didn't believe in ghosts.

I was an avid member of the National Trust. I'd been in many a manor and castle in that country (and others). The mustiness. The draftiness. The dank darkness or shadowed corners or secret passageways. I could absolutely see how people could convince themselves they'd experienced a haunting.

But that didn't make it real.

No, I was more worried about the patrician Richard. The withdrawn Jane. The ne'er-do-well Daniel.

The womanizer Ian.

And secrets.

Theirs.

And ours.

Yes, I was more concerned about the Alcotts than about their supposedly haunted country seat.

Them and us...we were not a good mix.

Dad had moved Portia and me to England twenty years ago. Although I went home frequently for visitations with Mom—and so Portia could have some sort of mother figure, I talked Dad into letting her go with me—for all intents and purposes, we'd never left.

We were still proud Americans and the beneficiaries of massive inheritances of new money. My mother, Dad's first castoff, had been and still was a schoolteacher. Portia's mother, castoff two, had been an incorrigible gold digger.

And then there was Lou, who was only five years older than me.

This sojourn felt more like Lou and I had been called in as reinforcements for a week in the English countryside at the very famous home of a very wealthy and illustrious family.

But nevertheless, we were still outnumbered.

And if you believed in that kind of thing, outclassed.

In other words, I was feeling some anxiety too.

It didn't help that we'd left the motorway forty-five minutes ago. We'd then turned off the A road twenty minutes ago, and not onto a B road, but a coiling, thin ribbon of C road. We hadn't passed a town or village in miles. And according to the satnav, we had another twenty-six minutes on this lane, twisting through...*nothing*.

This was a long way from anything—and call me a city girl (which I was)—I didn't like it.

Lou grew quiet along with me.

And we both (for my part, since I was driving, it was intermittently) watched the arrow on the satnav glide along the snaking road as we kept track of the countdown to arrival.

It was 2:37 and we were to arrive at 3:03.

We broke out of the hedgerows at 2:55 and into rolling countryside covered in green, with vast splotches of purple heather and jutting masts of gray, lichen-covered rocks punctuated here and there by an irregular tree malformed by wind.

Add some mist and I wouldn't have been surprised to see a frock-coated Heathcliff brooding astride his horse in the distance.

At 3:00, the moor gave way to a more cultivated and arboreal landscape.

At 3:02, Duncroft House became visible.

And...*wow*.

Okay.

Maybe Buckingham and Windsor were the biggest, shiniest jewels in England's crown.

But in my opinion, Duncroft shone brightly as jewel number three.

It was beautiful.

It was huge.

It was sprawling.

And it was overpowering.

"Right. Now *I'm* nervous," I admitted.

Lou reached out and squeezed my knee.

I drove my Mercedes between the tall, black, elaborate iron gates accented copiously by gold and attached on either side to a ten-foot-tall wall made of thick Yorkstone.

We'd officially arrived at Duncroft.

And I wasn't feeling sterling thoughts.

Because the second we drove through those gates, a shiver slithered down my spine.

Two

THE PEARL ROOM

L ou took her first hit within moments of our arrival.

I'd swung the car around the drive made of carefully-edged and manicured, blond gravel to come to a stop at the bottom of the wide front steps. We'd both gotten out of the car to see a tall, handsome young man wearing crisp, khaki pants, whiter-than-white trainers, and a light-blue, long-sleeved polo shirt bounding down toward us.

We'd also gotten out to be dwarfed into insignificance by the house and to be viciously bitten by the chill of a cloudless, autumnal, northern English afternoon.

The house had four wings in a cross shape, that being the Scottish cross, diagonal. It was said, the middle intersection was where the fortress had been and under which the bones of the pretender still lay.

It was four stories tall, a mix of red brick and Yorkstone, with two turrets at the ends of each leg of the cross, eight in total, all topped with green domes of tarnished copper. The rest of the roof was dark slate. There were parts of the structure on the ground floor covered in trailing wisteria. There were enumerable peaks and chimneys and gables. And in the center flew the Union Jack, underneath it, a light-blue flag with a golden shield on it.

It was sprawling, stately, handsome, but most of all, imposing.

It was not the genteel country seat of a long-standing aristocratic line.

It screamed wealth, importance...*dominance*.

It said, *You don't belong here.*

The king himself could stand where I was standing and maybe hesitate before he approached those wide steps.

The young man made it to us, and I saw there was a logo stitched into his shirt over his left chest. A golden shield, the same as on the flag flying above us. It looked to be a profusion of sprigs of heather adorning the top edges, the requisite helmet from a suit of armor at the top middle, and in the shield was the full body of a clawing wolf in profile.

He looked between the two of us and delivered Lou's first blow.

"Mrs. Ryan, welcome." He then turned to me. "Miss Ryan."

Lou couldn't quite hide the flinch.

Then again, from ages seventeen through twenty-five, she'd subsisted on coffee and cigarettes to keep her curve-less frame. As she aged, this turned to restrictive dieting and obsessive exercise, but neither of these done with a mind to health and nutrition, but instead keeping her size 0.

Because of this, her youthful glow and tremendous genes had slowly morphed to the look of desperation. Now, her forehead seemed too wide, her eyes too far apart, the rest of the features of her face scrunched beneath both, and nothing moved due to regular Botox injections.

She was still beautiful, she'd never not be (at least in my eyes), but she no longer was the young, energetic, rail-thin model. Instead, she was the gaunt thirty-nine-year-old woman who looked thirty-nine and as if she was wondering if a life of living a maxim, "nothing tastes better than skinny feels," might have been a life wasted.

I was thirty-four and apparently looked my age too, and I'd never met a treadmill I liked, so I avoided them, thus our relationship worked perfectly.

However, there'd been a time when people who didn't pay attention thought I was Dad's wife, and Lou was his daughter. It sickened me, and it never failed to irritate me that Lou would preen whenever it happened.

11

Things were different now, but I didn't celebrate her pain. It made me sad for her that something so mundane meant so much to her.

Everyone aged, and unequivocally, the more you had of it, the more blessed you became.

The years we lived, people didn't seem to understand, were the gift that kept giving.

Until they stopped.

"I'm here to show you into the house," he announced. "The other Miss Ryan is being informed of your arrival and she's to meet you in the Pearl Room for tea."

"What about our suitcases?" Lou asked.

It was then I winced as the young man quickly hid his expression of revulsion.

One did not touch one's own luggage in a setting like this.

Though, the distaste he was quick to hide was over the top, but perhaps not in a place like this.

Even so, I didn't like it.

Needless to say, Lou had not grown up with money either. She'd lived the first sixteen years of her life on a council estate. For the last thirteen, Dad took care of everything, except, of course, for the eighteen months since he'd been gone. In the years in between, her life was a whirlwind of jet-setting between fashion shows and photo shoots, parties and dating Hollywood actors. Weekends in the country with the hoi polloi wasn't on her agenda.

She didn't know the rules because she didn't have to bother to learn them.

I, on the other hand, had never been my father's favorite, but I'd been adjacent to his money, and as such had learned to make my own way in these worlds long ago.

It was too late to cover her gaffe, so I forged around the car, hooked my arm in hers and turned to the man. "We've been driving a long time. Tea and Portia sound perfect."

He nodded, threw an arm toward the steps, but preceded us, jogging up as we followed more sedately.

Hit number two landed on us both as we entered Duncroft.

Particularly me.

I felt a jolt of electricity hit the second I stepped over the threshold.

I'd traveled widely, and I honestly couldn't say I'd ever experienced something as audaciously beautiful, with the razor's edge of exquisite taste, as the enormous entry of Duncroft House.

It was the joint of the cross, the entirety of it, and the ceiling rose all four stories and was topped with a glass dome. The sweep of the elegant staircase spiraled round and round to the top floor, making the space seem cavernous.

And embedded that feeling that we were insignificant.

The floor was a sea of pristine-white marble, the walls a shade of lilac gray so pale, if the crown molding wasn't an immaculate white, I would have thought it too was that color.

In front of us, opposite the front door, beyond the sweeping staircase (also all white with a thick, dove-gray carpet runner clamped at the top edges of the treads by a thin rod of burnished silver, the color of that carpet having to be insanely difficult to keep clean), all you could see were windows that framed a massive conservatory. And well beyond that, barely discernable through the jungle of plants, were manicured lawns and gardens, and beyond *that*, heathered moors.

Four wide hallways led off of the foyer.

And at the foot of the stairs, atop the broad newel post, stood a figure carved in white marble.

I didn't know who she was, Aphrodite, Hera, Persephone, some other goddess. She was walking tall atop grass and flowers, the flowers rising up to mingle with the graceful folds of the shift that closely skimmed her feminine curves. Flowers also mingled in her flowing hair.

Her head was tipped back, and a serene expression was on her face.

Serene and...replete.

There was something sexual about her. It was nuanced, yet still managed to be overt. As if she was caught walking over the grass through the flowers while orgasming.

She was also tall. If she were on the ground, she'd be as tall as me.

She would seem curious and even wrong anywhere else but in that vast, bleached space, and if the person who sculpted her did it in that exact spot to make her proportions and impact as flawless as it could be, I wouldn't be surprised.

"Your keys?" the young man requested.

I turned to him.

"I'll get your luggage and park your car," he explained.

I nodded, took my car fob off the ring and handed it to him.

He dipped his chin and said, "This way."

I noticed that Lou tore her gaze off the statue when we followed him left, down the hall that led along the front southwestern leg of the house.

We walked to the very first door, and he stood outside it, again with arm extended, inviting us in. "The Pearl Room," he stated. "Miss Ryan, I'm sure, will join you shortly."

He did not enter the room, but we did.

The name of the room was apt. There were more colors here than in the entry, but they were all in the same theme, oyster, and the shimmering golds and pinks and silvers and greens of mother of pearl. The massive chandelier that fell from the ceiling rose in the center of the room looked made of swags of actual pearls.

"Holy shit," I muttered.

"Agreed," Lou muttered in return, moving her attention from the chandelier, toward the door.

I looked that way too, to see the young man was no longer there.

"Am I wrong?" she asked under her breath. "Should he have introduced himself?"

It wasn't the first time I wished my father had been less...*my father.*

It was his narcissistic, alpha tendencies that not only made his first wife bitter, twisted and angry, and his second wife banished and forgotten, it had also dispatched his last wife and youngest child as incapable of dealing with the world he'd left them in.

"Yes, he should have," I told her. "I can't even imagine how big the staff is in this place, but if he was sent to greet us, and he's taking care of our bags and my car, we'll probably see him around while we're here, and I should know who to ask for by name if, say, I want my car fob back."

"Okay," Lou replied, drifting further into the room while taking it in.

14

I stayed where I was, trying to put my finger on why all of this rubbed me the wrong way.

The room was spotless, as was the entry. There not only wasn't a speck of dust, but also nothing was out of place. And the two porcelain-white sofas looked like no ass had sat in them since they'd been laid facing each other. They were set perpendicular to the white marble fire-place with its veins of gray and lilac and gold. The same unused look with the two armchairs covered in pearlescent leather that sat at angles at the apex of the couches, facing the fireplace.

I knew the living quarters of houses like this tended to be a lot homier than the formal areas.

Daniel and Portia had been seeing each other just over six months. We were to be there for ten days. It wasn't lost on anyone what this week was about.

We'd barely stepped into the house, and the choice of this room to be our landing spot for tea upon arrival spoke volumes.

And every word was an insult.

"This room is...scarily beautiful," Lou noted.

She wasn't wrong.

"All the white is...a lot," she continued.

She wasn't wrong about that either.

"Daphne!"

I turned at my name, then froze, because Portia was sailing through the door.

Though, the reason I froze was spying this version of Portia, a version I didn't know, who was sailing through the door.

She was wearing an ivory sweater, the deep fold of the top made it off the shoulder, the matching skirt was a swish of falling ruffles of ivory tulle. It tumbled in an uneven hem to her ankles, exposing the ivory, velvet, Mary Jane ballet flats with a thin strap and delicate rhinestone buckle.

Her honeyed hair was pulled back at the crown, the rest toppled in waves and ringlets down her shoulders.

For a moment, I felt such an overwhelming sense of nausea, I was worried I'd throw up.

My sister did not wear tulle. Or ruffles. Or velvet ballet flats.

My sister was the cutting edge of Prada mixed with the nuanced macabre of McQueen.

Our citizenship and accent set us apart in this country, and Portia leaned into the rock and roll aspect to make sure no one forgot she was different, she was cool. She'd come over when she was young, but she carefully nurtured her accent so she'd never lose it.

And when it came to the American version of her that she wanted to convey, she was Miley Cyrus, not Taylor Swift.

She threw her arms around me and hugged me.

I was so surprised by her appearance, I had to force myself to return the gesture.

When she broke away, she grabbed both my hands, beamed up at me and said, "I'm so glad you're here."

I opened my mouth but didn't have the time to say anything before she let me go, turned to Lou and greeted disinterestedly, "Hey, Lou."

"Hello, lovey," Lou replied, sounding choked.

At the note in her voice, I glanced in her direction to see she wasn't injured by Portia's attitude (she was very much used to it). Her eyes were wide and aimed at Portia's outfit.

Yes, this version of Portia did not jibe.

"C'mon, they're going to be bringing tea in soon, we need to talk before they get here."

She dragged me to the porcelain-white sofas and completely ignored Lou.

I didn't, capturing her gaze as we moved, holding my hand her way.

When Portia noticed Lou coming with us, she instructed, "You can sit over there," and gestured to the couch across from us.

Lou was much better at hiding the hurt Portia's behavior caused her, so she didn't balk before she shifted her trajectory to the other couch.

"Okay, so, you have to be, like, *really cool* with Daniel and his folks, all right?" Portia demanded before I'd even settled into the sofa.

"Hey, thanks for taking off for a week and driving over four hours from London to meet my new boyfriend and his family in the middle of nowhere. And by the way, you both look lovely, but do you need

16

anything? I know you've been in the car for a really long time, so would you rather stretch your legs or something?"

I spoke these words and they were an admonishment because Portia should have said them.

Portia's eyes narrowed, and she stated, "Yes, things like that. Don't say things like that in front of Daniel and his parents."

She didn't miss my point, so I didn't belabor it.

"What are you wearing?" I asked instead.

She peered down at herself. "I'm trying a new look."

"For Daniel?"

She didn't quite catch my eyes. "He likes more feminine clothes."

"What do you like?" I pressed, even though I knew what that was, and it wasn't a ruffled, tulle skirt, as pretty as it was.

She caught my gaze.

"*Daniel*," she stressed.

"Portia—" I began, but I got no further because she leaned into me.

But it wasn't with anger or attitude, as it usually would be.

It felt like what had been filling the car from Lou on the way there.

Fear.

"I like him, okay? Don't mess this up," she begged. "I need you guys,"—she turned her head Lou's way—"both of you guys, to be really cool and not mess this up."

"How exactly would we mess this up?" I inquired.

"Portia."

At her name intoned in a man's cultured voice coming from the direction of the door, we all looked that way.

And I knew exactly what we might mess up.

Yes, Richard and Jane, the Earl and Countess Alcott, were the upper crust. Tall. Straight. He was ageing almost preternaturally well: his dark hair only touched with silver, his perfect bone structure offering the foundation for his continued good looks even though (I'd looked him up), he was nearly sixty-five. And she was a goddess. Cool and blonde. Ethereal didn't describe her. The house didn't need to be haunted, her beauty was haunting enough.

They walked into the room, and we all stood.

"Your family has arrived," Richard stated like an accusation.

"Yes, I sent word," Portia said.

"Which is why we're here," Richard replied frostily. He turned to Lou. "You must be Louella."

You must be Louella?

I thought they'd met.

Lou didn't remind him of that.

"Yes, yes. Hi. Hello." She moved forward, holding up a hand.

Both Richard and Jane stared at it for a scant moment as if trying to cypher some way to avoid touching it before Richard reached out and took it briefly and let her go.

Jane did not.

Richard also didn't look Lou in the face.

Then again, Lou managed the whole encounter with her eyes pinned to some point beyond Richard's shoulder.

Weird.

"Welcome to our home,' Richard droned.

"And this is Daphne," Portia declared, pushing me a bit toward them.

I, however, did not offer my hand.

"My Lord, my Lady," I said aloofly, matching their welcome. "Thank you for having us."

Richard's attention was sharp on me. Jane remained expressionless.

Richard looked to Portia. "You'll explain the rules?"

The rules?

And, hello, how do you do to you too.

Asshole.

"Of course," Portia assured quickly.

"We'll let you catch up," Richard declared. "And we'll see you at dinner."

With that, breathing not another word nor gifting us with another look, they left the room, Richard closing the door like he didn't want someone passing and seeing us in there.

Slowly, I turned my head to regard my sister.

She read my expression.

"It takes a while for them to melt," she explained.

"Have they melted toward you?" I demanded to know.

She shrugged.

Meaning: No.

Right, we'd get into that later.

I pressed on. "Rules?"

"I told you they dress for dinner." She suddenly appeared panicked. "Did you bring clothes to dress for dinner? They're sticklers about it. Cocktails at six thirty sharp, seating at seven fifteen, also sharp. The men wear suits and ties, the women, cocktail dresses at least."

I didn't mention we weren't on a cruise ship, and it was just plain weird that we'd be expected to dress up for dinner for ten days straight (for goodness' sake, I'd had to pack two suitcases for this shindig). I didn't do it now, and I didn't do it when she'd asked me to come and told me what to pack.

I just said, "Yes."

My sister showed immediate relief, the extent of which worried me.

"Portia—" I started again.

"You'll get a tour," she said. "Either from Daniel or Richard, not one of the staff. After tea, you'll be shown to your rooms to rest and freshen up and prepare for dinner. You aren't allowed to, um...wander the house until you're shown what areas are accessible and what are off limits."

"We'd hardly go poking around their home without permission," I noted.

"They just wanted me to make sure you wouldn't," she returned.

"Please assure them we're not going to ramble around the house looking for Instagram-worthy photo ops or filming video to splice into TikToks," I told her.

"That's another thing. No social media. At all," she replied.

I pressed my lips together, because...*obviously*.

"Right, of course," Portia mumbled, "I just...well, I promised them I'd make things clear."

"When you speak to them, you can share you did just that."

"For the most part you'll be guided where you need to be by staff," Portia stated. "Until, you know, you get the lay of the land."

"We'll be the perfect guests," Lou promised.

Even though she gave a slight nod to note she'd heard the words,

Portia barely looked at her.

I let that slide too and asked, "When are we going to meet Daniel?"

"He's at work," she told me.

"That doesn't answer my question," I told her.

"He'll be here by cocktails."

I nodded, wondering how she was there on a Friday afternoon. She had a job too, and it was in London.

I let that go (for now) as well.

So no tour, unless Richard decided to endure our presence for the hours it would take to show us his house. Then again, if he did that, we wouldn't have time to dress for dinner. Or, if it was as it seemed to be, for the few minutes it'd take to show us the small portions of his house we were allowed to inhabit.

"Daniel's lovely," Portia said softly.

He better be, I let my expression say for me.

The door opened and two women wearing dove-gray dresses with mandarin collars, white cuffs on the short sleeves and sensible black flats, came in bearing our tea on silver trays.

The tea service, I'd look up later and find was "Pearl" Nymphenburg, which was used exclusively by Bavarian royalty for a century.

But of course.

No scones and cream, instead, lifeless finger sandwiches and painstakingly decorated but completely tasteless petite fours that I could make better blindfolded.

During tea, I didn't say the many things I wanted to say or ask any of the myriad questions on my mind, because both my sister and step-mother seemed on pins and needles. They both needed to calm down.

And *then* I'd get into it.

But it would seem the shiver that went down my spine when we passed the gate, not to mention that bolt of electricity when I walked in, were an indication of intuition I didn't know I had until then.

And that same intuition was telling me it wasn't going to get any better.

But it could get worse.

I just didn't know at that time it was going to.

Or how bad it was going to be.

Three

THE WINE ROOM

My bedroom was a feminine extravaganza in the colors of cream, carnation pink and deep, rosy red.

It was mammoth. It was spotless. It had a bed with four posts that was so tall, I had to climb into it using the step beside it, and heavy, highly embellished but workable curtains. The room also had a seating area complete with a puffy, inviting couch in front of the pink marbled fireplace, and a delicate writing desk in the corner.

And the en suite was a dream.

If I were in a hotel, I'd be in seventh heaven, wouldn't leave the room for the entire week, and instead I'd read a half dozen books, take daily baths, and drink nothing but champagne from breakfast until I fell asleep.

I wasn't in a hotel, and I didn't enjoy the idea of liking the choice that was made for me, because this room wasn't insulting. It was the belated welcome Lou and I should have had when we arrived.

However, the weird part was that an hour ago, a maid had knocked on the door and asked if I needed any help dressing, "Or with your makeup and hair, Miss Ryan?"

Flabbergasted, hopefully politely, I'd declined.

One could take that as a very nice offering from the Alcotts, but who had lady's maids anymore?

Stylists for special events, sure.

Someone to help you do your hair for dinner at home? No.

But I was ready and it wasn't time to go down yet, so I grabbed my phone and texted Lou.

Can I come over?

It took mere seconds before she returned, *Sure!*

I left my room, walked across the hall and down two doors, and knocked on the one I'd watched the maid lead Lou to before I'd entered mine so I'd know where she was.

My windows faced the lawns and forest at the front of the house.

Hers would face the wing that made the other strike of cross.

She opened the door with perfect hair and makeup, but still in her robe.

"Hey," she greeted.

"I feel like I should leave a note on my door so our guide will know where to find me when they come up to get us," I replied as she stepped back, and I entered her room.

I stopped a few feet in, closing the door behind me and making the decision to do everything in my power not to let her see my allocated space.

Hers was not as big and it was oppressively filled with furniture, all of it high quality, maybe even priceless, but it was still mismatched. Likely discards from other rooms, or pieces that were too valuable to throw away, but where they used to reside had been updated and they were no longer needed.

It was fashioned into a usable room, the colors and fabrics were all in lovely shades of pale green and blue, with a theme of flowers, but it seemed close, disorganized and suffocating, not airy, artful and appealing.

In other words, I was welcome.

Lou wasn't.

"Rabidly private, as I said. I guess not a surprise," Lou noted as she shrugged off her robe and tossed it on a flowered chintz chair to stand unabashed in her underwear like she was backstage at a fashion show.

She reached into the opened wardrobe, and I saw she was unpacked, as I found I'd been after we were escorted to our rooms.

We hadn't asked them to do that, or not to do it as I'd have preferred.

I wondered what they thought when they put my vibrator into the top drawer of one of the nightstands.

It had been a wild idea to pack it, but I figured I'd need every avenue open to find ways to relax this week, so in it went.

And now the staff knew it did.

Fodder for discussion belowstairs.

"It's good you're here, you can zip me up," she said. "We're running out of time. They said they'd be here at six twenty to escort us down, yes?"

"Yes," I confirmed as I watched her step into a column of sequins and pull it up her body.

It was a midi sheath dress, fully sequined in burgundy, except the twin bands of silver around the waist. It was high necked and sleeveless.

And totally not Lou.

She looked like the mother of the bride, not like she'd walked hundreds of runways wearing haute couture and wasn't even forty years old yet.

I felt my heart warm and my temper flare, seeing yet again how badly Lou wanted Portia to like her. How badly she wanted to do what she could to make this go smoothly for her stepdaughter.

Lou looked the picture of appropriate, middle-aged-woman elegance when I didn't even think she'd admitted to herself she'd hit middle age.

I, on the other hand, was wearing a dress I'd thrown in as a spare, not expecting I was going to wear it.

It was pine green, totally simple, except it was skintight, had a plunge V that showed cleavage down nearly to my midriff, which meant my breasts were swaddled in support tapes to give them the perfect curve at the expanse of skin that was showing.

It hit the floor in a trumpet skirt with a high slit up the right leg, and I'd paired it with the fan-shaped, Divas' Dream Bulgari necklace of rose gold, diamonds and malachite Dad bought me, with its matching earrings, bracelet and ring.

My shoes were rose gold Sophia Websters with four-inch skinny stiletto heels and the requisite dramatic butterfly embossed with crystals at the heel. I'd likely have to take them off to walk back up to my room after dinner, but by damn, I was teetering in on those damned shoes.

And my hair was fashioned in a side bun that took four tries to make look nice.

It was in your face, the tens of thousands of dollars' worth of jewelry, the flesh bared, the shoes that were so far away from velvet Mary Jane flats it wasn't funny, and I had zero fucks to give that it was.

I zipped up Lou and she moved to sit on the arm of the chintz chair to put on her own high heels, pretty silver sandals that showed off her beautiful feet but made no statement at all.

"You should be you," I said quietly.

Lou didn't look up from her shoes. "I need to be what Portia needs me to be."

Dad had married Lou because she was famous for being gorgeous and she made him look to his cronies as cronies like Dad's envisioned the world. Like he could pull a beautiful young woman due to his looks, virility and prowess, and not due to the sole fact he had billions of dollars.

What Dad saw only at the very end, was that Lou may have married him because her career was waning, and she had a life she wanted to sustain. But she'd stayed married to him because somewhere along the line she'd fallen in love with him, and she was going to stick, no matter what wasted him away.

And she did, through cancer wasting him away.

"I'm going to talk to her tomorrow if I can get her alone," I vowed.

"You don't have to do that," Lou said.

"Part of growing up is learning how to treat people who've done not one thing to hurt you."

At that, she looked at me. "I know it was a shock to you girls when your dad married me."

"Louella, that was thirteen years ago. It's time she got over it."

"I get it. My dad spoiled me."

I didn't have to say her dad was a bus driver, so how she was spoiled was nowhere near the privilege Portia enjoyed, so I didn't say it.

But I never played poker, and not only because I didn't like gambling.

Thus, Lou read my expression.

"I don't want you two girls fighting about me," she asserted.

"We won't fight."

"It's obvious this boy is important to her."

"He's not a boy. He's a thirty-five-year-old man. And Portia is a twenty-eight-year-old woman. We're all grown-ass adults here, Lou. It's only that Portia isn't acting like one."

"I remember what it was like, that first flush of love."

I did too.

It was a trick of hormones and pheromones, and millennia of a dizzying number of behavior patterns, all designed so we'd find someone with whom to procreate to make sure we didn't allow the human race to die out.

Sadly, that first flush of love could hide what would someday become searing rivers of hate.

I just hoped my sister wasn't following in my mother's footsteps.

Or mine.

"What it shouldn't be like, is losing yourself to the guy you like and trying a different look because he likes more feminine clothes. He either likes Portia as she comes, or he doesn't. We're going to find out soon which way that goes."

"This, I can't debate," Lou replied, again appearing anxious, but not about our sojourn to the bucolic north and a possibly haunted house, but that perhaps Daniel Alcott wasn't the right man for Portia.

There was a knock on the door. I went to open it.

It was a uniformed maid, not the one who'd asked about my hair and makeup, nor one of the two who had brought in tea. She was the one who'd escorted us to our rooms in the first place.

It seemed this massive house had a massive staff.

Guess it was six twenty.

"Hello," I greeted.

"Miss Ryan," she said, glancing at Lou. She dipped her chin then asked, "Are you ready to go to the Wine Room?"

If it had alcohol, absolutely.

Lou rose from the arm of the chair and went to the bed to nab her evening bag.

Watching her do that, I realized I'd forgotten mine.

"I have to stop by my room to get my bag," I told the maid.

"Of course," she murmured, then her brows drew down and she called, "You don't have to turn out the lights. While you're at dinner, we'll be preparing your rooms for the evening. We'll take care of the lighting."

Lou halted in position of dousing a bedside lamp, her head turned to the maid.

"Um..." she mumbled.

Lou had her moral epiphany a few years after she came to understand what it meant in reality how ridiculously wealthy my dad was. Which meant, at first, she'd gone mad, but since then, she'd whittled down her charitable causes to being avidly climate change conscious and an animal rights activist, getting photographed repeatedly while protesting fox hunts and the like. She threw some of her billions of pounds at the same.

Now, I had to stifle a laugh at how in pain she looked to leave a room with the lights on.

"It'll only mean another day of flooding in Pakistan sometime in the future," I drawled.

"Not funny," Lou said, walking away from the lamp.

"I wasn't meaning to be."

When I glanced at the maid as we moved out of the room, her face was blank, and I knew the staff would not be coming in to turn off the lights, then rushing back up to turn them on when we headed to bed, all in an effort to make sure the globe didn't warm to the point of catastrophe in a few decades. But instead, they probably did turn down service, so although the lighting we'd return to would be subdued, at Duncroft House, they didn't care about flooding in Pakistan in the slightest.

We walked to my room, and I realized my mistake as we neared the door.

"I'll be out in a jiffy," I said while sliding through the door without fully opening it, nearly closing it behind me, then racing on my four-inch heels to the bed to grab my bag, teetering once on the brink of a sprained ankle, catching myself in the nick of time, and racing back out.

"I'm not going to throw a fit because you left your lights on," Lou assured me huffily.

I was relieved that was why she thought I wouldn't let her see inside.

The maid started walking.

We followed, and as we did, I pulled my phone out of my bag. I noted we had five minutes to get to cocktails, and even though we were a good walk away, I didn't think it would take five minutes.

Punctuality obviously was key at Duncroft House.

"Are you allowed to share your name?" I asked the maid's back.

"Brittany."

"Nice to meet you, Brittany," I replied.

She didn't look back as she said, "You as well."

I stared at her back thinking this maid was different. Chilly, instead of just formal and professional.

Lou and I exchanged looks, and neither of us spoke again as we followed Brittany to the Wine Room.

Newsflash: sadly, it wasn't filled with wine.

It was the color of wine: all burgundies and currants, with mahogany furniture. The walls looked papered in wine-colored leather (and I hoped they were not). The furniture was definitely leather, with some dark tapestry. And there was an interesting picture of a medieval couple on the wall.

Honestly, I didn't get to take much in before Daniel Alcott was upon me.

"The big sister!" he cried, moving my way, dragging my sister with him.

She was in ivory again, a full pleated skirt that reached her ankles and a pleated top, the halter neck a ruff of chiffon, her shoulders and arms bare.

And she definitely had help with her makeup and hair. She was good with both, but her elaborate updo was not something a layperson could do, no way, and her face looked like a TikTok influencer had been at it.

Daniel let Portia go in order to take hold of both my biceps and touch his cheeks to both of mine.

He smelled cloyingly of cologne that stated a little too boldly, *I'm a man!*

He pulled away but didn't let go as he looked down on me and smiled broadly.

Startling blue eyes. Thick, golden-blond hair, the same as his mother's color, if a shade darker. A healthy tan. He was tall. He was fit. He was handsome.

He was fake as shit.

I'd seen pictures of him, more when I started researching the whole family after Portia hooked up with him, then deeper when she'd asked us to this week at Duncroft.

He was not the financial wunderkind his brother was. He was his mother's light to his father's dark. And Daniel's reputation was more of a happy-go-lucky playboy than his older brother's inveterate philanderer.

But regardless of his effusive welcome, he did not want me there, and the fact he'd not even glanced at Lou told me how he felt about her.

In other words, the edge I was riding about this week got sharper.

Sharp enough to cut.

When I said nothing, he finally let me go and looked to Lou.

"Louella," he muttered far less enthusiastically, as was his touching only one cheek to hers.

I watched this and turned annoyed eyes to my sister before I moved in and did the touching cheeks thing myself. "Portia."

"You look pretty," she said.

We moved away and I let my gaze wander her head and hair before I replied with grudging honesty, "You do too."

I turned my attention to Daniel's parents, and I saw that Portia had told no fibs. Like Daniel and Portia, Lou and me, they were decked out. Exquisitely tailored suit and tie for Richard, a one-shouldered, deep-rose satin gown with a knotted waistline and some gathering to give it some interest, for Jane.

"Lord and Lady Alcott," I greeted.

"Oh, it's Richard and Jane, of course," Daniel invited, to his father's jaw growing tight, the same happening around his mother's eyes.

"Drink, Miss Ryan?" I heard said low, and I looked to my side to see a tall, thin man in a black three-piece suit and pale-blue tie that had the family shield emblazoned on it standing there, though also slightly behind me.

A new member of staff.

The butler.

That meant I'd seen four maids, whatever they called the guy who took care of the bags and car, and a butler.

Already a lot of staff, but I figured there was even more.

A number of them.

As I thought: massive house, massive staff.

I had no idea, but maybe the Alcotts were even more loaded than we were, and that was saying something.

"Champagne, if you have it," I ordered. I turned to the room at large. "We're celebrating, correct?"

"Absolutely," Daniel brayed cheerily.

Richard and Jane remained mute.

"Mrs. Ryan?" the butler asked Lou.

"Champagne too, please."

He dipped his head and floated away.

Daniel had retrieved his own drink, what appeared to be a G and T, and he lifted it my way.

"I'm not ashamed to admit, I'm addicted to your éclairs," he proclaimed. "When I'm in the city, I try to swing by your shop. This was even before I met Portia," he declared, sliding an arm along my sister's waist and tucking her to his side.

"Well, thank you," I replied.

"Best patisserie in London, even *The Guardian* said so," Daniel told his parents.

Portia piped up. "Daphne studied in Paris. *Grand diplôme* from *Le*

Cordon Bleu with an internship with François Perreault. He's known to have the best patisserie in Paris. It's in the Latin Quarter."

Unspoken by my sister, but probably known by all the Alcotts, was that I fell in love with and married François Perreault, and then, after the third time I discovered he'd cheated on me, I'd fallen out of love and divorced him.

The courtship lasted two years.

The marriage lasted two more.

The divorce was five years ago.

The bitterness remained.

Although everyone knew François, I suspect even the Alcotts—he was that famous because he was that good—they were completely unimpressed.

I wished I could have filmed their non-reaction at the mention of Frankie's name. He'd lose his mind that they hadn't sighed with reverence.

Though, Lady Jane had a figure like Lou's, so I doubted she'd had an éclair or a mille-feuille in a long time.

Or ever.

The butler handed me a coupé glass of champagne.

I checked to see if Lou had hers (she did), before I raised mine and asked, "Shall we toast to family and new friends?"

"Perfect!" Daniel cried. "I'll toast to that!"

Lou and Portia raised their glasses with Daniel, Richard and Jane slightly held theirs in front of them.

I ignored their lukewarm participation (they were still participating) and said, "Cheers."

And then I drank half the glass.

Four

THE TURQUOISE ROOM

I already knew something was going wrong, I just didn't know what it was, before we entered a dining room that was a study of turquoise.

The tablecloth was white.

The wood was cherry.

There was a massive tapestry on the wall that looked ancient.

But everything else, including the trim on the china, the vases that held extraordinary flower arrangements, the embroidery on the serviettes, and the cast to the crystal glasses and candelabra, was turquoise.

The table could seat three times our party, but even so, the fullness of it was set for us.

Head to foot.

Two place settings swimming in the long trail of the port side, three on the starboard.

We had not all been arranged at one end so we could easily see and talk to each other.

We were all going to have to yell at each other.

The thing was, there were only six of us.

Richard led Jane to the foot, Daniel leading Portia to the two-seating side.

Daniel explained things as Lou and I lingered in confusion at the door.

"Allow the seat between you, Ian will be here...eventually."

Hang on.

The prodigal son was returning?

And no one thought to mention that?

Of course, during our allotted forty-five minutes of cocktail time, the feel of the evening deteriorated as the minutes ticked by, but I thought it was because Richard and Jane were more and more beleaguered at having to spend time with us.

Now it would seem, considering the hard mask (or *harder* mask) that slammed down over Lady Jane's face at the mention of her eldest, it was because they were growing more and more annoyed that he'd broken the rules and not turned up at the appointed cocktail forty-five minutes.

And now we were to start dinner without him.

Which was what happened after Richard did triple duty of seating Jane, then moving to Lou to push her chair under the table, then to me, simply to stand there in a wasted display of chivalry, his hand on the back of my chair, for I was already seated and had tucked myself under the table.

His expression said I should have waited for him.

He was a man. Even if he'd seen my shoes, he couldn't know that no way was I standing on them for longer than I had to. Nor generally waiting for someone to help me do something I was perfectly capable of doing myself.

I ignored his expression, took hold of my napkin and flung it out to the side before draping it on my lap.

And thus, Richard had a hard(er) mask on his face when he finally seated himself.

He immediately turned to the butler who was hovering. "Soup, Stevenson," he murmured.

The man bowed then took off at a good clip to disappear behind a hidden door in the cherrywood paneling.

"This table is beautiful," Lou tried gamely, offering this to Jane.

The woman slowly tipped her head to the side in a regal, yet birdlike manner that had me glaring at Portia.

If recent memory served, Lady Jane hadn't uttered a single word since we'd met her.

Portia shot me a pleading look.

I took a fortifying breath.

And then another one.

"I hope our cook can impress the likes of a student of *Le Cordon Bleu*," Richard remarked.

I turned to him and saw his tone might have been dull, but he was attempting to be game too.

"You have excellent taste in champagne," I noted.

"I'm glad you approve," he replied.

"So I have every hope."

He jutted his chin toward me.

"Daniel's taking us to some ruins tomorrow," Portia announced as Stevenson returned with the young man who took my car. He was now wearing a black vest, matching trousers, a black tie (again adorned with the family shield), a crisp, painstakingly ironed, white shirt, and a long white apron tied meticulously around his waist.

He was also carrying a turquoise and white soup tureen on a gold platter.

"We're having a day of it. Starting with a tramp around the village. I hope you girls brought warm clothes," Daniel declared.

The soup was served to Jane first. I watched carefully as she helped herself. Although I'd been formally served before, the traditions of the house could vary.

I should have known in this house they would not.

The man went to Lou next, and fortunately she'd been watching too.

"Portia gave us deep insights on what to pack," I assured Daniel.

"Excellent," he squawked.

"I'm sorry, I don't know the story. How did you two meet?" Lou asked.

Portia blushed. Daniel fidgeted with his tie. I halted in the endeavor of serving my own soup, because Portia had told me they'd been set up by mutual friends, which should not earn a blush or a tie fidget.

"Weren't you set up?" I asked.

"Yes," Portia answered quickly.

Meaning: Lie.

I finished ladling my soup.

Nothing more was said on the subject of their meeting, though I made a mental note to bring it up when I had some time alone with my sister.

We all fell into uncomfortable silence as we sipped our soup.

It was a heavy, but delicious cream of brie.

I was on spoonful number three when a deep, droll, silky voice noted, "It seems the family text string has failed us yet again."

I had my spoon over my bowl and my eyes on the double doors that led into the Turquoise Room as Ian Alcott sauntered in.

Well, hell.

He wasn't just dark to Daniel's light.

He was two inches taller than Daniel at least. He was broader. He had the thighs of a rugby player. And if the Alcott blue eyes were startling with Daniel's fair coloring, they were disconcerting with Ian's dark.

Striking blue, the deep color of the Mediterranean.

I tore my gaze from him to see Portia's face pinched in a way reminiscent of when she was studying for an exam she should have started studying for days earlier, and Daniel's face was creeping with red, because his cover had just been blown.

Handsome, magnanimous younger brother was out the window.

He was the spare.

The real deal had just strolled into the joint, and damn, but if Ian Alcott didn't make that brutally clear.

I'd seen pictures of him too, and his good looks were not lost on me.

However, the man in the flesh was so much better, I was suddenly finding it hard to breathe.

He was magnetic.

And he knew it.

"And the family expands," he drawled, those preposterously beautiful, blue eyes pinning me to my seat. He stopped at my side. "I take it you're Daphne."

I put my spoon down and offered him my hand. "I am."

He didn't take my hand at first, not out of rudeness, he was caught up in the perusal of my cleavage.

And *that* was rude.

There was a slight smirk on his full lips when his fingers finally closed warm and tight around mine.

He also, I didn't fail to note, had big hands, and he might have been born with a silver spoon in his mouth, but somewhere along the line, he'd earned callouses on his fingers.

"Pleasure," he murmured, the word roaming my skin like a physical touch.

I pulled my hand from his and replied in a way it couldn't be mistaken I didn't mean, "Mutual, I'm sure."

The smirk turned into a sexy sneer.

While I dealt with that, he looked beyond me.

"The famous Louella Fernsby," he greeted Lou, moving her way.

She offered her hand.

He held it for a shorter period of time before he shrugged off his suit jacket and slung it with sheer and unmistakable in-your-face nonchalance on the back of the empty chair between Lou and me, a gesture that seemed like the smack in the face I was sure it was to his father. His tie was already gone, if he'd been wearing one, and his light-blue shirt was open at the tanned column of his throat. His blue suit was three pieces, the vest still in place, and the cut was superb and fashion forward.

He'd barely seated himself before the man was there with the soup tureen.

"Cream of brie," Ian stated, helping himself. "Bonnie isn't pulling any punches."

"Dinner is at seven fifteen," Richard asserted at this juncture.

The man with the tureen slunk away.

Ian shifted only his eyes to his father. "Thirty-seven years of that drilled into my brain, Dad, I didn't forget."

"It seems you did, since you're late. You were to meet us for cocktails. Those start at six thirty on the dot," Richard decreed.

"I texted I'd be late."

"We hardly bring our phones to cocktails," Richard sniffed.

"Perhaps you should," Ian suggested. "You'd not waste needless emotion at me running late if you knew that was the case."

It was then Lady Jane broke her long silence with a practiced, "Can we not?"

"Yes, can we not?" Daniel chimed in.

"Delighted to drop it," Ian murmured as he bent to his soup and took his first spoonful.

Richard wasn't delighted to do the same, I knew, when he declared, "We have guests."

Ian looked to me. "My sincere apologies for my tardiness," he said insincerely.

"You said you were going to drop it," Daniel reminded him.

"I'm apologizing to our guests," Ian retorted.

"Let's move on," Lady Jane requested.

"It's insufferable," Richard denied her.

"Jesus Christ," Ian growled to his soup.

"It's a simple request. Be in the Wine Room at six thirty, *properly attired*," Richard demanded.

Yes.

I knew that suit jacket thing was a slap in the face.

Ian rested the side of his hand to the table and said to his father, "I'm here now." He raised his dark brows. "Shall we eat?"

"Yes, let's eat. I'm happy you could make it, darling," Lady Jane put in.

"Thank you, Mum," Ian said to her.

"I'm going to vomit," Daniel declared.

"No need to be dramatic," Richard chided.

Portia was staring at me with big eyes that shouted, *Do something!*

But I had no idea what to do.

Someone else might find this amusing or be diplomatic enough to smooth things over by offering an interesting conversational gambit.

That wasn't me.

I detested confrontation, any I might be involved in, and even more, witnessing the same. I thought it was rude beyond bearing for anyone not to have enough control of their mouths to be able to leave it until they could discuss things in private.

And at that moment, I was painfully aware I not only didn't have my car fob, I didn't even know where my car was.

But from the moment my little sister's mother took the millions my father offered, she disappeared without the barest shadow of a care of what became of her daughter after her absence, and I'd slid in to do the best I could in that role.

Which was what I endeavored to do now.

"I know there was a castle here before Duncroft, but when was this home built?"

"Mason work started in 1617, and the house was finished in 1632," Daniel answered swiftly.

"Fascinating," I said.

And that was the end of my attempt at an interesting conversational gambit.

Ian made a noise in his throat that was part amusement, part something else, and the something else part I felt in my nipples.

He was bent over his soup.

I glared at his profile.

He ignored me, continued eating and, I decided, doing both knowing perfectly well not only that I was inept at salvaging a dinner party gone awry, but also what he did to my nipples.

"Was the castle razed before Duncroft was built?" Lou asked.

Ian answered her. "Yes. It and the murder and mayhem within its walls were swept clean away. Except the house might have been new, but the bent toward murder and mayhem remained."

"*Ian!*" his father snapped.

"If they have Google, Dad, they know the history of the house," Ian reminded him.

"We don't talk about such things," his father bit off.

"No, *you* don't. Everyone else in Great Britain and beyond does," Ian retorted.

"You goad him on purpose," Daniel accused.

"And?" Ian asked his brother.

I almost laughed, but not with amusement (well, not entirely).

And I thought Dad and his marital high jinks, Lou being my step-mother and young enough to be my older sister, Portia and her shenanigans, and me with my rabid bent toward cynicism were a mess.

These people put the dys in dysfunction.

It was my experience it was always the ones who thought they were superior who were, in reality, anything but.

And I still didn't know where my car was.

"Do you think that perhaps this dinner might mean something to me...and Portia?" Daniel asked.

"Portia, my love, I forgot about you," Ian drawled.

Oh...hell no.

"You may be the future king of all you survey, but that's my little sister, so be careful," I warned.

Ian turned instantly to me.

"Daphne, no," Portia begged.

My eyes clashed with pure blue.

And I didn't fucking back down.

It took some time before he said, genuinely this time, "My apologies." He looked to Portia. "Apologies, petal."

Her cheeks turned pink.

I harrumphed.

"Can we *please* just enjoy our dinner?" Jane requested.

At that point, it was an impossible request.

But I exchanged a glance with Lou, and we both sent careful smiles in Portia's direction.

Which meant we were going to try.

It ended up an epic fail.

But we gave it our best shot.

Five

THE CARNATION ROOM

"I think we should find a way to get Portia and leave."

I was standing at the window, cradling my snifter of Amaretto, and staring out at the shadowed landscape that, yes... was all but obscured by mist.

Britain's reputation for fog wasn't quite as true as everyone not in Britain thought it was, just as it didn't always rain. Frequent gray days and drizzle was more in keeping with the truth, and fog didn't happen often.

But when it settled, it didn't mess around.

And still, this was the worst I'd ever seen it.

Even with my foreboding about that fact, my attention cut directly to Lou at what she said about all of us leaving.

We were back in the Wine Room. She was seated in a leather wingback chair drinking port.

After-dinner drinks didn't happen for anyone but me and Lou. The minute we exited the Turquoise Room, an irked-looking Richard claimed an aggravated-looking Ian, and they disappeared somewhere. Portia and Daniel said quick goodnights, and they disappeared like they were advanced in age, it was midnight, well past their bedtime, not nine thirty and they were young and spry.

Jane just disappeared.

So now it was again Lou and me.

I walked to the chair at angles with hers and gladly sat in it, giving my feet the rest they needed. As worth it as they were, beautiful shoes could be a pain.

"I know. Dinner was a lot," I agreed.

"It's not that,"—she stared moodily into her port—"I just don't feel good about this place, this visit...these people."

My reception hadn't been exactly warm, but it'd been better than hers.

And she'd come into this week with trepidation, and nothing had happened since to make things better for her.

"Do you want me to take you to the train station tomorrow?" I offered.

Her head snapped up, an abrupt and even violent movement that alarmed me, and what she said alarmed me more.

"I think we three should stick together."

It had been a trying day, but unusually, in my opinion, Lou was overreacting to it.

"They're just dysfunctional, Lou. We aren't the soul of adjusted familial relationships either."

"Daniel is trying too hard. So hard, I don't trust him one whit. Richard and Jane are..." she trailed off with that, like the walls could hear us talking about our hosts, and she wasn't comfortable uttering her thoughts out loud. "And Ian is unbearable."

Ian was arrogant and conceited, arguably justifiably so, he was just that attractive.

He was also a thirty-seven-year-old man who didn't feel like being controlled by his pathologically controlling father.

Who could blame him?

I didn't.

In fact, I'd be the exact same way.

In fact, when my father was alive, I *was* the exact same way.

Though, not in company.

And my dad wasn't quite as big of an asshole as Richard was, and could often be quite loving, and was always generous.

"Portia is really into Daniel," I reminded her.

"You spoil her too, in your way," she replied. "There are so many girls who are not spoiled at all, in truth, so much the opposite, it hurts my heart to think about it. So, when one has the devotion that Portia has, I won't say a word against it. Except now, Daph." She leaned over the arm of her chair toward me and went on, "We're not safe in this house and specifically *she* is not safe with Daniel."

I leaned over the arm of my chair too. "Tell me why you say that."

She shook her head. "It's just a feeling."

I hated to say it, but it had to be said. "I have to have more than a feeling if I'm going to talk my sister into leaving the only man she's ever shown this kind of affection for."

Lou sat back, looking frustrated, and downed the last of her port.

I sat back too and suggested, "Let's give it another day, two, see how things go. If they don't improve, or you still feel weird, we'll talk, and in the meantime, I'll chat with Portia. Feel her out about all that's happening."

"All right," she mumbled.

I drank the last of my Amaretto.

Then I jumped because I'd barely taken my glass from my lips and Brittany was there, saying brittlely, "Allow me to escort you back to your rooms."

Okay, maybe I wasn't giving enough credence to what Lou said, because the maid didn't even hide she'd been lurking unseen in order to watch and wait for us to finish our drinks, and then we were to be tucked away like living dolls our owners no longer wished to play with.

Lou and I exchanged another uneasy glance before we dutifully got up, set our glasses aside, and followed Brittany out of the Wine Room.

Outside my bedroom, due to Lou's mood, I changed my mind about her not seeing my room and asked, "You want to come in? Keep chatting? We could ask Brittany to bring us another drink."

A peek at Brittany showed no reaction to this, approval or disapproval, or, perhaps, scant proof Brittany was other than an automaton.

"No, I'm actually pretty tired," Lou said. "That meal was heavy."

It *was* heavy.

The petite fours were a disaster.

The dinner was a buttery, cheesy, creamy, saucy, and in the end custardy triumph.

"Okay, see you in the morning," I replied, touching cheeks with her and giving her arms an affectionate, also hopefully restorative squeeze.

I stood in the hall and watched as Brittany escorted Lou to her room.

Only when she was inside did I duck into my own.

When I did, I found that earlier, I was not wrong.

Turn down service at Duncroft meant there was a soft light coming from the bathroom, the two large, tall, ornate lamps on the nightstands had been dimmed low, and all the others had been extinguished. The covers on the bed had been pulled back and smoothed, the pillows had been fluffed and arranged with the extraneous decorative ones removed and out of sight. And the heavy drapes at the windows had been securely closed.

I walked to the bed and saw there was also a tight, profuse carnation bouquet laid on the fold of the covers. The blooms were a pink that was an exact match to the shade used in the room, it was surrounded by a delicate, creamy netting and tied with an eerily perfectly matching bow.

Portia had told me during cocktails my room was known as the Carnation Room, while Lou's was known as the Floral Room.

And it looked like they took the room's namesake seriously.

Chocolates or mints would have seemed too hotel hospitality, for certain, but as with the sheer perfection of everything about the house (aside from its family), this, too, was incredibly weird.

In all honesty, it looked like a bridal bouquet.

And straight up, it gave me the creeps.

I wanted to know if Lou got one too, but then I didn't want to ask in case she didn't, and it was another slight.

I grabbed the bouquet, gazed around the room, found a vase with nothing in it, and went about the business of rinsing it out and then putting the bouquet in some water. I left it in the bathroom, moved to the bench at the foot of the bed, and with deep gratitude, sank to it, bent and took off my sandals.

I tossed them on the floor in front of the wardrobe and wandered back to the bathroom to prepare for bed.

~

I WAS COMING down the coiling stairs wearing a magnificent bridal gown and carrying a large bouquet of pink carnations ensconced in creamy netting and tied with a pink bow.

The statue on the newel post was bathed in an unearthly white light, so bright it blinded me, but my feet still descended the stairs, steady and true.

A man at the bottom waited for me, tall and besuited, but he was obscured by the bright rays beaming off the statue.

It was only when both my feet were on the marble floor did he come into focus.

Ian Alcott reached to me immediately, not my hand, but my face, cupping my jaw with great tenderness, his head descending.

I tipped mine back to receive his kiss.

And I was on my back in bed in the Carnation Room. There were frilly, pink petals covering the sheets and pillows.

Ian's hand was still at my jaw, his body warm and weighty atop mine, his mouth plundering my own.

The kiss was a juxtaposition of tender and carnal. My legs moved, restless with desire, trying to generate friction at the zenith, which was suffused with wet.

But the kiss needed to end.

I couldn't breathe.

Part of me wanted it never to end. It was beautiful. Exciting. Freeing.

But it was killing me.

I tried to turn my head, but I couldn't.

The hand was no longer on my jaw. Ian's weight was no longer on my body.

But my head had been immobilized. I couldn't lift it. I couldn't turn it.

There was a pillow pressed hard over my face, held down at the sides of my head.

I tried to struggle, but there was nothing to struggle against. No hands attached to wrists or arms I could push away, no body I could buck off.

I kicked. I writhed. I sucked in a desperate breath and pulled in nothing but soft, expensive cotton.

Frantic, terrified, I screamed.

The sound was blood curdling, but it wasn't my scream.

I heard a sick thud, my eyes sprang open, and I lay panting in the absolute dark, every inch of my skin tingling.

I felt the wet between my legs, the dream having an unconscious and undeniable physical manifestation.

But I was scared out of my brain.

I could still hear that awful screaming.

I heard that terrible thump.

And it felt like someone was in the room.

I sat upright and reached to the lamp, lighting it.

The first of three turns on the knob made the lamp illuminate very dimly, but it was enough to chase away the dark and for my vision to adjust quickly.

There were shadows, but nothing in them.

I was alone.

A bad dream.

Nothing but a bad dream.

Reasonable. It had been a weird day and I was worried about both Portia and Lou.

But damn, the dream had seemed so real. I'd never had a dream that real.

Used to the light, I turned the lamp one click brighter.

Better.

It was then I felt how cold the room was.

Freezing.

My nose was cold and so were my shoulders, which hadn't been under the covers. But now, with the bedclothes pooled in my lap, the rest of my body was catching up.

This was reasonable too. If I had to pay to heat this monstrosity of a house, I'd turn the boiler down at night as well.

But it couldn't be more than fifty degrees.

I got out of bed, went to the wardrobe, and pulled a carefully folded cardigan off an interior shelf and shrugged it on, yanking it closed tight at the front and keeping my arms crossed there.

Wide awake and knowing I'd need more than a few minutes to get myself together, find some calm and try to get some sleep, I moved to the windows in order to check on the mist. There was no reason why I did this, it was just something to do that seemed benign after that crazy dream.

I pulled a curtain back a few inches and looked into the night.

I then stood stock-still as I watched Daniel Alcott, wearing a heavy pea coat, walking away from the house, being swallowed by the fog, vanishing.

I didn't know how long I stood there, but it was my feet getting uncomfortably cold that made me drop the curtain and scurry back to the bed. I shoved my legs under the covers, pulled them up to my lap, and reached to the nightstand drawer.

Modernization had clearly been something that Richard took seriously, because inside the top drawer was fitted with a strip of sockets and USB ports. Both my vibrator and my phone were plugged in, charging.

I engaged my phone.

It was three oh three in the morning.

I felt bile rise in my throat.

Three oh three.

We'd arrived at three oh three that afternoon.

I swallowed down the bile, and that was chased by an involuntary shiver.

I mean, what the fuck?

Was that just a wild coincidence?

And why was Daniel walking into the mist in the wee hours of the morning?

Where was he going?

Why had he and Portia gone to bed so early?

We'd had tea, after meeting Richard and Jane, but I didn't even know where my sister's room was in this house. I hadn't been allowed much time with her, neither had Lou, including during cocktails, when Daniel didn't leave her side.

I didn't want to, but I had to.

I pulled my phone off the charger, opened Safari, and typed in DOROTHY CLIFTON.

I'd read the Wikipedia entry in my Alcott Family and Duncroft House research when Portia got involved with them, and again scanned it when we'd been asked to the house.

However, sitting in bed in the Carnation Room, I read it again.

Very closely this time.

Dorothy Clifton had been a silent film star. Platinum blond and beautiful. Very famous. Very glamorous. It had been rumored she'd had a torrid affair with the Prince of Wales years before he'd become enamored of his future wife, the woman he'd abandon the crown for, Wallis Simpson.

She had also, and these rumors were definitely true, been carrying on an affair with the handsome, dashing, but very married Earl Alcott.

For some inexplicable reason, still engaged in this affair, she'd agreed to attend a house party at Duncroft. Multiple attendees, after the fact, let slip that she and David, the earl, had continued their liaison in the very house where his wife lived and was in attendance.

On the last evening of the house party, wearing a stunning gown created by up-and-coming fashion designer Elsa Schiaparelli, Dorothy Clifton fell over the railing, at the very top of the grand staircase, to her death on the white marble floor below.

Guests and servants all shared she had been quite inebriated.

But many questions remained unanswered about this fall, foremost being why she was on the top floor at all. It housed staff quarters, the tutor's rooms, and storage. There was no reason for her to be there. With the house party requiring them to see to their duties, there wasn't even any staff up there.

And both David and Virginia Alcott had not been located until several hours after the incident. When they arrived at the house, they claimed to be engaging in a moonlit stroll that included David alluding to a marital tryst.

In the end, the incident was deemed an accident, regardless of the fact the balustrade twining along the entirety of the staircase was unusu-

TOO GOOD TO BE TRUE

ally high, nearly four feet tall. Practically impossible to topple over... unless you threw yourself over.

Or you'd been lifted and dropped.

Or pushed.

In the aftermath, for years, the scandal and scuttlebutt clung to the Alcotts and Duncroft like a pall, with ping-pong theories of Virginia doing the deed out of jealous rage, even though she was slight and petite, Dorothy being several inches taller than her, therefore it was doubtful she could manage it physically. Though, not impossible, considering the level of Dorothy's supposed intoxication.

So aspersions were cast on David, who it was said wished to end the affair, regardless that he very clearly continued to engage in it during the party.

There were whisperings that Dorothy wasn't even invited to the house, but showed of her own accord, and the Alcotts were too polite to turn her away (though perhaps not too polite not to kill her?).

For Dorothy's part, it was said she was worried that talkies were sweeping the globe and she'd be cast aside as other actresses had been. She was pressing David to divorce Virginia and marry her.

However, that theory seemed thin, considering the undeniable truth in all of it was, Dorothy was a well-educated young woman from an upper-middle class home. Due to her film career, she was very wealthy in her own right, and reports stated she'd managed her money well, and this bore true. On her death, she'd left over one million dollars to her younger sister, the equivalent of over sixteen million today.

Her sister remained vigilant of these funds, even after the crash that devastated the world in 1929. Indeed, the Clifton family had a penchant for finance and were now considered semi-old money by Britain's standards, because they were still loaded.

But she was by no means of the stock appropriate for the Earl Alcott.

The entry made no mention of the time she died, neither did several other listings I checked.

There were lots of pictures of her, however, and she was stunning. She didn't have the doe-eyed, simpering innocence that most female stars of that era possessed.

She was Britain's version of Mae West: sultry, hooded eyes, buxom, and explicitly sexual.

There were also photos of David and Virginia.

David had the thin-mustached, simmering sexuality and rugged good looks of Clark Gable. I could see shades of Richard and especially Ian in him, but not so much Daniel.

Virginia was a blonde version of Clara Bow, complete with wide, wounded eyes filled with vulnerability.

Apparently, David and Virginia never lived Dorothy's death (murder?) down, but David was rich and titled (as well as entitled) and didn't give two shits what anyone thought of him. He went about his business and life as if a woman he'd been having an affair with under his wife's nose (almost literally) hadn't died a horrible death in the entry of his ancestral home.

However, within months, Virginia had secluded herself in Duncroft, never to be seen on the London scene again. In fact, never to be seen again, unless someone went to Duncroft.

Something that sounded unnervingly familiar.

When I put my phone back on charge, it was nearing four thirty in the morning.

I considered my vibrator before I reached and turned off the light, plunging the room again in complete darkness.

I ruled against a self-induced orgasm, mostly because the dream with Ian Alcott seemingly marrying me, then making love to me, only to end up smothering me, was not something I wanted associated with a real-life climax.

Unsurprisingly, I had trouble sleeping, but eventually managed it.

Only shortly after to be awoken again.

And this time, someone was definitely in my room.

Six

THE TOUR

I jerked up in bed about the time the first set of curtains on one of the four windows in my room was slapped open by one of the maids.

I blinked as she moved to the next window, then whipped my head around when I sensed movement on my other side.

A second maid was approaching the bed carrying a legged breakfast tray, while the maid who'd offered to help me with dressing was finishing tucking my evening shoes into the wardrobe. She then turned toward the gown I'd thrown over the back of the sofa.

Brittany was not there.

"Breakfast," the maid who set the tray beside me on the bed said. She was now reaching behind me to gather pillows and fluff them for me to lay back on while I ate. "Lord Alcott will meet you at ten in the Conservatory to take you on a tour of the house."

The window maid was done with the curtains and was looking down at me, and it was her turn to talk.

"If you require any assistance, just use the bell pull," she instructed.

She then pointed to the wide, velvet ribbon ending in a silk tassel, which hung down the wall close to the bed.

The maid with my dress was walking toward the door.

"Hey," I called. "Where are you taking that?"

She stopped, turned my way and looked confused. "To the laundry, of course."

"It's dry clean only," I pointed out. "And I can see to that when I get home."

"We dry clean in house," the curtain maid sniffed, clearly affronted. "It'll be returned this afternoon."

All the maids were now heading to the door. Indeed, the dressing maid was already out of it, *with* my dress.

"Hold on," I snapped.

The breakfast tray maid slipped out, the curtain maid remained, arching her brows toward me.

"What's your name?" I asked.

"Laura," she answered.

"And the others?" I demanded.

"Rebecca brought in your tray. Harriet will see to your dress. I believe Brittany has already introduced herself."

Yes. They definitely talked among themselves.

"Please don't come into this room without knocking," I requested, *firmly*.

She hesitated, gave a slight bow to her head, and said, "As you wish."

And then she left, the door giving a soft snick when she closed it behind her.

I felt bad for being snappish, but for goodness' sakes. Who walked into a stranger's room, woke them up, fluffed their pillows and took their clothes?

No, in a team of three, who did all that?

None of this requested, after they'd unpacked personal belongings, again not requested.

I mean, honestly. If it wasn't for the USB ports in my nightstand, it'd feel like I'd been thrown back to the 1890s.

Still sleepy, feeling off, and definitely unsettled by what just happened, I looked down at the tray.

And for God's sake.

This was beginning to be too much.

The tray was large, like a small table. And the china appeared to be designed for the room, cream with carnation-pink edges clad in slender strips of gold.

Breakfast included egg in cup, impeccably toasted squares in an ornate silver caddy, coffee service, cup and saucer, creamer and tiny sugar bowl in the same cream and pink china. The silverware, as it had been at dinner last night, was gold-plated. There was half a grapefruit, several rashers of bacon, sauteed mushrooms, two delicious-looking sausages, two hash brown patties, and four small bowls, one of brown sauce, the others of ketchup, butter and marmalade. The only things missing from a proper English were the beans, blood pudding and grilled tomatoes.

There was also a small, gold vase, the top being tightly packed poofs of four pink carnations.

I grabbed the tray and set it aside so I could swing my legs off the bed. I went to the bathroom to brush my teeth, wash my face, and lightly moisturize (I could hardly eat with morning mouth).

I then went back to bed to enjoy breakfast in it.

But I did this with the steely determination to speak to Lord Alcott when I joined him for the tour in order to explain as politely as possible (even if he had not extended much of the same to me) my clothes and belongings were mine to deal with, I would prefer privacy in my room, and if that was too much to ask, I'd be leaving it and Duncroft, taking my sister and Lou with me.

And last, but most importantly, I would demand to talk, *alone*, with my goddamned sister.

∾

I WENT to Lou's room first, before I headed down to the Conservatory.

I knocked. She didn't answer.

I knocked again, no answer.

I didn't want to stick my head in, in case she was showering or had her earbuds in. I didn't want to give her a fright.

Truth, since I was purposefully running late (control freak Richard could wait five minutes for me, yes, that was snotty, but I'd had broken sleep and I was in a mood), and Lou was being very careful to make Portia look good, she'd probably already headed down.

Though, it would be strange she did that without knocking on my door first.

Nevertheless, I turned toward the staircase, walking down the flight of stairs on the inside (not close to the railing), entirely because I'd read about Dorothy Clifton a couple hours before and I wanted nothing to do with that railing. At least, not that morning.

I made it to the bottom of the stairs, rounded the newel post and statue while studiously avoiding looking at it, and headed to the back of the house.

To the Conservatory.

The doors to it were wide open and just plain wide, and tall, rising up ten, maybe twelve feet, and stretching across at least the same measure. There were curlicues of leaded fancies adorning the glass doors that swung inside the room. They were like iron summonses, guiding you inside, and the close, humid feel of a greenhouse could be felt several feet before I even arrived at the entryway.

It was nearly oppressive inside, plants hanging everywhere, some of them huge, with leaves and vines dangling twenty, thirty feet. They were so far up, I had no idea how they watered them. But they managed it: they were all almost grotesquely healthy.

I didn't spend too much time thinking about it, because no one was there to greet me.

I walked farther in.

The floor was a sea of stunning mosaic tile with inlaid paths twining through more plants, these potted and sitting on the ground, in planter stands or on ornate columns. The paths separated and reunited, until I hit the back of the Conservatory.

It was only here I could see the angled sweep of the expansive glass panes that started at least two stories up, led to the house and connected to it.

Also here was a cozy arrangement of comfortable-looking green velvet chairs and sofas intermingled with carved, glossy wood side tables. There were also Tiffany glass lamps, several of them.

Further, there were piles of books, as if this was someone's secret getaway where they lounged and read, away from the dysfunction of the occupants of the house. And there was a fully stocked drinks cabinet off to the side, hidden among a bunch of plants. It was beautiful, and I spied a small, expertly hidden refrigerator, which no doubt held chilled beverages so whoever hung out here wouldn't have to go too far, or be disturbed by anyone, if they wanted a cool drink.

Definitely a secret getaway for someone, and that someone appeared to be Ian Alcott, for he sat alone on one of the sofas, a book held open in his hand, a gold-filtered cigarette burning between two fingers of his upraised other one, his head turned and tipped back, his attention on me.

If he wasn't wearing jeans and a thick fisherman's sweater, I would have pegged him from another era, specifically considering that foul cigarette.

So my guided tour wasn't going to be conducted by stuffy, arrogant, pompous Lord Alcott.

It was going to be conducted by handsome, arrogant, vain *Lord Alcott*.

Not the Earl.

The Viscount.

He crushed the cigarette out in a heavy, cut-glass ashtray on the low coffee table in front of him, placed a leather bookmark in the book and tossed it on the table.

He then looked at his watch.

"Seven minutes late. Congratulations," he drawled.

"You shouldn't smoke," I announced.

"Ah, she worries about my health. How charming," he murmured, pushing up from the couch.

I ignored that and my reaction to his imposing height and the visual of him in all his glory, and I scanned the space.

When I saw we were alone, I asked, "Where's Lou?"

He looked genuinely perplexed when he said, "Sam took her into the village. She said she forgot some medication. She called her doctor. He phoned the prescription to the pharmacy there and they're off to pick it up."

She couldn't ask me to take her to get it?

What happened to *we three need to stick together*?

I didn't care what it looked like, after he was done speaking, I pulled out my phone and texted Lou, *Where are you?*

I then returned to Ian. "Where's Portia?"

"I'm afraid your plans for visiting the ruins today have changed. Something's gone wrong at Danny's work. Considering I employed him for three years, or shall I say *attempted* to keep him employed, but this didn't work, *spectacularly*, one can only assume he's the cause of it. He's been called in urgently, and Portia went with him, ostensibly for moral support. Which is a poorly hidden excuse for her not to be at Duncroft so you won't be able to get to her and talk some sense into her about being involved with my brother."

Well, one could say that was forthright.

"I see there's no love lost," I noted.

Though the brothers had given foreshadowing of that last night, still, with this current brutal honesty, I felt unhappy about pretty much everything he just said as well as the fact he said it.

My phone vibrated with a text, and I looked to it.

Lou.

I forgot my migraine tablets. I had a terrible headache last night. Fortunately, six tabs of ibuprofen and six of aspirin took the edge off. They said you were sleeping, so I didn't want to bother you. I'm in town picking up a prescription...and some more ibuprofen and aspirin. Do you need anything while I'm here?

No, I replied. Then sent, *Let me know when you're headed back.*

Okay, lovey, she returned.

I lifted my head to see Ian still standing where he'd been, but now he had his arms crossed over his wide chest. And as ever, his attention was focused on me.

"Well?" I demanded. "Your comments about your brother?"

"He's lovable. He's also a moron."

"My sister is lovable too, but she can sometimes make this difficult. Perhaps they're a match well made," I suggested.

"I inherit the house. I inherit the land. I inherit the accounts that come with them. My father has absolutely nothing to his name. The earldom has vast funds he can avail himself of, but they're monitored closely by trustees within the banks in which they're held. He cannot give to himself or others in any way that impoverishes the earldom. He can pay staff. He can pay to keep the home and lands maintained or make upgrades. He and my mother can take first-class vacations around the world, and clothe themselves in head-to-toe logo, but they can't spend outlandishly, and again, if they did something that endangered Duncroft's trust, they'd be cut off."

He took a breath in the midst of this, and I hated to admit it, but I was interested in what he was sharing.

He then kept speaking.

"In other words, Dad cannot land an inheritance on the second son. When Dad dies, it all comes to me. And then it'll be me who can't give money to Danny. Unless I feel like taking care of him as a matter of course should he wish to remain at Duncroft, and this would include me agreeing that he could do so, he needs to make his own way."

I supposed this wasn't a surprise. Bank trustees making sure the funds weren't squandered might be how Duncroft and the Alcotts survived all these years.

Ian carried on, "As you could probably read from our exchanges last night, Danny doesn't care much for me. He wants nothing from me, or my inheritance. Hence, he finds a woman worth one hundred billion dollars."

I heard the hissed-in breath I took at that, and I imagined Ian did too.

Because that was *viciously* forthright.

"So he's into her for her money," I whispered.

Ian shrugged. "My guess, yes."

"And you openly share this with me when we barely know each other, and it has nothing to do with some demented sibling rivalry?"

"Do you honestly think I consider Danny a rival?" he scoffed.

"I think you're possibly the most arrogant man I've ever met," I replied.

He smiled a wolfish smile. "Good. I'm doing it right."

Ugh.

He was terrible.

It was damnably attractive.

He was still terrible.

"Perhaps I don't want a tour."

"Oh, you want a tour, Miss Ryan. They all want tours."

"Who are 'they'?"

"Anyone, not us."

I studied him.

He let me.

Then again, he was probably used to all kinds of attention, completely comfortable with it.

It was his due.

"How often have you been around Daniel and Portia?" I asked.

"Since I dated her first, and he met her through me, often."

Holy crap!

"You dated her first?" I breathed in horror, shocked Portia hadn't shared this with me.

That put an entirely different spin on "some friends set us up."

"This isn't the first time it's happened. My brother can be very incestuous when it comes to availing himself of what used to be mine. It comes from his competitive streak. That streak runs in the family, fortunately skipping me."

I read between the lines and recited out loud what I read. "Then again, if you do everything perfectly, you don't need to be competitive."

Now I had a sly smile.

"You said it, I didn't."

Insufferable.

"Are you trying to chase me away?"

"Absolutely not, Miss Ryan. I like you. Very much."

"You don't know me very much."

"I know you were seven minutes late, doing this thinking you were meeting my father, and that tells me quite a bit."

It did, damn the man.

"You...and my sister," I prompted.

"Two dates, and we didn't fuck."

His coarse language was another test, and I realized he'd been testing me since before I showed up.

"I'm not a game player," I warned.

"I know this about you."

"Can I assume you've investigated me...*us*?"

"You're a size eighteen and you have very good taste in underwear and very poor taste in men."

I gasped.

"The dress last night was inspired, by the way," he continued. "I knew I liked you then. You're only confirming my good instincts now."

I shifted subjects.

"So Daniel stole Portia from you."

"No, Daniel *thinks* he did. Your sister is pretty, not beautiful, like you, but she's too highly strung, not grounded, again...like you. Both reasons why I didn't fuck her."

"Can you please refrain from talking about fucking my sister?" I requested.

"If you wish."

"I do."

"Fine," he allowed. "I let Daniel think she was stolen. Everyone needs some wins once in a while. Even if they aren't come by honestly."

I had nothing to say to that.

He had things to say.

"Your mother was...still is, beautiful, like you. Why do you think your father left her for Portia's mother?"

"Because Andrea was a whore with a particular skillset, and no matter Dad turned his father's hardware store into a retail giant that gobbled up the world online and in brick and mortar, he still solely thought with his dick."

When I was done speaking, Ian angled back his head and laughed.

The sound was deep and lush and thrilling, and I hated it almost as much as I absolutely adored it.

I scowled at him.

He finished laughing and whispered in a way that was both silken and sinister, "Yes, I very much like you."

"Are we doing this tour, or what?"

He uncrossed his arms to raise them to his sides. "Meet the Conservatory."

"It's oppressive," I told him.

"It would be. One of the four people who hung themselves in this house did it from a plant hook right over there."

He pointed.

I looked over my shoulder.

When I looked back, he'd gotten so much closer, and he'd done it in such utter silence and with such quickness, I jumped.

"You don't have to fear me," he murmured, gazing down at me with a languid look in his astonishing blue eyes that I felt *everywhere*.

"Yes, I do."

"And she's smart too," he continued murmuring.

"We're going to make a deal right now. We're going to give them a chance, you and me."

"Again, if you wish."

"I think it's real for Portia."

He appeared openly dubious.

But he said, "You control her money. You're intelligent and shrewd. You're successful and don't need a man or your father's money. If there's something to see through, you'll see through it. If her happiness means more to you than his games, you'll give her what she wants. Then it'll be on her. You don't care about the money. You've given half of yours away already."

Yes, he investigated me...*us*...thoroughly.

"You can live a long time on fifty billion dollars."

"I'd bet half my own fortune that half of the rest of yours will be in the hands of charities in the next two years."

He'd win that bet, so I didn't take it.

"Are we only allowed to be in our bedrooms, the Pearl Room, the Wine Room, this room and the dining room?" I asked.

"Of course not. I'll follow you to the hall."

This offer wasn't gentlemanly behavior. My ass looked great in these cords. And if I preceded him, he'd be able to watch it.

Whatever.

I led our way to the hall and stopped by the newel post.

"You get two questions here, petal," he stated, stopping a few feet away from me.

Petal.

I didn't like that he used the name on me that he'd used with my sister.

I let my expression convey that, he caught it, I knew because of his smirk, then I said, "You know my questions already, so answer them, please."

"She's Persephone, wandering the Elysian fields."

The woman of the statue was wandering the afterlife.

How fitting for Duncroft House.

"Of course," I muttered.

He moved away and stood what appeared to be dead center of the wide circle of the entryway.

"And she landed right here," he stated.

Dorothy Clifton.

Another shiver.

"Do you think it was an accident?" I asked.

"That's question three," he told me.

I tipped my head. "Actually, that was the first question I asked."

Something shifted in his eyes, on his face, an awareness, of me, of us, of this conversation.

It was uniquely thrilling.

He hadn't only been testing me and giving me shit to see what stuff I was made of, he hadn't been taking me seriously.

Now, he was taking me seriously.

He held an arm out toward the hall that led to the Pearl Room.

I only approached him and fell in step beside him when he started talking.

"There's a lot to that story that isn't on Wikipedia."

"And that would be?"

"Are you sure you want to know?"

"Why wouldn't I?"

"Because Dorothy was having an affair with David. She was also having an affair with William, David's younger brother."

"Oh my," I mumbled.

Tangled web.

And it would seem for Dorothy, poisonous spiders.

"Indeed," he agreed. "It's my understanding you've already seen the Pearl Room?"

"Yes."

He walked us to the other side and opened the door to the room across from it. "The Emerald Room."

It was much like the Pearl Room, except decorated in the rich jewel tones of that particular green stone.

"Every room on the ground floor of this wing is named and decorated for precious stones," he explained. "Sapphire, ruby, jade, amethyst, aquamarine, opal, pink topaz, garnet, moonstone, lapis lazuli, peridot, cat's-eye, and at the end with the turrets, diamond."

I was looking forward to the Cat's-eye Room.

"Are there themes on each wing?" I asked.

"Mostly, yes. The rooms in the wing your bedroom is in are all named after flowers. Carnation, rose, orchid, jasmine, daisy, poppy, dahlia, tulip, iris, narcissus, etcetera."

We'd moved out of the Emerald Room into the one next to it, what appeared to be the Aquamarine Room.

"What other themes are there?" I queried.

"The opposite wing of bedrooms from yours, trees. These have been converted into suites as it's the family wing. Mostly flowering trees. Dogwood, cherry, magnolia, hawthorn, jacaranda. I'm in Hawthorn, by the way, the exact opposite of your room, actually, on the southeastern side."

"Unnecessary information," I said, and he chuckled while leading me out of Aquamarine and across the hall.

"The opposite of this wing on the ground floor, as you may have guessed by now, are the wines and spirits. The Wine Room, Port Room, sherry, whisky, viognier, Bordeaux, brandy, chartreuse, starting the wing, obviously, is Champagne. As you know, the dining room is on that side. It used to be called the Chardonnay Room, but my great-grandmother, who detested chardonnay, thought that was common. So she commissioned custom china and had it repaneled. Underneath the tapestry that hangs there now is apparently an extraordinary hand-painted mural. But she loved turquoise, and even if it didn't fit in that wing of the house, she made it happen."

We were now in the Moonstone Room, and so far, it was my favorite.

"Mum's in the Cherry Room," he told me. "The turret room at the end of our wing. Dad's in Dogwood."

I stopped and stared up at him. "They don't share a room?"

He shook his head. "Not since the first time he fucked around on her."

I kept staring.

"Come, Miss Ryan," he began, looking and sounding disappointed. "Surely you know privileged men, or men in general, better than that."

He could be alluding to what he knew of my ex. He could be alluding to what we all knew, but never talked about, regarding Dad cheating on my mom, Portia's mom, and also Lou.

It could be both.

Or it could be he was enlightened to his gender.

His words and expression weren't acrid or sharp, meant to sting or tally a point.

There was something almost...*defeatist* about his expression and posture.

And I sensed this was about his father hurting his mother. Maybe even Daniel hurting other women. And maybe, considering what I'd recently learned of their triangles, Daniel hurting women that had once been Ian's, and he might have been done with them, but he didn't want them hurt.

However, none of this was Ian nor his own behaviors.

Then again, he went through women like water, and as far as I knew, had never even been engaged. He was open about his apparent commitment to bachelorhood. So much so, no woman at this juncture, with his reputation, could be surprised his attention would eventually wander. If she went in thinking she could "change him," his history proved her wrong from the start.

Thinking of it that way, Ian Alcott might be the last honest man standing.

He took my elbow and led me out of the Moonstone Room and down the hall, to the next room.

It was the Cat's-eye Room, and I didn't know why, but by far, it was my favorite.

The room was mostly a creamy, blueish, midnight green with the theme in the upholstery of the pillows and furniture of thin lines of white with a blue edge. It was clever, and it was warm. It was smaller than the other rooms, far cozier, even if, like all the rest, it didn't seem much used.

There was something cocoonish about it. So much so, I wanted to curl up with a cat and a book, a pot of tea, and eventually fall asleep in order to catch up on the rest I'd missed last night.

I knew what it was.

I felt safe in that room when, so far, I hadn't really felt safe anywhere in that house.

It all seemed, so far, to be traps, games, efforts at control, bonds and strictures.

I felt I could go to this room, and no one would look for me there: no maid, no Alcott.

No bad dreams.

When I finally had the opportunity, I intended to talk to Portia in that room.

"How did you know about your father?" I asked the room, speaking quietly.

"He shouted. She cried. I have excellent hearing. They're my parents, I'm their son, I'm going to feel everything, notice everything, especially about my mother. What might hurt her, what might keep hurting her. Most especially when I'm six."

Six.

Six years old.

For some reason, I shared, "It happened to me when I was four. Dad had just opened his twentieth store. We were leveraged to the hilt for him to do it. He took risks. Lived on the edge. Mom stood beside him even if we were eating ramen and she was cutting my hair, stealing from Peter to pay Paul to deal with bills, and she was a dab hand at begging for more time from creditors. But he was on the cusp. It would only take months from then when all his bets paid off and the profits started pouring in. When she found out about Andrea, Mom didn't move him out of her bedroom. She moved him out of our house. And then Andrea swooped in for the kill."

"She had something she could do. My mother doesn't. No woman should put themselves in that position. If there are no laws preventing them, they should be able to look after themselves. If there are laws, they should do everything they can to have them struck down."

Oh shit.

Was I beginning to like this guy?

I looked at him to see he was watching me.

"You didn't answer," I noted. "Who do you think killed Dorothy Clifton?"

At my question, without warning, he shut it down.

Completely.

His face. Our conversation.

He did this by saying, "You've had your quota of questions. Let's skip to the good part and go to the Diamond Room." He guided me out of the Cat's-eye Room, and we walked down the long hall. Along the way, he shared, "There are one hundred and fifty-four rooms in this house."

"Whoa," I muttered.

"And for the most part, two people live in it, two being the ones who can avail themselves of the fullness of it. There are ten full-time staff, as well as several part-time staff. However, they don't get to kick back and watch telly in the Port Room."

Again, was I beginning to like this guy, or was I reading into things?

I tested the waters. "What are you saying?"

"I think I said what I was saying," he replied enigmatically, and then he ushered me into the Diamond Room, which was certainly, at least in this wing, the pièce de résistance.

"Wow, this is gorgeous," I breathed, gazing around, taking in the prisms of light, the dripping chandeliers and wall sconces, the opalescent wallpaper, the delicate furnishings, the ivory grand piano in one of the turrets that had a runner draped over it that sparkled like diamonds, even in the dreary, weak sunlight that was struggling through the clouds.

I knew how shut down he was when he said, "You're welcome to peruse the rest of the house at your leisure."

This was surprising.

"But I thought—"

"However, the third door to the right of first floor, southeastern wing is mine, so if you're in there, be prepared for me to make a full perusal of your underwear firsthand."

I felt my eyes get big at this insanely forward comment.

Ian continued, "Next door is the Smoke Tree Room, that's Danny's. He's not in it much, seeing as he sneaks out to join Portia in her room in the northeast wing, something that irritates my father, for reasons I don't know, since he's still screwing around on my mum. Still, I doubt Danny would welcome your presence in his room. Portia is in the Robin Room in the northeast wing, which is where yours is, but flipped around."

At least I now knew where Portia was.

And the fact that wing seemed to be named after birds.

Oh, and the bizarre fact she was set in a different wing than everybody else, and far away from me.

"Cherry and Dogwood are the last two rooms on the southeast wing, Mum and Dad's room. Don't go there either," he demanded.

"But your father doesn't want—"

"Daphne, I'm quite sure you noticed, I don't give a fuck what my father wants."

And with that, and further apropos of nothing, the guided tour was over.

I knew that when the Viscount Duncroft turned and walked away.

Seven

THE PORT ROOM

uming, I left my bedroom and stalked down the hall.

I hammered on Lou's door.

She opened it, looking freaked, probably because I was banging on her door, only to stop looking freaked and start looking bemused when she saw me.

"You okay?" she asked.

"Where have you been all day?"

"I texted you. Since we were out, Sam suggested we nip to the ruins. It was farther away than I thought. We just got back half an hour ago. It was a lot of wandering and climbing. Then it started to drizzle. There was lots of mud. It was amazing, but I'm a mess. I have to hurry, or I'll be late for dinner." Her eyes went up and down my body and she asked, her voice pitched higher. "What on earth are you wearing?"

"Richard Alcott isn't my father. He can't send me to bed without supper if he doesn't like my outfit. Though I don't know if he's even at the house at all, since I haven't seen him, or Lady Jane, or *anyone* since Ian gave me a tour this morning then brooded off."

She seemed intrigued. "Ian gave you a tour?"

I didn't have time to get into how irritating his tests and games were, then making me think I might like him only for him to disappear in full Mr. Rochester, leaving me alone for the rest of the entire day.

Sure, the place was enormous, and it took almost two hours to get through it all.

But then *I was alone for the rest of the day.*

I hadn't invited my own self there, for goodness' sake.

"Do you know Portia is in fucking *London*?" I demanded.

"Yes, she texted. She said it couldn't be helped. Daniel had to go there for work. She'll be back tomorrow."

"I'd like to be in London, oh, I don't know...*running my business.*"

Lou made excuses for her, like normal. "This was unexpected for her and Daniel."

"This is another game," I snapped. "She knows we don't like him, or his family, or this crazy, beautiful, too damned perfect house. She knows if we have a chance to talk to her, we'll talk her out of being with him. And she's in London, where *we live,* and we're in the middle of goddamn nowhere, because she asked us to be here, and that is *not okay.*"

"I see you're upset," she said conciliatorily.

"You think?"

"Come in while I get ready, but I have to take a really quick shower. It'll be super quick, promise. I have to hurry."

"You're a grown-ass woman, Lou. Fuck Richard Alcott and his schedule. Don't hurry. I'll see you down there whenever you're ready."

I turned away as she called, "Where are you going?"

"To find a drink," I called back.

One could say I was a lot more comfortable tonight, at least in what I was wearing.

I had on an iridescent shirt in black that was unbuttoned so far down, you could see quite a bit of the very lacy cups of my black bra. I was wearing this with black tuxedo cigarette pants and patent black Christian Louboutin pumps. The only jewelry I had on were a pair of hoops that, on the outside, were traced with diamonds, and on the inside, were black diamonds. Those and a Roberto Coin Rock and Diamonds white gold ring on the middle finger of my left hand.

I was headed to the Wine Room, and I was half an hour early, but screw it. If no one was there to get me a drink, and I couldn't pour my own, I'd pull the cord and get someone to help me.

Since I had all day—*by myself*—as mentioned, I'd given myself the full tour.

So not only had I seen Portia's Robin Room was an incredibly pretty exploration of just how well you could use robin's egg blue, I also knew it was the Port Room where I heard the voices coming from as I closed in on the Wine Room.

"Who put her in Carnation?"

That was Ian, and he sounded pissed.

And one could only assume he was talking about me and my allocated bedroom.

The question was, why would that make him angry?

I stopped and stepped to the side of the hall, inching closer to the door, the better to eavesdrop.

"Household decisions are your mother's."

That was Richard.

"Bullshit. Mum wouldn't put anyone in there. It's ghoulish."

"It's a beautiful room. Outside Robin and Cherry, it's the best in the house. At least on the feminine side of things."

"So it was your decision."

"She's a special guest. She might be your sister-in-law if things go well for Daniel."

"So you put her in a dead woman's room?"

What the hell?

A dead woman?

"Please tell me you didn't tell her about that," Richard demanded.

"Fuck no, I didn't. Christ, Dad."

"It was nearly a hundred years ago."

Nearly a hundred years ago.

Oh my God.

Dorothy Clifton had been given my room.

"Not a single person has slept in that room for ninety-five years, until last night," Ian declared.

"I told your mother it was time to break the seal."

"So it *was* you who put her in that room."

"It isn't an issue, Ian."

"She's going to figure Danny out."

"I'm sure you helped her with that on your *tour*," Richard said snidely.

"Might as well save her some time."

"You can't see your brother happy."

"No, I can. I want that for him. What I don't want is for him to shit on yet another woman while he makes himself happy, just like his father taught him."

The viciousness of Richard's next had me holding my breath. "How fucking *dare you*," he snarled.

"Pretty fucking easy, *Dad*. Christ, she's a shell. You think I'm her son and I don't feel that for her?"

Richard's shift of subject felt like whiplash, and I wasn't even part of the conversation.

"She's in that room. She's fine. There's no reason to move her. It's a beautiful room."

"And Louella is in Floral, which is the shittiest room in the house. How stupid do you think women in general are?" Ian sneered. "Do you honestly think they haven't figured you out, at least Daphne? She had your ticket the second she laid eyes on you."

"I don't have a ticket, for God's sakes."

"You're worse than her father, and she smelled that on you before you entered the Pearl Room to greet her."

Well, surprise, surprise. Ian thought highly of me, because I didn't, but I also kinda sorta did, just not in the way he thought.

I must have passed his tests.

"This is a ridiculous conversation," Richard derided. "You're not needed here this week. You can go back to London tomorrow when Daniel and Portia return."

"If you think I'm going to leave those women to this pack of hyenas, Dad, you're dead, fucking wrong."

Yes.

I was beginning to like this guy.

Damn.

"Also, please, for the love of God, let this sink in," Ian went on. "You don't tell me what to do anymore. You haven't for twenty goddamn years. You never will again."

"Would that I could break the covenants," Richard taunted in an ugly voice.

I clapped both hands over my mouth.

Because...

The covenants?

That had to be...what?

What determined the succession of the earldom?

Richard was saying to his son's *face* that he didn't want him to inherit what was rightfully his.

Sure, it was by luck of the birth order.

It was still Ian's.

"Well, you can't," Ian returned. "But go for it. I could buy Duncroft twice and not blink."

"No one likes a braggart, Ian."

"You missed my point, Dad. I don't need the fucking title and I don't want the fucking house. I'm not stupid, it's worth a fortune, and since it's mine, I'll take it. But unlike you, and Danny, and everyone before you, I don't *need* it. And that's what pisses you off so goddamn much. Because I have something to brag about. And you've done not one fucking worthwhile thing in your life, so you've got dick."

Score!

I nearly cheered.

Instead, since this seemed to be winding down, I made sure to keep to the carpet runner and quickly made my way to the foyer.

That was marble, no rug, so I tiptoed as best I could around the staircase, then walked normally when I entered the Conservatory.

Because I knew where I could find a drink.

I was helping myself to a bottle of Champagne (Veuve, as a matter of fact) from the beverage fridge when I cried out and whirled after I heard Ian ask, "Making yourself at home?"

I stood, expensive bottle in one hand, fingers wrapped around the cork I'd already divested of its foil, caught red-handed.

"Uh..."

"Enjoy the entertainment?"

Shit, I could feel the blood rushing to my face.

"You couldn't miss it," I said carefully.

"You didn't have to listen."

True.

"You're freaking me out, how did you know I was there?" I asked.

"I heard your heels on the marble of the entryway. Coming and leaving. Even all the way from the Conservatory. It echoes."

Oh. Yes. Of course. How did I not think of that?

"Did your dad hear me?"

"My father lives in a bubble of his own importance that nothing penetrates. I'd pushed myself into it, necessarily, but regrettably. Since he's only capable of dealing with one thing at a time, and considering he'd have no issue calling you out for listening, I'd say no."

He came toward me, and I stood still, wondering what he would do.

He stopped in front of me and yanked the Champagne out of my hands.

Fair play. It was his, or his dad's, but actually it was both of theirs, really, in a weird way.

My mind stopped rambling when I heard the cork pop and he leaned into me.

His cologne wasn't cloying. It was elusive, but I smelled moss, clove and something fresh, maybe bergamot.

It was unusual: subtle (not him), yet still strong (totally him).

Oh dear.

When he straightened, he had two cut crystal Champagne flutes in one hand.

He offered them to me.

I took them.

He poured, set the bottle down, took one glass, clinked the one I held in front of me, looked me in the eyes, and said, "*Santé.*"

I kept eye contact and repeated, "*Santé.*"

If he'd opened his mouth over the rim and downed it in one, I wouldn't have been surprised.

He didn't.

He took a sip.

I watched...his face, his mouth, and in the end, that strong throat.

Oh yes.

Oh dear.

I took my own sip.

"I'll be telling Christine to move you and Louella into the bird wing tomorrow," he declared, not stepping away from me, standing very close.

"Who's Christine?"

"Our housekeeper."

"It's slightly creepy, knowing what I know now, I will admit, but my room is very beautiful. That said, Lou's room sucks. She loves irises, and I checked out that room on the solo part of my tour. It's right across the hall from mine and she'd like it very much. So maybe move her?"

"If you wish," he muttered, his attention having been captured by my lacy bra. "Is that for me?"

I didn't know it until that moment, but it was one thousand percent for him.

Argh.

"I thought it might annoy your dad."

He lifted his gaze to mine. "He's going to hate it."

"Then my work tonight will be done."

"Fuck, I wanna kiss you," he murmured, put that right out there, his gaze now on my mouth.

Well, *damn.*

And double damn because I wanted him to kiss me, goddamn it.

He didn't kiss me.

He moved to the couch and opened a sleek wooden box on a side table. In it was a stack of cigarettes rolled in dark-blue, watermarked paper, and they had a gold tip.

He took one, put it between his beautiful lips, then slid a long, thin, sleek gold lighter out of a special compartment carved into the box, which looked made for it.

He tipped his head to the side in a movement that had been made by many a gorgeous man over the decades, and had sold a million, trillion cigarettes, and he lit up.

He blew out a plume of smoke and only then did he down the Champagne in what was now two swallows.

"Trust you to have fancy cigarettes," I quipped.

He leveled his blue gaze on me in a way that had me rooted to the spot so firmly, in that moment, I wasn't sure I'd ever be able to move again.

"Only the best," he decreed in a throaty rumble of a voice.

"Ian," I whispered.

"Do you want to know more about Dorothy Clifton?" he offered.

I didn't, considering the last time she slept, it was in my bed.

"Um...okay."

He put the lighter back in its place, snapped the box closed, and turned again to me.

"David fancied himself in love with her, or at least that's what he told Virginia in an effort to make her jealous."

"Oh," I muttered, then took a sip of my Champagne.

"William was in love with Virginia."

"Oh!" I said much louder, caught by surprise by that nugget of information.

"William couldn't marry Virginia..." He shook his head. "Strike that. Virginia couldn't marry William because he was the second son. There was a third, but he was gay and moved to Paris when he was twenty, never to return to English soil again. William lived at Duncroft at David's leisure."

"All right," I said when he didn't go on.

"So, obviously, William had nothing. Not true. He was the local physician, but although a noble pursuit, it didn't give him much status. Not like David had. Virginia had no choice. It was her job to make the best marriage she could, and if lore is true, David was besotted, so she made it."

Ian had a beautiful voice, deep with that posh accent, mesmerizing.

"So, David loved her too," I noted.

"He was besotted with her, darling," Ian said softly, the last word sliding over my skin like velvet. So, so, *so* much better than petal. "That isn't about love. It's about something else. Obviously, after he had her, he was an Alcott. It appears he quickly lost interest."

I was beginning to get concerned about this self-deprecating bent he had toward his family line. I'd barely been there a day, but even so, it seemed to be deserved, though it wasn't like he'd personally broken promises along the way.

Certainly hearts, but I sensed not that first promise.

"This is a less fun story than it seemed, when all I knew about it was a woman fell to her death," I joked.

"It gets even less fun," he warned.

"Sock it to me," I invited.

His lips quirked, he took another drag from his cigarette and came my way, but only so he could refill his Champagne glass.

He leaned against the drinks cabinet, close to me, and I found it touching he made sure the cigarette smoke didn't get near me.

"William never fell out of love with Virginia. And not because he hadn't had her, and as such, he'd gotten bored. He was genuinely in love with her, and her him. Star-crossed lovers, living in the same house."

No wonder her pictures showed a wounded vulnerability.

Good God.

What a nightmare.

Poor Virginia and William.

"Dorothy toyed," he continued. "She was known for it. She was open sexually, very much. Things started expanding for a lot of people around that time in those ways, but not that much. However, she was fortunate. She had the studios to squelch any shady rumors, like the fact she was bisexual."

Another surprising nugget.

"Whoa."

"Yes," he agreed. "As for the rest, it only enhanced her reputation as a screen siren and femme fatale. It amused her to sleep with David and William at the same time. David was reportedly wild with jealously, for she'd tell him William was her favorite. William, it's thought, did it simply to hurt David as he'd hurt Virginia for years."

"So you think David killed her?"

"I think it was talked about openly, even written about, how callous, and even cruel Dorothy was to Virginia while she was in this house. She paraded her affair with both men under Virginia's nose, and Virginia, a product of a gentler time, living a genteel life and being of her particular gender, could do nothing but keep her upper lip stiff."

"So you think Virginia killed her."

"I think it's amusing how angry women are at the patriarchy, when so often they work so hard to tear each other down. Virginia and Dorothy were not natural enemies. They were both caught in their roles with limited power to break free. And yet Dorothy targeted Virginia as much as she did William and David, but at least the men got something out of it. I truly don't know if, today, women bend their entire lives around food and exercise so they can impress men in their yoga pants, or if they do it to make their sisters feel inferior."

He took another drag from his smoke and then kept talking.

"But I sense, for the most part, it's about the very sad fact that society has drilled into their heads the only power they have is sweating and starving themselves in order to have a firm ass, and that being to make men think they're attractive. In many senses, no offense, it's through little fault of your own, but you lot haven't come very far since Dorothy's and Virginia's time."

"You won't hear any argument from me on that."

A quick glance at my bra, my outfit, then a lip quirk, before he bent slightly toward me and went on, "And that's all you get for story time tonight, little girl."

I pretended to pout.

Though him calling me "little girl" didn't feel like velvet.

I had another reaction to that, and it was centered between my legs.

He grinned broadly, maybe because of my fake pout, more likely because he knew the reaction he caused. He took another drag from his fancy-ass cigarette and walked away to blow the smoke well away from my person.

"I hope this story doesn't end with you telling me you think Dorothy's shenanigans meant she got what she deserved," I said.

He shook his head. "Virginia was powerless. Dorothy was one of the first women in modern times who had scratched her way to holding a modicum of power, and I don't blame her how she chose to use it, or either of them for how they were forced to live their lives."

"Good answer."

"Hungry?" he asked.

"I think dinner is imminent."

"As much as I want to see my father react to your shirt and that fetching bra, I ran into Stevenson on the way here and asked him to request Bonnie set up a chef's table in the kitchen. Mum and Dad can stare at each other across a twenty-five-foot expanse. You and Louella and I are going where it's warm, it smells good, and people actually like each other."

"That sounds amazing."

He took another drag, crushed out his cigarette, and held his hand my way.

For some reason, I sensed taking it was a bigger declaration than just Ian leading me to the kitchen (and collecting Lou along the way) for dinner.

So I hesitated.

When I did, he turned it palm up.

He wanted me to take it.

He wanted me to make that declaration, not just follow him out of the Conservatory, or the other way around.

He wanted us connected.

And the way he was now holding his hand to me made him seem vulnerable.

Exposed.

Like he was taking a huge risk.

No, like he was teetering on the edge and holding that hand to me so I'd save him from falling.

I took his hand.

And we found Louella on the way to the kitchen.

Eight

THE CARNATION ROOM

I lay in bed, waiting for the book I'd just bought about the Dorothy Clifton possible murder/possible accident/possible suicide to download on my Kindle.

Ian had shared the Duncroft House Wi-Fi password over dinner.

Ian had done a lot of things over dinner.

For one, he'd charmed the pants (figuratively) off Louella, and in all honesty, me.

For another, he'd exposed us to an entirely different staff of Duncroft. Those who smiled, joked, called Ian by his first name, and were wholly comfortable around him as they went about their business.

Bonnie, the rounded, very pretty, middle-aged, classically trained chef (who Richard had called a "cook") even sat with us and ate dessert while she bombarded me with questions about my business and pastry-making secrets. All this while I inwardly squirmed because Ian watched as it happened, and he did this with great intensity.

We then moved back to the Conservatory (definitely Ian's favored space, and I didn't think it was only because that was where he could smoke). There, we had after-dinner drinks and I watched while Ian beat Louella in a game of backgammon.

I refused to play the winner and not only because I didn't know how to play backgammon.

No, it was because I didn't need any more of Ian Alcott's attention on me that night.

Now, I was in bed, wondering at my sanity for buying a book about a dead woman who had slept where I was sleeping, and also wondering if I wanted the full story, as told by Dorothy Clifton's great-nephew.

I wanted the full story.

I just wanted Ian to tell me.

Man, I was in trouble.

A soft knock sounded at the door.

"Yes?" I called.

Louella poked her head around the door.

Shit!

I hadn't come up with a plausible explanation why we were going to move her tomorrow, or a plausible reason why she was in the shittiest room in the house.

And now, that hour was upon me, and I was unprepared.

"Can I come in?" she asked.

"Sure," I said.

She looked around after she slid into the room and closed the door behind her.

"Uh..." I mumbled uncomfortably.

"I've stuck my head into a couple of rooms," she said, moving to the other side of my bed, then stretching out on her side next to me, up on an elbow. "I also know people like this have a nasty way of communicating things. They did it to your dad all the time."

That was news.

"Really?"

She nodded. "He wanted to be a Lord Richard Alcott. He thought money could buy that for him. He was wrong, and when he courted their favor, they liked to make sure he knew his place."

I didn't know that about Dad.

Still.

"Ugh."

"Yes," she agreed. Then she hit me with it. "What's going on with you and Ian?"

"Nothing," I said, too quickly.

"He liked his dinner. He'd have preferred to be eating you."

I batted her with my Kindle. "Lou!"

"Am I wrong?"

"He's flirty. It's not like he isn't known for his killer charm."

"Mm," she hummed.

"He's an ally in this mess."

She tipped her head to the side. "Is this a mess?"

"Um, wasn't it you last night at around this time telling me we had to get out of here?"

"No, yes. I mean, this is a mess. This house. Daniel. Portia. Richard. Jane. Ian, though, perhaps not so much."

"I thought you thought he was unbearable."

"I changed my mind. Sue me."

I didn't need this.

"Daniel's with Portia for her money," I blurted.

"Yes."

I blinked. "You know?"

"Portia is..."

She didn't finish.

"Not such a catch, if she didn't have billions of dollars," I filled in for her.

Lou avoided my eyes. "She's pretty. She can be sweet. She's smarter than she gives herself credit for. But she's difficult."

"She dated Ian before Daniel," I told her.

Her gaze shot to mine. "What?"

"A couple of dates. No intimacy. Ian let Daniel think he stole her from him. It's a game he plays. Throwing Daniel a bone."

"Portia isn't a bone," she snipped.

"I agree. That said, he was very forthcoming about Daniel's intentions. I don't think he wants Portia hurt."

"None of us do."

"I need to sit her down to talk."

"You do."

"I saw Daniel last night, out in the fog, at three in the morning."

Her chin went into her neck. "Sorry?"

"Yes."

"What was he doing out there so early in the morning?"

"Your guess is as good as mine. He wasn't here when I was able to question him."

"That's weird."

"It's all weird, Lou."

She fell to her back. "I'm upset Portia dated Ian."

I was too.

"Why?" I asked her, because the reason she was couldn't be the same as mine.

"Because now it's icky that you'll be dating him."

"I won't be dating him."

She turned her head my way. "He's into you."

"He'll get over it."

"You're into him."

"I'll get over it too."

"Not everyone is François," she said softly.

"Yes, they are, honey. Every man is François. All ego, all pride, all cock."

And if you haven't learned that yet, God help you, I did not say.

"You're too young not to reach for happiness, lovey," she said.

And what was your happiness? My father's utter devotion that came only when you blatantly showed him yours when he was dying? And then he was dead? Is that what I get? Proving myself time and again, earning their love, but giving it as it's supposed to be given, freely, without expecting anything in return...except to be honored with the same, but never having a chance at that unless forced by happenstance into some heroic display of undying devotion?

"Did you know," I started carefully, "it's a little-known fact, quite a number of husbands leave their wives when they get a terminal disease?"

"Yes. I also know the numbers are not the same the other way around. That's love, Daphne. For all of us. We decide what to give. What to take. What boundaries to build. When to stay. When to let go.

Do you think for a second your father didn't know at first I married him for his money?"

I wasn't comfortable talking about this.

"Lou—"

"Answer me."

I was getting angry. "So you're telling me he bought your devotion in the end? You may be dealing with some guilt now he's gone, but I know you better than that."

"I'm telling you there are ebbs and flows in all relationships. Power shifts. You must know that with how much you love your sister, and how much you put up with from her. You're in this bed, aren't you? You didn't get in your car to drive to London to tell her off or just to go home and let her make her own bed with Daniel."

"So are you saying I should have forgiven François?"

"No," she spat. "He was a piece of shit."

I smiled.

"Why do you think I was saying that?" she asked.

"I don't know."

"Because I put up with your father cheating on me?"

Oh God.

I *really* was not comfortable talking about this.

"Lou," I groaned.

"That was my bed. And his. And I only mention it because you have to let me lie in it. He was funny. He made me laugh. And oh, how he thought I was beautiful. He'd look at me and convince me I was the most exquisite creature on the planet. Good or bad, right or wrong, that meant something to me. And he gave it to me. In our way, we worked. No one can say whether the way something works is right, or wrong, except the person living it. Just as no one can say when a thing isn't working, and it should end, except the person ending it."

"Right, you're right. But now, are you saying we should let Portia have Daniel without interceding?"

"I think you should tell her what you feel and what you know...*carefully*," she warned. "You don't want to lose her. But then, yes. It's her decision. This life is her bed to make and lie in."

"And what about the money?"

"As always, I'll defer to you on that. Though, I will say your father put a caveat on the money that she can't have it if she gets involved with an unsavory character."

"So now you're saying I should use the money as a weapon to get her to do what I want."

She shrugged, but then said, "It certainly would be a test of how they feel about each other, both of them, if suddenly that wasn't part of the equation."

Oh my God!

Brilliant!

I felt my smile spread so wide, it hurt my mouth. "You're a genius."

She pointed to her face, "This is not just pretty."

"It's also pretty."

She pushed up, grabbed the back of my head, kissed the top, then rolled off the bed.

She was halfway to the door when I called, "Lou?"

She turned back.

"My mother was filled with bilious hate, constant. I'd go visit her and that's all I'd hear, *we'd* hear when Portia came with me. How much she gave up for him. How much she trusted him. How he'd used her and thrown her away. How men are all evil and selfish. That, coupled with Dad having piles of money, was why she lost custody of me. And then Andrea was a total waste of space." I drew in breath. "And then there was you."

I watched her suck in her lips.

She let them go to say a husky, "Stop it."

"Love you," I whispered.

"Love you back," she whispered in return.

Then she left my room.

~

I woke.

The room was total darkness.

I threw the covers aside, swung out of bed, went to the window,

81

pulled the drapes back, and looked down, searching for Daniel walking into the mist.

Daniel wasn't there.

Wearing a pale, beaded, flapper's dress, Virginia Alcott stood outside, looking up at me, those wounded eyes filled with longing. With pain.

I put my hand on the cold glass.

She lifted her hand to her throat.

Her mouth didn't move, but I heard her words.

What about Joan?

"Joan?" I whispered.

You're asking the wrong questions. You're asking about her. You should be asking about me. About Joan. About Rose.

"Rose?"

Light filled the room.

I turned to look toward the door.

Ian stood there, hand out, palm up, stretched toward me.

Don't take his hand. It'll be the end of you. They break us. They'll break you. They broke me. I couldn't be fixed. Don't take his hand.

I turned back to Virginia.

"Daphne," Ian called.

I looked again to him.

Don't. Don't take his hand.

"Daphne," Ian repeated.

You're not safe. Leave. Go. None of us are safe.

"Daphne!" Ian yelled.

None of us are safe.

"Daphne, come to me," Ian bid.

Suddenly, I was in his arms.

His face was stuffed in my neck, he shifted so his lips were at my ear.

"I'm going to eat you," he whispered there.

I shivered with delight.

"Eat you alive," he growled, his voice wrong, animal.

I pulled away in fear, and I was falling.

Falling and falling.

All I could see were stairs.

Spinning, never ending, white stairs.

I woke, truly woke, on a truncated scream.

I pushed up on an arm, reaching out to the light, turning it on dim.

The shadows slunk away.

"Holy crap, goddamn it," I muttered to myself.

The room was freezing.

I pulled the covers up to my neck, but I didn't lay back down. I needed to take in the room. Assure myself I was alone.

The Hawthorn Room, same as mine, other side.

How would Ian feel if I woke him up and said, "Hey, so sorry. I know we barely know each other, but I need to sleep in here because I'm having creepy-as-shit nightmares."

I'd tell him the truth. The dreams were so vivid, so real, more of both than I've ever experienced (a lot more), that they were freaking me out, and I couldn't sleep alone. Tell him that I needed his warmth in this cold, damn house. Just his warmth. His presence.

How would he feel if I asked if he minded if I slept with him?

Just sleep.

I just needed some sleep.

I mentally shook myself, and I did that hard.

I could go to a hotel and sleep.

I could go home and sleep.

My first thought being to wake up a guy I barely knew and ask him if I could sleep with him was just as freaky as all the rest of it.

Sure, he was gorgeous and charming and a fantastic flirt, but jeez.

Another important note, I'd spent another day in that house, for the most part alone, and I hadn't asked anyone about my damned car.

A strange noise sounded, and I jumped a mile.

Then I realized it was my phone vibrating with a text in the drawer.

"Note to self," I mumbled, "turn on do not disturb."

I opened the drawer and pulled out the phone, but before I did, I saw the fading text notification was from Portia.

Quickly, I pulled it up.

We're not going to be back until late tomorrow, but if it's too late before we can head out, it might be Monday. So so sorry! Love you and hope to be back soon!

I glared at my phone.

Then I stared at my phone.

Because it was three oh three in the morning.

And I hadn't noticed, but the text she sent that afternoon to tell me she was in London had been sent at the same time.

Exactly twelve hours earlier.

Nine

THE WHISKY ROOM

To say I was in a mood when I stormed down the white staircase later that morning was an understatement.

I hadn't been able to get back to sleep, and I was a sleep person. Two nights interrupted, and not enough, I was not in good spirits.

I'd told Bonnie last night that breakfast in bed was awesome, but it wasn't quite me.

She'd offered another seat at her chef's table for breakfast, which was a worktable in her massive, modern kitchen (again, Richard had spared no expense on those updates, that kitchen was a dream), and I'd taken her up on it.

She told me she'd cook to order when I arrived.

I was intent to arrive, specifically to drink lots and lots of coffee.

I'd checked in on Lou before heading down. She was still getting ready and told me she'd meet me down there.

On my way, I ran into Stevenson.

His eyes lit when he saw me, if he didn't allow his face to do the same (I didn't spend much time with him last night, he and some kid named Jack were serving the main dining room).

Still, he looked way more friendly then at our first meeting.

"Good morning, Stevenson."

"Good morning, Miss Ryan. Can I show you to the kitchen?"

"Actually..."

I looked down the southeastern hall.

As noted, yesterday, during my tour, I hadn't run into Richard or Jane, only heard Richard during his fight with Ian.

Now, I wondered why.

Had they known the tour was happening and hidden themselves in their rooms so they wouldn't run into me?

Ian and me?

Lou or Ian or me?

"Is Lord Alcott around?" I asked Stevenson.

"Yes. He's in his office."

His office.

I'd noted it yesterday. It was the Whisky Room.

Though, I wondered what he did at that big, baronial desk, since, as far as I knew, he didn't have a vocation.

"I'm going to pay him a visit," I said.

Stevenson hesitated, unsure.

He was right to be unsure, but I didn't tell him that.

"As you wish," he murmured.

I smiled at him then headed down the hall.

The door was closed.

I knocked.

"Come!" Richard called.

I opened the door and walked in.

At first, he couldn't hide his surprise.

Then he blanked his expression and rose from his chair behind the desk.

"Miss Ryan."

"Daphne," I corrected. "Where's my car?"

"I'm sorry?"

"Where's my car?"

"In the garage, where else would it be?"

"I'd like my fob back and to be shown where the garage is."

"You can have both of these by calling Stevenson. He'll have Sam or Jack show you."

In other words, *Why are you bothering me with this?*

"We need to talk," I told him, coming further into the room.

Inexplicably, he appeared panicked for a moment, before he schooled his features and queried, "And why would we need to do that?"

"Because I'm concerned about your son's intentions, and his true affections, and I have control of my sister's money. I figure you know this, but I'll tell you anyway. My father didn't come from money. He turned a dying local hardware store into a multinational company, and he didn't do it by being an idiot."

"No one said he did."

"And so," I carried on like he hadn't spoken, "when he carved his fortune up to give to the three women he loved in his life, he did it carefully, with forethought and planning."

Richard's eyes flicked behind me in a manner I twisted at the waist to look that way.

Ian was lounging in the doorjamb.

He looked good enough to eat.

Eat.

"Touché," I said.

He grinned at our inside joke about me eavesdropping last night, and him sneaking into this conversation now.

"Good morning," he replied.

It would be when I had coffee.

"Don't mind me," he prompted.

I returned my attention to Richard.

"I can't, for undue reasons, withhold Portia's money," I informed him. "Though, for due reasons..."

I let that lie.

"And what would those due reasons be in regard to my son?" Richard asked between gritted teeth.

"Well, I did mention not too long ago my concerns about his intentions and affections," I reminded him.

"Daniel is besotted with Portia," Richard declared.

Besotted.

I pulled my phone out of my back pocket and started tapping on it.

"Miss Ryan...Daphne—" Richard began impatiently.

I lifted a finger but kept looking at my phone. "A second. There we go. 'Besotted. Strongly infatuated. Archaic: Intoxicated. Drunk. From late sixteenth century, make foolishly affectionate.'" I raised my head, skimmed a glance through Richard and then twisted back to Ian. "You're right. It's not what it seems to be."

"I know I'm right, darling," Ian purred.

I felt that purr in my mouth.

And other places.

Jesus.

This guy.

I felt a wave of emotion, not the good kind, come tumbling at me from Richard's direction when he heard Ian's endearment.

I turned again to him.

Indeed, he didn't like Ian calling me darling.

I fought smiling and kept speaking.

"I'm going to need to be certain about Daniel's true feelings and his commitment to my sister. And I'm going to need this not only because I love my sister, but because my father did, and he trusted this to me. Now, in full disclosure, if she messes things up for a long haul, say, marrying someone who wants her for her money, then she doesn't get that money. Ever. It's absorbed into mine and Lou's trusts. She doesn't even get a stipend. She's cut off. Completely."

Richard blanched.

"Thus, this bullshit play that's happening,"—I whirled a finger in the air—"I'm not having it. Someone needs to tell Daniel to get his ass home and bring my sister with him. It's beyond rude they dragged Lou and I here then took off to regroup when things started off rocky. I have a life. I have a business. I have people who count on me. They're talented. Beyond competent, they can carry on without me. However, I love my work, and when I decide it's one of those rare times I'm going to leave it, I don't want to be jacked around like I'm a fool. I'm not a fool, Richard. I'm my father's daughter. And for more than one reason, it's time your son, the second one, stopped treating me like one."

On that, with Richard's face red with fury, I turned on my heel and walked to Ian.

"Are you coming to breakfast?" I asked when I stopped.

He took my hand. "Absolutely." We walked down the hall, and he didn't bother waiting until we were completely out of earshot before he said, "Well done."

"It was bitchy," I replied, beginning to feel bad I'd been so frank, and done it being so curt.

I probably should have found Richard after I had coffee.

"He would have disregarded you entirely if you'd been polite," Ian shared. "As he has been for the most part since you arrived. Disregarding you. He agreed to you being here. You're our guest. I've seen how he's been acting toward you. It's beyond rude. You have no responsibility to be nice to someone who's being rude."

Well, if you completely disregarded the most important rule of all, the Golden Rule, he was right.

But I made a note not to confront my host again, or at least not for the rest of that day.

Ian yanked on my hand, effectively stopping both of us.

I looked up at him.

His eyes scanned my face.

"Did you sleep?" he asked.

Great.

Apparently, I looked as shit as I felt.

"I'm having some bad dreams."

He tugged on my hand, and I hurried to keep up with him as he started prowling toward the servant's stairs all the while growling, "We're moving you out of that fucking room."

"It's not the room, Ian. It's worry about my sister. And sure, yes, this place and all that happened in it doesn't help. It's sneaking into my subconscious. No surprise."

He stopped abruptly, stopping me with him. "No more stories of murdered women."

I felt my eyes get big and pointed in his face.

"There!" I crowed triumphantly. "You think she was murdered."

"Christ," he muttered, continuing to prowl and dragging me with him.

"Admit it, you think she was murdered. It was no accident. So now you have to tell me who you think dunnit."

"No talk of Dorothy Clifton until you get a full night's sleep."

"No fair."

He stopped us again at the top of the stairs. "I'll tell you more if you let me help you sleep."

"And how would you do that?" I asked, though I figured I knew the answer.

"First of all, you wouldn't be in bed in the Carnation Room."

"Dearie me, Lord Alcott,"—I fluttered my eyes—"are you suggesting something untoward?"

"By untoward, if you mean fucking you until you're exhausted, yes. That's what I'm suggesting."

Take two with my eyes getting big.

"Yeesh, babe, you should try being honest once in a while," I teased. "All this roundabout talk is exhausting."

He tugged me down the stairs, saying, "You're cute when you're being a pain in the ass."

We hit the kitchen and Bonnie, at work at a bowl, and Harriet, sitting on a stool, eating some toast, immediately smiled at us.

What a difference a day, and a decent guy treating them like humans, makes.

Ian immediately spoke.

To Harriet.

"Louella is being moved to the Poppy Room and Daphne to the Rose Room."

For some reason, Bonnie gasped at this news.

"Oh, thank God. That Carnation Room gives me the heebie-jeebies," Harriet said.

"Hang on, Lou is going to the Iris Room. We decided. She loves irises," I reminded Ian.

"The Poppy Room is next to the Rose Room," he reminded me.

"They don't have to move me."

"You're moving."

"I'm not."

"You're moving."

"Am not."

"This isn't up for discussion."

"It so is."

"What's happening?" Lou asked from behind us.

"The girls are moving you and Daphne to different rooms," Ian told her.

"Why?" Lou asked, squeezing around us and sending greeting smiles to Bonnie and Harriet, also Rebecca, who'd just walked in.

"Because your room is shit," Ian, King of Honesty, announced.

Lou bit her lip, not about to confirm, but what he spoke was so true, she didn't have it in her to deny.

"And because Dorothy Clifton stayed in Daphne's current room," Ian went on.

"Oh my God!" Lou cried, her face draining of color.

"Now look what you've done," I snapped at Ian.

And Lou totally lost it.

It was nearly a shout when she exclaimed, "I can't believe they put you in her...her...*room*! That's *diabolical*!"

"See, samesies," Rebecca whispered to Harriett.

Harriet gave a fake shiver.

"Shh," Bonnie shushed.

"It's fine," I assured everyone.

"She's not sleeping," Ian told on me. "She's having bad dreams."

I tore my hand from his. "Oh my God, will you *shut up*?"

He was completely unperturbed. "Yes, when you stop fighting about moving rooms."

Lou spoke. "You're moving rooms. We're both moving rooms. This is...no."

Lou gave me the hand when I opened my mouth to speak.

I closed my mouth.

"We're moving," she decreed. "I like irises. I also like poppies. But I want to be close to you and you are not sleeping another night in that room."

Why was I fighting this?

KRISTEN ASHLEY

"Okay, whatever, everybody chill," I muttered.

"God, I have a headache," Lou complained as she moved toward Bonnie's workbench.

I squinted at Lou's back because that was headache number two so far. She had bad head pain, and it wasn't infrequent. But then she'd take something, rest, and be okay.

"You need coffee," Bonnie prescribed, turning toward the kettle.

"I'll take some of that," I said, starting to follow Lou, but I got caught short when Ian grabbed my hand again. "I'm mad at you," I told him when I looked back.

I was pulling at his hold.

He wasn't letting go.

"I have sleeping pills. You're taking one tonight."

"Oh, it's *Doctor* Alcott now, is it?"

He tipped his head to the side. "Shall I ask Lou?"

Bah!

"You fight dirty," I groused.

"You can't even imagine."

I rolled my eyes.

Finally, he pulled me to the workbench.

I looked to Sam. "Hey, after breakfast, can you show me where my car and key fob are?"

"Sure," Sam answered.

"Going somewhere?" Ian asked.

"No, but if you keep annoying me, after I murder you, I'll need a clean getaway."

Lou gasped.

Bonnie and Sam chuckled.

Harriet and Rebecca giggled.

But Ian?

Ian busted out laughing.

Ten

THE VIOGNIER ROOM

A fter Sam showed me where my car was (tucked between a black BMW and a sleek, British-racing-green Jaguar, which I hoped was Ian's, and down from a white Mercedes coupe, another BMW, this one silver, and ending with a muddy Land Rover), he also instructed me on how to get into the lockbox where all the key fobs were held.

I then told him I needed to take in some air, and I'd make my own way back.

He took off at a jog to the house, and I stood outside the garage, which was quite a clip away, tucked under the swell of a small hill so, even if it was huge, you couldn't see it. Not too far beyond it, and even farther from the house, were some stables.

Although I loved horses, I didn't head that way, nor did I go to the formal gardens at the back of the house beyond the Conservatory, which sprawled across the rear two strikes of the cross.

I made my way around the western side of the house.

The chill in the air was immense. It stung my cheeks, and I was glad I took a minute to run upstairs to grab a scarf and some gloves before Sam and I set out.

I noted immediately that, along the years, the Alcotts had tamed the forest and the moors around where the fortress had been placed. On the horizon, you could see trees, and beyond those, heather and the romantic swells that were part of what made Britain.

But on quite an expanse around the house, it was cultivated lawns and carefully placed trees, paths leading to shaded benches or through vine-covered arbors, with intermittent tall urns that had been turned out because winter was coming, but I suspected in the summer they tumbled with flowers and greenery.

Like the house, the estate around it was extraordinary.

Perfect.

But it would seem my feet weren't all that interested in it because they led me to the spot on the wide gravel drive in front of the house, beneath my bedroom window.

Or, not that any longer. Beneath the Carnation Room window.

I didn't look up.

I walked out, in the direction Daniel had been going when I saw him the first night we were there.

The manicured space gave way to forest, which was untamed in such a way it boggled the mind how the Alcotts had subdued it. Then again, they'd had centuries to clear trees and dig out rocks and make their mark on the landscape.

The forest didn't last long and opened up to the moors.

Here, the wind was biting, digging through my wool duffle coat, my thick cashmere turtleneck and scarf, and the long-sleeved shell I wore underneath it. My wool-lined, leather gloves held up, but I wished I'd put on a hat, not only for the warmth, but because the wind kept whipping my hair in my face, and it was annoying.

I kept going, and going, beginning to like the sting of the air, the freshness after being in that house for more than a day.

The thing was, the farther I went, the more I realized there was nothing out there. There weren't any trails. There weren't any cottages or farmhouses.

There was nothing at all.

So where was Daniel going?

Or more to the point, what was I expecting to find?

Many people had trouble sleeping and they did a number of things to remedy that. It wasn't unheard of for someone to put on clothes and take a quick walk to clear the cobwebs and maybe bring on some tiredness.

Perhaps Daniel was wound up about our visit, the dinner that didn't go so well, and he couldn't sleep. Thus, he took a walk.

"I'm an idiot," I muttered to myself, turning and noting how far I'd come.

In the distance, I could only see the chimneys of Duncroft.

I headed back, deciding, not only for Portia's sake, but my own, to cut Daniel some slack. To try to pull myself together and not let the house and its history and its atmospheric location get to me. I wasn't sleeping, all this was just amping up my anxiety, and I was doing it to myself.

When I made it to the house and was walking across what could be considered its front lawn (one a regulation football game could be played on), my intent was to go around the other side then head to the rear to look at the gardens.

I didn't want to go in yet. The sun was weak, but it was there, giving me much needed vitamin D. The air was crisp, and it felt like both were clearing my head.

However, as I began to traverse the drive, the front door opened, and Laura stood there.

I waved.

And she called.

"Miss Ryan! If you will!"

Laura, like Brittany, had not been in the kitchen last night, so I hadn't chatted with her and gotten to know her. She was several years older than the other girls. And right then, she looked severe and reminded me why I'd been letting my mind run away from me about this visit.

I switched directions and headed to the front door.

I was almost to the top step when Laura announced, "Lady Alcott would like you to join her for a light lunch in the Viognier Room."

She stepped out of my way so I could step inside, and in that yawning, marble entryway, I still felt the chill.

"Are Louella and Ian joining us?" I asked Laura.

I was taller than her, not by much, still, she tipped her head back to look down her nose at me.

No.

Not as sociable as Bonnie, Harriet, Rebecca, Sam, et al.

"The Viscount is working. However, Lady Alcott would like some time with you alone, as Portia's sister. Blood family with blood family."

Somehow, that made sense and was an insult to Lou at the same time.

It was Jane's house. I was her guest. I'd barely seen her and hadn't truly exchanged a word with her, and Lou seemed incredibly uncomfortable around her.

And honestly, I was curious.

So I pulled off my gloves, saying, "Sure."

"I'll take your outdoor gear."

I nodded, gave her the gloves, unwound my pink scarf, and shrugged off my pale-blue duffle.

I then moved toward the Viognier Room.

It was next to the Turquoise Room, and it was also a dining room, though much smaller and much brighter, with a beautifully varnished oval table that seated no more than eight. It would have been where I'd have my guests to dinner if I owned that house and our party was as small as it currently was.

But that was just me.

As I walked down the hall, I passed a girl I'd never seen who was even younger than all the others. She did not wear a dove-gray dress, but an outfit much like Sam's: khaki pants and a light-blue polo. She also had yellow rubber gloves on her hands and was carrying a round pail that was stuffed full of cleaning supplies and dust cloths.

She was coming out of the Whisky Room, Richard's office.

"Hey," I greeted.

She dipped her chin, avoided my eyes and rushed down the hall only to stop and disappear into one of the other rooms.

Shy.

Or weird.

I decided to have a more positive outlook about everything and chose to believe she was just shy.

Lou was famous. My dad was too. Ian as well. Daniel, Richard and Jane to a lesser extent, as all people with titles tended to be. And it couldn't be denied, in an even lesser way, I was too. I was Dad's daughter, and I was filthy rich, so that happened.

It could be intimidating, even if you worked in a house like this.

I made it to the Viognier Room and was surprised to see the door open. They had a thing about keeping the doors closed, and I knew from my tour yesterday that was more than likely about turning off radiators and containing chill in the vast amount of space that went unused.

The Viognier Room was not chilly. The warmth seemed almost forceful as I entered to see Lady Jane already seated at the head of the table.

She stood when I arrived.

"Daphne," she greeted in a vague way. "I'm pleased you're joining me."

She motioned to a chair beside her, the only open place setting.

I moved that direction, replying, "Thank you for the invitation."

She inclined her head and returned to her seat.

I'd barely sat before a panel in the pale, golden-yellow wall with white wainscoting opened, and Laura came in with a bottle of wine.

She poured while we remained quiet, then she left.

"I hear you took a wander," Lady Jane noted when the panel clicked shut while I was sipping the wine.

Viognier, of course.

"Yes," I replied, putting the glass back on the table. "The grounds are gorgeous. I'll have a look at the garden at the back after lunch," I told her.

"There isn't much to see. It's been readied for winter. But come spring and summer, it's extraordinary."

"Do you garden?"

She shook her head but said, "A little. We have two full-time groundskeepers. They do the bulk of the work. They live in the village."

"Ah," I said, because I didn't know what else to say.

Though, I thought I might understand why her voice and manner was vague. I couldn't be sure, but I had a feeling she and Valium had a close relationship.

No judge.

Whatever gets you through the day.

The panel opened again, and silence descended as Laura returned, with Brittany this time, both of them carrying a plate, Laura also carrying a beautifully woven basket.

Laura put hers in front of Lady Jane, Brittany mine, and I saw we were having a ploughman's. Well, a posh ploughman's. The basket was filled with slices of fresh bread and homemade crackers, both looked divine.

Lady Jane waited until the panel snicked shut before she spoke again.

"It's my understanding you and Ian are growing fond of each other."

I took a slice of baguette. "Your son is charming."

"He is that," she murmured. "He's on quite a tear with the house."

This was an unexpected comment.

"How's that?" I queried.

"Updates. Modernization. His father and he have been butting heads about it for years, I'm afraid."

What?

"But Ian is determined to bring Duncroft into the twenty-first century," she carried on. "It annoys him, for some reason, to have to plug a cord into the wall. He'd rather these things be built into the infrastructure of the house."

So it was Ian who was behind the plugs and USB ports built into the nightstands, and possibly elsewhere.

"Even if it took three months for it all to be done, Bonnie was in fits of glee when she was able to move into her new kitchen," she went on.

And he was behind the new kitchen too.

"Apparently, next spring, we're having solar panels added to the back pitches of the roof," she shared. "And possibly one or two of those windmills installed on the northern moors. More, if he can manage it. He wants to offer sustainable and affordable power solutions to the village."

"That's...actually really cool."

"I'm sure these panels will be hideous," she said, delicately smoothing pâté over a piece of melba toast.

"The roof is tall, and at the back, hardly anyone will see them."

"We don't have a lot of sun in England," she pointed out.

"Any move away from fossil fuels, your grandchildren will thank you for."

She lifted her hazy, green eyes to me but said nothing.

I cut into a wedge of cheese.

We ate in silence for a while, and it was uncomfortable.

Lady Jane broke it by mystifyingly informing me, "Stevenson oversees the entirety of the staff."

"Oh?" I asked, after swallowing some pâté covered in thinly sliced cornichon and minced red onion.

"The hiring, sacking, advancement. He keeps a very close log of our possessions, everything from the art and the china and crystal, to the wine in the cellar and spirits in the cabinets. He also sees to any maintenance. And you can imagine Duncroft constantly needs taken care of. He deals with the plumbers and electricians and roofers, and such. He further looks after Richard and myself. A secretary, if you will. Making certain we have all we need, from booking Richard's train tickets and hotels when he travels, to seeing to our clothing."

"Okay," I said.

"Christine is more of a day-to-day person. Scheduling the cleaning so everything remains tidy. Working with Bonnie on menus and making certain the marketing is done. Her days off are the weekends, which is why you haven't met her yet. Bonnie's days are Monday and Tuesday. Christine and Laura will see to our meals while Bonnie has her time."

"Right," I muttered, interested, but still weirded out by her sharing this.

"It was another argument, that Ian won, the renovation of the top floor," she stated. "We have less than half the staff that was needed in olden days to take care of the house. And the children raised here are no longer tutored here. But Richard prefers live-in staff, obviously. The comings and goings of bikes and vehicles is distracting. And due to our location, if they don't stay onsite, it left the pool of possible help only to the village and the town, which isn't optimal. They're paid very well.

Especially when they have no living expenses. It's quite a coup to be employed at Duncroft."

I didn't believe that for a second.

I still nodded.

"We had loads of space on the top floor," she continued. "Ian had it gutted, and he made suites for the staff. They now all have kitchenettes, sitting rooms, bedrooms and their own ensuite bathrooms. Little apartments, as it were. They get free, erm...internet and TV. And they're allowed visitors, if they come in the servants' entrances, promise not to access the main house and Stevenson has approved them, of course."

"Of course," I mumbled.

"I've been up there. Ian took me on a tour when it was done. These suites are quite roomy."

"That's nice."

"Your sister is not appropriate for my son."

Well, hell.

Sneak attack.

I stared at her and said nothing.

"You cannot strive to achieve class and refinement. You either have it, or you do not," she proclaimed.

"And you don't think my sister has it."

"She's flighty and spoiled."

I couldn't argue either, damn it.

"She's also a schemer," she went on.

All right, now I was getting mad.

Fortunately, before I could say something rude, she put her knife down, gave me her undivided attention, and continued.

"My first son needs a woman who knows her own worth, but especially has a pure heart. She cannot look to him to give her value. She has to understand herself. She needs to stand independent, even as she stands at his side. She needs to work *with* him to build the life Ian and she will share, holding up her end all the while. The same to create the family they'll make when they have children. She'll need to be confident and, there's no other word for it, have grit as she plays host with him in this house. Duncroft has consumed many a Lady Alcott. Those who fell to her, they didn't understand. It is not you pitted against this house. It is you and Lord Alcott who *are* this house."

"We're not talking about Ian," I said carefully.

"Are we not?" she asked.

What on earth?

"You'd just insulted my sister," I reminded her.

"Ah, then," she said. "My second son. Now, *he* needs a taskmaster. He needs a keeper. He will need to be taken care of until his dying breath. He doesn't have it in him to take care of a woman, or a family. The woman he chooses will have to bear the brunt of it all, and she'll have to go into it knowing she will."

"This is much what Ian had to say," I murmured.

"Daniel is blinded by envy, Daphne. Perhaps even tortured by it," Lady Jane told me in what sounded more like a rather ominous warning. "You would do well to remember that. Ian loves his brother. Adored him when they were younger. And Daniel worshipped Ian. I can't quite put my finger on when that twisted. When it changed. When it became ugly. But it did. I think Ian is wounded by it. Duncroft is remote. They only had each other. They were playmates when they were very young. Then they became friends. Ian wants the brother he grew up with back. I fear this won't happen. I fear it for the both of them."

It didn't take a psychologist to ascertain Lady Jane played favorites.

"You're being very frank," I noted.

"People mistake me for distant. It's the quiet ones who observe the most, Daphne. Advice that might serve you well in the future. But please don't mistake me, I love my sons equally. Ian is proud and smart and strong, and has the curse of the eldest. He seems to be able to do everything right and people get the erroneous conclusion he doesn't have to work for it, it simply falls in his lap. I assure you, he works for it. Daniel is kindhearted and fun-loving and free-spirited. But things are harder for him. I've no idea why, perhaps it's just the way of the world. They both have their strengths and their weaknesses. And I love all that is them."

With that, even though neither of us were finished eating, she stood.

"I believe I have some correspondence I need to see to."

She began to swan to the door, and I watched her go, baffled by this whole episode, and a little weirded out by it, but she stopped and turned back to me.

"Ian was right. The cords are hideous and it's most irksome to have to roam around to find one when one is needed. I have a phone. I have a laptop. Time marches on. But that doesn't mean tradition isn't important. We've made changes. We've made do. We've made advancements. We don't need a dozen footmen and scullery maids because fires need to be laid and the vacuum hasn't been invented yet. But places like Duncroft *need* to exist, Daphne. They *need* love and care. They *need* traditions to stand. They *need* Stevenson and Christine, and Bonnie and Laura just as much as they need Lord Alcott and myself. And Ian must see this. He must teach his son the same. He doesn't think so, but he has things to learn from his father. He needs to start paying attention."

"Are you...do you..." my words sounded strangled, "do you think I hold some sway over Ian?"

"Of course not," she sniffed, but oddly, I felt her response was a blatant lie. "I'm just making conversation."

"And it's been a most interesting conversation, Lady Jane."

"Do you know your British history?" she asked.

"Of a sort," I answered.

"The most famous Lady Jane in this country was queen for nine days. She was educated. Intelligent. And she wanted what was best for Britain. Her head was taken as a traitor when she was anything but. Before that happened, she blindfolded herself." She drew in breath while I struggled to digest words that were disturbing before she finished. "Duncroft is a country on its own, in a way. And many a lady has been found traitor to it and paid the price, even when she wanted nothing but the best for it and did her part, giving her own blood and bone to ensure its future."

And with that unnerving message, the Lady Jane of Duncroft House swept from the room.

Eleven

THE ROSE ROOM

I was barefoot in the Rose Room, about to nip out to go to Lou's to ask her to zip my dress.

I was also wondering why I'd fought against being moved.

During the tour, I noticed that this was the prettiest, most spacious, most decked out room of the lot in this wing. The only rivals it had were the Carnation and Robin Rooms.

It was the turrets that won the match. One had a chaise longue in it, a perfect spot for reading or napping or gazing over the estate. The other had a beautiful secretary, perfect for those times when you needed to "see to your correspondence."

The seating area was bigger, as was the fireplace. It had an actual closet, a walk-in one that was enormous, thank you very much, and if the bathroom in Carnation was a dream, the one in Rose was sheer heaven.

And the ridiculously beautiful wallpaper didn't suck.

I loved it there. I felt right there.

At home there.

It was weird, but even though my lunch with Lady Jane was curious (I decided to consider it that rather than creepy), I was still hell bent on making the best of the rest of this visit.

103

A mammoth task, but I was psyching myself up for it.

I was on my way to the door when there was a knock. Probably Lou needed a zip up too.

I opened it, and Ian was standing there.

"You're decent," he murmured, his eyes on my dress. "Pity."

I opened the door further. "Stop it and get in here. I need a zip up."

"At your service," he said, coming in and closing the door behind him. I turned my back to him, and as he did me up, he remarked, "I'm used to this going the other direction."

"I already know you're a scoundrel, no need to beat the horse dead," I said as he finished, and I turned around to face him.

"A scoundrel?" he teased.

I walked to a beautifully upholstered, rose velvet chair and sat. "A scoundrel. Are you here to tell me Portia and Daniel have returned?"

"Alas no," he replied. "Allow me," he then said, coming to stand in front of me and holding out his hand for the gold, stiletto sandal I'd picked up to put on.

Mutely, I handed it to him, feeling a frisson of sexuality in the gesture.

"Give it here," he muttered, snapping his fingers toward my feet, his eyes aimed that way.

Marvelous.

He was going to give me an orgasm by being bossy and putting on my shoes.

I lifted my foot.

He cupped the heel in his big, warm hand.

Yes. Careening close to orgasm.

"I'm here because father informed me, we have guests for dinner," he shared.

"Yes?"

He was a dab hand with the slender straps and buckle, because he managed it in a trice.

"Yes. The Dewhursts. Michael and Mary, and their daughter, Chelsea."

"Okay," I said after he bent to retrieve the second shoe and I offered him my other foot.

"They're good friends of my father, at least Michael is."

"All right."

His gaze lifted to mine. "Several years ago, I saw Chelsea for a few months."

And the murkiness clears.

"Ah."

"And after we finished, Daniel saw her for a few months more. At this juncture in delivering my message, I feel it's important to note it was Dad who extended the invitation to them."

And the vision came into stark relief.

But I could not believe what I was hearing.

I tried to be diplomatic. "Your father's kind of not a very cool guy."

"He's an asshole," he muttered to my shoe.

He finished with it and let me go, which was a shame.

"I had lunch with your mum," I told him.

He pushed his hands in his trouser pockets, which brought something else into stark relief: the utterly delectable dark-gray suit he was wearing, again with a vest and a beautiful shirt, this one snowy white, and no tie, collar open at his throat.

He gifted me with the attention of those beautiful blue eyes again. "I heard."

"She told me about solar panels and windmills and kitchenettes."

He appeared openly surprised at that, but replied, "I see."

"And indicated your father was not at one with all your plans."

He jutted out his strong, cleanshaven chin. "No. He wasn't. He told me the house was fine as it is and shared we have plenty of money, so the fact we'd shave what would amount to at least ten thousand pounds a year off our heating and electrical bills installing the solar panels alone was unnecessary."

I *knew* it was a bitch to heat this place.

"Short-sighted too," I noted.

"Yes, I mentioned that and how the slowness of our great country in modernizing and thinking forward is rapidly shrinking our once vast empire. He didn't take my point. He told me if I wanted the changes, I'd have to pay for them myself."

Interesting.

"Did you?"

"Fuck no," he replied. "It cost a fortune and it's not for me, it's for Duncroft. Duncroft should pay for it."

I couldn't argue.

"Dad flatly refused," he continued. "I went over his head to the trustees. They're in the business of being forward-thinking, so they approved the expenditures. But along with the living expenses as Mum, Dad and Danny like to live, it was noted those new outlays might well dip into the principal. This meant they advised us other cuts needed to be made."

"I'm sure that didn't go over very well."

"No, considering two of the expenditures the trustees pointed out would be easy to let go without most who lived in and served Duncroft suffering were Dad's apartments in London and York."

This was confusing, specifically York, considering that city was very close to Duncroft. An easy day drive if you had business there.

"Does he need to go to those places very often?"

"He did if he wanted to fuck the mistresses he kept in them."

Oh boy.

"Ian," I said softly.

"Obviously, I explained to Dad that Mum should not be asked to cut costs when such other costs could be more easily, and discreetly, cut," he spoke over me. "So Dad told his special friends he'd be unable to provide for them in the manner in which they'd become accustomed. They took their esteemed services elsewhere."

Listening to his words, something occurred to me.

"Do you keep an eye on your father?"

He nodded. "Though, I don't have an army of men in Inverness capes and deerstalkers following them around," he joked, and I laughed.

When I was done, he went on.

"But I do keep a finger on the pulse, as non-invasively as possible. Dad. To a lesser extent, Daniel. It's unnecessary with Mum." His gaze suddenly grew sharp on my own. "I think we both know how other people's peccadillos can be annoying to put up with. If I know in advance some shit Danny pulled is going to bite me in the ass, I can deal with it."

"Smart," I said.

Sad, but smart.

"I left things with Chelsea as best they could be," he shared. "We'd known each other since we were kids. She had high hopes. It didn't work out. I can't say Danny left things on the same footing."

"Great," I mumbled.

"Chelsea will be fine, at least to me, you, Lou. She might have a few digs to get in if Danny shows. And beware, if she scents she can draw blood from a weaker creature, she'll go after Portia."

I stood, which put me very close to him. "I'll not be able to allow that to happen."

"I'll run interference," he promised, sliding his eyes down my dress, which was blood red, form-fitting, fell to mid-calf, had a high neck, long, fitted sleeves, some shoulder pads, and some angular pleating that helped it fit perfectly to my curves and gave the material interest. It also had a cutout at the side waist that showed skin, front and back. "Poor girl," he said, as if he was talking to the dress. And with his next, I'd find he was. "It's simply that the two that came before you were so stellar that you're ranking third on my favorites list."

I burst out laughing and Ian smiled at me when I did it.

His smile was warm and open and beautiful, just because it was, but more because he was so obviously enjoying the fact he'd made me laugh.

It was a perfect moment, I felt it in an instant. An absolutely perfect moment in our otherwise decidedly imperfect lives.

It was the kind of moment you lived for. It was the kind of moment that was one of the last beautiful things you remembered before you died.

It was everything.

And then the door flew open.

Instinctively, Ian stepped in front of me, which was entirely unnecessary, and absurdly attractive.

"Well, isn't this fucking *cozy*."

I leaned to the side to see around Ian because that voice was Portia's.

Her eyes were darting between the two of us and there was something very wrong in her expression.

She wasn't upset, or mad.

She was *enraged*.

As one might be, when they were threatened with losing one hundred billion dollars if they didn't shape up.

But my sister knew me.

She knew I'd never hang her out to dry.

I didn't do it when she was fifteen and I caught her in my bathroom snorting coke.

I didn't do it when I learned where she got the coke and how much danger she put herself in to get it.

I didn't do it when Lou donned that Oscar de la Renta dress that was specifically made for her and found one of the straps had been snipped and poorly stitched together to hide it until it was put on, then it broke loose, making the dress unwearable. This, so that at the very last second, for an important event, Lou had to dig in her wardrobe to find something else to wear and redo her hair and makeup in order to wear it.

Needless to say, Portia had been the one to snip and stitch.

And further, I didn't when I found her out after she went on a tear of eBaying Dad's very expensive stuff when he got pissed at her and cut off her allowance.

The list went on.

In other words, I didn't the many times she deserved it.

Including now, when she'd lured Lou and I away from our homes and lives and then left us with people who didn't like us (save Ian, but when she left, she didn't know we'd make friends with Ian (or with their history, did she?)).

She was not the one who should be angry.

It should be me.

And seeing her so damned pissed, I was.

"I'm here, *herr kommandant*," she declared, clicking her heels and saluting. "As ordered."

"I'll just leave you to it," Ian murmured, turned his head, caught my eyes and finished, "Good luck."

Sadly, Portia didn't let him get away unscathed.

As he shifted to squeeze past her when she didn't get out of his way, she snapped, "Does she taste better than me?"

Ian stopped dead and looked down his nose at her.

"I don't know yet, petal," he said dangerously. "But I'm a betting man, and I'd let it ride the answer to that is yes."

Portia looked like he'd slapped her.

A reaction of her own making.

Ian disappeared into the hall.

Portia turned on me.

"Not another word," I warned.

"Or what? You'll take away all my money?"

"Dad's money."

She jackknifed my way. "*My* money."

Enough.

"Girl, you didn't earn a dime of that, so keep those words out of your goddamned mouth," I bit.

Her face colored and she bit back. "What are you doing with Ian?"

"What do you care?"

She looked flummoxed for a second, which I found strange, and then she said, "He's my boyfriend's brother."

"And you dated him."

"He told you?"

"If he didn't, you just did with your ill-advised comment. Obviously, in the short time you were with him, you didn't learn as easy prey not to toy with the apex predator."

And again, she looked like she'd been slapped. "Easy? You did not just say that to me."

"I did, Portia. Good God, what did you think would happen when you left me and Lou in this house? That the Alcotts would eat us alive? I didn't spend the time you were away cowering in my room."

"What I *didn't* think was that in, oh, I don't know...*a day*, my sister would be fucking my ex-boyfriend."

"Was he your boyfriend?"

More color stained her cheeks.

What was going on here?

I narrowed my eyes on her as if that could help me figure it out.

"Well, we're back, and Daniel's nervous as hell," she announced. "He's worried he's upset you and you'll make *me* pay for it."

"I don't know whose idea it was for you two to skip this idyllic interlude in the middle of fucking nowhere, but whoever that was, I can confirm. Yes, they've upset me. But no, I won't make them pay for it. However, there's going to be some work to be done to repair the damage."

"Always kissing Daphne's ass," she mumbled irately. "I've had a lifetime of it."

Oh no she didn't.

"Really? Like when I covered for you when you took off with your friends that night you were grounded? Then, when Dad found out we both lied, I got grounded too. Was that *you* kissing *my* ass?"

She glared at me.

"Or when I talked Dad into not losing his fucking mind when you had your friends over and you drank and then puked up the entirety of his fifty-thousand-pound bottle of Cognac?"

She started to look uncomfortable.

"And was it you kissing my ass when I spent all last week working with my staff to manage the patisserie while I was away so I could be here for you and Daniel?" I demanded.

"You've made your point," she clipped.

"I hope so," I retorted.

"And somehow, in...like...*a day*...you've managed to insinuate yourself into the queen's quarters."

That threw me.

"What?"

"The Rose Room is Lady Alcott's room. It always has been."

"Not always, as it isn't now."

She stared hard at me. "The heir is almost of age."

"I don't understand what you're saying."

"It's part of the covenants."

"What is?"

"When the heir apparent reaches age thirty-eight, they inherit everything. If the current earl is still living, he can remain at Duncroft, but only with the permission of the new earl."

Holy shit!

Really?

"Ian turns thirty-eight next month. It's tradition, so Jane moved out of this room only a month ago," she concluded.

No wonder Bonnie gasped when Ian announced I was moving into this room.

"I...that's weird. Isn't it weird?" I asked. "Charles waited seventy-four years to succeed."

"Sorry, Daph," she sneered. "I haven't memorized the history of the Alcott earldom. But somewhere along the way, it happened, and it's unalterable. Daniel told me many an earl tried to change it before his time was up, but it's carved in stone."

She threw both hands out before her and separated them, like a car model showing off a new car.

"Congratulations," she finished. "Two days in, and as usual, you win." She turned and said, "Now, I have to hurry and get dressed so I'm not late to cocktails."

And with that, she was gone.

But I remained, standing in the countess's room with my clothes in the countess's closet.

And I was not the countess.

Twelve

THE DIAMOND ROOM

E ven though it was farther away from the formal dining room, I soon discovered when friends of the earl came to call, they weren't relegated to the perfectly adequate (and quite comfy) Wine Room for the Cocktail Forty-Five Minutes, like family and lesser mortals, such as Lou and myself.

They were entertained in the Diamond Room.

This, Jack—tonight wearing a suit like Stevenson's, but with a black tie, again with the shield on it, and standing sentry at the bottom of the stairs—told me after I descended them.

All I could think when I saw him looking like he was at attention, rather than smiling and friendly as he had been when he was in the kitchens with us last night, was Lady Jane's all-important *tradition*.

I wasn't one of those people who dismissed other's beliefs because they were not my own. I might not agree, or even understand, but I wanted to listen, to be able to turn it over in my head, to have the words and facts and feelings so I could make a decision.

So honestly, all afternoon, Lady Jane's words had been rumbling around in my head.

Was there still a place for pomp and circumstance in this world?

Was it necessary for a young man to stand alone in a massive foyer for the sole purpose of telling a couple of people which hallway to walk down?

It kept him employed.

But there were dozens of bedrooms that went unused every night in this house, when one hundred fifty million people worldwide were homeless.

Solar panels and windmills should have been raised a decade ago.

And as beautiful as this place was, as much as it stood as a testimony to a different time, and we should never lose hold of our past so we don't repeat mistakes in our future, it could be a hospital. An orphanage. At the very least, broken up so multiple families lived in it, not one.

Lady Jane would probably be horrified at the thought.

But how had we, as a human race, come this far and not seen there should be far less of a divide between the ones who have too much and the ones who don't have anything?

And yes, this included my own self, sitting on billions of dollars.

This was on my mind. Lady Jane's lunch was on my mind. The fact Ian put me in the countess's room without telling me it was the countess's room, was on my mind. All of that was on my mind as I walked down the long hallway in my thousand-pound-sterling high heels and then entered the Diamond Room.

If it sparkled during the day, it glittered at night. Perfect low lighting mixed with candlelight made every facet shine to its brightest.

Score one for Lady Jane, because this room should never have a single thing changed about it.

And in blood red, I stood out like a stain.

Eight sets of eyes turned to me when I walked in, and I noted several things at once.

Daniel was there, appearing abashed.

Michael and Mary Dewhurst were good, solid, Yorkshire gentry.

And if all of Ian's flirting was actually real, he had a type.

Chelsea Dewhurst made Jayne Mansfield look subdued.

She was pinup perfection in a skintight, strapless, bangled dress in the colors of Champagne and crystal, like she'd dressed for the room. It was held up at her burgeoning, ample chest by what could only be a miracle.

Her eyes shot down to my gold sandals and up to my golden hair, and it concerned me greatly when obvious jealousy crossed her features like a dark shadow before she hid it behind a sip of Champagne.

So, Ian was a cocky-as-all-hell flirt, but still, he didn't know women inside and out.

He'd been wrong.

That woman wasn't going to leave me alone tonight. No way.

Making this worse, Ian moved forward to claim me, and I wished he hadn't.

I was not exactly angry at him, but he was spoiled for choice as to rooms he could have put me and Lou in. His choice was...if not wrong, then not right.

Furthermore, I wasn't his to claim and I was perfectly capable of walking into a room alone.

"Daphne, allow me to introduce you," he said, placing his hand on the small of my back so that I could feel the tips of a few of his fingers against my skin at the cutout and drawing me deeper into diamonds.

During the introductions, Stevenson hung back as I endured Michael and Mary's superciliousness, this piled onto Richard's, Jane's distracted but this time far warmer brush of cheeks, Daniel's customary overenthusiastic greeting, and finally, Chelsea's catty glare.

It looked like it was turning out to be another fun night at Duncroft.

"Where's Louella Fernsby?" Michael Dewhurst demanded, lifting up on his toes (he was rather short, also rather balding) to look over my head toward the door. "And your little pip, Daniel?"

"His little pip has a name," I said. "She's Portia. And she and Daniel just returned from London. She's freshening up for dinner."

Michael, clearly not accustomed to someone calling him on his shit, glowered at me.

I dismissed him and warmly thanked Stevenson, who was hovering while holding a tray of glasses of Champagne.

"As for Lou, I checked on her on the way down," I went on after I took a sip. "She's having some issues with headaches. She said she hopes she'll be well enough to join us for dinner."

Michael appeared crestfallen, which didn't make Mary too happy.

Daniel sidled close and requested under his breath, "Can we talk?"

I looked up at him. "Now isn't the time."

"It really was a work thing," he replied.

"Mm," I hummed to the rim of my glass before I took another sip.

"You're friends with your stepmother?" Chelsea inquired.

I nodded. "Good friends."

"Would stand to reason," she noted to everyone and no one. Then aimed at me, "She's your age, isn't she?"

"Chels," Ian warned low.

"Am I lying?" she asked mock-innocently.

"Yes, though not exactly," I answered her calmly. "She's five years older."

"Is that bizarre?" Chelsea inquired, then again to everyone and no one. "I mean, if it were me, I'd find it hard to handle."

"I loved my dad. He loved Lou. I met Lou and fell in love with her too. He died too young, and we grew even closer as we nursed him until the end. They didn't have a lot of time together, and perhaps our family isn't normal, but tell me whose is, and I'll uncover the rocks to prove it untrue. We are who we are, do what we do, and we have two choices. Live in glass houses and throw stones or live outside them and get stones thrown at us."

Chelsea squinted her eyes at me irritably.

I took another sip of Champagne.

Ian settled his hand on the small of my back again, this time both proudly and possessively.

I squinted at him irritably.

His brows rose.

"I'm here, so sorry, what a rush," Portia called out breathlessly, scampering in while smoothing down the skirt of her blush-colored cocktail dress, which looked to be made entirely of tulle and boning. It had a swirly skirt, and I was pretty sure the costume designers said it was too girlie for Baby to wear when Johnny asked her to dance, but it was a close runner-up, and now it had somehow found its way onto my little sister's body.

"Oh, *delicious*," Chelsea purred.

"Is she for real?" I asked Ian, not quite low enough I couldn't be heard.

"Maybe I should ask *you* to behave yourself," he suggested.

"I will if others will," I returned, again, meaning to be heard.

He grinned rakishly.

Even if it was a great grin, I fought rolling my eyes.

"Oh, Stevenson, you're a lifesaver," Portia declared while accepting the last glass of Champagne on the tray.

"Let me introduce you, love," Daniel waded in.

I stepped back to allow them room, and since Ian was still claiming me, he came with me.

He then dipped his mouth to my ear. "Have I done something to annoy you?"

I turned my head so he had no choice but to pull away to catch my eyes.

"I'd like an after-dinner rendezvous in the Conservatory."

"This can be arranged, though I'm thinking what you're thinking we'd do there is not as titillating as what I'm thinking of doing to you there."

Such a damned flirt.

"It isn't," I confirmed.

"I'm also thinking you aren't going to ask me to teach you backgammon."

"Nope."

He drew me farther away from the others.

Much farther.

"We don't know each other well," he said low when we were out of earshot. "So I'll share something. I'm not a patient man, and I particularly don't have a lot of it when a woman is pissed off at me and makes me wait to find out why."

I tipped my head to the side, put my Champagne to my lips, didn't release his gaze, and asked, "The Rose Room?"

"What of it?"

I dropped my Champagne hand so it was out of our way and got closer to him. "It's your mother's room."

"No. Right now, it's your room."

"It's the countess's room."

"No," he repeated. "Right now, it's your room."

"You know what I mean."

"I know it's the best room in the house. I know you've been sleeping, essentially, in a dead woman's bed. Or not sleeping, as you're having bad dreams in that dead woman's bed. I know that I like you and this is my home and I want you to feel comfortable here, and you haven't been made very comfortable for a variety of reasons. And I know I don't give a shit about the traditions this house has carried for four hundred years. If I ever have a wife, when I'm earl, I'm not going to sleep in the Cherry Room while she's all the fucking way across the house in the Rose Room, like every earl and countess have done since Thomas murdered Joan in their bed in the Cherry Room. Instead, her body will be in *my* bed in whatever room she likes. I don't give a shit which room it is."

Always, without fail, every single one of his answers was a good one.

It was annoying.

But...*Joan*.

How could I forget about *Joan*?

"Are you over your snit?" he demanded.

I quit thinking of Joan and the fact Virginia mentioned her in my dream last night and I focused on Ian.

"My *snit*?"

"Yes, your snit."

I got even closer to him. "You installed me in the countess's room, and, oh yeah, I forgot, you're going to be the earl *next month*. Something else you failed to mention."

He shifted even *closer*, so our bodies were touching, and I could swear I felt his nose brush mine.

"I'm sorry, darling, we've been so mired in your shit, I must have missed when you were asking about me and my life in an effort to get to know me."

See!

So annoying!

Every single one of his comebacks were good too!

I clenched my teeth.

"No reply?" he mocked.

117

"You're infuriating," I ground out.

"Infuriating?"

"Yes."

"How so?"

"Because you have rational answers and good comebacks and everybody knows, *darling*, that's the absolute *worst* when you're having words with somebody."

He scowled down at me.

I glared up at him.

Then he hooked an arm around my waist, plastered me to his long, hard body, threw his head back, and laughed.

"That's the worst too, don't you know," I groused. Then went on to grumble, "And we *do* talk about you."

He righted his head, but only so he could duck it so his mouth was again at my ear.

"I'm sorry, Daphne, but it's your own fault you're remarkably amusing."

I jumped and would have jumped out of Ian's hold if his arm didn't tighten when the voice came from our side.

And I was shocked as shit to see Lady Jane had gotten close.

She put her hand on Ian's arm, gazing up at him with a benevolent expression that wasn't overtly adoring, but it wasn't blank either, and she said quietly, "I just love to hear you laugh, my dear."

I looked at her, stunned.

Then I looked beyond her.

Everyone was staring at us.

The summation:

Richard: beside himself with fury.

Michael and Mary: shocked.

Daniel: confused.

Chelsea: venomous.

And last, Portia: again enraged.

Of all of those, the only one I didn't understand was Portia's.

I didn't get a chance to wrap my head around it.

Richard announced tersely, "I believe it's time to eat."

Thirteen

THE TURQUOISE ROOM

At seven fifteen on the dot, as we were selecting our chairs (Ian again claimed me, this time as dinner partner, no matter how hard Mary was pushing Michael my way so Ian would be stuck with Chelsea), Lou showed in the Turquoise Room.

Michael lost his mind, fawning over her, which was revolting.

I didn't have much interest in that (outside of saving Lou and making sure she sat on Ian's other side), considering Lou had slapped some makeup on to try to hide it, and she looked beautiful, but I knew her, and I could tell she felt like hell.

For more than one reason I did not like this.

She suffered migraines the entire time I knew her. We'd all learned how to help her when that happened, mostly leaving her alone. But when Dad wasn't around and I was, I'd change the cool compress over her eyes and guard against any sound or disturbance until she was past it.

They came too often, considering how much they pained her.

But days of back-to-back headaches was not how it normally worked.

Stress was probably triggering it, so I was going to be a lot pushier

119

tomorrow about getting her to the train station so she could get out of this train wreck.

Michael dominated the conversation loudly through soup and salad.

It was the fish course when Chelsea had finished sharpening her claws and wanted to test them to see whose blood she could draw.

She started with Portia.

"We're in a sisterhood, you and me," she said across the table to my sister.

Oh, right. The table.

Important to note.

Head, Richard. Foot, Jane. Obviously.

Down one side were me at Richard's left, Ian, Lou, then Chelsea.

Down the other side, Mary to Richard's right, Michael, Portia, then Daniel.

I heard Ian sigh.

Then I heard Portia ask in all innocence, "We are?"

"Chelsea," Daniel said low.

"Men," Chelsea huffed then leaned forward to look at me. "I bet you know how well Ian knows me."

"Do you read bad romance novels? Or is it maybe too much Real Housewives? I mean, I'm truly curious. What is it?" I asked in return.

Her face twisted.

Ian caught her expression and murmured, "What's that about dishing it out?"

Chelsea tossed a poisonous look at Ian.

"What are they talking about?" Portia asked Daniel quietly.

"I'll tell you later," he replied in the same tone.

"I'm only saying, I've known Ian and Daniel *very well* for a *long, long* time," Chelsea told her.

"Yes of course," Mary rushed in to save the situation. "They've known each other since they were children."

I glanced at Richard to see his reaction to the devilry that he'd designed.

He was using his knife to push sauce and halibut on his fork, not a care in the world.

Until...

TOO GOOD TO BE TRUE

"Chelsea, tell us how your design business is going," Lady Jane requested.

Richard's head snapped up and his gaze was sharp and unhappy on his wife.

"She's having just a few growing pains," Michael quickly answered for his daughter.

And there it was.

According to Richard, Chelsea was here to dish it out so we'd take it.

Surprisingly, Lady Jane had other ideas.

And it seemed the person most surprised about this was her husband.

"Oh?" Jane inquired. "Too bad."

"She had hoped," Mary put in, "with all the work you've been doing here at Duncroft—"

"Oh no," Lady Jane cut her off before Mary could finish her pitch. She inspected Chelsea from hair to spilling décolletage in a guileless parody of the famous Sofia Loren, Jayne Mansfield photo. "I believe Chelsea's talents don't quite fit in Duncroft."

I choked on my halibut.

Ian needlessly rubbed my back. However needless, it felt nice.

"Daphne?" Lady Jane called.

Behind my hand, as decorously as I could, I coughed my throat clear and answered, "Yes, Lady Jane?"

"Are you all right?"

"Perfect."

She smiled munificently at me and noted, "I know you're on holiday, but I rarely get to London—"

"As in never," Michael snorted under his breath.

"Dewhurst," Richard hissed.

"—and I would love to try some of your pastries," Lady Jane finished as if the byplay didn't happen.

"You're in luck," I told her. "Bonnie asked me to show her a few tricks while I'm here. We're going to work together on Wednesday."

"Excellent," Lady Jane decreed.

Ian was smirking at his fish.

Chelsea looked to be sucking a lemon.

"Who's Bonnie?" Portia asked Daniel.

"Our cook," Daniel answered.

"She's studied at River Cottage and the School of Artisan Food," I told Daniel. "This after she sous-chefed for Topher Lambeth for three years, and he's won four Michelin stars. You're tasting her food right now and have eaten it countless times before. So you must know, she's not a cook. She's a chef."

"Semantics," Richard scoffed.

I turned to him. "I can assure you the cooks who nourish school children and the chefs who make a study of the art of food would disagree," I returned. "Both are important, but only one studies deeply before laboring under often-times exacting taskmasters for years before they earn their first kitchen." My gaze moved to Stevenson, who was wandering the outskirts of the table with a bottle of wine wrapped neatly in linen, his eagle eyes sharp for the glass that needed filling. "Those who manage your house know precisely what they're doing."

A flush crept up Stevenson's neck at my compliment, but otherwise, he didn't falter in his duties.

"Well, all I can say is, this is utterly delicious," Portia declared.

"Agreed," Michael grunted.

We all fell into silence, but when Sam and Jack, with Stevenson overseeing, started clearing our dishes for the next course, Chelsea exclaimed, "Right, girls! Let's have some fun. Which morbid tales of the women of Duncroft did Ian and Daniel use to do their wooing?"

My back snapped straight.

Ian emitted a low growl.

"I know Ian's favorite is Joan, and Daniel favors Rose," Chelsea shared.

Joan.

And Rose.

Joan and Rose.

Who was Rose?

"So?" Chelsea pressed.

"My dear, we don't speak of such things at Duncroft," Richard proclaimed.

"Oh Richard, of course you do," Chelsea rebutted. "I know firsthand."

"Chelsea, love," Mary said in soft warning.

But her warning came too late.

Ian was done.

"I'm uncertain you understand," he stated in a cutting voice I was instantly happy he'd never used with me, I felt lacerated, and it wasn't even aimed my way, "how much of a fool you're making of yourself."

"Listen, son—" Michael began heatedly.

Ian turned to him. "You'll know when I'm speaking to you. Now, I'm not."

In affront, Michael's eyebrows hit what should have been his hairline.

Ian's attention returned to Chelsea. "You're no longer in my bed, nor are you in Daniel's. If this was something you desired again, I can assure you, with your behavior tonight, you've blown any chance. I can't begin to imagine why you're acting as you are. It has no goal but to wound, which isn't nice at all and says terrible things about you. I held affection for you, Chelsea. But right now, I think you're acting like a bitter cow."

Chelsea's face went slack in shock.

"My God," Mary breathed, aghast.

"You've been sitting right here, Mary," Daniel noted, his hand covering Portia's on the table protectively. "You can't have missed how she's been behaving."

"Is this how Duncroft will be run when you take over?" Michael demanded to know.

"If you mean when I ask someone to join me in my home to drink my wine and eat my food and grace my table, and they act like a vicious shrew, am I going to call them on their fuckery?" Ian asked in return. Then he answered, "Yes."

I sat back with my wine and said, "I've gotta say, you Alcotts sure know how to throw a dinner party."

Lou choked down a hysterical giggle.

"You're not helping," Ian murmured to me.

But Daniel was smiling at me.

123

And Portia was watching me closely.

She turned her hand under Daniel's and linked fingers.

The panel opened in the wall and Stevenson ushered Jack and Sam in.

We'd already had a lot to chew on.

But for now, we had to set that aside.

It was time for the main course.

NEEDLESS TO SAY, when we left the dining room, Portia and Daniel, Lou, Ian and I didn't follow the others to the Wine Room for a digestif.

I walked Lou up to her room and made sure she took her migraine tablet and drank a whole glass of water besides. I then pulled the bell, and when she arrived, asked Harriet to fill her water carafe so she could have some close at hand in order to stay hydrated.

I could tell it was getting worse, so I helped her get undressed and brushed her hair into a ponytail while she took off her makeup and did her skincare regime.

Once she was tucked in bed, and I'd had a word in the hall with Harriet about keeping an eye on Lou tonight as she dealt with her migraine, and she promised she'd look in again before she was off the clock at eleven, I went back downstairs to the Conservatory.

Ian was alone with a cigarette and a brooding expression.

"Can I have one of those?" I asked.

"Do you smoke?" he asked in return.

"No."

"Then no."

He was sitting in the middle of the couch.

I sat in a chair opposite him.

"Where are Portia and Daniel?" I queried.

"Who knows? Who cares?"

I cared, obviously. Since I asked.

Though, with his oppressive mood, I didn't share that.

I gave it a few minutes, and in those few minutes, Ian set his burning cigarette in the clean ashtray, pushed out of the couch, went to the drinks cabinet, came back, and reaching across the low table between us, he handed me a snifter of Amaretto.

Thoughtful. Funny. Gorgeous. Protective.

Ugh.

I took a sip while he folded back into his sofa, reclaimed his cigarette and continued smoking pensively.

Then I noted carefully, "She's very beautiful."

"If that's your effort at trying to make me feel better I fucked that bitch, I'm afraid, my darling, it's not going to work."

"Is that why you're in such a mood?"

"I'm not telling you about Dorothy Clifton to get you in my bed. I'm telling you because you want to know."

"I know that."

"As I told her about Joan because she wanted to know."

"Will you tell me about Joan?"

"You didn't do very well with your research if you don't know about Joan and Thomas, Daphne," he chided.

"Well, I do. The Cuthbert affair. You just seem to know so much more than the internet."

"My great aunt considered herself an Alcott historian. She listened avidly, researched single-mindedly, and these efforts bore fruit. There are about twelve of her handwritten diaries on the history of Duncroft and the Alcotts."

"Have you read them?" I queried.

"Every last one."

"Is that a prerequisite to becoming an earl?"

He stopped watching the smoke curl lazily from his cigarette and turned his attention to me.

With the brand of that attention ("brand" being the operative word, for I felt scorched), I braced.

"No. It was a young man's desperate attempt to learn all the reasons why his father was an inveterate adulterer in an effort to circumvent that happening to myself should I fall in love with a woman and make her my wife."

"You're not your dad," I said gently.

He inhaled and blew a cloud of smoke over his head.

It floated behind him, away from me, like he could even will smoke to go where he wished.

What he didn't do was respond.

"Tell me about Joan," I urged.

"Bored with Dorothy?"

"I sense that story is more about Virginia, and no. I'm not bored with it. But tonight, I want to hear about Joan. And Rose."

"You only get one, love."

"Then Joan," I picked.

He launched right in.

"The beauty of the Season. The Exquisite. The Prized Jewel. She should have gone to a duke. Maybe even a prince. She stupidly fell in love with an earl."

"I sense this story isn't about her infidelity."

He studied the burning tip of the cigarette, which was almost to the gold paper.

Then he leaned forward and snuffed it out.

After that, he got up and went to the drinks cabinet. "Fair warning, it's scandalous."

"I'm not easily scandalized."

"Thomas liked to fuck and be fucked."

Okay, maybe I was easily scandalized.

"He liked to fuck Joan and watch others fuck her too," Ian carried on.

Definitely, I was easily scandalized.

"So he was bi?" I asked.

He came back with what appeared to be Cognac and resumed his seat.

"No, he was pan. Men. Women. Pain. Bondage. Giving and taking. He held orgies in this house. He had whores of all persuasions on his payroll. No maid was safe from his attentions. No footman safe from buggery. He was a sexual menace in a time while holding a class where that went entirely unchecked. He could do whatever, and whoever he wanted with impunity. Even if they didn't want it."

Awful.

Fiendish.

"And Joan was into this too?" I inquired.

Ian shook his head. "Not at all. She hated it. Enter poor Cuthbert."

Poor Cuthbert.

"She fell in love," I guessed.

Ian nodded, but said, "He was a favorite of Thomas's. An actor. He lived in this house with them for years. The Owl Room. Reportedly, he was very handsome. Tall. Built. Dark." He stared intently at me. "With eyes as blue as the sea."

I felt my heart stutter in shock.

"Holy fuck," I whispered.

"Well stated," he agreed. "However, there came a time when Joan had had enough. She went to her father. She begged his mercy and him to intervene. A devout man, he was outraged. He went to the king."

I sipped, watching him.

He sipped and kept talking.

"She was pregnant by this time, and Thomas suspected it wasn't his. He fucked everything that moved, and as yet, had no progeny. My aunt is certain he was sterile. The idea that Joan would birth someone not of his line sent him into a rage. He too went to the king."

"Oh boy."

"Mm," he hummed. "Though, Joan had a card up her sleeve that Thomas could never imagine. No one could. It was a secret closely held."

"That being?"

"She was a direct descendent of Henry the Eighth. He had a number of children that were not from his wives. Some were secreted away. Some were carefully homed. Some given land and titles. Joan was Henry's great-great granddaughter. A secret well-kept, issue well protected, even by King James. You see, if one was thrown under the bus, others could be too. No monarch wanted to see their seed wasted, especially when it laid no claim to the crown and was not a threat. So Thomas was ordered to love and cherish her and the babe in her womb."

"Are you telling me that you're—"

"Royal blood? A direct descendent of Henry the Eighth? Yes."

I couldn't believe this!

"Oh my God, Ian."

"Perhaps that's where it all began," he said musingly to his Cognac. It was a valid question. Henry was an asshole.

"Another reason Duncroft survived where other aristocratic houses dwindled or blinked out of existence," he remarked. "Until the twentieth century, we had royal patronage."

"This is huge," I uttered my understatement. "Are you sworn to secrecy or something?"

"All anyone would have to do is read Aunt Louisa's diaries."

"But they're in your library."

"Copies are also in The British Library for anyone to check out. I suppose the ramblings of a dotty spinster aren't interesting to some, no matter how meticulously researched and referenced they are. Another indication of how foolhardy it is to ignore intelligent women you deem superfluous simply because they were unwanted by a man. That said, it's my understanding from her diaries, it was the other way around. She found men vain and tedious. Nevertheless, she had affairs and 'men friends' until she died at age eighty-three."

I felt my lips curve. "I think I would have liked her."

"I can guarantee she would have liked you."

How sweet.

"So, with the king's protection, how did things go so poorly for Joan and Cuthbert?" I asked.

"I suppose there's only so much a vain, tedious and privileged man can take. Thomas came home one day and found Joan and Cuthbert enjoying each other in a session that was not ordered by him. He lost his mind, gutted Cuthbert and turned the bloody blade on Joan. Fortunately for the Alcott line, by that time, she'd given him a son and two daughters. All with dark hair and sea-blue eyes."

"In other words, the real Alcott line died with Thomas."

He threw back his Cognac then asked. "I don't think that was much of a loss, do you?"

I studied him closely, noting, "This is a lot of history to be lugging around."

"You know, the most amusing aspect of it is that Dad has never read those diaries. I'm not sure anyone has, but me. Louisa didn't shout it from the rooftops. I think her uncovering of it, and how it's there, *right there* and no one knows, was amusing as hell for her too. Dad has no idea in his veins runs the blood of a common actor and male prostitute who spent his adult life as a sexual plaything. He also has no idea he has royal blood. He has no idea this blood, the blood he'd deem important, didn't come down the paternal side of his line, but the maternal. He has no idea, for all intents and purposes, he's a Tudor, not an Alcott. He's convinced of the nobility of his blood, not understanding his many-times great-grandfather was the one who proclaimed the divine right of kings."

"So, you haven't told him," I drawled.

That coaxed a small smile out of him. "No, I haven't shared this with Dad."

"What happened to Thomas after he disobeyed the king?"

"She'd birthed a son by then. What do you think?"

"Nothing," I mumbled.

"Nothing," he confirmed.

I changed the subject. "Any fun plans for your birthday?"

"Mother has a party every year. My sense, this year, Chelsea's being uninvited."

I started laughing.

He was a gentleman, so he waited until I wrung all the enjoyment out of that before he asked, "How'd your talk go with Portia?"

"Not great."

"I think one of our meetings in the Conservatory needs to include some history. You two couldn't be less alike, and you've shown quite the efficiency with dealing with inanity and idiocy. And yet you haven't marched to your car, roared away in a spray of gravel and called your solicitor to lock down her inheritance."

"You have a flair for the dramatic, Lord Alcott," I teased.

"You have patience and loyalty that seems unearned, Miss Ryan," he parried.

I shrugged. "I try to do what Dad would do. He had a lot of patience with Portia. And it's his money." I took another sip to gather the courage, and then I asked, "Did you look into Portia too?"

"You know I have."

"Is she working?"

"Working?"

"Employed."

"No. She quit her job last month to be Daniel's full-time girlfriend."

I looked beyond him to the moonlight shining through the vast expanse of windows.

"Why?" he asked quietly.

I looked back to him. "I was wondering how she could be here this week. She's held down a job for eight, nine months. It's required for her to draw from her fund."

"Well, shit."

I tipped my snifter to him. "Now it's well-said to you, my friend." I sighed. "I was giving her thirty thousand pounds a month. When she hit her year anniversary at work, I was going to increase it to fifty. Now, it'll return to two. And that won't be at my decree. That's Dad's."

"Is there any hope she's set aside any of those two hundred and forty thousand pounds to get her through a long, cold winter?"

"None whatsoever. The shoes she was wearing tonight cost twenty-five hundred pounds, and they were new. Everything she's worn that I've seen in this house is new. Is Daniel in a position to buy her a diamond bracelet?"

"Not that I know."

"So there's another fifteen K, at least."

Ian just watched me.

I just sighed again.

"This is a lot for your father to saddle you with," he remarked, a low rumble of annoyance in his deep voice.

"Honey, I've been saddled, though I don't like that word, with Portia since she was born. Her mother took off with a huge settlement and we've never seen her again. At least, not anywhere near Portia. On yachts with her most recent sugar daddy. Drinking in Corfu. Frolicking in Capri. Walking out of the Ritz. I can't imagine. My mom hates my dad and isn't afraid to say it, but she loves me. She also took in Portia and gave her love. But my mom isn't her mom. I think if they're pains in our asses, we can convince ourselves we're happy they're in Capri and not in our lives. But I doubt that's the real way of it."

"Unquestionably."

I threw back the last of my Amaretto.

Then, feeling slightly woozy, which probably had to do with bad sleep and lots of wine at dinner, I said, "I want to go check on Lou and get some rest. I need to tackle Portia tomorrow, and to do that, I need to have all my pistons firing."

He set his Cognac on the table and stood, coming around to offer a hand to help me up.

This time, I didn't hesitate in taking it.

"First stop, my room for your sleeping pill," he stated.

"Ian, your thoughtfulness is lovely, but those weren't prescribed for me."

"I have a pill cutter. We'll halve it. Take half. If you need more, take the other half."

"All right," I agreed.

We held hands all the way up the stairs and down the hall to his room.

I hadn't poked around too much on this, his wing. Just stuck my head in a few rooms, worried that I'd run into someone's private quarters.

But I'd noted they were all like my current one. Much bigger. Sitting rooms. Huge closets. Massive bathrooms. Not rooms as such, but suites.

That was the family wing, created so they each had their own personal space to escape to, and a lot of it, or at least, somewhere in modern times, it had been fashioned into it.

Ian's suite of rooms was handsome, masculine, and looked like a tornado went through it.

The double doors that framed his massive bed in the bedroom area —a tall bed made taller because, for God's sake, it was on a dais, of all things—showed that space was tidy. As such. At least the bed was made.

The rest was an absolute mess.

"This is a disaster," I said, taking in the papers, folders, portfolios, two laptops, graphs, printouts, an overflowing, if attractive attaché. This mess was on his toffee-colored button-backed leather couch. The end tables. The coffee table. Stacked on the floor by the big desk. Stacked *on* the big desk.

"I have a lot of projects on the go. Diversity is the key to making a fuckton of money," he called from his bathroom. "And my assistant isn't here to keep it in check."

"Have you not heard of a cloud?" I called back. "I think the amount of paper in here is responsible for the extinction of two species of birds, one of squirrels, three chipmunks, and an adorable class of owls."

He came out of his bathroom grinning.

He stopped in front of me. "Do you know you're at your most fuckable when you're giving me shit?"

"A girl tries," I quipped.

He reached, grabbed my wrist, lifted my hand and dropped the two halves of a small blue pill in my palm. He then curled my fingers around them.

"Go. Sleep. When I finally seduce you, I want you firing on all pistons too."

I rolled my eyes. "Flirt."

"Tease."

I winked at him then got up on my toes and kissed his cheek.

After that, I headed to the door.

"Daphne?"

I stopped and turned back.

"Dad orchestrated tonight. He wanted me, you, Danny, Mum and Portia uncomfortable. He also put Chelsea in that position. Mary. Michael. Michael is his closest friend."

And there was the reason for his earlier Mr. Broody.

"I know," I said gently.

"And then came you, making me end the night smiling."

"Don't get soppy on me, Lord Alcott."

"Never."

I stopped bantering and said, "Sleep well, honey."

"You too, Daphne."

I shot him a smile. Then I went to my room.

I was still feeling woozy.

I was also feeling warm. I was feeling happy. I was feeling confused at both. I was trying not to feel worried about the fact I was beginning to feel a lot for the very-soon-to-be Earl Alcott.

What I was not feeling was, after I checked in on Lou (who was thankfully sound asleep), when I hit the Rose Room and saw how fabulous it was when the girls had prepared it for me to relax for the evening, another bridal bouquet being placed on the turned-back fold of the sheets.

And this one I knew wasn't right.

But it was sending a message.

I just didn't understand what that message was.

Because it wasn't roses.

It was an exact replica of the one I left in the bathroom down the hall.

But bigger.

And it was carnations.

Fourteen

THE HAWTHORN SUITE

I sat in bed, Kindle in hand, unsure if this was the right thing
to do.

That bouquet.

The story of Joan.

I did it.

I opened Steve Clifton's book, *The Woman in the Orange Dress*, on
my e-reader.

He'd dedicated it to, *Aunt Dorothy, for all the talent you weren't
given the time to share.*

Also, *To Mum and Dad, for believing in me.*

Then I hit the Preface.

It began:

*To understand what happened to Dorothy Vera Clifton, you have to
understand the stories of Virginia Alcott, Joan Alcott and Rose Alcott. The
broken three.*

On a spiked heartbeat, I immediately closed the cover.

The broken three.

The broken fucking *three.*

I had not read that before Virginia said the same thing to me in a
dream.

No, I had not read that before she said the *same damn thing in my dream.*

My heart was beating too fast, and my hands were shaking.

Those flowers weren't right.

Someone was toying with me.

I had no idea how, or why, but they were.

Or maybe, two nights, not enough sleep, I needed to get a handle on myself and a good night's rest.

Ian had been sharing about Virginia. I'd looked up and read about Joan. I must have read about Rose somewhere, since Virginia mentioned her in the dream. I just forgot. I'd done a lot of reading about Duncroft. I'd read about Dorothy. And the word broken wasn't a rarely used word.

The bouquets, who knew? Maybe they only had carnations. It wasn't like they were right next door to a flower shop. It also wasn't like they weren't generous with food, drink, in-house dry cleaning. They could give whole bouquets as gifts for guests. It could be their thing. All I had to do was ask.

I was blowing this out of proportion.

It was dark and it was time to go to bed, and it'd been another roller coaster day.

And truth, I was anxious about having another bad dream.

I'd accepted Ian's sleeping pill, but I hadn't taken it.

I got up, went to the bathroom where I put the two halves in a pretty, crystal dish set out either because it was pretty, or to put jewelry in.

I took half of one.

There was a multitude of lighting in the bathroom, including dim light that shone on the floor under the vanities.

I turned that on and left it on.

It lit my way back to the bedroom, and, once I turned off the lamps on the nightstands, the light coming from the bathroom took the edge off the dark.

I did one better, going to all the windows and pulling open the curtains.

The moon shone in.

Good.

I was learning.

I crawled into bed.

I'd never taken a sleeping pill. I didn't know how long it would take to work.

I pulled the covers up high.

And within minutes, I was out like a light.

WE WERE ON THE MOORS, walking and holding hands.

"It was a perfect moment, wasn't it?" I asked.

"Perfect," Ian agreed.

The wind swept my hair into my face.

I shook my head to shake it away.

"Why don't you give me heather?" I asked.

"Because you're carnations."

"Not roses?"

"Roses are for countesses. You're nothing but easy pussy."

I turned to him, pulling my hand away.

He lunged at me like he wanted to harm me.

I started running.

I made it to the stairs at the front of Duncroft in a blink.

It was now dark.

I had to get there.

I had to stop it.

Or she'd be broken.

I leaped up the steps two at a time.

I made it to the foyer, but the chandelier and sconces were all lit and all that light bouncing off the white, it was so bright, it was blinding.

I skidded to a halt.

That was when I heard the scream.

I looked up.

The dress was orange.

So orange.

She was falling so fast, the silk was beating against the air, slapping against her body.

She hit with a thud, the same thud I'd heard my first night there, and a nauseating *crunch*.

I screamed.

Her head was turned my way, eyes open and lifeless. Then the blood came out of those eyes, her mouth, her ears, creeping across the white marble, mingling with her platinum hair, the orange silk of her dress. All that orange and red, stark against the white.

The diamonds wrapped around her forehead and her wrist twinkled expensively in the lights.

Her arm was twisted wrong, as were both of her legs.

Even so, she lifted her head.

I started backing away.

One side was caved in, the blood dripping in thick globs from the wound.

Her jaw came unhinged as her mouth moved.

"Broken."

I turned and ran into Ian.

He was now in old-fashioned eveningwear, staring down at Dorothy.

"No more carnations for her," he said.

A tap on my shoulder and I looked that way.

Marble-white Persephone had left her post.

"Will you come with me?" she asked. "It's time to go to the fields."

I shook my head, heart in my throat, fear coating my skin, and raced by Ian and into the night, onto the lawn, through the trees, to the moors, going in the direction I saw Daniel take. Running. Running.

I saw them, all three of them, pushing and fighting among the night-time shadows of heather. Virginia in a pale dress that shone in the moonlight.

It was blue.

"*You pushed her!*" she screamed.

"No, you pushed her!" David shouted back.

They both turned on a shadowed man, just a body wearing evening clothes, no face.

William.

"*No, you pushed her!*" They yelled at him.

Virginia then looked to me, and her screech felt like it shattered my eardrums, "*BROKEN!*"

I whirled in fear and found myself in a big space made from stone. There were large fireplaces. Coarse furniture. Hanging tapestries.

My eyes went direct to her.

She smiled at me.

Rose.

"They'll burn me alive for this," she said gleefully. Then, like she was of my time and not wearing a gown and kirtle, her hair hidden behind a structured hood and veil, she cried, "Worth it!"

She cackled.

Wet splashed on me.

I spun and more hit me.

Blood.

Everyone in the room was vomiting blood.

I tried to back away and slipped on it.

Fell.

It was all over the stone. I couldn't get my hands under me. I kept falling into the blood.

I felt a presence loom over me.

I looked up.

It was Rose.

She was burning.

"Broken," she said, smiling as her skin blistered, blackened, fell away. She reached toward me. "Be broken with me."

I shot up in bed, then shot out of it.

Bare feet hitting the floor, I ran to the door, threw it open, dashed out, down the hall, around the landing, to Ian's room.

I pounded, loudly, frantically, then pulled the door open.

The light switched on just as I ran into his sitting room.

I stumbled clumsily to a halt and looked left.

He'd thrown off the covers and was angling out of bed but stopped when he caught sight of me, his expression freezing.

"Daphne?"

"Do you put bouquets of flowers on guests' beds?"

"What?"

"Do you put bouquets of flowers on guests' beds!" I screamed.

He moved quickly to me—pajama bottoms, drawstring, navy...bare chest, wide, great chest hair, all over, even on his flat, boxed belly.

I backed away.

He stopped.

"Come here, love," he coaxed gently, holding a hand to me.

"Do you? Answer me," I demanded.

"I don't know," he said, dropping his hand.

"How did Rose die?"

"Rose?"

"The one who poisoned her fiancé, her family."

"That was Margery."

Margery.

Yes.

That was her name.

"Who's Rose?" I asked.

"You need to calm down."

"What's happening?"

I reeled toward the door. It was Lady Jane in a beautiful cashmere dressing gown, looking like a deity.

I'd never seen her face so expressive. She was watching me, her beauty etched in worry.

"Do you put bouquets on beds?"

"Bouquets on beds?" she asked.

"Carnations."

Her eyes darted to Ian.

"Tell me!" I shrieked.

She looked again to me. "No, dear, I don't. We don't. Is someone leaving carnations on your bed?"

While Jane asked this, Ian stalked out of the room.

"Yes. The first night. And tonight," I told her.

"I don't know who's doing that, Daphne, but we'll get to the bottom of it. Come," she motioned to Ian's couch. "Sit. Let me call down for some hot cocoa."

I was shivering. So damned cold.

I raked a hand through my hair, shook my head. "I'm having nightmares."

"It's a cruel joke. Perhaps a prank. Not funny," she murmured irritably. She got close, touched my arm lightly. "Will you sit with me?"

"Don't wake anybody up. I just need to calm down."

"All right. I won't wake anyone up. But will you sit with me?"

I nodded.

She led me to the couch, carefully moved some papers, and we sat down.

"I'm so sorry this has happened," she said. "I can't...there's no excuse. But I can assure you it'll be dealt with."

It hit me.

Daniel.

And maybe Portia.

Probably mostly Portia.

They were here the first night, and tonight.

But not last night, when I didn't get any flowers.

Both nights, they'd disappeared early.

It was Daniel, but probably Portia.

I knew it.

I sucked in a breath.

It was then I realized Jane was holding my hand on her knee.

"I'm sorry I woke you up," I mumbled.

"This house can be overpowering. You get used to it, though."

Never.

I was having my talk tomorrow with Portia, then I was taking Lou, who this house and the people in it was giving migraines, and we were getting the fuck out of there.

I jumped nearly out of my skin when I saw movement at the door.

Daniel in nothing but boxer briefs, and Portia, in a baby-pink, short, lace-edged, obviously expensive nightie.

Ian brought up the rear.

The new arrivals both looked disheveled and that groggy-alert you get when you're woken up by something important: you're awake, but you're still half-asleep.

"Tell her," Ian demanded.

Daniel was staring at me.

"*Tell her!*" he roared.

"It was just a joke," Portia said in a small voice, also staring at me, looking ludicrously guilty.

Goddamn it.

Portia.

"Oh my Lord," Lady Jane breathed angrily.

"Get out of my sight," Ian ordered.

"Ian—" Daniel started.

"Danny, get her...out of my...*sight.*"

Straightaway, Daniel herded Portia out the door.

But my sister kept looking back at me.

Guilty.

Ian turned to his mother.

"I've got this," he declared.

"All right, darling," she replied readily, giving my hand one last pat, putting it in my lap and rising with the grace of a ballerina.

She floated to Ian. He dipped down to get her peck on his cheek.

She turned at the door. "I'm truly so sorry, darling," she said to me. "But as ever, tomorrow is another day."

Trust her to quote Scarlet O'Hara and not sound like a twit.

"Thanks for checking in, Lady Jane."

The ends of her lips curled minutely.

She closed the door behind her.

A glass of liquor I smelled instantly was whisky was shoved in my face.

I looked up at Ian. "I don't like whisky."

"Drink it."

"I—"

"Drink it, Daphne."

I gave him a glare and took the glass. Then I threw back the entire contents.

I nearly retched. I did breathe with my mouth open like fire would come out.

Whisky.

Bluh.

"I didn't say chug it, for fuck's sake," Ian muttered, taking the glass from me and slamming it down on the table on top of some papers. "Up. In bed."

I stood. "I'm sorry I woke you up."

"I'm sorry about why you woke me up."

"I'm sorry I woke your mum up too."

"It doesn't matter. It's over. Get in bed."

"How did you know it was them?"

"You don't make two billion pounds before you're twenty-eight not knowing how to read people. Your sister has a nasty streak. Hence only two dates."

And no fucking, he thankfully left unsaid.

"Thanks for...well..." I lamely threw out a hand to finish that statement.

"Daphne, get in bed."

"All right," I mumbled. "Thanks again."

I started to the door.

His arm around my belly stopped me.

I looked up at him.

"Where are you going?" he asked.

"To bed."

He jerked his head to the left. "The bed is that way."

My mouth dropped open.

"You think I'm going to let you sleep alone?" he demanded.

"I—"

"You shrieked at me."

Oh God.

How embarrassing was this?

"I'm fine now, Ian."

"You'll be more fine if you have another nightmare that wakes you up, terrified, and you don't have to race through the house in the dark to get where you feel safe. You didn't go to Lou. You didn't go to Portia. You came to me. That shares all I need to know. Now, get in my bed."

"I don't want to—"

I stopped talking when he looked to the ceiling.

This had to do with him being clearly exasperated, and I felt bad it was me exasperating him.

This also had to do with the fact his throat and shoulders and collarbone and chest were on display, all of that was close, and I was no longer freaking out (so much), so I could process it, and what I was processing was making me weak in the knees.

He looked down at me and his voice had gentled when he urged, "I need sleep. You definitely need sleep. And honest to fuck, I need you in here with me. Swear to Christ, the way you looked when you rushed in here, I thought the devil was on your heels."

"God, I'm so sorry," I whispered.

He pulled me into his arms, close, giving me a comforting hug and a soft urge of, "Come to bed."

His arms felt good, and I didn't have the energy to fight it any longer.

"All righty," I mumbled to the skin across his bulging pecs.

He let me go but took my hand and guided me to bed.

I climbed in and scooched over. He folded in after me.

He turned out the light, pulled the covers high over us both, then found me and tucked me to his warm body.

It could be, all the muscles he was no longer hiding under his clothes were just hard normally.

But I sensed he was tense.

"Did I freak you out?" I asked.

"Yes."

"Stupid question," I muttered.

"No, it wasn't. I'm fine," he assured.

"So am I. I'm okay. It's all okay. It was just a very bad joke and me winding myself up about things."

"I'm not freaked out anymore, Daphne."

"You're tense."

"Yes. Because I'm out of my brain angry at your sister."

He could say that again.

"I just—"

His hand came to rest tenderly on my cheek, good aim, because it was dark as pitch in his room.

"Daphne, what might hasten this process is if you'd be quiet."

I shut up.

He slid his hand back into my hair and then commenced running his fingers through it.

That felt nice.

I started to unwind.

I felt his body begin to relax.

He switched to stroking my back.

I unwound more.

He stopped stroking and pulled me close.

I cuddled my cheek to his chest.

And fell asleep.

In the dark, on the face of the tablet by Ian's bed, the clock ticked the minute change.

It was three oh three.

Fifteen

THE SITTING ROOM

I woke without opening my eyes and instinctively gliding my hand across the sheet to find what I was looking for.

My hand came up empty.

I opened my eyes.

When I did, I saw one of those tablets that a lot of hotels had these days sitting on a stand on the night table.

It was one of those smart room tablets, that in my personal experience, never really worked. Apps that turned on and off lights, dimmed them, opened and closed curtains, and adjusted temperature.

This one appeared to have a current events window.

And it also told me it was ten fifty-seven in the morning.

I'd slept in, by a lot.

I sat up in bed and looked through the double doors to see Ian on the couch, twisted to look over the back at me.

Last night (or more aptly, early this morning) came crashing into my brain and I didn't know whether to be embarrassed about how I'd lost it or terrified out of my head at how much I was beginning to feel for Ian Alcott.

While my just-awake brain was sifting through these things, Ian got up and walked toward me.

I watched as he came right up to the bed then reached beyond the nightstand to pull a wide velvet ribbon that, considering the room was so masculine, was the odd color of white with a faint stripe of pink down the middle. The silk tassel at the bottom was a bright, leafy green.

It hit me.

The colors of a hawthorn blossom.

"I overslept," I announced.

"Correction," Ian replied, standing beside the bed looking down at me and also looking pretty scrumptious in some gray joggers and a navy, long-sleeved shirt. His feet, I'd noted, were encased in some OluKai, gray shadow slippers. "You caught up on sleep," he finished.

I nodded.

"They know if I ring the bell, you're awake. They'll be bringing up some coffee and food for you in a minute."

"Okay. I'll head back to my room."

To that, he went to the end of the bed and picked up my camel-colored, merino wool duster cardie, which was so long, it hit my ankles.

Someone had been to the Rose Room.

"You'd only have to come back here," he said. "They brought your bathroom things too. They did this because I asked. I want you with me for a while, if you don't mind. I want to make sure you're okay."

So sweet.

That said...

"I'm okay, Ian."

"I'm asking you to humor me."

I'd been really freaked out, and I'd brought that right to Ian's door, as it were, and freaked him out too.

Now, understandably, he was worried.

There was no reason to fight it, so I didn't.

I nodded again.

He held out the cardigan like it was a coat.

I slid out of bed and turned my back to him, shoving my hands in the arms.

He settled it on my shoulders then used those shoulders to guide me down the dais toward a door. He ended putting his hand on the small of my back and giving me a gentle shove before flipping a switch, which artfully lit a bathroom that was a study of rich browns with stark-white porcelain bathroom accessories and gold fixtures.

Once I was inside, he shut the door behind me.

I used the facilities, and when I got to the sink, I saw a silver tray with a thick, rose-colored hand towel draped over it, on top of which were my Sonic toothbrush, toothpaste, box of dental floss, cleanser, toner, moisturizer, my hairbrush and a scrunchie.

Easy to use here, easy to carry back with me.

The staff really had it going on in Duncroft.

I gazed at myself in the mirror.

Although my eyes were puffy, they didn't seem hollow like they'd been getting of a morning, and the shadows I'd needed to use concealer to cover were gone.

Sleeping in four hours clearly did me some good.

I took care of business then wandered out, past the bed, to where Ian was on the couch.

A TV had been exposed behind a panel, and it was on but muted, set to some station that was nothing but a tape of stock indexes running at the bottom and rapidly shifting graphs and numbers on the screen.

A laptop was open on the coffee table, what looked like a half-drafted email, on it.

And the long swath of the rest of the coffee table had been cleared so the tray could be set there. It had a coffee service resting on it that was ivory with a wide green band, along with some croissants, butter, jam and a bowl of berries and yogurt sprinkled with granola.

Ian, still seated in the far corner, stretched an arm to his side in invitation.

I didn't know why, maybe I was still a bit fuzzy, maybe it was too tempting of an invitation to turn down, but I accepted it, sat close to him, and he curled his arm around me and tucked me closer.

I rested my head on his shoulder.

He was strong and warm, I liked his slippers, and I really liked his room. It was beautiful and dark and male, but still relaxed and homey.

Unlike pretty much every room I'd encountered in this house, this room felt lived in, even though I knew Ian lived his real life in London. It smelled like him. Like moss and outdoors, and wealth and man.

After a few long moments, he asked, "All right?"

I nodded yet again, my head moving on his shoulder.

"Are you angry?" he asked.

"Livid," I answered. "She's a grown woman acting like a teenager. Playing pranks, who does that? And I don't like to be scared. I don't like horror movies. I don't read horror thrillers. She knows that. It was just...*mean*."

"Can she be mean to you?"

And this was the question.

"In all honesty, throughout our lives, most of it seemed like acting out. I think she feels her mother abandoning her. I think Dad was about making money and spending it, and he didn't have a lot of time for us, and without her mom, she needed him. I think he knew that, and instead of giving her what she needed, his time, he chose to compensate by giving her things, spoiling her, coddling her, and when it was time for her to mature and take responsibility, the damage was done."

I took a deep breath, let it out, and finished.

"And I think the relationship she and I have, never having been very strong, has gotten worse since Dad died. She wants her money and to live her life, and she doesn't want anyone telling her how to do it. Yet I have no choice. If I tried to go against the parameters of her trust, the other trustees would step in and stop it. If I tried to hide something, like the fact she's no longer working, I'll be removed as the primary director. Dad died understanding the flaws of his parenting when it came to Portia and putting into place a plan to fix them. It's too late, really, but in truth, what he's asking of her is not that much. Portia knows all of this. Like she knows, if she's not working, any funds beyond her two thousand stipend will be suspended. But she still chooses to target me when it's his rules she's breaking, not mine."

"Mm," he hummed.

It sounded nice when I was that close and could feel it come from his chest, but I knew what that noise wasn't saying.

"And okay, I'll stop making excuses for her and answer...yes. She can be mean to me. But pulling a prank like that, knowing I'm sensitive to those kinds of things is another level."

Ian leaned forward, taking me with him, but he had to remove his arm from around me in order to pour me some coffee.

"Cream? Sugar?" he murmured.

"A little cream."

He splashed, stirred, handed it to me in its saucer, then rounded me again with his arm and relaxed us back into the couch, but now I had caffeine.

Seriously. He might be the perfect man.

I sipped.

Bonnie knew her food, she also knew her coffee.

Excellent.

"You just woke up, but do you have an idea of what you're going to do now?" he asked.

"I'm going to have a chat with her, then pack Lou and me up, and leave."

His arm tightened in what felt like an unconscious spasm.

Except not quite a spasm, because it stayed tight.

"Will you trust me?" he queried.

After another sip, I took my head from his shoulder and tilted it back to look at him. "Pardon?"

"Will you trust me?" he repeated.

What a peculiar thing to ask.

"I already do. Shouldn't I?"

"I mean, don't leave." He shook his head but went on, "I have a gut feeling about something, I just don't know what it is. And if you leave, I don't think I'll be able to figure it out. Because, if you and Lou are gone, there's no reason for me to stay and there's no reason for Portia and/or Danny to pull their shit. But I sense whatever is behind what's happening needs to be outed. Now."

"It was just a prank. A mean one, but just a prank. What shit are you talking about?"

"That's what I'm not sure about. But I think they're up to something. That wasn't just a mean prank, Daphne. It was cruel. You were out of your mind terrified last night. But I don't think that's the end of it. When I woke them, they knew immediately something was up. They both looked guilty. But a lot guiltier than just setting some flowers on someone's bed would make them feel."

"Portia knows how badly I'd react to that."

"I still sense it's more."

Fabulous.

"I saw Daniel walking into the fog the first night I was here," I blurted. "It was three in the morning."

His brows drew together. "Where was he going?"

I shook my head. "No clue. I walked that way, far that way yesterday, and there's nothing at all on the trajectory where I saw him disappear into the fog. Does he have trouble sleeping?"

"Not that I know of."

"Is he prone to take walks?"

"Not at three in the morning. Also not at other times. He used to run. But now I think he plays tennis and squash to keep fit."

I nodded, vaguely wondering what Ian did to keep fit, having now seen and felt just how fit he was.

"I don't want you to leave," Ian declared.

My mind flew from his muscles as my belly fluttered.

"I think it's important for me to say that," he continued. "I'm enjoying getting to know you. I like to spend time with you. I don't want it to be over. Not how it is for us here, in this house, where we have time. We live in the same city, but life intrudes. I like this for us. I like it a great deal, Daphne."

I liked that he did.

I liked that a lot.

Because I liked what was happening between us too.

Perhaps too much?

"Ditto," I whispered.

He visibly relaxed a little, which was incredibly endearing.

"But I also want to figure out what those two are up to," he went on. "The whole house feels...off. It has since I got here for this visit."

Interesting.

And I'd never been here before, but I could sure as hell say it felt the same way to me.

"So it's not always picture-perfect yet filled with familial dysfunction?" I quipped.

He smiled. "It's always that, this time it's just more."

"But you don't know what that more is?"

"Mum's quiet, but she's quieter than normal. I don't think she likes Portia, but it isn't only that. Dad is actively being an asshole, rather than generally being one. He tried to hide who put you in the Carnation Room. I thought it was him being a dick. Now I wonder if it was Danny's suggestion and Dad generally being an asshole went along with it. Laura is Mum's favorite maid, and she can be watchful, looking after Mum, but now she's being...strange. Brittany's new, and I don't have a good feeling about her. She's not friendly like the rest. She doesn't seem to fit in, which makes her an odd choice for Stevenson. He's good with building a tight team. It's everywhere, Daphne. And I don't like it."

"My, but you do sell horror, country-house holiday like no other, Lord Alcott," I fake simpered. "But of course I'll join you on the continuation of our Great Adventure of Mischief on the Moors."

He chuckled and gave me a squeeze.

But I got serious. "Truth, Portia's acting weird too. I noticed it the minute I saw her when I got here. I don't know what she's up to and I don't know if I *want* to know. All I know is, if I stymie her by leaving, she'll just hatch some other scheme later, and I'd rather have it done with now than have something else sprung on me down the line."

"At least now we can be more vigilant and communicate. You can tell me what you see and hear, like Danny taking a walk in the early hours of the morning, and I can do the same."

"Right. But I have to say, I'm going to try to talk Lou into leaving. She has chronic migraines, but this is crazy. I think Portia is stressing her out. She needs to go home."

"Agreed."

"So it seems the game is afoot, Lord Alcott."

"It seems it is, Miss Ryan."

I was looking up at him. He was looking down at me. We were cuddled together. We'd slept in the same bed.

It was the perfect time for a kiss.

And it happened.

It was just that the kiss was Ian pressing his beautiful lips to my forehead.

Ah well.

That felt nice too, I supposed.

He pulled away but tipped his head toward the tray. "Get something to eat. Lou checked in a little bit ago. She seemed better, said she had a hint of a headache, but that happens after a migraine. She was going out to take a walk."

"Okay," I replied, pulled away and was loading up a croissant with butter and jam when there was a restrained knock on the door.

"All right?" Ian asked me.

I looked over my shoulder at him and nodded.

"Yes?" he called.

The door opened and Laura stood there.

She studiously avoided looking at me when she announced, "Lady Alcott would like for you both to meet her in the Sherry Room at one o'clock."

There was resignation in his voice when Ian said, "We'll be there."

Laura nodded smartly and strode out.

The door clicked.

I totally got what he meant about her. She was so formal, she was borderline creepy.

"Always the ceremony," he muttered under his breath, taking my attention back to him.

So that was what had him resigned. That it couldn't be Lady Jane knocking on the door, or, in a place this huge, sending a text.

No.

She had to dispatch Laura.

"What's that about, do you think?" I asked.

"We're going to find out," he answered, taking the bit of croissant I'd prepared and popping it into his mouth.

I frowned at him.

He smiled while chewing.

Fortunately, Bonnie put three croissants on the tray, so I smeared butter and jam on another section and enjoyed.

Sixteen

THE SHERRY ROOM

I'd already figured out the Sherry Room was the countess's room. Her office, of sorts.

Although decorated in a lot of wood and heavy, dark-green velvet curtains, the stain of the wood was lighter than other rooms on that wing. And there were deep slashes of buttery yellow, not to mention the walls above the wood wainscoting were a mellow linen to soften the darkness and drive home the feminine in a wing like the one above it, both of which veered masculine.

The main feature of the room was the beautifully carved writer's desk that had inlays of ivory.

This was gross now, and it was gross then, but that didn't stop the desk being made in another age when they did that kind of thing. Nor did it stop it from being a testimony (but not an excuse) to why so many elephants gave up what they were forced to give to create such beauty.

This was the showstopper, but there were also two large and extraordinary paintings that looked like Turners (and very well could be), and as such, they were stormy and turbulent and morose.

Along with its beauty, there was a melancholy to that room.

And at one o'clock that afternoon, standing at the window looking out to the late autumnal desolation spreading to what seemed forever at the front of the house, I wondered if the spirits of Virginia and Joan, and even Margery somehow permeated the atmosphere.

Past countesses (and a countess's daughter) who suffered for their status.

Suffered for Duncroft.

Ian was sitting on one end of the yellowish-green velvet couch sipping an espresso, Lou on the other side looking nervous.

She, too, had received a summons from Lady Jane.

This was weird, but then again maybe it wasn't. When everything seemed weird, when did weird stuff stop being weird and just become the norm?

I'd had croissants and yogurt, and then for about an hour, I'd chilled out and quietly hung with Ian while he worked, before I took my bathroom tray and headed out, going to the Rose Room to take a shower and prepare for the day.

When I got there, I was grateful to see someone had taken away the bouquet.

I hadn't seen Portia or Daniel yet that day, but after I paid this respect, whatever it was about, to Lady Jane, who had been really cool with me last night, I was finding Portia and sharing a few things.

Then I'd work on Lou.

In other words, I had a packed afternoon planned of fun and revelry.

Not.

However, that morning, Ian had passed his laptop to me, and I'd checked. There was a train headed to Leeds from a town about half an hour away that left at four. And from Leeds, Lou would be in London in two and a half hours.

And that'd be one thing off my mind, and I could spend the week focusing on Portia's latest shenanigans.

The door opened and Lady Jane came in.

I hadn't mentioned yet, but it should be noted, Lady Jane made everyday, landed-gentry elegance seem effortless.

Today she was in light-gray slacks with a cream turtleneck and a gray and yellow scarf under a pale, pale-pink sweater blazer. Her blonde hair was appropriately teased and curled and gorgeously swept away from her face from a side part, in a manner it looked like it'd dip over her eye at any moment. Her lips were lined and filled with a becoming neutral that had just a hint of gloss. Her Clash de Cartier hoops were gorgeous, but not overdone, and best of all, unless you knew what they were, you wouldn't know they cost seven thousand pounds.

The hallmark of true wealth: when you didn't feel the need to scream you had it.

Although I had more of an edge to my look, and at that moment in my life I'd rather wear nothing than wear a sweater blazer, I took note how you could be you, and flawless, even when you were sixty-one years old.

Alternative thought, Richard was a fool.

Jane was regal. Stunning. Stylish. Mysterious. And I'd also learned... sweet. She knew and loved her children, and even if she communicated that in ways I wasn't used to, she still communicated it. And she was loyal.

So many men had such treasure in their hands, and yet they chose to cast it aside to chase the sunrise of their lives, which was always fleeting.

"Thank you for coming," she said, avoiding looking at Lou, per usual, and seating herself with a straight back, ankles crossed under her and hands folded in her lap in one of the two chairs across from the couch. "If you don't mind, we'll need to wait until Portia and Daniel get here. They're on their way to the house. They're just back from riding."

Riding?

My sister and her man were enjoying their country sojourn, off on a horseback ride?

I felt my blood heat.

Ian looked over his shoulder at me because he knew that would make me mad.

Lou wasn't aware that anything had gone on. I hadn't had a moment alone with her yet.

I gave Ian a look that told him I wasn't going to get in a hair pulling fight with my sister when she showed (I hoped) and kept my silence.

It was only a couple of minutes before Portia and Daniel arrived, in full riding gear, and Portia (who I'd never seen in such a getup), looked like she was a goddamn Olympic equestrian.

At least she didn't have the hat on.

Though, that outfit had to be another hit to the money she should have saved if she intended to quit her job.

She lived in a posh, two-bedroom flat in Chelsea, for heaven's sake. If she had no money, she wasn't going to make the next month's rent.

Her gaze raced quickly between Ian, me, then Lou, back to linger on Ian before she visibly startled when Lady Jane spoke, because she couldn't see the woman as the high back of her chair was facing the door.

"Good, you're here. Please, come in."

Hesitant, like the two naughty children they were impersonating, Portia and Daniel slunk into the room.

They barely stopped in front of the cold fireplace when Lady Jane launched in.

"Dorothy Clifton was a vital woman with a thriving career. She lived. She had family. Friends. It was a long time ago, but no matter the time that's passed, the tragic fact she lost her life in this house is not a joke. It isn't fodder for a prank. Frankly, I find it vile that anyone would think so."

Daniel was contritely studying his muddy riding boots.

Portia was white as a sheet and staring at Lady Jane.

I only had Lou's profile, but she appeared confused.

As for Ian's profile, he was regarding them both like they were a mildly interesting play, but even so, he didn't take his eyes off them.

"Portia," Lady Jane continued, and I turned my attention, catching my sister's nervous swallow. "I'm not impressed. I wasn't impressed with your exit from this house, leaving your family behind with people who don't know them at all well and expecting us to carry on like the integral connecting piece hadn't vanished into thin air. But the results of your cruel plotting are abominable. I can only assume your hope for this week was for all of us to learn of each other, including learning to like each other. I can assure you that's happening, the problem for you is, I'm not learning to like *you*."

Harsh.

Fair.

But harsh.

Portia's attention rushed to me, like I could save her.

Like I often saved her.

I pressed my lips together.

"You disrespected your sister," Lady Jane went on. "Your step-mother. And me. Making matters worse, you invited them into my home to do it. It's intolerable."

"Mum—" Daniel began.

I shifted my attention to him and saw his cheeks were ruddy, and he looked miffed.

Then again, his girlfriend was getting a dressing down, one she deserved, but they were both adults, so this had to be humiliating.

Top that, there was an audience, and the brother Daniel was jealous of was part of it.

"Now," Lady Jane cut Daniel off, standing. "We have a whole week to learn how to treat each other with respect. I hope I have your assurances there won't be a repeat of some version of last night."

"It was just meant to be a joke," Portia said weakly.

"What was meant to be a joke?" Lou asked.

"Did your sister look amused last night?" Lady Jane demanded.

Portia cast her gaze to the floor.

"Do I have to ask again?" Lady Jane prompted.

"There won't be a repeat, Mum," Daniel said.

"Good," she replied. "Now, I'm certain your sister has a few things to say. I'll leave her to say them among family."

With that, she dipped her head to Lou, acknowledging her for the first time, and she gave her version of a warm look to her son, and also, I thought was nice, to me, before she swanned out.

I was surprised she had all that in her. Surprised and impressed.

Then again, it was Lady Jane who said Daniel needed a taskmaster. I just hadn't put it together at the time that all his life, that role so far had fallen to his mother.

It was Daniel who stepped up first.

"Jesus Christ, Ian," he sniped, glancing at me briefly while saying, "No offense. I saw you last night and I could tell it went too far,"—back to Ian—"but it was just a goddamned joke."

"Was it you who asked to put Daphne in the Carnation Room?" Ian returned coolly.

"Oh my God," Lou whispered.

"I don't have to explain myself to you," Daniel bit.

"May be nice, though, if you explained yourself to me," I butted in.

Daniel's jaw rippled.

"Did you?" I pushed.

Daniel said nothing.

Portia said nothing.

"Answer her," Lou demanded of Portia.

Shocker.

Even though Lou was family, she never butted into family stuff, not even when Dad was alive. And she never pushed anything. Ever. Particularly with Portia.

"What happened last night?" she asked.

"Danny and Portia left carnation bouquets for Daphne the two nights they've been here. The same type of bouquets David would leave for Dorothy because she loved carnations. Hence, she chose that room. And when David's wife was away, and Dorothy would come to play, that's where they'd tryst. Even Virginia came to understand that had become Dorothy's room."

And there was the explanation behind the reason Lady Jane seemed so shaken when I mentioned the carnations last night.

I didn't freak out about all this new knowledge that only made what Portia did worse.

But Lou sure as hell did.

"You know your sister isn't good with that kind of thing," she snapped.

Actually snapped.

"Lou, it doesn't have anything to do with—" Portia began.

Lou interrupted her. "I'm a part of this family, whether you like it or not. I care about you and your sister. So it has something to do with me, knowing you'd be so thoughtless. I mean, honestly, Portia. What do you think your sister does all day? And she's here. Do you not get what that means? You can't," she answered her own question. "If you did, you wouldn't be playing your usual mind games."

"Mind games?" Portia spat.

"Mind games," I said calmly.

Because...yes. Spot on. I finally got it, and Lou obviously already knew it.

That was what it always was.

Portia getting into trouble, and dragging me in. Portia pushing Dad and getting something out of the fact his need to become stricter and more demanding of her meant he did the same with me. Portia playing on my sympathies and my big sister loyalty and Lou's need for her love and approval. Portia pulling shit like she did last night for whatever she got out of doing things like that.

It was all just mind games.

Portia opened her mouth.

But I was done with this.

"It was you and I know it. Daniel doesn't want to throw you under the bus, and you sure as hell don't have the maturity to cop to it, but it was you. Daniel told you the story of Dorothy and David, and you knew I'd look into things when you asked us here. It's tragic, mysterious and spooky, with Dorothy supposedly haunting this house, a famous story I couldn't miss. You hatched your scheme and got Daniel to play along with it."

As it had been last night, the guilt was written all over her face.

I was done with Portia's guilt too.

So I kept going, "It wasn't nice. It hurt my feelings. But it's over, and we're moving on. Not with forgiveness," I hastened to add when Portia seemed to settle down and the familiar I-got-away-with-it smirk started to form on her mouth. "You haven't said you're sorry. But I have to share I am so...fucking...*done*. With all of it. And there's more. And I want that done too, so we're moving on."

"There's more?" Portia asked.

"Are you employed?" I shot back.

"Dear God," Lou moaned when Portia's expression again gave us the answer.

"You know what that means," I noted.

"I also know you two can talk to the trustees," Portia returned.

"What does it mean?" Daniel asked.

"We can't and you know it," I said to my sister. "You also know you're supposed to report to them, Portia, if there's a change in your employment status."

"I'm taking a break."

"Fine. Your life. Your choice. But you know if you do, your stipend reduces."

"It does?" Daniel looked down to Portia. "To what?"

"It's preposterous," Portia snipped, to him, to me, to the universe.

"It's what Dad wanted."

"You and Lou could do something."

"We can't."

"You haven't tried."

"And should we now?" Lou demanded irately. "When you're putting your sister in a dead woman's bed and fucking with her mind? Is it now we should step up for you, Portia?"

"What's the matter with you?" Portia asked snidely to hide her shock and dismay that Lou was growing a backbone when it came to her.

"I'm tired," Lou retorted. "My head hurts. I've been trying to prove how much you mean to me for nearly fifteen years, and I, too, am done." She stood and turned to me. "I'll call the trustees."

"I can do it," I replied.

"No." She glanced at Portia. "This time, I'll do it."

And without another word, she stormed out.

"How much does your allowance reduce?" Daniel asked.

Portia glared at him.

"She gets two thousand pounds a month until she's gainfully employed and then it's up to Lou and me how much we'll augment that," I shared.

Portia turned her glare on me.

But now it was Daniel who was white as a sheet.

Telling.

And sadly for Portia, her tricks opened the door for me to test the waters of her and Daniel's relationship to see how deep they ran.

But now...

Onward!

"And, I've made a decision," I said to my sister. "I'm going to talk to Lou, and if the trustees don't receive paystubs for six months straight, you won't get more. And when you do, it'll only be five thousand for six months beyond that."

"That's crazy!" Portia cried.

"This was all Dad's last effort at tough love, sis," I replied. "And since it hasn't been working, now's the time to get tougher."

Portia told me something I already knew. "I can't even pay my rent with that."

"Then you'll either need to get a job quickly or downsize."

She was looking panicky. "Daphne, you can't do that. I can't even pay movers."

Yup.

She'd squandered it all.

"Then you shouldn't have blown what amounts for a normal family to about five years' worth of income in eight months." And just because I was in a foul mood, I remarked, "Nice riding boots, by the way."

She didn't even respond to my dig. She was in full-blown panic now, then suddenly her gaze dropped to Ian and her entire face flamed red.

And something else hit me then, though it'd been staring me in the face since the start.

Goddamn.

She then looked up at Daniel, hooked her arm in his, straightened her shoulders, and like a dare that I honest to God in that moment didn't know if it was aimed at Daniel...or Ian, she declared, "I'll move in with you."

Now it was Daniel looking panicked.

Ian folded out of the couch saying, "How about we leave these two to wade through the aftermath of their bad decisions. I think there's a conversation you need to have with Lou."

It'd only been days, but the sight of Ian holding his hand to me was an endearingly familiar one.

I moved his way, accepted his offer, and he guided me to the door.

"I'm sorry about the flowers, okay? I honestly didn't think you'd freak so badly," Portia called to my back.

Ian stopped us as he felt me turn to her.

"You know, that hurts most of all," I said in a voice that shared how deeply it did just that.

Portia flinched. Even Daniel looked alarmed at the tone of my voice.

I carried on, "That you haven't bothered to pay enough attention to me over the years to know how much that would mess with me. Lou knows. My own flesh and blood doesn't. Yes, honey, that hurts."

After saying that, I looked to Ian.

And he guided me out the door.

Seventeen

THE TURRET

I was lounged on Lou's bed in the Poppy Room.

Lou was packing.

I didn't have to talk her into it, she'd made the decision herself to leave, (yes, she was that angry at Portia and that done with bending herself into pretzels for my sister). By the time Ian escorted me to her room, she was on the phone with the trustees, her laptop open in front of her, booking tickets for a train to Leeds tomorrow morning.

"The train this afternoon leaves too late," she told me. "I don't want you driving in the dark, and I'm just knackered, Daph. So I'll go down and ask Bonnie if she wouldn't mind making me a tray for dinner. I'll take a bath tonight and have a quiet night up here. I'll say my goodbyes and we can head out in the morning."

I was concerned she was knackered. She shouldn't be. She'd been resting a great deal lately. Though I knew her headaches took a lot out of her, the aura that always happened after never lingered like it'd been doing at Duncroft.

But mostly I was relieved she was getting out of there.

"Sooooooo..." she drew that out and said no more.

"So?" I prompted.

"You ran to Ian in your fright last night?"

163

She looked at me and batted her eyes.

"I needed to know about the bouquet," I explained lamely.

"When I asked Rebecca where you were this morning, she told me in Ian's room. It took him that long to explain about the bouquet?"

"Shut up," I mumbled.

"Another reason for me to leave, I'll no longer be the third wheel. You have him all to yourself to *play backgammon*."

I threw a poppy-red silk bolster pillow at her.

She smiled.

That made me feel better.

"He thinks Portia and Daniel aren't done with their games," I shared.

"He thinks right," she replied. "A trait of hers is being radically counter intuitive. Instead of learning from her mistakes, she pushes harder, which only digs her hole deeper. I don't get it."

I didn't either.

And I'd turned that over enough in my head, I knew no discussion with Lou about it would serve up any answers.

"Ian wants to work together to figure out what they're up to and thwart it," I told her.

"I bet he does," she teased.

"And yes," I said seriously. "He made it clear, when I told him I wanted to take you and leave, that he wanted me to stay because he wanted time to get to know me better."

She straightened from pressing down on the mound of folded sweaters in her case and exclaimed, "I knew it!"

That almost made me smile, but I cautioned, "Don't get excited. We like each other. But he hasn't even kissed me."

"Poor play to make a move on a woman who just ran screaming to you in the night," she remarked.

"I didn't scream," I told her.

I did, just not while I was racing to Ian. Only after I got to him.

"Well, it's good you're out of that room and you know Portia and Daniel have been screwing with you, so you can sleep tonight. And it's good you're staying to get to know him, because you already know, I like you two together and I'm tickled pink you're giving a man a shot again."

Especially a man like Ian, and I don't mean how drop-dead gorgeous he is."

This was the thing.

Because it was flirty and there was hand holding, and Ian had made me sleep by his side last night.

But it was also easy and friendly, and my sister was seeing his brother, and I had more than one concern about that. She'd also dated Ian, and this could all end up a mess.

And then there was that forehead kiss.

Ulk.

Bottom line: was I reading into the flirty when I should be reading into the friendly?

"And there you go, talking yourself out of how blatantly into you he is," Lou noted, watching me closely.

"I think I need to get some things straight," I admitted.

"Do that. Be honest. I sense he'll appreciate it and want you both on the same footing from the jump, whatever that is. Though I know he likes you, and in future, you'll be spending more time in the southeast wing."

I rolled my eyes.

She ignored this and carried on, "But also, one of us, and obviously that's going to be you, has to stay and see how things turn out, because Portia played into our hands. Daniel was not best pleased her allowance plummeted. He might come from money, but that doesn't mean he has it. She could already be acting as his sugar mama."

"Mm," I hummed my agreement, because from what I saw between them not twenty minutes ago, that was a definite possibility.

"So now that you've erased any possibility of the high life for both of them, we'll see the real of their relationship," she concluded.

"Yes," I agreed again.

"It's all going to be okay, Daph."

Her change in tone, reassuring and sympathetic, made me focus fully on her.

"Do you think it was just a joke?" I asked.

Her expression altered, grew harder at the same time contemplative. And then, like it was difficult for her to force out the words, she

165

said, "You know, it might be the headache talking, the drama of all this, but some things seem to be coming clear. I hate to say it, but I'm not sure I'd put anything past your sister. So keep your chin up, lovely, and your eyes open."

Indeed.

The strange and intrusive request for an entire week in the country. Dragging Ian from his life too, so we were all drawn into the game. Daniel walking into the mist in the dark of night. Them throwing us together, then disappearing for nearly two days. The Carnation Room and carnations. Whatever was standing between Lou and Richard and Jane, something that was still her secret, and I wasn't going to pry, but I had to admit, I was curious.

Ian was right.

He knew more about how this house should feel.

Even so, I felt it too.

Something was off.

Something was coming.

At least Lou would be out of it.

And Ian and I were a team.

"I've done what I can here. I'm going to pop down to see Bonnie, maybe get a snack and a bottle, then come up and take a bath," Lou said.

My cue to roll off the bed and leave her to it, something I did after stopping to give her a quick hug.

After I slipped out of the Poppy Room, I kinda wanted to go to the Brandy Room to look for Aunt Louisa's diaries, but I didn't.

I went to the Rose Room, mostly because it was closer, and I was feeling lazy.

I threw myself on the chaise longue and watched the unchanging gray horizon.

That was numbingly boring, so I got up to grab my Kindle.

Not to read Steve Clifton's book about his aunt. I was giving dead women stories a rest. I got my e-reader to go back to the book I'd been reading and take a couple of hours to myself before I had to start to get ready for dinner that night.

I walked my Kindle back to the lounge, stretched out, opened and woke it, only to stare at what came up on the screen.

The hairs rose on the back of my neck.

It was an old-timey picture of a group of people standing in front of Duncroft House.

"What the...?"

I looked at the header, and it was Steve Clifton's book.

I went to the table of contents and saw that there was a section of photographs.

I let out my breath.

I'd opened the book last night. Somehow, I'd hit something that forwarded it to the photo section. I'd never done anything like that before, and I'd never known the Kindle to jump around either.

But that had to be why that photo came up.

Since I was there, I went back to the photo and lifted it to my face, looking closer.

It was an old black and white, not sharp to begin with and even more difficult to see on an e-reader. The people were mostly dark forms wearing the height of twenties outdoor fashion: the women in big, boxy coats, some with fur trim, and cloche hats with feathers or rosettes or ribbons, the men in suits with wide-shouldered overcoats.

Dorothy with her flair and platinum hair was easy to spot off to the side. She had a leg kicked back and she was leaning into both hands she was resting on the chest of the man beside her.

His head was turned, not her way, in the opposite direction. The picture was taken while he was moving, making his face a blur. But he was tall and dark, and his shoulders were broader than others, because the shoulder pads in his coat were augmented by the real thing underneath.

And I knew it was William because Virginia and David were front and center.

David had his arm around his wife, and he was smiling at the camera, the man of the house, the king of his castle, the god of his domain. Devilishly handsome and stylish and living his best life with an injured beauty at his side and a vixen in the wings.

Virginia had her eyes cast down to what looked like a few feet in front of her, which was the gravel of the drive.

The others were striking gay poses too, like Dorothy. Arms flung up or out, one man in the back had jumped up high, one man on the opposite front side to Dorothy was hunkered down, looking like he was pumping his muscles for the camera. Some were holding up coupé glasses of champagne or full bottles of it.

Good times.

Fun times.

Happy times.

And then tragedy would strike.

I was about to try to figure out how to enlarge it so I could get a better look when two things happened.

One, my phone vibrated against my ass with a text.

The other, I noted a woman in the back row. All you could see was her head. She was short-ish and mostly hidden.

But she was not striking a jolly pose.

She was gazing at Dorothy and William in a manner that I looked back to William to see if he might not be turning his head to look at his brother and/or Virginia. But to look at whoever that woman was.

My phone vibrated again, so I slid it out and saw it was a text from Ian. One of the things he did other than work while I mindlessly watched stock info I had no hope of understanding on his TV, was put my number in his contacts.

With a little thrill at getting his first text, I set the Kindle aside and pulled it up.

I'm heading your way.

I typed in, *From where?*

"Here," he said a couple seconds after my text whooshed, doing this after opening the door and sticking his head in.

When he saw me in the turret, he fully came in.

"Am I driving Lou to the station?" he asked as he sauntered my way.

"She's leaving in the morning. She's going to kick back tonight. She's still a little headachy. Her train leaves at nine thirty."

"Right. I'll let her know I'll be ready at eight thirty to take her to town."

"You don't have to do that, Ian. I can drive her."

"You can come with, but I need to get out of this house."

That sounded awesome. "Then I'm coming with, because I do too."

After I said that, I quickly moved my legs because he was aiming his ass at the lounge where they were resting.

"Are we hanging out?" I joked.

He sprawled, legs stretched in front of him, crossed at his ankles, and linked his fingers behind his head. "I showed you mine, your turn to show me yours."

All right.

Flirty banter aside...

Were we doing this?

And if we were, what was *this*?

I rotated to sit on my ass and scooted up so I was leaning against the high back swoop at the corner of the lounge, my legs crossed in front of me.

"I think it's kinda important I know what's happening here, Ian," I said quietly.

He watched closely as I moved and spoke, his expression shifting, and he replied in the same tone, "I think I'm distraught you don't already know, Daphne."

"You're a huge flirt. You have been since the beginning."

"I am. But not unless I want to sleep with the woman I'm chatting up."

He unlinked his hands and held one palm out my way when I opened my mouth.

I shut it.

He went on, "I'm understanding at my request this morning you're now needing full disclosure, so allow me to share that yes, in the beginning, I simply wanted to fuck you. But unfortunately, you're plucky and witty and I have this damned weakness for a woman with an American accent. Not to mention black lace bras, flawless skin, fantastic fucking hair and zero patience for fuckwittery. So I'm afraid the bad news is, I like you for more than a brief week-in-the-country fling."

"Plucky?" I asked.

He shrugged.

"Do you really have a weakness for women with American accents?"

"A development I discovered Friday night."

I smiled at him because he was funny, and I was super, mega relieved that he was where I was with what was happening between us.

"I have a lot of baggage, honey," I warned.

He looked around and then peered out the window before he came back to me and raised his brows.

I chuckled.

He reached out to wrap his fingers around my ankle and gave it to me straight.

"I'm absolute shit at relationships."

And again, that was a relief. The honesty, and that we shared that trait.

"My father was a cheat. My ex-husband was a cheat."

"I know," he said gently.

"I don't know what it does to a man to see a woman he cares about suffer because of behavior like that, but you haven't made a secret you're struggling with processing it with your dad. I will say, that's a one and done for me. I admire women who have that forgiveness in them. I tried it with François. I lost five years to that forgiveness when I should have been living my life without the heartache he brought into it. It's a mistake I probably won't make again."

"I would not ever do that to you or any woman, darling," Ian assured. "It's my staying power you need to be warned about."

I covered his hand on my ankle. "I might not have investigators like you do, but I'm hell on wheels with a Google search, babe. So that isn't lost on me. Now I'm warning you, my mom was bitter, and I have some of that ingrained in me. Dad imploding our family. François making a fool of me and killing the love I had for him. Watching Lou fade and shine depending on whether Dad had a mistress or remembered he had a wife. You might think me plucky, but it's the circumstances. Normally, I'm a resolute cynic."

"So we're both going in eyes open."

"Yes. Eyes open."

He stared at me.

I stared at him.

We kept doing this.

The longer we did, the more my nipples tingled.

Because this was happening. Really happening. The friendly *and* the flirty.

And I wanted it badly.

I also wanted to jump him, and I wanted that badly too, but the minute the thought entered my head, he whispered, "Tonight, after dinner, in the Conservatory. I want to kiss you first there."

"Why?" I whispered back.

"Because I knew I wanted to fuck you when you said, 'Mutual, I'm sure.'"

I smirked.

"Though it could have been your cleavage," he admitted mock ruefully.

That made me laugh.

He continued, "And I knew you were interesting when you called me on my shit and took your sister's back. But I knew I wanted to know you when you met me in the Conservatory."

That was wonderfully romantic. Because it was, I felt elation.

But I fake pouted.

And gave in.

"Okay. After dinner then, I suppose."

"Poor baby," he murmured, pulling at my ankle until my leg was in his lap. Then he pulled at the other one. "Sexual frustration is hard on us all. I should know."

"And how long has it been for you?" I asked flippantly. I really didn't want to know, and I didn't expect him to answer, except as a joke.

"Since yesterday evening, after you left my room. I came for you all over my stomach."

My vagina clenched.

He knew it and grinned roguishly.

This made my vagina clench even better.

Bastard.

"I'm glad I brought my vibrator," I replied blithely. "After you kiss me tonight, I can come up here and finish myself off."

His hand still around my ankle squeezed.

"Bad girl," he murmured, staring at my mouth.

"Down boy,' I returned. "It's your rule about delayed gratification, and you were the one who brought up touching yourself."

His hand went up my cords along my calf.

He had a light touch.

I shivered.

It was his turn to smirk.

"Now who's the tease?" I asked.

"And who's the flirt?" he returned.

I dropped my head to the back of the lounge and cried, "Ugh!"

He slid his hand out of the leg of my pants and promised, "I'll be good."

I looked at him. "That's the problem."

He chuckled.

"Shall we change the subject to one that won't require cold show-ers?" I suggested.

"Shoot."

"It's not going to be fun, but it's on my mind."

"Then get it off your mind, darling," he invited.

"What did you mean when you said Daniel shit on women?" He appeared confused for a moment, before I reminded him, "You were talking to your father. I was listening in the hallway."

Humor lit his eyes at the reminder, then, as usual, he didn't delay or prevaricate.

He socked it right to me.

"I mean, like your sister hasn't grown out of pulling nasty pranks, when it comes to women, my brother hasn't grown out of laddish behavior. What do you Americans call it? Frat boy."

"Has he ever had a serious girlfriend?"

"Yes. Portia."

Good God.

Daniel was thirty-five years old.

Not good.

He rounded my legs with one arm while he turned to me and rested into an elbow on the back of the lounge, giving me his undivided attention.

Not that I didn't have it before, but he was definitely settling in to share.

So I relaxed with him and settled in to listen.

"I've not been a choir boy," he confessed. "And when I end things with a woman, and there have been many..."

He paused to watch my response.

But since I already knew about the many women from my Google search, I didn't have one, so he carried on.

"I cannot tell you they were all in agreement that our relationship had run its course. But I learned to be careful about leading a woman on. I had a girlfriend when I was eighteen and I was not serious, but I liked her. Our relationship was intimate, and it was the first time I had that with a longtime partner. I liked getting it, so I wasn't as careful with her emotions as I should have been when I put in the work to keep her. This meant, when it was over for me, she was blindsided. It might have been over, but I cared about her still, and I felt like an ass. To this day, if we're ever in the same space, she avoids me. And to this day, I still care about her and I'm aware I hurt her so much, it still stings, twenty years later. And that, my darling, doesn't feel very nice."

I hated he hurt her, even inadvertently.

And I hated they both still suffered for it.

But I loved that he got why that was.

"I bet not," I said, because he'd stopped talking and I needed to say something.

"So I take pains not to do that again. It isn't to say a woman hasn't been ugly because she's not getting what she wants from me. But I always know I gave her no indication I intended to give it. If she misread things, that's one thing. The other side of the coin..." He gave my legs a squeeze. "We'll just say, I'm careful to make sure the other side of the coin never happens."

"I like your honesty, Lord Alcott."

"Eyes open, love," he reiterated his earlier warning.

I nodded.

He kept speaking.

"To finish, I would hope you'd understand that if I'm with a woman, she means something to me, during and after. So when Danny would swoop in and toy with someone who used to be mine..." He shook his head. "I don't know what word to use to express it. But it isn't fun to know my brother shits on any woman, but one who means something to me is far less fun."

I could see how it would be, and I was reading between the lines his words were a vast understatement.

"I'm sure," I said softly.

"I sense we'll soon find out where he's at with Portia, but from what I saw earlier, I'm not sure, at this juncture, who's shitting on who. But it looks like a watershed moment happened in the Sherry Room. I just hope we don't get caught in the spillage."

"Mm." I hummed. After I did, Ian studied me for so long, I asked, "What?"

"Ask it."

"Ask what?"

"Ask about what you've been noticing, but I can't ask about it, because if I do, I'll sound like an arrogant prick."

Well, damn.

"It's not a question," I said.

"It's an observation, so say it."

"Portia is pining for you."

He drew in a big breath through his nose, expanding his chest, then he let it out.

"So it's not just me feeling that," he remarked.

No, it wasn't.

And it might explain a few things.

Why we were there for a full week, all the more time for Portia to rub her relationship with Daniel in Ian's face. And the fact Ian was there at all. It was a meeting of the families, of course, but he was a busy man, who it was my understanding managed a vast empire.

Lady Jane never left Duncroft. We'd have to come here to meet her.

If there was going to be a sibling meet, we could have had dinner with Ian in London.

"She looks at you a lot," I remarked. "She was furious you were in here with me last night. Some of her only displays of affection for Daniel are when she show one to me."

"Yes. Yes. And yes."

"Shit," I muttered.

"Thus, this is what we're working with," he began.

He then ran it down.

"My father is about to lose his title, so he's acting more of an ass than usual. My mother is off, maybe because of that, maybe because of Portia, maybe for an as yet unknown reason. Danny's future lies in the balance because it'll soon be up to me, not only his status here at Duncroft, but if I'll continue to allow him to be a line item on the estate's balance sheet. And instead of having a man-to-man chat with me about it, Danny has some play he's making, we don't know what it is, but I sense it's coming."

All true.

Ian kept going.

"And now there's the possibility that whatever it is, is independent of what Portia is up to. She wants me. She may or may not have been using my brother to attempt to make me jealous. This backfired. Worse, she threw you in my path. Now you have me, which could exacerbate whatever she has on her mind to do. And the stakes that hang in the balance of all of this are hearts, minds, family ties and the small matter of a hundred billion dollars, which two of those players want their hands on pretty badly. Neither have control of it, but you do, and they just tied your hands in confiscating it. At least for the next year. Have I covered it all?"

He'd been pretty thorough.

Though my favorite part was, "now you have me."

And none of the rest was favorite at all.

"I think that sums it up nicely," I replied.

"My brother told me about your éclairs before I even met Portia. I've been to your shop. I'm partial to your Viennese whirls."

I loved that.

And I loved he'd tasted my work, he'd had a part of me, even before he met me, and he liked it.

I didn't tell him that.

I said, "Those are simple."

"There's nothing simple about excellence. Especially the kind that's no muss, no fuss, just sweet and decadent."

"You're being flirty again, babe."

"No, Daphne, I'm not."

What?

Wait.

Pow!

Right to the heart.

Argh!

"I'm not loving this kissing date we have for later when you're right fucking here," I groused.

"It's better to wait. Promise."

"I hope so, for your sake," I muttered.

He grinned at me and the promise in his eyes made me shiver again.

"Okay, changing the subject..." I began, starting to reach toward my Kindle to show him the picture I found, but stopping dead when we both heard a spine-chilling scream.

And if I wasn't wrong, it was coming from Lou's room.

Before I could blink, Ian was up, bent to me, finger in my face, growling, "Don't leave this room."

And then he sprinted toward the door.

Eighteen

THE POPPY ROOM

I wasn't proud that when I popped off the lounge after Ian raced out, I froze.

This was because thoughts collided in my head as adrenalin rushed in my veins, and I couldn't decide what to do.

That scream was close. It was horrible. Ian had rushed toward it. I wanted to know if Lou was all right. I wanted to know if Ian was all right. But I wondered if first, I should find a weapon or call the police.

My decision was made for me when I heard Ian roar, "*Daphne!*"

I dashed out and instinctively went right to the Poppy Room.

Lou's door was open, and when I arrived, my chest caved in.

Rebecca was standing, face ashen and filled with fear, a phone to her ear, her eyes cast down to Ian, who was kneeling over Lou.

Lou.

She was in her robe and thrashing on the floor, only the whites of her eyes showing, the skin of her neck and jaw stretched thin in a grimace, the rest of her body uncontrollably convulsing.

It was hideous.

It looked painful.

I dropped instantly to my knees and reached out to her, but Ian barked, "*No!*"

In a panic, I looked to him.

"You could hurt yourself, you could hurt her," he said curtly. "We just need to try to make sure she doesn't run into anything. Does she have epilepsy?"

"No," I forced out through a tight throat.

"Has this happened before?"

"No. Never. Or at least, not that I know."

Rebecca got closer. "The ambulance is coming."

"Pull the bell. Get me a wet cloth," Ian issued orders to her, then to me. "Darling, go grab a pillow and that throw from the couch."

Like Rebecca, I rushed to do what he said.

When I came back, again on my knees, helpless to do anything else, I kept flicking her robe over her legs as she kicked it off, doing this so she remained decent. It was unimportant, but I had to do something.

It didn't take long for the seizure to start to subside.

Immediately, and with great care, Ian lifted her head and put the pillow under it.

Equally immediately, I moved to lay on my belly on the floor beside her.

I grabbed her hand and felt it covered when Ian tossed the throw to cover her.

Her head fell to the side toward me.

It was a little death to see she was unfocused and so out of it, she was drooling.

Ian tucked the throw around her while I squeezed her hand and whispered, "I'm here, Lou. We're here. We've got you."

Gently, Ian reached in and wiped the spittle from her mouth with a wet cloth.

"I brought the tray up from the kitchen. Nibbles and wine from Bonnie. Something to tide her over until we brought her dinner. We were chatting," Rebecca babbled. "She was totally normal. Smiling. Joking about how Bonnie was trying to fatten her up. Then she got this faraway look on her face. It was terrifying. She was standing there, but she wasn't in the room at all. After that, she just went down."

"You need some fattening up, Lou," I told her, my voice trembling. "Bonnie's doing God's work."

My world righted when, weakly, her fingers tensed around mine.

"There you are, lovely," I whispered, close to tears as her gaze, still very hazy, started to focus on mine. "I'll pop the cork in a second. We'll hang down here."

"I feel weird," she mumbled.

"That's what happens when you thrash around on the floor, beautiful," I quipped, but it fell flat, mostly because my voice was still trembling, and nothing was funny about this. "Just hang tight. Help is on the way."

"Have Jack bring my car 'round," I heard Ian demand, and I didn't move, just angled my gaze to see he was talking to Brittany, who was standing at the door, eyes wide and staring at Lou and me. "Tell Stevenson an ambulance is coming. And gather Miss Ryan's coat and purse."

Brittany didn't move, and I was too in my emotions to process how there seemed to be something strange, both chagrined and morbidly curious, written on her face as she stared down at Lou.

"Brittany!" Ian clipped impatiently. "Now!"

She jerked then took off.

I went back to Lou. "Ian's being bossy. It's very sexy."

"Has he kissed you yet?" she whispered.

Ah.

There was my girl.

"We have a date for that. Tonight, in the Conservatory. I guess it's a thing in gothic mansions, the tortured viscount making his long-suffering heroine wait for his embrace. After that, we're going to murder Colonel Mustard in the Ruby Room with a pipe then go meet Professor Plum for a pint. I'm psyched."

I was relieved to feel her fingers close more firmly around mine as she muttered, "Always the card."

"Honey, has this happened to you before?" I asked carefully.

She closed her eyes like she was exhausted, and she probably was. All that movement, it was unnatural. It had to hurt and take tons of energy.

"No," she answered.

"Okay, rest. Help will be here soon, and we'll figure out what's happening."

She opened her eyes. "You need to get up. You can't stay down here with me."

"Watch me."

"Then I'll get up."

She made to move but Ian's hand came to her shoulder, and he said gently, "No, Lou. Please stay where you are, love. I want professionals checking you out before we go anywhere."

The house was far away from everything. It'd take half an hour for them to get there and the draft on the floor was something fierce. Not to mention, the silk, likely priceless rug we were lying on was thick, but it was damned uncomfortable.

I lifted my head to protest. "You can carry her to the bed."

"I can, but I don't know if she did harm to herself, darling," he said tenderly, the same expression on his handsome face, and I really wanted to take time to enjoy it, but I couldn't. "There's an ambulance service in the village. They'll be here in only five minutes more. I promise."

This mysterious village must be a lot closer than I expected and somewhere tucked away, since I saw hide nor hair of it driving to the house or on my walk on the moor.

"My goodness!" I heard Stevenson exclaim.

Ian rose. "Good. You're here."

He moved away.

I squeezed Lou's hand again because her gaze had grown distant.

She focused on me, and I let out the breath I started to hold. I was terrified she'd seize again.

"Did you hear that? Five minutes," I told her.

Her fingers tightened around mine so hard, there was pain, and shock, since I didn't think she had that in her right then.

"You know I love you," she said, a fierce undercurrent running alongside her feeble tone.

For the second time since I hit that room, my chest caved in.

"Shut up."

"You do, right?"

Tears stung my eyes.

"Yes, Lou. And you're going to be fine. Just fine. Four minutes now, okay?"

"Okay, lovey."

I lay on the floor, held her hand and her gaze.

Ian had not lied.

Within a few minutes, rolling a stretcher with them, the paramedics were there.

~

THE GOOD NEWS about hanging with an up-and-coming earl at the local community hospital while your stepmother was being looked over by doctors, you didn't have to brush shoulders with the rabble in any old waiting room.

We were in an office. A nice one. Probably the hospital administrator's or the head of medicine. Likely a doctor if the degrees on the wall were a reliable clue. And we'd been brought coffee and biscuits.

I didn't touch them.

I stared out the window at the drab parking lot while night descended.

Ian and I had been mostly silent as we followed the ambulance to the hospital, and I remained so as he dealt with things for Lou, and then for me, which ended with us being ushered into this office.

Though, for the whole car ride in his fabulous Jaguar, pure Ian, he held my hand.

The door opened and I whirled to it, only for my shoulders to sag in despair when I saw it wasn't news forthcoming about Lou. Portia and Daniel walked in, and surprise of surprises, Lady Jane was with them, carrying a large basket covered in a tea towel.

Portia rushed to me. "How is she?"

"I don't know."

"Why didn't you tell me what was going on at the house?" she demanded.

My temper instantly flared. "I don't know, Portia. I was more concerned with being with Lou after she flailed around on the floor in the throes of a violent seizure. Sorry you weren't the first thing on my mind."

She withdrew, mumbling, "No need to get nasty."

181

I couldn't deal with Portia right then.

I looked back out the window.

"Bonnie sent some sandwiches," I heard Lady Jane say.

"Thanks, Mum," Ian replied.

"No word yet?" she asked.

He didn't answer, but I suspected that was because he shook his head.

Daniel inched close. "Do you need anything, Daphne?"

It was a nice thing to ask.

"I'm good, Daniel, thanks," I answered distractedly.

I heard noises, maybe sandwiches being passed around, people settling, I didn't much care.

You know I love you.

Why did she say that?

The door opened and I did the whirling again.

It was the doctor this time.

"Miss Ryan, Lord Alcott," he started, glanced around and saw three women in the room, "I mean, a Daphne Ryan."

I stepped forward. "Me. I'm here."

"Mrs. Fernsby-Ryan would like to see you and Lord Alcott."

I moved forward instantly, snatching my purse off the desk where I'd put it, and about an instant after that, I felt Ian's strong, guiding hand pressed to the small of my back.

I was a woman who could make my own way, but damn, that hand felt nice right where it was.

"We'll wait here," I heard Lady Jane say as we left the room.

Nothing from Daniel or Portia.

Ian kept his hand on my back as the doctor led the way down the hall.

"We're going to keep Mrs. Fernsby-Ryan with us tonight. We're not equipped for some things in a hospital this size, but we can keep an eye on her and transport her to a bigger facility far faster if need be."

This did not do anything to alleviate my dread.

He stopped at a door. "In here."

I rushed by him.

It was a private room. Lou lay on the bed with oxygen tubes in her nose but that was it. No IV in her arm. No beeping machines. Though, she had one of those things clipped to the tip of one of her fingers.

And her color was good, her affect alert, though understandably she was still a bit wan. She had her robe on still, but now she had a hospital gown on under it. The covers were tucked precisely around her waist.

I stopped at the side of the bed and took her hand. "Hey."

"Heya," she replied, giving me a small, weird smile. She transferred it to Ian. "Hi."

"Hello, love," his silken voice rumbled as he came to stand at her bed opposite me. "You look better."

She lifted one shoulder and dipped her ear to it, but that was all.

I heard the door whoosh shut behind me, looked that way, and saw the doctor had left us alone with Lou.

I turned back to her. "They're going to keep you here tonight. Did they run any tests?"

"They didn't need to."

What?

"Babe, you had a seizure."

"I also have a brain tumor."

My head swam, and it felt like the floor buckled and the only thing that kept me standing was Lou's strong grip on my hand.

"It's benign, and not large," she continued hurriedly. "My migraines were coming more often. I went to get checked. They found it about two weeks ago. I'm scheduled for surgery next month to have it out."

"Why didn't you tell me?" I asked, making grave effort to keep my voice measured.

"Well, I told my mum, dad and brother, and they lost it, so I wasn't all fired up to do that again."

"Oh, Lou," I whispered.

"They told me the headaches would probably keep coming, and in extreme cases, something like what happened today would happen. I'm supposed to not stress about anything. Stress can cause flare ups and flare ups could mean anything from losing feeling in my limbs to passing out to seizures."

Fucking Portia.

"Has any of that happened, outside of what happened this afternoon?" I queried.

"Some tingles. A lot of exhaustion. It's why I decided to leave Duncroft. I thought I could hack it, but with Portia being Portia and the frequency of the headaches, I knew I had to throw in the towel."

"Well, once we get you out of here tomorrow, I'll get you home," I decided.

"I've called Mum and Dad to come get me," she said and turned to Ian. "And I'm trusting you to look after her."

Before Ian could reply, I spoke.

"I'm coming home with you," I declared. "It's you who needs looking after."

She returned to me. "That's what I don't need."

"Lou—"

"I'm scared," she whispered, breaking my heart with her tone. "And I want normal. I want people to treat me like normal. They said it's in as good a place as it can be, for a tumor. There are hardly any good brain tumors, but if there is one, this is it. It's called a glioma and they said it's probably what started the migraines. It's really slow growing and won't spread. But they want it out, and I might have some interesting hairstyles for the next year or so, but they say it's a relatively easy procedure and it shouldn't return."

She tugged my hand and kept talking.

"It's still scary and I want everything to be normal until it has to be not normal for a while. I'm fine. You know Mum would push you out of the way anyway, so she can wait on me hand and foot and drive me crazy, all the while fighting with Dad, since he'll be trying to do the same thing. So I'll need you fresh when you come and relieve them after you and Ian are done taking care of things at Duncroft."

"I'm going to stay here tonight with you, then."

She shook her head. "No. I already called, and Mum and Dad are on their way. Go home. Have your date in the Conservatory. But please don't murder Colonel Mustard. I need you unincarcerated to help me pick short haircuts that will look cute on me."

I started to say something, but she tugged on my hand.

"Don't," Lou begged. "I don't want people fawning over me,

worrying about me. There's going to be a time for that. Please, Daph, don't make that time now."

"Whatever you want, honey," I said immediately.

"Would you like us to bring you anything?" Ian asked, so damned thoughtful. I mean, maybe he *was* the perfect man. "A nightgown? Book? Your phone? Can we get you some magazines and candy?"

"I'd take the magazines and candy. It might be nice to have a break from my phone." She gestured to the one on the nightstand. "My parents have the hospital number. They can call me if they need to." Her head moved on the pillow so she could look at me. "Would you finish packing for me? Mum and Dad and I'll swing 'round tomorrow to get my things."

"You got it."

"Okay, then, not to be rude, but...go. Get on with your night, but mostly, I'm shattered, and I need a nap."

"Okay, but just so you know, Portia, Daniel and Lady Jane are here," I informed her.

She looked stunned. "Jane?"

I nodded. "Quick visits? Or do you want me to tell them you're napping?"

"It's sweet they came, but could you tell them I'm napping? I'm not being a bitch. I really am tired."

"Absolutely."

There wasn't much more said. I gave her a hug. Ian kissed her cheek. He asked if she wanted one of Bonnie's sandwiches, and she shared she wasn't hungry. Ian promised we'd return with provisions and then we stepped out.

"We need to hurry. Boots will be closing soon. Though, it's just around the corner," he said.

"Okay. How about I dash out and take care of that, you talk to your mum and the kids?"

His lips twitched when I referred to Daniel and Portia as "the kids," but he replied, "That'd be most expedient. If I'm quick enough about it, I'll meet you at Boots."

"Right."

I turned to go to the hospital entrance, but he caught my wrist.

When I looked back, his gaze intent on my face, he asked, "Are you okay?"

I felt the tears threatening, so all I had in me was to whisper, "Not now, baby."

Understanding swept his features, and God bless him, he let me go. "See you at Boots."

I nodded and took off.

I didn't run but I didn't dally either. I was on a mission.

That didn't mean my mind wasn't filled with thoughts, mostly about the fact Colonel Mustard wasn't going to die that night.

But I might throttle my sister.

Nineteen

THE CONSERVATORY

I an was again holding my hand as we walked up the front steps of Duncroft.

The door opened before we got there, the bright light from the white foyer streaming out, the shadow of the long, straight body of Stevenson filling it.

It was at once beautiful and akin to the poster of a horror movie.

He stepped aside.

We stepped in.

"How is she, Ian?" Stevenson asked with open concern before he even closed the door.

I loved it that he called Ian by his given name. It made it seem like they were family like I thought it should be, not staff and employer, when they essentially lived in the same home.

"Good. Better. Resting," Ian answered. "They're keeping her there tonight. She's going back to London tomorrow."

Stevenson didn't hide his relief.

"I believe she's mostly packed. Brittany and Rebecca are on for tonight," Stevenson told Ian while closing the door.

He turned to us and held out his arm.

I understood why when Ian shrugged off his overcoat and handed it over.

All while Stevenson kept talking. "Do you want me to ask them to finish packing for Mrs. Fernsby-Ryan?"

"She'd want you to call her Lou, Stevenson," I said.

Stevenson nodded to me on a warm smile.

"Give him your coat and purse, darling," Ian prompted in an undertone.

I started to do that, finishing, "I'll pack for her."

"You're joining me for a drink in the Conservatory first," Ian declared. "I need a smoke."

"It's not much and they don't mind," Stevenson said low, giving me a smile and a wink and taking my coat and bag.

Ian reclaimed my hand and pulled me to the back of the foyer.

I avoided looking at Persephone as we walked by. I didn't want her to get any ideas. She could have her Elysian fields. Lou and I were staying in the here and now for a while.

We hit the seating area in the Conservatory, which was dark. He let me go to move to the drinks cabinet, then I saw a tablet light in his hands, and shortly after, the Tiffany lamps, all of them, illuminated the space.

I hadn't noticed the tablet before, and I wondered if all Ian's favored spaces had been smart-ified. Neither the Carnation nor the Rose Room had.

Or maybe they just hadn't gotten around to setting up the whole house.

"Champagne, wine, Amaretto, or something stiffer?" Ian asked.

"Amaretto," I ordered, throwing myself on the couch and only realizing how badly I needed that couch when I was on it.

Ian handed me my snifter, his highball was definitely loaded with whisky on ice, and he folded his long body beside me and reached to his cigarette box.

He lit up while I sipped and watched.

It was horrible and alluring at the same time, the way he went about his habit.

After he returned the lighter, he murmured, "It's a turn-off, I know.

I smoke only at Duncroft, only in here, and only because my father knows I do and detests it."

I lifted my snifter in salute, "Then carry on, milord. Got any lines of coke I can snort? I'm sure Richard would detest that even more."

He gave me a small smile. "Sadly, no."

The smile died and his head turned, then abruptly, he stood up, all before I noticed we were no longer alone.

Portia, Daniel trailing her, emerged from the foliage.

"You're back," she declared, her gaze doing what was now customary, bouncing back and forth between Ian and me.

"In the flesh," I pointed out the obvious.

"And you're in here relaxing and having a drink and not coming to talk to me?" she demanded.

"What do we have to talk about?" I asked.

"Lou has a brain tumor!" she shouted.

I sat very still, mostly because I was controlling myself from losing it with my sister, and if I moved, that control would snap.

"Calm the fuck down," Ian said with quiet menace.

"Excuse me, but my stepmother is dying," she snapped.

Daniel rounded to her side. "She's not dying, Portia. You heard Ian when he told us what was happening, and we looked it up when we got home. It's a glioma. It's benign."

"You can tell me how to behave when a member of *your* family has a brain tumor," she retorted.

"When someone has a glioma, stress can cause seizures. Did you read that when you were looking it up?" Ian asked sardonically.

"We—" she started.

"And what stress has Lou been experiencing recently, Portia?" Ian drove his point home.

"Oh my God!" she cried. "Now *I'm* responsible for Lou's tumor?"

"No, but you do bear some responsibility for the episode she endured tonight," Ian replied.

"Portia, let's go somewhere and get a drink," Daniel intervened.

Arm stiff, she pointed to the drinks cabinet. "There's alcohol right there."

Daniel looked beleaguered.

Ian took a drag from his cigarette, blew the smoke to Portia's right side, not in her face, but his intent was clear, and he instructed, "Duncroft lesson, petal. With plenty of space available, we've all claimed our own. This and the Brandy Room are mine. In case you're interested, Mum's are the Viognier Room and the Sherry Room. Dad's are the Whisky and Wine Rooms. Daniel is partial to the stables and the Bordeaux Room. We respect each other's space. And if you intend to spend any time in this house, you'll do the same."

"Will I get my own space?" she asked snottily.

"It's been a generation since anyone used it. Mum flew in the face of convention and wanted her babies close. But the Nursery is available in the northwest wing," Ian drawled.

Portia's face turned red.

I sipped Amaretto.

Suddenly, her attention came to me, and she watched with bizarre intensity as I swallowed the almond liqueur.

"What's your space?" she whispered in an ugly voice.

I didn't get the chance to answer.

Ian did it for me.

"I'm particularly fond of the time she spends in the Hawthorn Suite."

Portia looked like her head was going to explode, so I shifted my efforts from trying not to lay her out to trying not to laugh.

"Fuck it. Fuck this. It's been a shitty day. I'm going to get drunk," she declared, turned and flounced out.

Daniel, either being a decent person behind the seemingly clueless puppy dog he'd been since I met him, or having learned that day I held power and it'd serve him well to curry my favor, looked to me and said, "I'm really sorry about Lou, Daphne. That's terrible news."

"Thanks, Daniel," I replied. "But according to her, although it's going to get hairy, she'll be okay."

"I'm glad to hear it," he muttered.

Ian, demonstrating he had a soft spot for his brother, or perhaps being like me and capitalizing on the rare times Daniel wasn't acting like an asshole, offered, "Would you like to have a drink with us?"

"I should probably make sure Portia's okay," Daniel said. "She doesn't know how to act when she's feeling too much."

"Sadly, I've noticed that," Ian returned. "Though it appears she feels too much on a constant basis."

Daniel gave him a look I couldn't decipher, though I was mildly surprised to note it wasn't unpleasant, before he nodded to his brother, dipped his chin to me and took off.

Ian folded back into the couch.

"Is that true about the space?" I asked.

"Yes," he answered.

"You picked the best spots, though this is kinda creepy, especially at night."

"The better to have the damsels I lure here cowering in my arms."

I shot him a smile and relaxed deeper into the couch.

Ian shifted to one hip, lazily hooked one knee over the other and reached out to wrap an arm around mine and draw them up to the couch so I was curled into a cocoon of Ian.

It was a smooth as hell move.

I loved it.

I was also a lot more comfortable this way.

He then said, "There was a debutante named Adelaide. She was sheer perfection. Her coming-out season, a triumph. It was rumored the Prince Regent himself was enamored of her, and if it wasn't for his pesky marriage to Caroline, he'd have fallen over himself, royally of course, to offer for her hand. However, it's likely this would have been rebuked because everyone said the moment she laid eyes on Augustus Alcott, she was lost. This being good for her, because Augustus told his mates he would stop at nothing to have her. He didn't have to make any grand gestures. He offered, and she and her family didn't hesitate to say yes."

"And?" I asked to urge him to continue telling his story.

I loved story time with Ian. Yes, even when the stories were scary.

"He brought her to Duncroft, and it was some time, they were very busy at first, before her missives flooded her friends. 'My home is the jewel of Britain,' she said. 'I live in a palace of dreams,' was something else she shared. She was so proud of her new home, and Augustus proud of her, they threw balls and hunts, and everyone travelled all the way from wherever they were to this distant house to make certain they didn't miss them. The bedrooms were filled often, and everyone spoke of how very clever Adelaide Alcott was, showing off what she called Britain's jewel, and entertaining in rooms she had decorated in precious stones."

"So that was Adelaide's idea," I remarked.

"Yes," he confirmed, and carried on with the story. "Amused at her cleverness, Augustus turned his attention to the family's quarters. The southeast wing, ground and first floor. Trees and spirits. While Augustus created his legacy, Adelaide turned to the rest of the house. Flowers and birds."

I sipped.

Ian continued narrating another tale of his home.

"They had one ongoing argument. You see, she loved being in this house, Augustus loved being in his wife."

I grinned.

"As such, she gave him eight children. They both doted on their brood, but Augustus thought Adelaide doted on them too much. She put them among the trees, and at the barest whimper, would leave their bed to see to her babies. He preferred her in his bed, so he moved the children's rooms to the northwest wing. This didn't make her happy and they fought, but she could no longer hear her children in distress, so her attention was no longer divided. As Augustus and all highborn people knew was the right way of things, their nannies took care of them when it was needed, not their mother. And Augustus again had her undivided attention in order to go about the business of giving her more."

"Please tell me this story doesn't have an ugly ending," I begged.

"No, darling. They wrote love letters to each other until Adelaide died at sixty-seven. And when I say that, I mean Augustus wrote her his last letter on the day she died. They've been kept. They're under lock and key, partially because they're fragile, mostly because they're raunchy as fuck."

My mouth dropped open.

I snapped it shut to ask on an actual giggle, "Really?"

Ian sipped whisky then shared, "He was partial to going down on her. He called her 'nectar' his 'life force.' My favorite quote, 'I sit here, my darling, my bride, my wife, with the taste of you still on my tongue, your song of pleasure in my ears, and I want nothing more than to bury my flesh in yours, and I was in that heaven but ten minutes ago.'"

"That's both sweet and hot," I stated the gods' honest truth.

"Mm," he hummed his agreement.

"They loved each other?" I asked, the wealth of hope in those words surprising even me.

"The good kind of besotted, darling," he answered. "Augustus may have moved the children, but Aunt Louisa found other letters. Letters from Adelaide's mother, her mother's friends, all of them admonishing her, and urging her to press Augustus to stop being so 'unseemly' in their open devotion to their family. They picnicked in the parkland and took holidays together. Augustus taught his own children to ride, his sons to hunt. They had many friends. They had a great many parties. They filled this house with love and happiness."

"So it isn't all dead women and grossness."

He smiled. "No, not all dead women and grossness."

I went cautious when I asked, "Did you have love and happiness here?"

His long legs still angled my way, he twisted so his back was to the couch, resting his head there, and he took another drag off his cigarette.

Blowing smoke straight into the air, he kept his eyes aimed to the hanging plants and glass ceiling when he said, "Danny and I were close. Inseparable before we went to school. Once at school, we were still tight, even if we made a lot of friends. We'd play rugby on the front lawn and track mud in because we both liked to ride in the rain. Mum's old-school British. Reserved, keep calm and carry on and don't touch the queen's person. But she threw extravagant birthday parties for us every year, always has a huge Christmas bash and gave us a ridiculous amount of presents. And she helped us with our homework personally. She was interested. I felt loved. I knew my place in her heart."

"Your dad?" I asked quietly.

He turned only his head on the couch to face me. "Earliest memories, idyllic. He doted on her. Like he didn't believe she was real. As if she might vanish in an instant, like a dream. Same with us. We were happy. Then, and I can't know if it was the first she knew of or the first he had, but it was the one she couldn't abide, she learned he was stepping out on her, and she called him on it. He was outraged. I remember that argument and I remember he said more than once it was not her place to question him."

He took another drag, blew out the smoke, then looked back to me.

"It turned to shit after that. She withdrew, even from us in some ways. And he seemed to make it his mission to show us what a 'real man' was and drilled that into us both."

"And what's his version of a real man?"

"One who does what the fuck he wants, when he wants to do it, and no one has the right to tell him any different."

"Are you going to kick them out of the house?"

His brows shot up. "Hell no. It's their home."

"Does your dad think you will?"

He sighed.

Deeply.

"His allowance will be defined by me. That doesn't exactly say, 'Do what you want when you want.' I'm not going to make them live like paupers among splendor, but part of me understands a man's son controlling his finances would be humiliating. Which is why he should have found some way to make his own money."

"Like you did," I noted.

He nodded. "Even when my son, if I have one, turns thirty-eight, I won't need to rely on him. Far from it. As it should be. My grandfather saw the writing on the wall. He knew the covenants. He was an architect. When his time was up, he moved my grandmother to a beautiful home he designed himself over on the coast, continued his work at his firm, and I don't think he took another penny from the estate. Same, in a sense, with my great-grandfather. He ended his career as an admiral in the Royal Navy when he was in his sixties, and he retired in Cornwall."

"Impressive. You come from good stock."

His eyes twinkled.

It was fabulous.

Yeesh.

He seemed too good to be true.

However, the twinkle died. "Granddad was disappointed in my father. I have two uncles and an aunt. One is a solicitor. One is a retired pilot in the RAF. My aunt's still a practicing psychologist. But Dad always lived off the estate. The only one of the four. In fact, my uncles and aunt all moved out for college and never came back. Dad went to Oxford. All the Alcotts do. But he didn't do anything with the degree he earned."

"Did you go to Oxford?"

He nodded. "And Eton. Same with Danny."

"And again, I'm impressed."

This time, he shook his head. "Don't be. The Alcotts have endowed both. We had guaranteed places."

"I bet you were a good student."

"You'd bet wrong. I spent more time taking my mates' money and investing it in the stock market, and losing most of it, than I did studying while I was at Oxford. It was a game to me, but I was fascinated with it."

"That losing streak obviously ended."

One side of his mouth went up. "It did."

"Hm." I took the last sip of my Amaretto.

When I did, Ian took my glass.

He reached to the table to set it down, crush out his cigarette, set his glass aside.

Then he came back to me.

"Come here," he ordered gently.

I looked at his face and my chest got tight.

Because it wasn't first kiss time.

It was something else.

"Ian—"

"Please, come here, sweetheart."

I'd been holding it together. All that was me told me I needed to keep holding it together.

But when Ian lost patience and pulled me into his arms, I gave up the fight.

Shoving my face in his sweater, my shoulders racked as the sob came.

Ian gathered my hair in his hand and held it at the nape of my neck as he held me, and I cried for what Lou was going through.

"D-dad would lose his shit," I stammered. "He wasn't the greatest husband. B-but he loved her the way he could. H-he'd hate he wasn't here to be there for her."

"I'm sure," he murmured.

"It's not an 'easy procedure,'" I mumbled into his chest, referring to how Lou described her upcoming surgery.

"I expect not."

"She just doesn't want me to worry."

"No, she doesn't."

I tipped my head back and looked at him with watery eyes. "I'm worried as fuck."

He shoved my face back into his chest. "I know."

I cried more, he held me through it.

Eventually, I got my shit tight, turned my face, and rested my cheek against his chest, but otherwise didn't move.

Ian's thumb stroked the side of my neck.

"Thank you for being so cool," I said.

"You're most welcome."

"We're not going to kiss tonight, are we?"

"I taste of cigarettes and your friend has a brain tumor, so no. I don't think our timing is right."

"Ugh," I grumbled.

He stopped stroking my neck so he could squeeze me with both arms.

I was still grumbling, even if the words were, "It's annoying, but I'm glad you want to make it special."

"Mm."

"I need to go check if the girls have got all of Lou's things packed, and then I want to call Lou's mum. She's probably beside herself and it's a long trip. She won't be here for at least another hour, and I want her to know Lou's okay."

"All right."

His arms loosened, and I pushed away and up to my feet.

I looked down at him. "Thank you for tonight, and especially for earlier. When Lou was seizing. At the hospital. I was a mess, but you knew exactly what to do."

"It was my pleasure, darling."

I sensed he told no lies.

Which was beautiful.

"So far, this visit has been a trip, but I'm sure glad I met you."

His big body jolted with surprise at my words, and I took advantage.

Bending, I placed one hand on his chest, one on his jaw, and my mouth on his.

Ian didn't pull away.

He sifted his fingers into my hair and curled them into my scalp.

And then my kiss turned into Ian's as his tongue slipped into my mouth.

He tasted of smooth, expensive tobacco, smoother, more expensive whisky, and Ian.

I was addicted in a flash.

Our tongues danced, but he was a strong lead, carrying me away into a shadowed, secluded corner where he could see about making it so he could do as he wished with me.

And then he pulled away.

Instead of climbing into his lap, like I wanted to, I brushed my lips along his jaw, straightened and made note that post make out, Ian was the best Ian of all.

"I'm taking up smoking," I announced.

He burst out laughing.

No.

I was wrong.

Ian laughing was the best Ian of all.

I smiled while he did it.

And then I blew him a kiss before I wound my way out of his lair.

Twenty

THE DOGWOOD SUITE

I was in the gallery on the third floor, or in British terms, the second, since the first was known as the ground floor.

I'd checked the Poppy Room, and Rebecca and Brittany had taken care of all Lou's things. Her bags were lined up beside the door, ready to be carried down in the morning.

I didn't want to go back to the Rose Room for whatever reason, possibly because the last time I was in it, I'd heard a woman scream.

But also because of the story of Adelaide and Augustus.

I hadn't spent a lot of time on the second floor. When I did, I saw it was clearly unused.

This was because it contained the ballroom and a variety of parlors to mingle in, when people did that kind of thing in the days of massive house parties where hundreds of guests were invited.

There were more bedrooms up here, much smaller, they hadn't been modernized (not a one), and back in the day, they were probably used for those with lesser titles or even overflow staff.

There was one, sunny, beautiful room at the end of the northeast corner, which was unmistakably the Music Room, what with the harp, the pianoforte, and a flute that lay in a bed of cobalt-blue velvet sitting on a side table.

There was also a gallery of portraits of past earls and countesses and their progeny, and this was what I wandered as I talked with Jo, Lou's mum, and shared what happened, spinning it as best I could when there wasn't much to use to spin it that way. But I made sure she knew Lou was in fine fettle when we left her: covered in *Hello!* And *OK!* magazines, KitKats, Maltesers and Crunchies.

I continued wandering when our conversation was over.

I hadn't paid much attention to the gallery when I took my own tour, but one could say now that the legacy of Cuthbert was marked.

Earlier earls were all fair.

After Cuthbert, they were all dark.

That gave me a giggle.

Now I found Joan and Thomas easily, and not simply because all the portraits had little gold plaques screwed into the bottom of the frame to tell you who they were.

They were hanging together in one lasting form of control: him seated, turned slightly to the left, facing her, who, in her portrait, was seated, turned to the right, forced to face him.

She was pretty, she looked delicate, and the usual empty stare of people in older portraits was tinged with sadness.

His with condescension, and it might be what Ian told me, but his lechery clung to him like a cloak. Gazing at him gave me a shiver.

Thus, I didn't do it for very long.

Adelaide and Augustus were also easy to spot: the only earl and countess who'd had their portrait painted together *with* their children. It was huge, by far the largest painting in the gallery, taking up one whole end of the room. She was seated, a babe in her arms. He standing at her side, his hand resting on her shoulder.

Also like very few of the others, they were smiling outright, and the artist had captured a toddler in baby hose and a ribboned cap scampering across the carpet while one of his sisters laughed.

I could see it with those two. He was straight and handsome, she was exquisite. Knowing their thirst for each other, knowing their undying love had created all that was in that portrait was not only beautiful, but titillating, and almost erotic.

I wanted to read his last letter to her.

And I loved that Ian told me that story about Duncroft, a happy one, a bedtime story that wouldn't lead to nightmares.

I kept moving and came upon David and then Virginia.

But I moved by them swiftly until, not far down the line, I got to Richard and Jane.

He was in a hunting outfit, red coat and all, and I couldn't help my lip curling, because of course he'd set out to chase down, exhaust and allow his dogs to tear apart a fox.

Jane's portrait, like David's, was painted when she was much younger. Probably late twenties. And although the bloom hadn't gone off the rose to this day, when she was younger, she was astonishing. A goddess. An angel. Sitting, the skirt of her gown a sea of filmy pale pink wafting around her, the perfection of her face effortlessly composed, I felt myself start to get angry that Richard was the kind of man who would break her heart with impunity.

But I was glad to know he didn't break her spirit.

There was space for more, the room was vast, so Ian would have his place, and I loved that for him. With all his stories, his knowledge of this house and the people in it, it was obvious he was proud of his home, and he deserved to be part of its legacy because of that, along with simply being born to it. And I hoped somewhere down the line, some ancestor told happy, and maybe even juicy stories of the love he created in this house.

Although it might seem weird, if I had more time in Duncroft, I could see myself coming up and spending it here, sitting on one of the six button-topped, cerulean velvet, Queen Anne benches lined down the middle of the room.

It was quiet. Peaceful. Like a museum that was closed and only you were there to breathe in the peace.

I was about to head out, thinking maybe I'd have a hot bath before I got in bed, when an odd-woman-out portrait, mounted away from the rest, caught my eye.

I'd noticed the Earls Alcott had good taste in spouses, and she was no different.

But she was openly haughty.

It was a common trait in others, but hers was explicit. Almost a dare. Even a threat.

I looked to the plaque.

JOAN KATHERINE, 10TH COUNTESS ALCOTT
1920-1922

I stared at the plaque.

I then moved back to Virginia's.

VIRGINIA ELIZABETH, 10TH COUNTESS ALCOTT
1922-1959
DOWAGER 1959-1963

I looked to David's.

EDWARD "DAVID" FREDERICK THOMAS, EARL ALCOTT
1918-1959
DPSD. 1959-1960

Dpsd? What did that mean?

I moved to another painting of an earl.

There was also the *Dpsd.* note.

Dpsd as in *deposed?*

I continued on.

All of them had the same, either *Dpsd.* or *Dowager.*

Except Thomas and Joan and the ones before them.

Good Lord, did Thomas's shenanigans lead to the covenant that ousted the earl at thirty-eight?

And how were there two 10th countesses?

Who was Joan? And how was she countess at the same time David was earl? From her portrait, she unquestionably was not his mother.

I jumped and twirled when I heard a throat cleared.

Brittany was standing there.

She didn't give me the creeps like Laura did, but she was certainly a cold fish.

"Lord Alcott requests you to attend him in the Dogwood Suite," she announced.

The Dogwood Suite?

"The *actual* lord," she finished.

The...?

Richard?

Richard was asking me to his bedroom?

"Why?" I queried suspiciously.

"I'd hardly know," she replied. "Do you need me to show you the way?"

I didn't. I knew it.

But something about her pushed me to be catty.

"Yes, since I don't make a habit of going to an old man's bedroom at"—I looked at my phone, thumbing the screen to activate it—"nine thirty at night."

"Then follow me."

She stood with her hand on the light switches.

I walked to her.

She turned the lights out before I got there, plunging the room into shadows.

Not a cold fish.

A bit of a bitch.

She didn't say anything as we made our way into the hall, down the stairs, or to Richard's room. She still didn't say anything as she knocked softly.

She then gave me a lip curl and walked away.

The door opened.

Good news, he wasn't in his underwear or a gaping dressing gown.

Bad news, I didn't know what this was about, and I'd had a trying day. I didn't need his shit.

"Are you all right?" I asked. "Do you need something?"

"Yes, please, Daphne. To talk to you."

I had a feeling Daniel had been at his dad, told him the jig was up with the carnations, and Portia's money, and Daddy-o was intervening.

He stepped aside so I'd enter his room.

I did, but when he went to close the door, I said, "I'd rather you keep it open, please."

He appeared startled, then pissed. "I'd hardly be inappropriate."

"That's not what I've heard."

He scowled at me but did as I wished, leaving the door open before he walked into the room.

It was much like Ian's, except a lot bigger. There was an additional room that was a study, another baronial desk he did nothing at. The furniture was heavier, more ornate, darker, even lugubrious.

And there was a lot of white, with flashes of surprising pink, though somehow made masculine, both colors of dogwood blooms.

"Would you feel comfortable sitting?" he asked.

I would, actually. I was feeling off. It was the day. Lou's situation. Amaretto on an empty stomach.

"No," I answered.

"Can I get you a drink?"

"No again, and no offense. I've already had one and I was about to go to my room and get ready for bed."

"So be it," he murmured.

He then glanced at the door.

Though it wasn't a glance since it lasted a long time.

I expected someone to come in, like Daniel to plead Portia's case, but that didn't happen before Richard spoke.

"I'm sure you know by now that Louella and I had a...liaison."

I jolted, like I'd been struck by lightning.

He smiled a slippery, obnoxious smile. "I can assure you it was before your father." He lifted his shoulders in a mock-indifferent shrug. "It was when she was casting about for a patron. She married your father not long after I ended things with her."

I didn't know what to say.

I didn't know why he was telling me this.

Though, sadly, I didn't disbelieve him.

Even when Lou was at the height of her career, she dated older men. After years of thinking on it, I put it down to her trying to find her father, who adored her and made her feel safe, and it wasn't wrong to search for something like that.

Whatever made you happy.

"Obviously," he continued, "I'd never leave my Jane for her."

"Why are you telling me this?" I asked, my voice a lash.

"Why?" He seemed shocked at the question.

"Yes. Why?"

"Because Daniel's told me what's befallen her, poor girl. And I wanted you to know how sorry I am for her, your family, and tell you if there's anything at all I can do…"

He let that trail.

"Are you a neurosurgeon?"

"No."

"An oncologist?"

"Daphne—"

"In other words, no. I don't believe there's anything you can do. But thanks, Richard. Though, I hope you don't mind, I won't share this tête-à-tête with Lou."

"The affair may have ended, but it was enjoyable while it lasted, and—"

"Please, don't," I hissed, moving to leave.

"I'm concerned about her," he stated.

I stopped. "I don't know you very well, and I'm in your home and it pains me to be impolite, but you must know I don't believe you. More, it sickens me that you'd use the awful thing that's happening with Lou to do something petty and spiteful like you're doing now."

I moved toward him.

He stood staring at me and not backing down.

I stopped close.

"Do you think it makes me think less of Lou, that she was with you? Is that what this is? To shock me and make me upset that my step-mother had an affair with a married man? Doing that within a few hours of me finding out she has a tumor in her brain?"

"Hardly. As I said. I'm concerned. I thought she told you about us."

"She came here for Portia, the question is, why on earth did *you* allow her in your house with your wife here?"

And now the Richard, Lady Jane and Lou uneasiness was explained, and I wished it wasn't.

Dear Lord, somehow *Lady Jane* knew Lou had an affair with her husband.

God, I felt for them both.

But in this instance, I loved Lou, but I mostly felt for Lady Jane.

"Portia is high-strung," he explained. "You probably know, she's

TOO GOOD TO BE TRUE

been here before. More than once. Jane and she weren't meshing. I called Louella personally—"

The second time that night, my head spun.

This time with fury.

"Oh my God. You're a fucking piece of work."

"No need for foul language," he bit. "And if you'd let me finish a single sentence, and perhaps listen when I speak rather than making judgments before hearing, I could get my point across."

I crossed my arms on my chest. "And what point is that, Richard?"

"As I said, she means something to me. I'm concerned. My sons don't know of our past relationship, obviously. It's clear you and she are close. Dear friends. Which was why I thought she told you. So I had hoped you'd keep me informed about her condition."

"How's this?" I suggested. "I'll keep Ian informed, and Portia can keep Daniel informed, and you can learn news of Lou from them."

"I'm not entirely certain why you've taken such an adversarial stance with me, Daphne," he remarked shortly. "I'm hosting you and your sister in my home. I believe you've been made comfortable."

I leaned back and tossed out my arms. "Ah yes, sleeping in a dead woman's bed and getting her floral bouquets delivered at night."

"Jane told me about that," he said, now appearing sincerely regretful. "I believe Jane has shared both of our feelings on that subject with Portia and Daniel."

"So you had nothing to do with me being in that room? Oh, and while we're talking about this, Lou being in the Floral Room?"

"Daniel made all the arrangements at Portia's behest."

Sadly, I could believe that too.

"Though, when I discovered where you were both assigned, I was dismayed," he informed me. "But by then, it was too late."

"It's the matter of packing a suitcase and moving a room away, Richard," I pointed out. "Or, if we weren't really welcome, finding a hotel or inn nearby."

"Staff prepare those rooms, Daphne, and they have other duties as well. You can't understand the running of a house like Duncroft. Nothing is as easy as you think."

That was probably true too.

Though Ian managed to get us moved without much trouble. I was there when he ordered it, and none of the staff seemed overwhelmed with the additional duties.

"I think Ian shared he wasn't pleased at the arrangements, and you didn't tell him it was Daniel and Portia's idea," I reminded him.

"He was angry. They don't get along. Jane and I both try to run interference. I knew if he knew it was Daniel, this would cause problems between my sons."

Shit!

That was a good excuse too.

"And while we're on the subject of Ian," he began.

Here we go, I thought.

"I'm pleased you two are getting on so well."

Well, knock me over with a feather.

He looked sincere about that too.

"Your patisserie is well-known and well-regarded. I heard your pastries were even ordered by Buckingham Palace for some event or other."

He heard right.

That was a huge coup.

I didn't confirm.

Richard kept talking, "Ian needs a woman who...how shall I put this, has her own pursuits."

Well, hell.

"He's a busy man," he continued. "He travels often. And I believe he'd become bored very easily with a woman who waited at home for him, or tagged along, demanding his attention."

Well, hell again, because that wasn't where I thought this was going.

I thought he was insinuating Ian needed someone who had something to take her attention so he could fuck around on her at his whim.

It seemed I was wrong.

I studied Richard closely.

Cripes, did I have this guy's approval?

"And Jane likes you enormously," he concluded.

That felt nice.

"I like her too," I muttered.

"We don't have to be enemies, no matter what my son has told you about me," he said. "Obviously, if he finds a woman with whom to settle down, create a family, she and her children would be my family as well."

Regrettably, not a selling point for Ian.

But we'd just kissed. I'd known him mere days.

And oddly, it seemed Jane was grooming me to take over for her, and Richard already had us married off.

"I'm honestly concerned for Louella," he said quietly. "Whatever you think of me, she had an alarming incident in my home. I understand how you can't understand how difficult it was for me to learn of that, and why you wouldn't. To have everyone off to the hospital to be with her. And it was inappropriate for me to come along. And yet, outside of you, I'm the one in this house who holds the most affection for her."

I looked hard, and I couldn't believe it, but it appeared he wasn't lying.

As such, I matched his tone when I said, "I didn't know about you two. I wish I still didn't. But I get it, and you have my apology for being unkind when I came in here. It's been a bad day."

He appeared mollified. "Yes, it has. It's upsetting for all of us, but I know, especially for you. I hope the drama is over for you, and the rest of your stay at Duncroft is far more enjoyable than it's begun."

He held his hand out to me like we'd shake.

Détente with Richard Alcott?

I had enough going on. I didn't need to be feuding with the father of the man I was...what? Seeing? Dating in a Conservatory?

God, this was all *so weird*.

I took his hand.

He squeezed minimally and let me go.

"Enjoy the rest of your night and sleep well, Daphne," he bid.

"You too, Richard."

I took my leave and almost stopped at Ian's room on the way to my own to tell him what just happened, but I decided against it.

I wasn't sure he needed to know any of that.

Also, I was tired, worn out actually, and my head felt almost woozy.

I hadn't had dinner, but I'd had a lot of drama.

I needed a bath and bed.

And hopefully a good night's sleep.

I headed to the Rose Room to get that, knowing that things had been very strange.

But not knowing it was about to get much, much worse.

Twenty-One

THE ROSE ROOM

The first text came when I was in the bath.

You disappeared and didn't say goodnight.

I haven't gone to bed. I'm relaxing in the bath. I returned.

Torture, he replied.

I grinned.

The next came when I was undoing the work of the girls by slapping open all the curtains in the bedroom.

Breakfast in the Hawthorn Suite?

You're on, I replied.

Text me when you wake. Goodnight, darling.

Goodnight, honey. And thanks again for being awesome today.

No worries. Sleep well. You need anything, you know where I am.

Yeah, this guy was too good to be true.

I got in bed with my Kindle, but I did it with thoughts of our kiss.

And thoughts of what Ian told me while we were talking on the lounge.

I was tired, and the bath helped to relax me, but I knew what would unwind me the rest of the way.

I opened the drawer to put my phone on charge and grab the other thing that was in there, but found the drawer empty.

Except for a note.

In bold handwriting, it said, *Don't even think about it. If you want to use what was in here, you have to come fetch it. It's in the Hawthorn Suite.*

"I'll be damned," I whispered, smiling.

I pulled up my texts again, *You're a rascal.*

He knew exactly what I was talking about. But of course he did.

I've noted it's fully charged.

Plans have changed. Breakfast in the Rose Room. With you returning my precious belongings, I shot back.

Only if it's breakfast in bed, he returned.

Such a flirt!

That can be arranged.

Go to sleep.

That'll be hard without my friend.

I can return it now.

You wish.

I do.

My fingers work.

So do mine.

Gah! Talk about torture! I don't know what to do with you!

Open to suggestions?

Go to sleep, Lord Alcott.

Sweet dreams, Miss Ryan.

Still smiling, I put my phone on charge, turned out the light and snuggled under the fluffy duvet on probably ten million thread-count sheets (by the feel of them, and I knew good sheets, these were the best).

And yes, my friend was awesome.

But with Ian's kiss a ghost on my lips and visions of his chest dancing in my head, my fingers worked just fine.

~

I STOOD at the altar in my wedding gown.

There were so many flowers, you couldn't see the church. Walls of flowers. Flowers covering the high, arched ceilings, petals ankle deep on the floor.

I looked to my groom.

It was Ian, his head turned the other direction.

I looked to my bridesmaids.

They consisted of Virginia, Dorothy, Joan and Margery, and they all wore mourning black, defiling the beauty of the flower-festooned sanctuary.

When I turned back to Ian, I saw he had one groomsman. But I couldn't see his face. It was moving. Blurred. Like it was in perpetual motion, his head vacillating side to side so quickly I couldn't make out his features.

It was nauseating.

Ian turned to me.

But it wasn't Ian.

It was David.

He leered and became Thomas.

I lifted my skirt and turned to flee, and like a streak, a figure moved from the back of the church, down the aisle, to stand at the foot of the altar.

I couldn't make out her face.

She was wearing a fur-trimmed coat and cloche hat.

"But what about Rose?" she asked me.

I felt something touch my cheek.

I woke.

The room was dark as tar.

But there was someone in there with me.

I knew it.

I felt it.

My blood ran cold.

"Ian?" I whispered, knowing it wasn't him.

Whoever it was closed the drapes, and he wouldn't do that.

Through the dark, I saw a shadow move.

Blonde hair.

No.

Platinum.

Oh my God!

I reached for the light.

It knocked my hand away.

I was awake.

This was real.

And whatever that was, was close enough to *touch me*.

Horror-stricken, I scrambled over the bed and fell off the other side, slamming my head into the nightstand.

Pain darted through my temple into my eye as I crashed to the floor.

The door opened and weak light came in from the hallway, but the bed was between me and it, and I couldn't see.

Something trickled in my eye.

I dashed at it, and it was wet.

"Oh my God, oh my God," I chanted, scurrying to find my feet and backing up.

I hit the wall and let out a scream.

The door remained open.

The hall was empty.

No one was anywhere near me except...*that thing*.

I scrambled to the bed, turned on the light, then crawled over the bed, turning on the other one. I opened the drawer, yanked out my phone, and shivering like a lunatic, I called Ian.

"Please don't have do not disturb on, please don't have—" I chanted as it rang, drawing my legs up and holding them to my chest.

"Daphne?" he answered, sounding sleepy.

"Someone was in my room," I breathed, sounding as frightened as I was.

"Where are you?"

"In bed. They ran out. Down the hall."

"I'm coming."

"Ian, I'm not making this up. I saw them. It *touched me*."

"I'm on my way, darling. Breathe."

"It wasn't a dream."

"Breathe, Daphne."

"I'm being very serious."

"I can tell. Can you breathe for me?"

"I'm scared out of my mind."

"I can tell that too," he sounded funny, jerky, like he was running. "Breathe for me, sweetheart."

I got one shaky breath into my lungs before I had my suspicions confirmed and Ian ran into the room.

"Jesus fucking Christ," he snarled, racing the final few feet to the bed.

"She was here."

He sat on the bed while I spoke, reaching to me.

"She was here," I repeated.

Tentatively, he touched my temple.

I flinched.

"You're bleeding."

"I fell off the bed."

"Stay here." He got up, went to the bathroom.

I started rocking, still shivering, hugging my legs, staring at the hall.

He came back with a wet cloth, talking into his phone. "No. Get to the Rose Room. *Now.*"

He tossed his phone on the covers, then sat in front of me again and carefully dabbed at my temple.

"I need to see how bad this is," he murmured.

I grabbed his wrist. He quit dabbing and looked into my eyes.

"Dorothy was in here. I saw her hair. I'm not kidding. I'm not making this up. And I'm *not* crazy."

"Okay, sweetheart," he soothed. "All right, darling. Just try to calm down and let me see to this cut."

"She touched me *while I was sleeping.*"

Ian had no time to react to that.

I screamed and pushed away from him, starting to dash across the bed, when movement came at the door.

I stopped when I saw it was Daniel, Portia running in after him.

They both stopped dead, but only Portia cried, "Oh my God! You're hurt!"

"Go wake Stevenson. Sam. Jack. I want this house searched, top to fucking bottom," Ian ordered.

"What? Why?" Daniel asked.

"Daphne was attacked."

213

I was freaking, but I still saw Daniel's sheer shock, then his face suffused with anger and he sprinted out of the room.

Portia darted forward. "How bad is it?"

"I don't know," Ian answered. "She might need stitches. I need to join the search. Clean it and stay here with her. I'll send someone in with first aid, and if she needs a doctor, find me."

He handed the washcloth to Portia, leaned in and kissed me quickly on the lips, then he ran out.

"Oh my God, Daphne, this is crazy," Portia said, sitting on the bed and reaching the cloth to me.

"I'll do it." I took it from her.

"I can help," she said petulantly.

"I know, honey. I'm just freaking. Let me think," I mumbled, pressing the cool, wet cloth to my head.

"You were attacked?"

"I...I don't know. Someone was in here. I can't think straight. I need a second."

"I'll get you some water. Do you want some water?"

I focused on my sister.

Another short nightie, expensive, this one green satin. Pretty lace.

"Cuddle in bed with me?" I requested. "I'm shivering and you have to be cold too."

"Okay," she agreed.

Moving carefully, like I was made of china, she shifted with me, and awkwardly, because I was still holding the cloth to my head, we both got under the covers, backs to the headboard, bedclothes pulled up high.

She wrapped an arm around me and leaned her weight into me, like she wanted to share her heat.

"There. Let's get you warm. You're freezing," she said.

She rubbed my arm, fast, up and down.

I'd had a dream. I was marrying David.

No, Thomas.

And then something touched my cheek.

But did it?

I looked to the windows.

All the curtains were closed.

All of them.

Closed.

Someone was definitely in here.

A tremble bolted through me.

"I don't like this," Portia said in a small voice. "You're never like this. You're scaring me."

I dropped the cloth and put my arm around her too.

"We're okay. We're safe."

"It's supposed to be me saying that." She gazed at my temple. "It doesn't look bad. You need some plasters. I'd get some, but I have no clue where they are."

"It can wait."

"What on earth?"

Both Portia and I started and looked to the door.

Jane in her cashmere dressing gown again, this time with Richard, who was wearing full pajamas.

He took one look at me, his face turned to stone, then he spun on his foot and marched out.

He barely cleared the door before he started jogging down the hall, bellowing, "*Stevenson!*"

Jane came to the bed.

"My word," she whispered.

"We need a first aid kit," Portia said.

"I'll get one. Stay with her?"

"Of course," Portia replied.

"Be right back, dear," Jane said to me.

I nodded.

She floated out the door, but quickly.

"It's swelling," Portia noted, staring at my cut. "I should have told her to get ice too. I know where that is, but I don't want to leave you."

"No," I said urgently, holding tight to her. "Don't leave me."

She put her other arm around me and held me, cooing, "I'm right here, Daph."

Jane came back, incredibly quickly, but I knew why. She was with a lady, a redhead, but her hair was turning white, a little older than Bonnie.

She was holding a rather large case that looked like a fishing tackle box, but it was white and had a red cross on it.

She was also wearing a nightgown with a dressing gown over it.

"Good God," she said when she saw me.

"Have you met Christine?" Jane asked and didn't wait for my answer. "This is Christine. Christine, Daphne. Christine takes care of us. And now she's going to help me take care of you. Portia, can you let us in there?"

Reluctantly, Portia slid out of bed. She rushed toward the bathroom.

I scooted over to the edge of the bed, staying under the covers.

Christine sat down with me, eyes to my temple.

"Everyone's saying lovely things about you," she murmured, turning to the box, flicking it open. "I would have liked to have met you before you were bleeding and given a fright."

That almost made me laugh.

She turned to me. "It's not bad, but I'll have to clean it and that might not feel good."

"Do what you gotta do," I invited.

Portia returned, having helped herself to my merino duster.

Christine was right. With Portia and Jane watching like hawks ready to swoop in for the kill if Christine put a gauze swab wrong, Christine cleaned the wound with alcohol and it hurt like heck. Then Jane moved in to add some fingers as they held it together and plastered it over with two strips.

Christine came back with a clean gauze she'd squirted sterile solution on, and she gently washed the blood away from my temple, eye and cheek.

"There you go, fit as a fiddle," she decreed when she was finished.

Not even.

"All right, now that's done," Jane announced efficiently. "Let's get you to bed. Up with you."

I stared at her, confused, seeing as I was *in* bed.

And I was never sleeping again *in my life.*

"Come, dear." She held a hand to me. "We're moving you to the Hawthorn Suite."

"What?" Portia asked.

"What?" I parroted.

"You can sleep in there, with Ian," she stated. "Which I'm certain will be his decree. Or in the Robin Room with your sister, or in my room, with me. Your choice, but my guess would be Ian will circumvent it when he returns to us if you don't pick the first."

That would be my guess too.

"You do need to move. With Lou gone, you're all alone in this wing," Portia noted.

"I can have one of the girls prepare Magnolia," Christine offered. "It's got an adjoining door to Hawthorn."

"That might be all right, but I'm uncertain she should be alone," Jane replied.

I was certain.

No way in fuck did I want to be alone.

"I'm sixty-one, not ninety-one. I didn't grow up in the fifties," Jane stated bafflingly in my direction. "I know what's going on with you and my son. It's the way of things now as it was in my day, for goodness' sakes."

Okay.

All right.

I mean, really!

What the hell?

"We've only kissed once!" I cried.

"You stayed with him last night," Jane pointed out.

"I was freaking out."

She raised her brows.

Point taken.

"And he made me," I added sulkily.

"Let's not cause undue shuffling about," Jane decided. "We'll wait until they're done...doing what they're doing."

That would be finding some piece of shit who, for reasons unknown, dressed up like Dorothy Clifton, came into my room, closed the curtains, woke me by touching my cheek, and then, when I was going to turn on my lamp and their jig would be up, knocking my hand out of the way and running when I lost it and crashed to the floor.

"Maybe some sherry?" Jane suggested to Christine.

"Right away," Christine replied, closing the first aid tackle box.

"Be sure to bring a glass for yourself," Jane invited.

"Oh, I was going to," Christine said as she got up and walked out.

"Daphne doesn't drink sherry," Portia shared.

"She will tonight." Jane looked to me. "Don't worry, dear. It's dry. I don't like the sweet stuff either."

I collapsed against the headboard.

Jane floated around turning on lights.

Portia crawled back into bed with me.

Thus, sometime later, there we were, Jane, Portia, Christine and me, sipping awful sherry, when Ian prowled in wearing a face like thunder.

"Why did no one invite me to the party?" he drawled, but the joke was underlined with a thick vein of fury.

Still.

That made me smile.

"You might wish to go to the kitchen, Christine," he suggested. "Dad and Stevenson are right now sacking Brittany. Someone will need to make sure she's fully packed when she's kicked out because, if she leaves something behind, she sure as fuck won't be coming back."

Christine appeared horrified for a split second before that morphed to anger, and she stormed out, taking her sherry glass with her.

"What's this?" Lady Jane asked, and I had pulled it together (it was having some time, and I hated to say it, but the sherry helped), but I shivered at her tone.

Now I knew where Ian got it.

Dangerous.

"She was pretending to be asleep, but she hadn't had time to fully change, and Jack found the wig shoved in a broom closet," Ian told her.

"The wig?" Jane asked.

"She dressed up like Dorothy Clifton and came in here to frighten Daphne," Ian said.

"Oh my God! Why would she do something like that?" Portia cried.

Ian looked at her but didn't answer.

Jane set her glass aside, and with a mask of fury, wordlessly, she left the room.

I didn't think she was headed to the Cherry Suite.

I thought it was highly likely she had a few things to say after Stevenson sacked Brittany.

Ian turned his attention to me. "You're moving to the Hawthorn Suite."

There you go.

Figured.

Twenty-Two

THE BEDROOM

I was pacing.

Ian had gone to do something, telling me he'd be "right back."

He was not "right back."

I was in his bedroom.

Alone.

I was okay with that. This was a much more populated wing, and as far as I knew, everyone in the house was awake. Anyway, on the way there (by the way, I didn't walk there—get this, Ian *carried me*) I did not fail to note that it seemed like every light in Duncroft had been switched on.

Ian finally stalked in, carrying one of those ice packs with a screw top. It was blue.

"You're out of bed," he growled, sounding ferociously pissed.

Yes, he carried me right to his bed. Then he tucked me in and everything.

But, obviously, I got out.

"I couldn't sit still," I replied.

That made him look more pissed.

But he approached me, and for once, I wasn't sure that was a good thing.

Yes, he was that pissed.

"It's probably too late to do anything about the swelling, but we're going to try," he announced.

Even with his mood, when he used the side of his fist under my chin to move my head so he could look at my temple, his touch was remarkably gentle.

"Not bad, not great," he said to my wound, then again gently, he placed the ice on it. "Hold that there as long as you can."

I lifted my hand to take the bag. "What's happening?"

"I'm sorry, darling. I had to stop and try to talk Dad out of pressing charges. Then I wondered why I'd try to stop that, Bonnie got me your ice, and here we are."

"Pressing charges for what?"

He stared at me like I'd gone temporarily insane.

"It's unhinged what she did, and I'd like to understand why she did it," I went on. "But I'm uncertain the police need to be involved. Though, maybe a psychologist."

"She's an ex of Daniel's."

My mouth dropped open, and I left it hanging that way.

"Yes," he grunted. "Daniel ended it, but apparently she had some pictures of him. I believe the kids refer to them these days as dick pics?"

I kept the ice where it was but still looked to the ceiling and prayed for Daniel's salvation, and maybe for someone to give him some brains in his head, not solely housing them in some other organ.

I did this by using the words, "Oh my God."

"Mm-hmm," Ian agreed. "She lives in the village. Not a lot of opportunity there. She demanded he get her a position here. Blackmail. He leaned on Stevenson when Maggie got pregnant and quit to get married and move to Newcastle. This still left why she targeted you a mystery, until Dad started threatening the police. She then confessed the get-up was supposed to be used on Portia, but Portia was never alone at night. She heard talk of what happened to you last night and decided it was the perfect atmosphere to make her play. Since you're Portia's sister, she figured, if she scared the absolute fuck out of you, this would cause you to leave, and Portia would leave in camaraderie. I've no idea why she'd want to send Portia away. Possibly jealousy, possibly sour grapes. It doesn't matter. In the end, it was you who got the Dorothy Clifton treatment."

There was nothing else I could do but let out a massive sigh.

Therefore, that was what I did.

"Are things settling down?" I asked after I did it.

"No. Dad is beside himself. I've never seen him so angry. Stevenson blames himself. Danny feels like shit, and I want to say he deserves it. That was fucked up, what he did. We all know we don't meddle with staffing. It takes a great deal to run this house and none of us have the skills. But Stevenson was up against the wall, the earl's son asking him a favor and to keep it confidential. Even with all that, Daniel could never know she'd do something so radically bizarre."

"This is true," I muttered.

"Portia is pissed at Danny, as she would be. Brittany's been doing her hair."

Now I was pissed.

That woman was doing my sister's *hair*?

"This is a disaster," I snapped.

"Agreed. Mum tore a few strips off Brittany. We exclusively get our meat at the local butcher in the village. Our groceries from the small market there. Mum's flower arrangements from the florist when our garden is out of season or when she's throwing a party. Stevenson even orders our liquor through the off-license. It isn't like it used to be, where that village was almost entirely dependent on us in one way or another, but it's not ancient history that Duncroft puts more than a small amount of coin in their pockets. And the village wouldn't even be there if it wasn't for Duncroft. We not only endowed the school and library, we built both. And that ambulance service that could get here so quickly for Lou?"

"Yes?" I prompted.

"It's helped to stay afloat from a very generous yearly donation from Duncroft. There's not enough population for the NHS to operate that service in this area. But there are a lot of farmers and herders here. Some of them are even farther away and much more remote than we are, which makes the hospital dangerously far if something happened without at least paramedics to wade in. It was needed. Duncroft made it happen. Most of our staff is from the village. We have groundskeepers who work here and live there, and they earn a very good wage. In other words, people like us, and they might not depend on us, but this house is important to them. And it's Duncroft. They have pride in it, even if it isn't theirs."

"You're telling me this because?"

"I'm telling you this because Lady Jane Alcott is pissed as shit at Brittany, who's from the village, and the girl I saw downstairs is scared out of her mind she's going to be a pariah. And she's right to be. Mum could make it impossible to live there if she had a mind to do it. And she's of that mind right now."

This made even less sense than the rest of it.

"Then why did she do it?"

"Because she didn't think she'd get caught," Ian told me. "She also thought we'd think you were crazy when you said you saw Dorothy. It isn't like we're immune to the ghost stories. But I've lived in this house for thirty-eight years, maybe not daily, but I'm no stranger. And I've never seen a single ghost or even had the minutest experience."

At least that made me feel better. The house wasn't *actually* haunted.

"You can't arrest someone for scaring someone," I pointed out.

"You can for blackmail."

Whoa.

"Is Daniel okay with people knowing he was blackmailed? And how that could happen?"

With his hands at my waist, Ian started herding me to the bed, saying, "Dad's not going to press charges. But he's also not an idiot. She was being stubborn. The threat of police and Mum getting involved loosened her mouth."

He pushed me carefully to sitting on the bed.

I looked up at him. "Do you think that was where Daniel was going that early morning? To tryst with her or talk to her or, I don't know, maybe she made some other threat or demand, and he needed to bargain with her?"

Ian suddenly looked reticent.

Uh-oh.

"Ian?"

He crouched in front of me. "When Daniel admitted to getting her hired and why, I had that same thought. So I took him aside and asked him. He said he wasn't outside that morning. He seemed sincerely confused by the question." When I was sure my expression shared how much I didn't like that, he quickly added, "It's likely he's lying. He can be a good liar when he needs to be, and he's in hot water right now. He's not about to make it worse by confessing to...whatever he might have to confess to."

"So at least now we know why you thought Britany was off."

"At least now we know that."

After he said those words, unexpectedly, he cupped my jaw.

And then he rocked my world.

"Come home with me."

"Wh-what?"

"We've both arranged to take the week. I'm working, but not full steam like normal. We can go back to London." He smiled rakishly. "I have a big flat. I can't say you'll see much but the bedroom, but we can take the time we have left to get to know each other better and see where it goes from there."

It was an amazing offer. And I was tempted.

That said.

"It wasn't twenty-four hours ago you talked me into staying here."

"I've changed my mind."

"Why?"

He sounded incredulous when he repeated, "Why?"

"Do you think Portia and possibly Daniel don't have anything planned anymore?"

"No, I think I raced through my own damned house in the middle of the bloody night to get to you, only to find you in bed with blood all over your face, looking like you'd stared evil right in the eye. And all this shit is just shit, but it keeps happening. *To you.*"

"Tonight wasn't fun—"

He interrupted me to mostly repeat after me again, and continued to do it incredulously, except a lot more incredulously, "It wasn't *fun*?"

"But it's been explained."

He stood, and scowling down at me, asked, "Are you out of your mind?"

"I'm tired. And my head hurts a little. And I fell on my hip, and that doesn't feel great either. Maybe we can talk in the morning?"

"It is morning."

I looked to his tablet.

It was nearly five.

A chill slid over my skin because I wondered when all this started. It had to have been a couple hours ago.

At around three.

"Daphne," he clipped.

I looked up at him. "Okay, then later. Can we talk about it later?"

He appeared frustrated, then he stalked to his bathroom, came back with a glass of water and a clenched fist.

"Hand," he ordered.

I held out my hand.

He dropped some pills into it. "Ibuprofen."

"Perfect," I whispered.

I took the pills while he walked around turning off lights.

He came to me, divested me of the glass, then I scooted into his bed while he kicked off his slippers, pulled off the long sleeve T-shirt he'd donned somewhere along the way and entered the bed with me.

He turned out the lamp on the nightstand and turned me into his arms.

I guessed he was giving in, and we were going to talk about it later.

I settled against him.

"If we stay, you're moving in here," he declared into the dark.

"You're fresh," I teased.

"I'm not joking. This isn't sexy teasing texting. I'm being very serious."

He sounded very serious.

"How about I move to the Magnolia Suite? We can leave the adjoining door open."

"No."

I lifted up. "Ian!"

He pulled me back down. "No. We'll talk more later, but that's the caveat. If we stay, you're with me."

"This is the zaniest courtship on record," I griped.

"I'm not courting you. I'm trying to keep your mind in one piece so you can pay attention when I fuck you. You'll want that too, just to say."

"Arrogant."

"Maybe, also true."

"I'm not talking to you anymore."

"Good. Then sleep."

I humphed.

Ian held me closer.

I was still holding the ice to my head, which was a good excuse not to hold him back.

I thought I'd stay awake, but I woke up from a snooze when the ice bag skidded into my face.

Ian took it and tossed it to the floor.

"Go back to sleep," he murmured drowsily.

It was only then I slipped my arm around him.

And I went back to sleep.

Twenty-Three

THE BEDROOM

I sensed a kerfuffle and opened my eyes to see Rebecca and Harriett moving through Ian's bedroom.

With my suitcases.

I got up on an elbow, wincing a bit due to a twinge in my temple.

"You woke her up," Rebecca said under her breath.

"Sorry, Daphne," Harriett said to me.

"That's okay," I mumbled.

"We'll just get on with this," Rebecca replied.

And then they disappeared into Ian's bathroom, and, my guess, beyond, where his closet probably was (I hadn't snooped, but I was clearly going to need to change that this morning).

I turned my head when I saw movement out of the corners of my eyes and watched Ian striding to me.

He was ready to face the day. Jeans. An oatmeal T-shirt. An army-green, shawl-collar, cable-knit cardigan.

Scrumptious.

"So it appears we're *not* talking this morning and you've made the decision I'm moving to your suite," I remarked.

He grinned.

Then he reached to grasp me around my ribs and hauled me toward him.

My body collided with his, and I had no choice but to hold on to his shoulders as I dangled in his grip. And then I had to do it because his mouth came down on mine.

I had no thoughts of morning-breath kisses when his tongue swept inside, and I became aware that he'd been holding out on me the night before.

This kiss was hungry, no...*greedy*, demanding and commanding, and I was powerless to do anything but wrap my arms around his neck and give all he required.

And he required everything.

He lifted his head, and it took a couple of seconds, but eventually my eyes fluttered open.

"Good morning," he murmured, those throaty two words rasping in a delightful way over my skin.

"Morning," I replied.

He sat me in bed, sitting there with me, my hip to his, pressed tight, our arms still wound around each other.

"How are you feeling this morning?" he asked.

"Better," I didn't lie.

His gaze lifted to my temple. "Your head?"

"It's okay."

"They're here mostly so you have your things to get ready and not have to go back to the Rose Room," he explained. "And now, fast, give me five reasons that will convince me I should allow you to stay at Duncroft."

As good as his kiss was, it wore off quickly on the word "allow."

"Allow?"

"I said fast, Daphne. If you don't convince me, I'm bundling you in my car in your pajamas and driving you to London myself. Jack or Sam can drive your car down."

I studied him and realized he was dead serious.

Okay, last night had freaked me, but it seemed it had freaked Ian more.

"Reason one for *you* to stay," I began. "You need to talk to your dad."

It wasn't my place to say, but that didn't negate the fact it was plainly past time for those two to have a sit-down and iron things out.

I wasn't going to get into the whole Lou thing. I hadn't had time to think on it, but I wasn't sure I'd ever tell him, and that sucked. I didn't want to keep anything from him. It felt like a lie, holding that secret.

But the truth was, I didn't want to do it, mostly because I didn't want him to think badly of Lou. Though, I had to admit, I also didn't want him to have more fodder to think badly of his father.

That said, he might already know. He told me he kept an eye on his dad and brother. It wasn't something he was going to pipe up about either.

"I know you don't get along," I continued. "But you're both adults, something big is about to happen, and you need to hammer out the details so he knows his place in this house is secure. I suspect it'll help both your parents to be less on edge."

That and the fact Lou was gone, but again, I wasn't going to get into that now (or ever?).

"That's one," Ian rumbled.

"Two is, if I leave, Lou will want to know why. And I don't want her to know about last night. It'll upset her."

I could tell that was a good one with his tone when he said, "That's two."

"Three is, Portia and I had a moment last night. If she's staying, I feel I should stay with her. She's justifiably angry at Daniel. She's upset about Lou. Yes, it's in her way and it's not a good way, but she is. And I think, if we had a breakthrough last night, I should push my advantage. Maybe now I can talk some sense into her, give a little, tell her I'll convince the trustees to give her enough money to cover her expenses, say for a month, until she finds a job. And maybe attempt to counsel her on finding her true calling in life. Something she enjoys. Something she'll stick with so we don't have to go through this again."

"All right. I don't quite agree that you should give in when it comes to teaching Portia a lesson, but you know her better than me. And she was openly upset about what happened to you last night and stepped in like any sister should. So that's three," he said when I stopped speaking.

"Four is, I'm curious about this village everyone keeps on about. I want to see it."

"It's weak, but yes, that's four."

I felt my lips curl up but carried on. "Five, call me crazy, but I like Duncroft. One can say things sure aren't boring here."

I could see the flare in his eyes, sharing how much he liked that I liked his ancestral home, regardless of all that had been happening.

I wasn't going there with us right then, but the bigger truth in that was I liked getting to know Ian while we were there.

He'd *become* Duncroft for me. A beautiful, strong, endlessly interesting fortress where I felt safe.

He was right. All the shit was just shit, but it was happening to me.

That said, I didn't feel unsafe here.

Not exactly true, there were times, obviously, when I'd been petrified.

But then, he was right there, and I had the exact opposite feeling.

I hadn't had time to think on this either, but it was even more.

I was beginning to get the sensation that something else was happening. It was like the house was communicating to me, with my tours, meanderings, my dreams, and most especially Ian's stories and the time I spent with him while he was telling them (and besides).

And what the house had to say, it was necessary for me to hear, and I couldn't hear it if I wasn't there.

It was weird (it was *all* weird), but I felt, deep down, I was *supposed* to be here. That it wasn't yet time to leave.

It wasn't time for Ian and for me.

"Then the girls are unpacking you," he gave in. "Because you know the deal."

"Ian," I said softly. "It isn't like I'm not that girl. I'm that girl. Proudly that girl. I go after what I want. But we haven't even had a date."

"This will be rectified when I take you to the village this afternoon, and then we'll have dinner at the Italian place. They have four restaurants. That one, an Indian place, Chinese takeaway, and a chippie. And

I'm not standing on a street corner eating a battered sausage for our first date."

I loved battered sausages, but no. That wouldn't do for a first date with Ian Alcott.

Still, I said, "I think you know what I mean."

"You've been here with me the last two nights."

"With extenuating circumstances."

"Right, love, I don't get this. Because I'm a man. But I understand the way of it is that women have been trained to consider these things as a matter of course and be cautious about them. But let me educate you about where I'm at. You hold the power, all of it, when it comes to intimacy. If you're not ready, I won't push you. When you're ready, I'll be waiting. I want you here because I want you safe. I want you here because I like being with you. I want you here because you feel good beside me in my bed. I've also made it clear I want to be inside you. But I'll be inside you here when you decide it's time. *Only* when you decide it's time. Now, will you please move into my suite?"

"Yes," I whispered.

His relief was so great, I wondered why I protested it.

I wondered that more when he kissed my nose as a reward for giving him what he wanted.

He then said, "I called the hospital. They were processing Lou's release. They transferred me to her room, and she told me she and her parents are going to have breakfast then make their way here. She thinks they'll be here around ten thirty, eleven. If you want to be ready to see her and not go down in your fetching nightclothes, you best be rousing."

I looked to the clock.

It was just after nine.

I looked back to Ian.

"You think my pajamas are fetching?"

I was in a racerback tank, bralette under it to keep the girls under control, and a pair of loose shorts with a deep edge of lace, all this in a blush pink.

It wasn't exciting. It was comfortable.

231

"It's damned sexy when a sexy woman knows she doesn't have to try to be just that."

Interesting.

He reached to pull the bell cord. "Again, they know to bring up breakfast for you if I ring. I'll leave you to get ready."

He gave me another kiss, this one on my lips, a quick one, but still sweet.

He was up and moving toward the door when I called, "Ian?"

He stopped and turned back, raising his brows.

"I took a meander up on the gallery when I was talking to Lou's mum."

"Yes?" he asked.

"What's the story about Joan, the other tenth Countess Alcott?"

His expression shifted, I didn't like the shift, and I liked it less when he said, "Not for now, darling, okay?"

"Now I need to know," I told him.

"It might be best we lay off ghost stories for a while."

Terrific.

"I'm now in here with you," I reminded him, throwing a hand out to indicate his room. "Safe. Right?"

He sighed and crossed his arms over his ridiculously attractive cardigan and even more attractive broad chest.

"She was David's first wife. And she was a beast."

Oh boy.

And...David had another wife?

How on earth did I miss that in my research?

Though, I supposed with a thousand years of history in that house and Dorothy Clifton hogging the limelight, I'd miss things.

"A beast?" I queried.

"Hideous to staff. Authoritarian. Stuck-up. In other words, a total bitch."

"Did he divorce her?"

Ian hesitated, but caught my expression and said, "No."

"So what happened to her?"

"She was found hanging in the buttery."

I blinked. Slowly.

Then I asked, "She killed herself?"

"That was what it was ruled. A suicide."

I stared hard at him. "I sense there's more to this story."

Another sigh from Ian and, "It was known by everyone she was not the kind of person to suffer suicidal ideation. She was the queen of her castle and loved that role, flaunted it, lorded over the house, the village, even her social set, because of her beauty, wealth, her position in society and this house. She also wasn't the kind of person to ever be caught belowstairs. That was beneath her in more ways than locationally. If she were to do what it was ruled she did, she wouldn't have chosen the buttery to do it in."

"So someone killed her?"

He shook his head, but said, "That's the gossip. The staff hated her. Everyone in the village hated her. Her supposed friends were not friends because they hated her too. And by then, David had fallen in love with Virginia."

And then I remembered.

1922.

The end of Joan's tenure was the same year as the beginning of Virginia's.

David hadn't even waited a year to replace his first wife.

"Are there more happy stories about Earls and Countesses Alcott?" I asked, maybe a little desperately.

"My grandfather worshipped my grandmother. I've heard stories, and it was much the same with my great-grandfather and great-grand-mother. Then there's the story of Earl Walter Alcott, who was rumored to have a part-time hobby as a pirate and was the one who significantly augmented the wealth of Duncroft, likely from his efforts at illegally acquiring booty, and his lady wife Anne, who he loved so deeply, he ordered his body be buried in her coffin when he passed a year after she did."

If that didn't scream gothic romance, nothing did.

"Well...*shoo.*"

Ian smiled.

Then he asked, "Are you going to get ready for Lou?"

"Yes."

He lifted his chin at me, a gesture I'd never seen him make. It wasn't a jerk or brusque movement. It was tender, affectionate, intimate, and I liked it a whole lot.

"See you when you're ready," he murmured.

"Okay, honey," I replied.

He left.

I got out of bed to see if the girls had unpacked my toothbrush.

But in my head, all I could think was David Alcott might have had a habit of killing the no-longer-needed women in his life.

And he didn't mind taking care of that particular business in his own home.

Twenty-Four

THE PINK TOPAZ ROOM

I was in search of my sister.

Lou and her folks had come and gone.

Things had started poorly, considering the plasters on my temple. But I deftly sidestepped that concern with a little white lie of clumsiness due to Amaretto on an empty stomach and taking Lou aside to tell her Ian and I had kissed...twice. This last capturing her attention, and plasters were forgotten.

Lady Jane swooped in to finish my brave efforts by greeting Lou and her family with her brand of warmth, offering them luncheon and a tour of the house, which both Jo and Kevin, her dad, couldn't hide they were eager to accept.

Lou and I chatted in the Cat's-eye Room while Lady Jane guided the tour, with Lou holding court to Portia coming in and awkwardly, but still sweetly, giving Lou a hug and telling her she was there if Lou needed anything. Then a studiously separate visit from a sheepish Daniel for him to ask after her and share his goodbyes. This led to an uncomfortable visit from Richard, where I had more proof he did not lie the night before, his concern evident. And finally, Ian, who stayed with us for a while, then took off because he had a phone meeting, but he didn't leave before he told me to be ready to go to the village at three.

This last made Lou very bright and cheery.

Oh, and by the way, it was clear Ian took them all aside and made sure they didn't share last night's incident, because no one said a thing.

Richard joined us for lunch, but Daniel and Ian didn't, and Portia and I alone gave hugs and kisses at Jo and Kevin's car, with Portia's hug for Lou lasting longer than mine, and me having good thoughts about how Lou closed her eyes and held on tight throughout it.

However, it was only me who stood at the base of the steps of Duncroft and watched their car drive away until I couldn't see it anymore, Portia dashing up the steps and disappearing into the house.

There was nothing to make me feel great about it all, but I felt better. Lou seemed in good spirits. I knew her mum and dad would take excellent care of her. And she'd be home soon and safe from all the stress of Portia and Richard and Jane.

Though, when I did walk back up the steps, Richard was waiting for me.

I worried about another uncomfortable conversation, but he took the opportunity to, rather formally, apologize for what happened the night before. Although the apology was stiff, I could tell he was still angry about what happened, and it seemed authentic.

Since it wasn't his fault, I didn't think he had anything to apologize for, and although it was nice he did it, I thanked him and told him an apology was unnecessary.

He finished by requesting, "Please don't think too badly about my son. We all do things that are imprudent when we're backed into corners. Daniel's learned now, lamentably through something upsetting happening to you, he shouldn't have done any of it. Not from the start of getting involved with that young woman. But I can assure you, this won't be repeated again."

He couldn't assure me of that, he wasn't Daniel. But since we both very much wanted our talk to be over, I accepted his assurances, and the talk was over.

Now, it was nearing three and I needed to have a chat with my sister before Ian's and my first date, and I couldn't find her.

My efforts were rewarded when I looked into the Pink Topaz Room.

This was another smaller, though not cozy room. The pinks were bright and blinding, almost overpowering.

But my sister, curled into a window seat, resting against fuchsia taffeta throw pillows and a magenta cushion, wearing another long, flowing skirt, this one shining silk the color of a ballet slipper, with a matching fluffy turtleneck sweater, looked designed for the space.

"Hey," I called.

Listlessly, she turned her head to me. "Hey."

I made my way to the window seat and wedged my ass in with her.

For her part, she tucked her legs tighter to give me room.

"Are you all right?" I asked.

"I should be asking you that."

"As you can see, I'm perfectly fine," I assured her.

"I can't even leave," she said as a belated and perplexing answer to my opening question, turning her head back to the window.

"Pardon?"

Her gaze remained at the window. "I don't have a ride to the train station. I don't have a car. I don't *own* a car. And I'm too angry at Daniel to ask him to take me. They don't have Uber here. And even if I could get there, I need the money I have left to pay rent, not buy train tickets."

This was my cue, but I didn't get to take it. She turned her face to me.

"That isn't a ploy to get you to give me money or something. I'm just realizing..." She took a big breath. "I get myself in muddles sometimes," she whispered.

Okay, it seemed we hadn't had a breakthrough last night.

She'd had a revelation.

She peered back out the window. "I lied to him, you see."

Now I was confused.

"To Daniel?"

She shook her head at the glass. "To Ian. I told him I was thirty-one. I thought, if he knew how young I was, he wouldn't ask me out. When I met him, he was so...*Ian*, I had to have him. So I pretended to be someone else." Her voice got quieter. "I pretended to be like you."

Oh my.

Well, from the way things currently stood, at least that explained why Ian dated her, something I'd wondered about but hadn't yet asked.

"We ran into Daniel on our second date. It was a fluke. But Ian asked him and his party to join us. There were five of them. They were rowdy. They took over. Daniel was flirty. I thought it was weird, him flirting with his brother's date. But me being me," she said self-deprecatingly, "first, I was angry that Ian asked them to join us and then didn't seem too broken up they were horning in on our time. So then I thought it would show Ian what a hot ticket I was, and I leaned into Daniel's flirting. I got cocky. I also got drunk. Which led to me, for the first time with Ian, actually being me. It also led to me letting it slip how old I really was to Daniel, and Ian heard."

And that explained how Daniel thought he'd stolen Portia from Ian.

She rested her head against the glass and kept speaking.

"Ian is a gentleman. When he took me home, he didn't call me on my lie. He kissed my forehead and said in a really nice way that I only see as nice now, we weren't going to work. At the time, I didn't understand what was happening. I'm not used to, when it's over, guys just ghosting me. It's more usual, me ghosting guys. And it made me mad. I'd worked hard on him."

Hmm.

I didn't know what "working hard" on a man entailed, but then, I wasn't Portia.

"Like, the next day, Daniel called me," she shared. "I don't know how he got my number, but when we were talking the night before, we found we have mutual friends. It wouldn't be hard. He asked me out. I was mad at Ian, so I said yes."

"So now, how do you truly feel about Daniel?" I asked.

Both her shoulders went up, but she didn't take her attention from the window when she answered, "I don't know. I sure am mad at him about Brittany. So I must feel something."

"Do you still feel something for Ian?"

That was when she looked at me. "Who wouldn't?"

Who wouldn't, indeed.

She waved a hand dismissively. "I'm over it. Last night, I got over it. The whole Brittany thing and how completely dumb Daniel was about it. How I saw Ian was with you, protective and angry on your behalf. You know, I never liked Frankie. He was so up himself. Sure, his pastries are great, but he's not the Michelangelo of custard and cream and dough."

That made me grin at her.

"You need a decent man in your life. Someone better than Frankie." Her tone changed. "Someone better than Dad."

"You know Dad loved you," I said softly.

"I know," she replied. "But he was also a big, stupid jerk. I know it's wrong, but I really wish what's happening to Lou happened while he was alive. He needed to be shook. He needed to see what he had right in front of his face, and that there were ways he could lose it that all his money and the rest of the money in the whole world couldn't buy it back for him."

It *was* wrong, but I understood what she was saying.

Thus, I agreed, "Yes."

She flipped out a hand, an indication of her coming subject change. "I've been going over it in my head. I'm not good with numbers, but I still have some money. Enough to squeak by for a couple of months. I'll find a job. I'll be okay. It's all getting so boring anyway, the clothes and fancy dinners and stuff. It might be good to cook at home. I want to learn how to make Indian food."

I decided it best to ignore her sense of entitlement in saying clothes and fancy dinners were boring and replied, "That sounds good. But I wanted to talk to you about maybe not finding something because you have to, and instead, finding what's right for you."

"What am I good for?" she asked. "I'm a rich man's daughter who doesn't have any real money. I'm semi-kinda-famous because of that. That's all I have going for me."

My tone was firm when I stated, "That isn't true."

She straightened a bit. "Really? So what is there to me, Daph?"

"You dress great. You know designers." I smiled at her. "You're really good at shopping. You could be a stylist. Get a job at Liberty, Harrods, work your way up."

Something lit in her eyes even as her face brightened with excitement.

She hadn't considered she could do something she liked and make money at it.

"Same thing with getting a job at a fashion magazine. It'd have to be entry level, but you could give it a shot. Or try working at a designer boutique. You like to travel. You can be a travel agent. Or a flight attendant," I suggested.

"I like the idea of helping people shop better."

"Then go with that."

Her enthusiasm held on, but only for a moment before the despondency set back in, and she again gazed out the window.

"Daniel," I surmised.

"I'm surprised at how much it hurts, knowing he fucked that woman. Knowing he put her in this house and brought me here, let her touch me, do my hair. Knowing what kind of person she was, how she'd use what he gave her to get what she wanted, then she'd do something as whacked out as what she did to you last night."

"You're surprised to find that you were using him to try to get Ian back, but somewhere along the line, you started liking him."

She turned again to me and shocked me by admitting openly, "Yes." She reached out and grabbed my hand. "What he did, with Brittany, how it played out with you, that happening after we found out about Lou. He couldn't know it would happen, but my God, Daphne, how fucked up is that? It's a terrible coincidence, but in the end, it was Daniel who orchestrated it. And that's not cool."

"Tell him you're disappointed in him and talk it through. If you don't like how he handles it, I'll take you to the train station and buy your ticket home."

When she was going to interrupt me, I shook her hand.

"No," I kept going. "You'll accept. It's my prerogative to take care of my little sister when she gets herself in a jam."

She shook her head ruefully. "I don't know how you put up with me."

"I love you, that's how."

"You shouldn't, you know. I'm terrible."

I felt a quiver of trepidation snake down my spine at the weightiness of her words.

But I said, "How about you let me make that decision?"

She held my gaze when she confessed, "It hurts to see how into you Ian is. How well you two get along. How perfect you seem to fit. I shouldn't be surprised. I *was* being you when he asked me out. It still doesn't feel good."

I could only imagine.

And not totally over Ian, I could see.

I could also imagine that.

"I like him, Portia. A lot," I informed her.

She let me go and said to her lap, "I can tell."

"And I know it seems confusing, but somewhere along the line, you've fallen in love with Daniel," I pointed out.

My sister looked again to me. "I think you're right, which is the bitch of it. Because he's kind of a moron."

I started laughing.

It took her a second, but she laughed with me.

When I sobered, I ventured, "Do you know where he's at with you?"

She was blunt when she inquired, "You mean, does he want me for my money?"

I didn't verbally confirm, though I was pleased she understood that was a possibility.

She still answered, "It seems I'm going to find out."

She was correct about that.

"I can tell he's freaked. I say, make him worry," I advised. "At least a little while longer. Stay distant but don't leave. Talk to him tomorrow."

She nodded. "I think that's a good plan." Then she asked, "Do you think, truly, Lou's going to be all right?"

What I thought, truly, although I was sure Portia coming to my room in the middle of the night to find me scared out of my mind and bleeding was part of it, the thing that was bothering her the most was Lou's diagnosis.

And that said a great deal about my sister.

"I think we have to have a lot of hope for her."

"Well, at least that's something I can do," she mumbled.

"Hey," I said, feeling my phone vibrate in my pocket. "Stop talking about yourself like that. It hasn't been easy to find your way, but it seems you're getting closer to the right path and that's all you. You're putting the work in. And that's something to be proud of."

"You always had more confidence in me than me."

"And again, that's because I love you."

She gave me another funny look and my phone vibrated again.

I pulled it out.

It was a text from Ian.

Ready?

"I've got to go," I told my sister.

She didn't look happy, probably guessing who the text was from, and I didn't get how she could be with one and have feelings for him, at the same time having the same for the other, but I knew it'd be confusing.

"Go," she urged. "Will I see you again tonight?"

"I don't know, maybe not. Ian and I are having dinner in the village."

"Have fun," she said apathetically, but at the same time, oddly, it seemed earnest.

"I will. While I'm gone, don't be too hard on yourself."

"I'll try."

I could tell she'd fail, but maybe a little self-pity would do some good.

At least it seemed to be making some inroads already.

I pulled her into my arms and gave her a hug.

I then kissed her cheek and left the room.

Ian was waiting for me in the foyer, wearing his camel coat over his cardigan, a pine-colored scarf tucked through a half-fold around his neck. He was holding my duffle and purse.

Testimony to how hot he was, a man waiting for a woman while holding her purse, and he looked fabulous doing it.

But his attention wasn't on me as I approached.

It was down the hall from where I'd come.

When I arrived at him, he simply looked down at me and raised his brows.

And jeez.

We were here, already, because he didn't have to say the words and I knew what he was asking.

"Portia and I had a chat. I'll tell you on the way to the village."

He nodded and handed me my bag, then shook out my coat to help me put it on.

It was only then I noticed he also had my scarf and gloves.

Yeesh.

This man.

No hand holding as he walked me down to his Jag, which was waiting for us at the foot of the steps. No. He slung his arm around my shoulders, and I slid mine along his waist.

He held the car door open for me.

With the sun of the first cloudless day we'd had since arriving glinting against British racing green, the sleek car purred down the drive of Duncroft on its errand of taking us to the village.

And I wasn't paying attention.

But Ian and I took off on our first date when it was exactly three oh three.

Twenty-Five

THE VILLAGE

The village, called Dunmorton, was picture perfect.

I shouldn't have been surprised.

It could only be its remoteness that meant it wasn't on the tourist track. It was just that postcard pretty, with buildings made of the stone that partially fashioned Duncroft, tight alleys of mews that spoke of modernization with respect to a different era, pretty flowerboxes and hanging planters that, even in late October, were a profusion of health and vibrant color.

There was a quaint church with the requisite graveyard surrounding it gracing the swell of a knoll. The freestanding schoolhouse was adorable. And there was a triangular park in a fork in the road, which was tiny but had huge trees that shaded the benches underneath.

And there was a lot more to it than I expected.

It was bigger, almost a town (but not quite), and it was clear the locals patronized it, and it was an attraction for the farther flung, but still local.

Along with the Italian place, the Indian restaurant, the Chinese takeaway and the chippie, there was a pretty tearoom, a bustling pharmacy, a florist with tubs of blooms outside, a fresh veg stall with crates of bright vegetables, and a pub with picnic tables and a bowling green at the back.

Ian and I walked all along its lanes, stopping for coffee and a custard slice at the tearoom (both very good), wandering the cemetery (he showed me the Alcott section, it was highly populated and had the most impressive tombstones). And the spag bol I had at Luigi's was exemplary.

We left there and huddled close in the cold night air as Ian walked me to the pub at the other end.

And now we were at a booth in the back, seated beside each other, facing the quite lively pub (for a Tuesday evening), Ian with an expertly pulled pint of Guinness and me with my half pint of cider.

What I was also experiencing was something curious. Something that, even as long as I'd been living in England, was something I'd never quite understand as an American.

The class structure ingrained in those who were born to this sceptered isle.

The lord of the local manor was in attendance. And as I sat there I realized, all afternoon and evening, from passersby on the streets, to staff at Luigi's, to the assiduously unobtrusive observing of us here in the pub, Ian commanded a deference that had nothing to do with his looks or manner or money, and everything to do with the blood he'd been born with.

I wanted to say I was immune to the appeal of it, that one should always live their lives earning that kind of respect, rather than happening into it by chance of birth.

But I couldn't say that.

Although there was every possible plotline available to readers of romance novels, when something like this was on offer, the vast majority of them had the, yes, plucky heroine stealing the heart of the duke, or earl, or baron, not the man who pulls a good pint of Guinness at the local pub.

Rationally, it made no sense. All wealthy or privileged folk were not thoughtless or entitled and out of touch with the common person, all working-class folk were not slovenly and ignorant and undeserving, earning their low station by not working to get out of it.

People were people.

But the truth of it was, the amount of privilege Ian had, and the long, storied history of the family that went before him that carried the same, made him mysterious, fascinating...*other*.

That was it.

He was a rarity.

It was not that they were in the presence of their *better*.

Simply of their *other*.

A man who lived a life and came from a line that they couldn't fathom, that would never be theirs, no matter if they made a lot of money or garnered tons of fame.

The beauty of it, the thing I found extraordinary and astonishing with the extent of his wealth, the vastness of the history of his family, was that Ian was clearly not out of touch. He realized this, and in the subtlest of ways, moved to alleviate it. Eye contact. Please and thank you. Compliments to the chef. Smiles to people who passed him on the street. Stopping to scratch the head of a dog or tell a woman the baby in her pram was beautiful. Taking his time for those who wanted it to assure them that Lord and Lady Alcott were doing very well, thank you for asking.

It was no surprise I found him enormously attractive.

It was just, in that village, was where I was both terrified and exhilarated to understand I might just be falling in love with him.

At the same time, the turn of my thoughts was about the other members of his family, particularly Daniel, who had dipped his toe in this pool.

I, too, had a life of wealth and privilege. I couldn't imagine what it would feel like to turn the son of the earl's eye and take him to my bed, and what hopes I might pin on that. Only, after he was done with me, to find myself serving his house, his family and new girlfriend, and him not giving any indication he'd shared that integral connection with me.

That didn't excuse what Brittany did to me, but a part of me understood it.

And even if Daniel gave off the air of the bungling, handsome, likeable lad who would never quite grow up, I hoped Portia moved on from him.

She couldn't be a taskmaster. She couldn't keep him in line, some-thing, Lady Jane was correct, he seemed in need of having. Portia was a woman who needed to be taken care of, not the other way around.

And she deserved strength and devotion, but she also deserved someone who wasn't a bumbling idiot who careened from mishap to mishap, leaving damage in his wake.

"It happens, and you should know it," Ian said low, taking my attention.

I turned my head to him. "What happens?"

"This, while being out with me."

Okay, now I was feeling strange, in good and bad ways (mostly good) at how in my brain he was already, because I knew exactly to what he was referring.

"Truthfully, it's at its best here, in the village," he shared "Also in some senses, the town. People know us. We're not a curiosity. In London, other places..."

He didn't finish.

I did it for him. "You're *Lifestyles of the Rich and Famous*, Aristoc-racy and Secret Royalty edition."

His lips tipped up. "Something like that."

I tipped my head to the side. "Have you been with women who found it difficult?"

"No. But I have been with women who've grown addicted to it."

I pulled a face.

"Precisely," he agreed.

"I haven't escaped that, you know. Dad was a big personality. He did not shrink from the limelight. It was the opposite. And Lou's famous."

"And you're beautiful."

I shrugged and took a sip of my cider, but those words sure were nice coming from his lips.

"When you're with me, and we're not here, we'll be photographed. Often," he warned.

I drew in a breath on that.

But there was nothing for it. It came with him. I wanted him. So if we got to that point, I'd suck it up.

However, Ian needed reassuring. I knew it when he said his next.

"Portia lives life boldly. You, privately. I didn't need investigators to tell me some things. A simple Google search, even on your name, brings up more pictures of her than you."

"It might not be an everyday thing for me, but it is for Lou. In London, she can't walk down the street without people staring. Dad needed security. It's been part of my life."

"Darling, you can't duck your head and look cute trying and failing to hover in Lou's shadow. With me, it'll be inescapable."

He had an uncanny knack at saying all the right things.

If I wasn't falling for him, I'd find it scary.

"I feel I've failed after surviving multiple, attempted fake hauntings to communicate to you I'm made of some stern stuff," I joked.

"That hasn't escaped me. But our motto is eyes open, no?"

"I haven't forgotten."

"Multiple, attempted fake hauntings aside, this is our idyll. One of the reasons why I wanted you to stay here with me. When real life intrudes, things will be much different. Far more challenging."

"I'm not the type to get addicted to that kind of attention, Ian."

"I don't think you are. I think you're the type to get sick of it."

Dear Lord.

Was he sharing vulnerability?

Even insecurity?

Only Ian could make that attractive.

"How about, with eyes open, we just be in this without worrying about what might become of it? Whatever that is will happen, no matter how hard we try to shape it," I suggested.

He looked away, took a sip of his stout, and murmured, "She's wise, along with gorgeous, humorous, and achingly loving."

I pressed into him where I was settled in his side and teased, "Achingly loving?"

He was in no mood to be teased.

"You lay on the floor with Lou until the paramedics came, holding her hand and talking to her. I don't know a single soul who would do that. And I'll never forget witnessing it, Daphne. Not until the day I die."

I stared up at him, throat closed.

TOO GOOD TO BE TRUE

"You come with baggage, yes," he carried on. "But I'm profoundly aware I bring the same, and along with it an abiding inability to find my way around the rather imposing obstacle of living in complete fear that I'll turn into my father."

Well, goddamn.

One could say *that* was putting it out there.

"Honey—"

He shook his head. "No. It's there. You need to know about it. I've had a lot of women. I've always ended it. Always, Daphne. And I hope you know with me being with you, I have exceptional taste."

Yes.

Always saying the right thing.

"So there were many thrown away that a more adjusted man would have known better and kept," he finished.

It was time to nip this in the bud.

"I appreciate this heartfelt honesty. It means everything, honey. Really everything. But what you're not cyphering into this conversation is first, I'm a part of this equation, with free will and a brain in my head to make decisions for myself. And second, I'm making decisions based on the fact you haven't hidden any of what you're talking about. You've been what you promised you were. You aren't leading me on. You aren't hiding anything. It's common knowledge that women want or really don't want to grow up to be their mothers. The same with men. You've made it clear which way you swing. Attempting to observe this clinically, your awareness of it and ability to talk about it speaks volumes for you."

"I haven't run you off yet, although in a sense, I've tried. Perhaps it's testing, though I hope it doesn't feel that way, it doesn't mean I haven't been unconsciously doing it."

"And again, you know yourself," I pointed out.

He lifted his chin in acknowledgement of my words and carried on, "So prepare for this, I've never discussed any of this with another woman."

"Oh," I breathed.

"Yes," he replied.

Wow.

That was big.

I grinned at him, clasped my hands in front of me and twisted his way, leaning against him and saying, "He likes me. He really, *really* likes me."

He grinned back and said, "You're a nitwit."

I batted my eyelashes at him and returned, "Why, Lord Alcott, you say the *sweetest things.*"

He kept grinning and urged, "Drink up. Mum's very aware of my age, but she's still my mum. The roads are winding and dark. She doesn't like us driving them at night. The sooner we're home, the sooner she can stop worrying."

I took up my cider again, noting, "You're a very good son."

"She needs one decent man in her life," he murmured, taking a sip of his own drink.

But in taking mine, I watched him, struck to my core in learning something new about this man.

Mr. Honesty, Self-Own, Say the Right Thing, Thoughtfulness Personified Ian was all of this for his mother.

She had a husband with a wandering eye and a younger son who was about as deep as a bowl of water.

Ian filled in the gaps.

So yes, damnit, I was falling for him.

And even though we'd shared a lot in a short period of time, we were still very new...

But I didn't mind in the slightest.

Twenty-Six

THE DREAM

That day the wind was more like a breeze.

The sun was out.

At long last, winter had passed.

The warmth thawed the bones.

It was spring.

I heard children's laughter, and I turned my head from gazing at the moors.

He was there with them frolicking about him, on his back on the blanket, the detritus of our picnic littering the wool, our youngest gurgling and giggling as he tossed him in the air and caught him.

I saw this beauty before me, but my mind was on that morning. The vision of his dark head buried between my thighs, the love he made to me with his mouth, the rapture he gave me replete on his face in just watching the culmination of it, knowing it was him who gifted me with that, and I hadn't yet given the same in return.

My breasts were heavy with the longing for more.

Five children, and my hunger for him wasn't close to slaked.

I used to fear it.

It lived in me now, alongside my days, seen to in our languid nights, our indolent mornings.

He put our son down, rolled to his side and got up on an elbow, facing me, as if he felt my regard.

Our youngest scampered into the heather, but he lounged there, that long firm body, so full of energy always, now at rest, his gaze on me...heated.

Basking in it, I could feel the phantom touch of his fingers, his tongue, his shaft surging inside me.

And I could see the promise in his eyes of what was to come.

I knew, if our children weren't there, if he hadn't insisted, under the censorious eyes of the nannies and the tut-tutting of the staff that we were taking them out of the schoolrooms and onto the moors on this, our first warm day in what had seemed an interminable winter, he and I would still be here.

But both of us would be on that blanket.

No, I would be. He would be covering me, moving inside, gazing in my eyes, in as many ways as he could, telling me the vastness of his love for me.

I thought of that morning. Of the time after he pleasured me. Of turning him onto his back. Of pitching my leg over his hips. Of watching the carnality saturate his expression as I lowered myself on him and took him inside.

And I thought of that evening, when I would ask him to sit on the edge of the bed, and I'd kneel before him, worshipping with my mouth the long, thick shaft he used to pleasure me. Of taking it in my hand when I heard he was close and stroking it with my head tipped back in awe, in wonder, watching his handsome face as I coaxed the pearls of his love for me to jet onto my breasts, my neck.

He loved that.

He loved everything.

And I gave him everything.

There was no opening he hadn't breached without my heartfelt invitation and welcoming of him inside. There was no fantasy he could whisper in my ear that I would refuse him.

I gloried in the memory of when, not long after we were wed and he'd already thoroughly introduced me to our lovemaking, how I tempted him, teased him, pushed him beyond the endurance of his control, forcing him to snap and bend me naked over the desk in his study in our rooms, pressing oil up my backside with his fingers before he invaded it with his cock.

Oh, the growl that came when he sunk completely inside, his grip on my flesh leaving bruises I wore proudly for days. The power I had over him, and he over me, him and me, always.

I gloried in every time after, when he'd turn me to my belly and fill me there.

I thrilled in remembrance of the heady looks he sent my way at Marlborough's ball, before he secreted us to a dark parlor, pressed me against the back of a settee, sunk to his knees and dove under my skirts.

I rejoiced at recollecting the night he ordered the staff out of the dining room, swept my wedding china to shattering on the floor, my beef and sauce a stain for the maids to clean, and he'd planted me on the table at my setting. He'd tossed my skirts up, and I watched the savage intensity of his face as he held me still just at the waist and pounded inside. And I delighted in his surprise when I climaxed for him, simply with the brutality of our lovemaking. How he'd then torn my bodice down and pulled at my nipple, making the sensation last for hours, days, decades.

Eons.

Oh, how I reveled in him enjoying the fruits of our love, our children who raced to him every time he was anywhere near their vicinity with excited cries of, "Papa! Papa!" their arms stretched out for his touch.

But I cared not what it said of me as a woman, a mother, a lady, that as much as I loved this, what was ours, only ours, what we'd created, our family.

It was him.

Only him.

I had nothing in this world that was mine. Even my children would grow and leave me.

But I had him.

I would always have him.

"Addie," he called, stretching a long arm to me.

"Coming, my love," I called in return, not hesitating to make my way across the moor to my husband, my lord, my love.

Augustus.

My eyes snapped open to see only dark, and I felt the slumbering heat of Ian's body spooning the back of mine.

And I lay there, at first feeling good and right, perfectly both, the like I'd never had in my life. This faded to feeling funny, strange, right and wrong, knowing and bewildered, scared and safe.

I remembered. I remembered the dream.

No.

I remembered everything.

I remembered the memory.

I remembered that day on the moors. I remembered the morning orgasm. I knew that night I'd have another...and another.

And I knew I hadn't been dreaming.

Nor had I been remembering.

I'd been possessed.

No. That wasn't right either.

It was me doing the possessing.

I had been Lady Adelaide.

And she had been me.

Ian and I had returned earlier and gone right to the Conservatory for one last drink.

Lady Jane had stopped in to say goodnight, the first time I'd seen her in that space. Portia chose to text from wherever she was in the house to do the same. We saw nothing of Richard or Daniel.

I again started feeling off, unable to put my finger on how, but I put it down to all that had gone before, and a belated reaction to it now that I had a chance to process it after an uneventful and pleasant day.

I told Ian how I felt, though, and he decreed it was bed for me. He came up with me, and because he wasn't sleepy, told me he was going to do some work.

I got ready for bed and went to him in his sitting room for a goodnight kiss that became somewhat of a make-out session before he scooted me to the dais and kissed my cheek after he tucked the covers around me.

Now he was here, and I was here, but I'd just been *there*.

Two hundred years earlier, on the moors with my husband, *her* husband, thinking her thoughts, feeling her feelings.

And I lay there in the dark, cradled in Ian's body, for the first time since I got to Duncroft House, genuinely and completely terrified out of my brain.

Twenty-Seven

THE BRANDY ROOM

I t was not lost on me, when I slipped into the Brandy Room early the next morning, that Ian's chosen places were the most expansive in the house, outside the ballroom, gallery and foyer.

The Brandy Room dominated the end of the southeastern wing. Two turrets and the high ceilings had been used to their utmost in storing books and displaying artwork, notions and ornaments.

Including the handsome balustrade, which protected the balcony that wrapped around the room and gave access to the second level of bookshelves, and the vaulted ceilings, it held the studious grandeur of Professor Higgins's library, except it was better, because it was the real thing.

The varying seating areas and workspaces covering the floor were all fashioned to coax you to want to stay.

It smelled of leather and pipe smoke, the mustiness of old paper and the moss of Ian.

And I had no way of knowing where to begin.

There wasn't an obvious lockbox I'd need Ian's thumbprint to open.

And there had to be thousands of books. Everything from leatherbound volumes with gold leaf to contemporary novels by Grisham and Gaiman and Hornby.

I looked anyway, and I tried not to be frantic in doing it.

I'd woken very early, sliding carefully out of Ian's slumbering embrace, and slunk into his bathroom, which beyond it, did indeed have a walk-in closet, where now, I had a small section. But it was nearly full of Ian's clothes, something that made packing to go to the country very easy for him. Just load up buckets of work, and off he went.

It also laid testimony to the fact Ian was a clothes whore.

I brushed my teeth, washed my face, moisturized and swept on some powder, a hint of blush and some mascara (because, odds were, I'd eventually see him, and although he'd seen me bare-faced, when one had the power to do so, one must do what one could).

I'd then dressed and crept past his somnolent body, resisting the intense urge to round the bed and watch him sleep. His back was to me. I'd never seen him asleep. I was dying to witness it.

But it had to wait for another day.

I couldn't waste this opportunity.

And I needed to have it, without him, or anyone else in the house, muddying the works.

I needed coffee, and maybe one of Ian's cigarettes to calm my nerves after my dream-not-dream of the night before.

And I needed more.

I was meticulous in searching, but the letters weren't to be found, not in the many drawers in the many tables and desks scattered around.

So now, I was searching for Aunt Louisa's diaries.

Surely, she'd have long passages about Augustus and Adelaide, and maybe even extracts, or whole recountings of their letters to each other.

Although I'd noticed the books were strictly organized, lots of fiction on the bottom floor, and even that was separated by genre, I found no joy there, not even discovering a history section.

I wondered if maybe Ian had tucked Louisa's work away, the better to keep it from his father (because, Lord knew, Richard was pompous enough without knowing he had royal blood), and was about to alight one of the two sets of spiral staircases to peruse the upper shelves, when the door opened.

I shot straight, looking as guilty as I felt, as Lady Jane swanned in.

"Why, Daphne, good morning," she greeted.

She looked fresh as a newly opened rose.

It was cool, and intimidating, and for the first time I was around her, I considered it frightening, all of this at once.

And the fact, in a house with over one hundred and fifty rooms, she wandered into the one I was in, was just plain weird.

"Did you sleep well?" she asked, like she knew.

She knew.

Or...

Was I going crazy?

I had slept well, and part of that dream-not-dream that was creepiest was how, until the fullness of it hit me, I woke with an utter contentedness that was unreal. And when I fell back to sleep, that time dreamlessly, not an hour ago I woke up the same.

I studied her and thought, *fuck it*.

I was tackling this head on.

"Yes. Thank you. But I'm here because Ian told me about Adelaide and Augustus. Do you know of them?"

"Of course."

"Apparently, there are letters?"

"Oh yes," she said, unaffected by my question, in fact, seeming to presume it, and glided to a wall that had a recessed area cut into the books that housed a large painting of a woman in a green and ivory dress, a big hat with a dramatic plume angled dashingly atop her wig. A piece that I would not be surprised was a Gainsborough.

And of course, touching the side of the frame, the painting sprung slightly away from the wall for Lady Jane.

I stood watching as she opened it, exposing the large safe behind it.

But of course, they had a safe hidden behind a painting.

Lord God.

This place.

"We have several of these in the house," she said. "False walls are a thing in Duncroft. Has Ian told you?"

Since, in my current mood, my new knowledge of that felt creepy as fuck, my voice was croaky when I answered, "No."

"Yes. Along with the safes and other hidey-holes, servants were not seen or heard back in the day. There's a rabbit's warren of hidden corridors and stairwells to the belowstairs."

I'd seen Stevenson and Laura, etc. slip behind hidden panels in the wall, but since I didn't avail myself of what I considered the staff's space during my tour, I hadn't seen the fullness of it, outside the kitchen, so I hadn't put it together.

"And there was a time when you couldn't trust banks," she said, turning the huge dial on the big safe. "But jewels have always been jewels and money has always been money, and everyone needs a safe place for them both. Ah," she uttered as the lock clicked, and she swung the heavy safe door open. "Here we are."

She reached in but withdrew a pair of pristine white gloves. She put them on, and came out with another pair, as well as two tall stacks of letters. One tied in a fading blue ribbon. One tied in faded pink.

She came to me and set the letters down on the narrow writing desk I was standing beside.

"Is it Adelaide's letters you're interested in, or Augustus's?" she queried.

Both.

But I said, "Augustus's. His last."

"That would be this one," she told me, pulling an end of the blue ribbon. It came untied and fell away. She removed it entirely and then offered me the second set of gloves. "If you don't mind," she murmured.

I said nothing. I simply took them from her and put them on.

She handed me the letter that was on top of the stack.

"Is that all?" she asked.

I took her in.

It was like she'd come in here to do just this for me.

It was a strange feeling, and I didn't like it in the slightest.

"Since I got here, every night, I've had dreams," I shared.

"Yes. I told you. This house can be overwhelming."

"I don't think it's the house."

"What would it be?"

"An overactive imagination. Ian telling me stories. Portrait galleries and carnation bouquets. Subliminal messages."

She tilted her head to the side much like she did to Lou that first night at her dining table.

"Do you think the people who lived in a place didn't leave anything in it, even after they were gone?" she inquired.

"Do you mean ghosts?"

"Oh no, there are no such things as ghosts. Do you think you've seen a ghost?"

Was she trying to make me feel like I was as crazy as all this seemed?

"No. I think someone, or someones plural, are making me want to believe there are ghosts."

"Brittany?"

"Whoever," I said vaguely.

"The house likes you, Daphne," she stated decisively.

What.

The.

Fuck?

That certainly defined my "whoever."

I mean, I felt the house had something to say to me, but not *in reality*. Doing it by invading my dreams.

How creepy would that be?

No, it was about experiencing it.

Like Ian said, this was our idyll.

I'd never have this first time here again. And if this whackadoodle, rollercoaster of a visit meant down the line Ian and I somehow worked, that this was the start of something, something lasting, this would be my home.

That was what I meant.

Not that I needed to give the house the chance to decide if it liked me or not.

So again...

The fuck?

"I know," she said softly. "I know how odd that sounded. You must think I'm mad. But have you never been someplace, like the Tower of London, in the spot where Anne lost her head, and not felt it?"

"Anne's ghost?" I scoffed.

"The residual essence of her, and many others, who were pawns of

TOO GOOD TO BE TRUE

powerful men? It's particularly powerful, I find, in places where the heights of emotion are reached. Great sadness. Great tragedy. Great injustice. Even great happiness. In fact, walk into any church, which will have seen as many weddings and christenings as its seen funerals, and it gives a certain feel."

I'd been to the Tower of London, and other places, and felt that same thing, so I couldn't deny it.

"Maybe it's fanciful," she continued. "Maybe it's the selfish need of a mortal for some sense of immortality. But I think every creature on this earth has left something lasting. Not their spirit. Not their ghost. Not their bones. Just...*something*. And this house has stood long, and before it a castle, so it's bound to have it too."

"So you think this house is giving me dreams?" I asked disbelievingly, or I was hopeful in my disbelief.

She watched me closely for a moment before she said, "No. I think Ian loves this house and its history, even more than he knows, or will admit to, and I think he's telling you stories. Between that, and other occurrences, which I wish you had not had, you're manifesting these dreams. Doesn't it tally to you that you had a lovely evening with Ian, and then you dreamt of Adelaide and Augustus?"

Finally, she was making me feel better.

Because that totally made sense.

I'd dreamed of the moors and a picnic and the children, all of which Ian told me about, and the last of which I'd seen a portrait of my owned damned self. It was my subconscious, no matter how real it seemed, how it felt I was hearing her thoughts, like I was in her head, in *her*, *was* her.

It was just a very real-seeming dream, a sexy one, after I had a date with a handsome, sexy man, who, it was important to add, often talked about the sex he wanted to have with me.

So it wasn't real.

(Was it?)

"Yes," I confirmed resolutely. "That makes sense. But it was very real. And then you showed up in here."

"I was having my coffee in the Sherry Room. You passed by. You didn't look in to see me. You also didn't return so I found you. There's no mystery to that."

I let out a breath.

No, there was no mystery to that.

"I don't say it to scare you," she went on. "I say it because it's true. This house is overwhelming. It's large. It's filled with beautiful things. It's filled with history. It's also filled with flawed people. It has seen birth and death. You are existing in history, doing it leaving your own mark. I write in diaries too, which will be entombed in this room or elsewhere in the house for someone to unearth along the way. And they'll read my entries of when the lovely Daphne Ryan, daughter of the great retail magnate Robert Ryan, came to visit. At least."

She leaned slightly toward me and finished.

"It helps, especially when you reach my age, to know your story will live on, Daphne. I want you to learn that, especially now."

"Why 'especially now?'"

She leaned back. "Because Louella will be fine. I'm certain of it. But until you know that, until you and she are both living it, you need to understand, she lived, she'll live on, she'll be remembered, long after, quite some time from now, when she's gone."

And now she was being sweet.

"I'll leave you with the letters, dear," she bid.

And then she wafted out of the room.

I sat down and, nervous, folded open the first letter that had an elaborate "A" written on the outside.

My darling,

Right now, you lay above me, after slipping into eternal sleep.

What do I do, my dearest, without your warmth at my side? Without the promise of your laughter but a quip away?

The children are inconsolable, but I gave you my vow I'd see to their sorrow, even while hiding my own when this dreaded day arrived.

But what impossibility! What hopelessness!

Thus, I've secluded myself in Brandy, barred the door against their intrusion.

You must forgive me. I must have time.

Time to remember your gentle touch. The beauty of your eyes. The first time I saw you, your gown was blue, your eyes were bluer. The last time I saw you, that blue unfaded.

Just memory?

No.

You faded naught for me. Your hair may have grown silken with white. The creases may have formed on your hands. The lines may have burrowed around your eyes. But is this fading? It is not. You were a beauty to me from the moment my eyes lighted on you and your beauty isn't extinguished even now, when your eyes are forever closed.

You will hate me, you will be most cross when we meet again, but oh, how I wish for that time to come quickly.

Yes, please know to your soul I will see to the children. To their children. Mama and Grandmama will live on for them through me.

But when the hour is upon me, know, my bride, my beauty, my beloved, I will not fear it.

For I know it will bring me back to you.

Forever, my Addie,

Your August

THE FORCE of the sob that tore up my throat after finishing that letter was painful.

He'd written it here, in this room, *secluded myself in Brandy.*

While she was upstairs, in Cherry.

Gone.

I felt her love on that moor in my dream-not-dream. I felt his love when he was watching her while reclining on the blanket.

At least I thought I did.

What I knew was what I felt, and for the first time understanding the purity of it, I wanted it for me.

After I pulled myself together, carefully, I folded a beautiful letter that tragically was never read by its intended recipient and reached for another one.

I was on my third when my phone rang.

I gently set the letter aside, pulled my phone out of my pocket, and saw it was Ian.

I took the call.

"Hey. You're awake."

"Where the fuck are you?"

He sounded *ticked*, the level of it tweaking me.

"Downstairs in the Brandy Room."

"Why didn't you wake me?"

"Because it was early."

I heard his big breath.

Then, "Daphne, I don't wish to cast aspersions on how much I like your lovely body beside mine in bed, but the primary goal of you staying in Hawthorn with me is so I can have you close and know you're safe. Waking up with you vanished defeats that goal."

Shit.

Guilt was heavy in my tone when I said, "I'm so sorry, honey. It's morning. I didn't think you'd worry."

"Obviously," he replied tersely.

"I'm fine. Your mum got Augustus and Adelaide's letters for me."

"You're not allowed to read them."

What?

"Why?" I asked.

"Because, trust me, it's flowery, but it's dirty as fuck, and a total turn on, and I'd like to be waiting in the wings when you're done."

That made me laugh, and the release of it after the tenseness of the morning was awesome.

"I haven't read many. I think they're later and they'd slowed down by then. I'll leave the spicy ones for when you can do something about them."

"Excellent," he muttered.

"Come down and have breakfast with me. I want you to show me where Aunt Louisa's diaries are."

"I don't keep them in the Brandy Room. Dad might find them. They're stacked in the Conservatory. He never goes in there."

"Ah. Well played, milord. You're the true progeny of Cuthbert and Joan, wily with well-guarded secrets."

More muttering with, "Pain in my ass. You do remember they were murdered while engaging in one of their secrets?" Then, before I could answer, "I'll be down in a few."

"I'll pull the cord."

"See you soon, darling."

"Okay, honey."

We rang off, and I was about to finish the note I was reading before tying them up again when the safe caught my attention.

It was still wide open.

There was an internal light, which must have been activated when the door was opened.

And right now it shone on the framed photograph resting upright against the back of the safe.

The same photograph that began the picture section in Steve Clifton's book.

The photograph of the guests of David and Virginia's house party the weekend Dorothy Clifton died.

Twenty-Eight

THE BRANDY ROOM

M e, and a layout of coffee, almond croissants, late-yield berries, buttered crumpets, and tureens of jam, yogurt and oats were waiting for Ian when he arrived.

And I was prepared, including the fact I'd already downed a whole cup of joe.

"Excellent," he said when he entered the room. "Bloody coffee. I slept like the dead and I can't shake it."

Hmm...perhaps an excuse as to why he woke in such a foul mood.

I tipped my head back, and he pressed a hard but brief kiss on my lips before he threw himself on the sofa beside me and reached for the coffeepot.

"How late did you work?" I asked.

"Too late," he murmured. "Email is the bane of my existence. It feels like I can delete fifty, and a hundred more will have arrived. I should never have made investments in Asia and Australia. The time difference means I never stop receiving emails."

This was one of the myriad reasons I liked my job. It didn't really depend on email. It was about face-to-face interaction.

"How did you sleep?" he asked, resting slanted sideways toward me against the back of the sofa with one finger hooked through a coffee cup that was squat, masculine, and ivory with a wide swath of what looked like tortoiseshell, banded in thin lines of gold, stating plainly what I thought from the beginning.

Each room had a matching service.

In his other hand, he held a croissant.

"I had a dream about Adelaide and Augustus."

His brows drew down. "Is that why you asked Mum for their letters?"

"Yes. It was a very real-feeling dream."

His smile was wolfish. "Were you doing naughty things to Augustus while you were lying beside me, darling?"

"They were picnicking with their kids, but yes, Adelaide's thoughts rang the top bell on the saucy scale."

He chuckled.

I twisted to reach to the table beside me and flipped the photograph I took from the safe toward him.

His gaze fell to it, and he halted in taking a bite of his croissant.

"Where did you find that?"

"It was in the safe."

His eyes drifted there.

"Who's this?" I asked, reaching over the top and pointing to the woman in the back with her head turned toward William. The same woman who came racing down the aisle in the dream where I was marrying David/Thomas.

He leaned forward, taking a bite of his pastry, and narrowed his eyes on the picture.

He sat back again, chewing and swallowing, and blithely stating, "It's Rose. Rose Alcott. William's wife."

I nearly choked.

So I had to force out, "Rose is William's wife? Record scratch and go back. *William had a wife?*"

He took a sip of his coffee, studying me, and then said, "Yes. As you know, some Alcott men have a tendency to stray. Why are you reacting like that?"

"I've asked about her before."

"I wasn't keeping anything from you, Daphne. I just hadn't got 'round to telling you that part yet." Another downward dip of his brows. "Are you angry with me?"

I set the photo aside and didn't answer his question. Not because I was angry at him, because I was weirded out and needed answers myself.

So I asked my own.

"What happened to Rose?"

"Well, she was briefly considered a murderess after Dorothy took her fall," Ian told me. "But she was quickly discounted."

"Why?"

"Several reasons, the primary one was she had an alibi."

"Do you know what that was?"

He seemed stricken for a moment before he said, "It was her husband."

By damn.

"Tell me now, Ian, who do you think murdered Dorothy?" I demanded.

He stared me in the eyes, reading my tone, and said, "I think she became too messy for David, so he had her killed. I don't think he did the deed, like he didn't kill Joan, because he probably wouldn't be caught dead belowstairs either, absolutely no pun intended. But he needed her out of the way to marry Virginia, so he killed her. And he was sure to be out with Virginia when Dorothy was pushed to her death."

"Have you read her nephew's book about her?"

"Certainly."

That morning's tenseness came back again, a thousand-fold, especially after last night's dream, and what that might mean about the other ones besides, and you could hear the strain in my voice when I asked, "Did she die in a shocking-orange dress?"

"Although you will never fucking see them." My tone had been tense, his voice was a growl. "I have. The police took pictures of her dead body. Possibly it was about the investigation. The fact they made the rounds and are easy to find even to this day, it was more about her fame and the macabre thrill of her death. But although it's black and white, it's known she was in a custom-made Schiaparelli sheath. And it was black."

I let out a huge breath.

"What's this about?" he demanded.

"I'm having dreams."

"I know. You've said."

"They're very vivid. Last night, unbelievably real."

"You've said that too."

"I dreamed she died in an orange dress."

"Because you know of Clifton's book. But have you read it?"

I shook my head.

"Well, if you had, you'd know he came to a different conclusion than I have. He concluded Rose killed Dorothy, and that night, Rose was wearing an orange dress."

I sunk back into the couch.

There it was. That was it.

Decisions my subconscious was making about what I was feeding it were filtering into my dreams. I wasn't seeing what actually happened. My mind was making it up.

Maybe Ian was right. Maybe we needed to stop talking about this.

Even as I thought that, Ian kept talking about it.

"Clifton was fascinated by Rose, Joan, David's first wife, and Virginia, almost more so than Dorothy. But he betrays a healthy dose of misogyny, because not simply did he pin all the dirty deeds on women, even if he dedicated the book to her, he was derisive of Dorothy's lifestyle, the power she wielded through her sexuality, and looked down on her bisexuality. He even tried to argue it was vile conjecture when it wasn't. Several of her female lovers' letters and diaries made it clear she enjoyed her own sex as much as the opposite one. And he surmised that Virginia did away with Joan, which is ludicrous. Joan was tall and stately, country stock. I believe she was five eight. Virginia was petite and reed thin, as flappers tried very hard to be. She couldn't hoist Joan up in a noose from a twelve-foot ceiling."

"He thought she did the deed herself?"

He nodded. "In the dead of night during another, smaller house party. The problem with his theory was, at the time, Virginia was engaged, supposedly to a man she cared for very much. He got scarlet fever, which led to meningitis, and died. Some say she married David in a fugue state, such was her grief she lost her fiancé, this coupled with the fact she couldn't have William, her first love, and was being married off to David, who she did not love. David certainly capitalized on it one way or another. He had his ring on her finger within months of Virginia's fiancé's death, which was within months of Joan dying."

He took a sip of coffee and then kept speaking.

"Many women then had little say in who they married, especially those who were highborn. The story goes, the love sprung up between her and William, under the jealous eye of David. He was taken, but her parents put a stop to any hope William had of being with her, and Virginia with William. In the meantime, William found Rose. Virginia's parents found her a fiancé they approved of. He then found himself dead. David, in my opinion, found a way to rid himself of his wife. He approached Virginia's parents, and she was married off unceremoniously to her first love's brother, and forced to live in a house with him, and his wife, and at times her husband and lost love's paramour."

I thought of the dates on the portraits, painfully did the mental math, and they didn't add up.

Particularly when David was deposed as earl.

"Was Virginia pregnant when she married David?"

"No. They didn't have any children. The earldom was inherited by David's only child. A son he had with Joan."

Holy crap!

"So you're a product of Joan, not Virginia?"

"I am."

"Whoa. This is making Daniel and Portia and Brittany look tame."

"Agreed, however, what I'd like to talk about now is, do you always dream like this?"

I shook my head.

"Only here?"

I nodded. "I dream, and I've had a few nightmares along the way, but I don't dream every night, or I don't recall them. And I do here, and I could tell you everything that happened in them."

"So tell me," he ordered. "Now."

I opened my mouth to do that, or I'd get to it, after I asked about his current intensity, but I didn't get any words out.

Because, regrettably, he said his next.

"But also, although I doubt you can answer this query, I'd like to know why that photograph was in the safe. It's not kept there. Aunt Louisa had a meticulously organized filing system with all the history of Duncroft she kept in a room on the top floor. That picture was in it. The only reason Adelaide and Augustus's letters are down here is because I want them to have privacy, and when we allow outsiders access to our papers, I don't want them read. That room is locked. Temperature controlled. Has an expensive air filtration system, so the pictures, papers, daguerreotypes, slides and photographs in them will be preserved, as will Aunt Louisa's tireless work on them. And, for the most part, unless a historian contacts us, that room remains untouched. In fact, I think the last person Dad let in there was Steve Clifton, when he was researching his book."

Cue another chill gliding over my skin.

Before I could react to it...

"*So it's about the money!*" was shrieked from down the hall.

Ian and I sat still, listening, and I'd again tensed up.

Because that was Portia.

We heard nothing and then.

"*I don't believe you!*"

I stood.

"Don't," Ian urged.

I looked down at him. "I don't know if I can't. She's a guest in your home, Ian. At the very least, she shouldn't be shouting in the hall."

I went to the door with Ian calling, "Daphne."

But what I saw at the end of the hall had me running.

Twenty-Nine

THE CAT'S-EYE ROOM

It wasn't just due to Ian's long legs that he passed me.

He saw what I saw.

Therefore, he got to Portia and Daniel in the foyer before I arrived, and immediately wrapped his fingers around Daniel's wrist, which was attached to his hand that was curled around Portia's arm in an attempt to drag her, unwilling, back to the stairs.

"Release her," Ian snarled.

Daniel didn't move.

"*Release her!*" Ian thundered.

Daniel let go and Ian instantly shifted between him and Portia, planting a hand in Daniel's chest and shoving him back.

I rounded them and went to Portia, pulling her in my arms.

She was trembling, but I didn't think it was from fear. Instead, anger.

"I need her to listen to me," Daniel said. "She's not listening to me."

"You're old enough to know by now that when a woman doesn't want to listen, you wait for when she's ready to listen. And if she's never ready, tough fucking luck," Ian retorted.

"She froze me out all day yesterday and barely let me get a word in

272

when she allowed me to speak with her this morning!" Daniel returned heatedly.

"Are *you* listening? Did you hear what I just said?" Ian asked.

The brothers stared each other down.

Both Portia and I started when we heard Richard order, "Go, Daniel. Walk it off."

Everyone looked toward the mouth of the southeastern hall to see both Richard and Lady Jane there.

"Go," Richard repeated inflexibly, disappointment heavy in his features. "Now."

"I'm going for a ride," Daniel bit, glowered at Ian, glanced at Portia, then he stomped off toward the northwest wing.

Portia suddenly pulled from my arms while watching Daniel leave, then she whispered, "I'm sorry." She covered her face with her hands, let out a sob, and cried, "I'm so sorry!"

She then dashed to the stairs.

I headed after her, hearing Richard demand of Ian, "Follow your brother. Make sure he doesn't do anything foolish and hurt himself."

I was running up the steps but still saw Ian walking in the same trajectory as his brother.

I didn't have time to think about how that would go.

I had to see to Portia.

≈

IT WAS EARLY AFTERNOON.

I was in the Cat's-eye Room after trying for a short period of time to console Portia, who wanted to "...just be left alone, just for a little while. I need to get my head straight."

I got a text from Ian who said he was going riding with Daniel, and I hoped that went okay as I headed down to the kitchen to keep a date with Bonnie.

She ordered in pastries from a small bakery that operated out of a local farm, but she wanted to do them herself. She had some experience, but it was an area of cookery she hadn't yet fully explored. So we made some rough puff together and then moved to choux, both of which she was familiar with, but I showed her some shortcuts that still produced delicious results.

She then had to focus on lunch, but I had nervous (and angry) energy to spare, and I felt at home in any kitchen, so I asked if I could make dessert for dinner that night.

She agreed. I checked her larder. And then I created my fiddly orange custard cake which Americans would recognize as reminiscent of a Creamsicle.

Richard and Lady Jane had Dover sole up in the Viognier Room. I munched on a bacon and brie baguette in the kitchen while I lost myself in the warm comfort of baking.

Now I was in my favorite room of the house (outside the Conservatory and Hawthorn), my Kindle in my hand but my eyes staring unseeing at the cold fireplace.

This was when Ian sauntered in.

For the second time that day, I watched him throw himself on a couch, this time the one across from me, but these movements were even more beleaguered than the last.

"How is she?" he asked.

Back straight, prim and pissed, I answered, "I don't know. She was too upset to talk. She wanted to be alone. I texted her when I finished in the kitchen with Bonnie, and she said she was feeling better, and she was going to talk to Daniel when he returned."

"Well, he's returned."

I glared at him.

"I have no excuses for my brother," he said on a harassed sigh.

"I'm not angry at you. I'm angry at him."

He slouched in the couch so his head was resting on the back, lifted his hand and pinched the bridge of his nose.

I felt for him. His brother was a mess.

I was still angry Daniel put his hand on Portia in that manner. Granted, it hadn't been violent, but when someone didn't want to be where you wanted them to be, unless they were in a situation where they were possibly going to harm themselves, you didn't physically make them be where you wanted them to be.

But regardless, Daniel had far from been impressing me since I arrived, so I might be overreacting, but with cause.

Ian dropped his hand, kept his pose, but lifted his head to look at me.

"Danny and his mates have created some app."

I tipped my head to the side, still pissed and knowing nothing he could say would change my mind about his brother, but willing to listen.

"He's working his job, but he was also the one responsible for getting the funding for startup. As you know, I keep an eye on him, and I knew he was hitting people up for funding. I just didn't pay too much attention because Danny is, well..."—big sigh—"Danny. He wasn't being a nuisance to mutual friends or people I have business relationships with, and the project wasn't outlandish. They get capital requests like that all the time. But mostly, I didn't think anything would come of it and he'd eventually lose interest."

I nodded when he paused.

He carried on, "He managed to get the funding needed, and they launched a few months ago. Things are going better than expected, much better, so they've decided to expand. Too quickly, in my opinion. But it isn't my project. It has something to do with football, and they're adding cricket and rugby. They needed to hire another coder, and that takes money, and still seeing to his regular employment, he was also trying to see to that. He was burning the candle at both ends, and I think we both know this is just me relating the story, with no judgment because you won't be surprised at this, but Portia wasn't having it that he didn't have as much time for her as she'd like."

Fabulous.

But he was right. I wasn't surprised.

Ian kept going. "So she offered the money."

"God damnit," I mumbled.

Ian nodded. "She pledged to cover their shortfall and saw to that for the past two months, but now she's cut off, she can't continue because she needs what she has left to pay her own bills. They've already hired the coder, announced the launch of the additional arms of their app, dumped money into marketing them, people are expecting them to release in three months. It was already a tight timeline, and Daniel's sunk everything he has in this thing, his mates are leveraged up to their necks, they have nothing left to give. They need that money."

I said nothing.

"He showed me the app. It's interesting. It's good. Hundreds of thousands of people have downloaded it. They've tried to keep investment minimal so they don't have to dole out the dividends they want to put in their own pockets to too many shareholders. Now, he needs to find the shortfall and he needs to find it yesterday."

"So he's with my sister for her money," I remarked.

He sat forward, elbows to his knees, and replied, "No. I believe he genuinely loves her. He's actually in deep for her. Deeper than I suspected. Deeper than even he suspected. Now he's worried he's fucked it up beyond redemption, especially after this morning. He didn't ask her for the money, he swears it. He said she offered. He's upset that it won't be forthcoming. However, when she was angry about Brittany, and as such, he should never have broached the subject, at least not now, and like the imbecile he can be, he brought it up. And now she's convinced he's with her for the money."

I had nothing to say to that either.

He pushed up from his knees and announced, "I told him I'd cover the shortfall."

I was surprised at that. "It's not my place to advise you how to deal with your brother, but is that wise?"

"It's not your place?"

That was unexpected.

"Are we there yet?" I inquired.

"He's seeing your sister, you're sleeping with me. You're smart. You have a thriving business of your own. You care about her. I hope you care about me. Isn't that what relationships are? You have each other's backs and advise when it's needed?"

I went cautiously when I asked, "Are we in a relationship?"

"Aren't we?"

We'd had one date, but had spent so much time together, it amounted to fifty (maybe an exaggeration, but it felt like that). And we'd slept together repeatedly, but we hadn't yet had sex.

It was wild, but there was only one answer to his question.

We absolutely were.

"Okay, then, allow me to rephrase," I requested. "Is that wise?"

He seemed appeased and shared, "The app is good. I negotiated a percentage. I'm giving them more than they need so they can hire a further coder and launch on time. He's written a business plan. He shared the basics of it with me, and they have a solid, if risky and aggressive marketing strategy. A plan for future growth, even beyond these new arms they're launching. This is a serious project. It isn't a lark. He's using words I've never heard him use and he's using them correctly. And it sounds like he's worked his ass off to make it happen. This has potential to be rather successful. I'd be proud of him if he wasn't acting like such a bloody idiot."

I returned my gaze to the fireplace, but I looked back to him when he stood.

"I'm not going to state his case. If he patches things up with Portia, he'll have to put the work into convincing you he'll treat her right. But he did promise that would never happen again and it wasn't his intention to hurt her. Just get her to listen and stop her from shouting at him in the hall."

"That's stating his case, Ian."

He gave me a rueful smile.

"What can I say?" he asked softly. "Danny's my brother. The ride was long, we talked about a lot of things, but mostly Portia. I think he's considering marrying her, and he's an absolute mess, worried like fuck between this and Brittany, he's blown it."

I knew Ian loved his brother, but I hoped he'd blown it.

Although it sounded like Daniel had put his attention to something that was worthwhile and he was finding his way, both of those two bumbling along the right path, however right, they were still bumbling, didn't give me good feelings.

"I had barely any breakfast," Ian said. "And no lunch. I'm going to go down and get something to eat, then I need to find Dad and set some time to talk about the handover of the earldom."

"In other words, it's shaping up to be another sterling day for you, baby," I murmured sympathetically.

He made no comment to that. He just came around to my couch, bent to me and kissed the top of my head.

Then he said, "I'll have to see to some work after that. But I'll see you at dinner?"

"You will."

"I'm looking forward to whatever you'll be wearing."

I decided just what that would be, and I smiled.

He let out a low growl at my smile, a growl I felt in several places in my body, before he moved to the doorway.

He stopped before he used it and turned back to me.

"I feel shit he didn't come to me from the very beginning. Worse, because I knew he was looking for funding, but I dismissed it not really knowing what it was or how dedicated he was to getting it done. He said he wanted something of his own, but I know I've made him feel like the idiot he acts a lot of the time, and he believes in this project, put everything he has behind it, time and money. Thus, he didn't want me throwing what I thought about him in his face."

My poor baby.

"This isn't your fault, Ian," I assured him.

"I miss my brother, and I've convinced myself he's the whole of the issue that's keeping us disconnected, not seeing I might have a part to play in it."

I didn't think it was the time to remind him that his brother thought he'd stolen Ian's girlfriend and then went about the effort of parading that in his face with this long visit. That same girlfriend he now might be considering marrying. And all the other rash decisions Daniel had made after reckless actions he'd committed, one of which meant I still had plasters on my temple.

Instead, I said, "You're a good brother for thinking that way. And now it seems this visit for us both has us reconnecting with our siblings in good ways, so let's just go with that."

He did that affectionate chin lift I loved so much, this time with a lovely, soft expression on his face, before he left the room.

Thirty

THE BED

I gauged it was time to emerge out of the closet (literally) after I gave it some time when I heard the shower turn off.

I was in there when it went on, struggling with my dress in an effort to get ready for dinner, and I didn't think it was prudent to walk through the bathroom with the possibility of seeing a naked Ian in it. If the rest of him was as good as his chest, I'd jump him for certain, and we'd never make cocktails in time.

I'd come up earlier to prepare for dinner to find to my surprise that Ian was not in the room, but even if I was surprised, I took advantage.

So now I was fully dressed, rather than slipping my black Louboutin pumps on and putting on my jewelry in the sitting room as I'd planned to do, and he'd had plenty of time to get decent, I walked into the bathroom.

And stopped dead.

Ian was bent over the basin, finishing shaving, hair wet and combed back, wearing nothing but a towel.

I started salivating immediately, and it got worse when he turned his head to look at me, razor suspended, and he froze, the look in his eyes driving so deep somewhere pleasant, I grew wet just staring at him.

I was in a strapless black shift. Simple but form fitting, with cleavage at the top that I considered not too much, not too little, just right.

Ian apparently agreed.

I paired this with my ruby pendant, earrings and bracelet, and the pumps. I'd left my hair down but curled it so it was big and bouncy, and the deep part I put into it, I thought, made it a sexy sweep across my forehead, serving double duty to hide my wound.

And I'd gone full smoke with the makeup.

I'd done all of this as kind of a joke, considering our banter, but also because it made me feel wanted and pretty, how Ian reacted when I decked myself out.

It appeared my efforts worked.

Too much.

We both stood immobile, staring at each other, the steam in the room seeming steamier at what was passing between us.

An undeniable pull. A need.

The wave of an obsession neither of us quite realized we were riding until we found ourselves at the crest of it breaking, in that very moment, right there.

"If you take one step toward me," Ian said in a rough voice that was like a physical touch, "we're going to be late for cocktails."

I knew with all that was happening with the people in that house, I should head to the sitting room. We needed to be at cocktails.

I didn't head to the sitting room.

I took one step to Ian.

He snatched up a towel, wiped the remaining lines of shaving cream off his face, and then he was on me.

We were kissing, lots of tongues, lots of hands, while Ian backed me out of the bathroom.

He had the zip down on my dress in the doorway and we paused just long enough for Ian to shove it over my hips. It fell to my feet, and I stepped out of it, still kissing him as he guided me to the bed.

I tripped over the lip to the dais, and with an arm around my waist, he lifted me up, then I was on my back in the bed with Ian on top of me.

Oh boy, that felt good.

Heaven.

He went up on a straight arm, angling away from me, his eyes devouring my body in my strapless, black lace bra and matching cheeky panties.

His gaze came to mine, dark and hungry.

So fucking hungry.

At the same time, we attacked.

And then it was an out-of-control tussle. I wanted to touch every inch of him. Taste it. He wanted the same. It was consuming. It was beyond anything I'd ever experienced. The bed didn't exist. His room. The house. The planet.

It was just him and me.

Planting my pump in the duvet and bucking, I managed to turn him to his back, then I straddled him. He tried to push up, but I shoved him back down then went at him with my mouth. His strong jaw that smelled deliciously fresh from his shave. His throat. Collarbone. Down to his nipples.

I'd made it to trace my tongue along the groove of his hip muscle and was tugging at the towel when I cried out because he yanked me up.

I landed in my hands and on my knees over his head.

His hands were on my hips, yanking me down on his mouth.

He sucked on me over my panties then shoved the gusset aside and there was no barrier between his lips and tongue and me.

Oh God.

Oh *yes*.

I straightened, arched back and rode his mouth, and Lord God, what he could do with it should be illegal.

I was close, dear God, I was right there, when he pulled me off, tossing me to my back beside him.

"Fuck," he clipped. "Be right back."

He kissed my rounded belly and left the bed, leaving me muddled and desperate, but he was Ian. He did as he promised. He came right back.

He pulled a condom out of his wallet, tossed the wallet on his nightstand and then yanked off the towel.

I whimpered and squirmed at the sight of his big, beautiful dick standing proudly from a thick nest of dark hair and then squirmed more as I watched Ian expertly roll the condom on.

Finished, he reached in and ripped my panties down my legs. It was a smooth move, forceful and expert, and it left me with my heels still on and the area between my legs quivering.

I opened for him, even as he shoved my legs apart, and in one elegant, powerful surge, he was there, and he was inside.

I let out a big gust of air at the heady feel of my body accommodating the size of him, never having taken so much, never having a connection feel so right, and I was concentrating on that before I realized he wasn't moving.

I focused on his face to see he was smiling down at me.

A beautiful smile.

Exquisite.

This man, I was correct.

He was perfect.

I melted underneath him as I rounded him with all my limbs, because I'd never had that either, that smile and what it communicated in a time like we were sharing.

We were here. We were as together as two people could be.

And he was happy.

I moved a hand to rest it on the side of his face.

"Make love to me," I whispered.

His eyes gentled and his hips moved, and it started in that vein with kissing and touching and gazing lingeringly into each other's eyes.

But then Ian slid his hand between us to work between my legs, and things changed. In the end we panted in each other's mouths, his strokes bold and aggressive, my touch frantic and demanding.

My orgasm was crashing toward me. I raked my nails down his back, he groaned, his head angling back, and I cried out as I exploded.

My world blanked in a bright light that rushed out, placing me in a cocooning dark, experiencing nothing but Ian's cock moving inside me.

I felt him unleash then, thrusting powerfully, and with an animal sound that rolled from deep in his throat that I felt driving up my sex, he followed me.

His lips worked my neck as we both came down, and finally, he lifted his head.

"Alas, my love, that was my only condom," he announced.

Happy, outrageously, unencumbered and completely happy, I clutched him to me and let out a giggle.

"Well, someone is going to the chemist first thing in the morning," I replied, still chortling.

He grinned and then lingered over kissing me, doing it until he naturally slid out of me.

"Don't move," he whispered, exiting the bed.

He went to the bathroom to deal with the condom and came back out, still naked, to find I'd moved. I was sitting at the edge of his bed, the pumps I was still wearing spiking into his duvet, holding my legs to my chest.

For a moment, he did nothing but stand there in all his naked, powerfully masculine glory.

When he moved, he unfolded me deftly by putting his hands to my waist and tugging me deeper into the bed, then falling on me so I wrapped him up in me again.

"Did you not hear the part about one condom, darling?" he asked drolly.

"We'll see if Daniel has any."

"We won't right now, and you in nothing but a bra and spike heels, with just-been-fucked hair and a bruised mouth waiting for me like that in my bed means I need inside you again."

"Really?"

He shifted.

I felt him semi-hard.

My eyes got big. "I'm impressed."

"You need to be good, at least until I can raid Danny's stash."

"I'm surprised you don't have one."

"I don't usually go out on the pull in Dunmorton."

Yes, but he'd had girlfriends.

"If I brought a woman here, I'd come with provisions," he explained, again reading my thoughts. "I don't fancy going into the local chemist in the village to buy prophylactics. It'd be news that reached the coast in an hour. And it's rare I bring women here."

I didn't want to talk about his women. I didn't want to do anything but cuddle and then fuck again.

However...

"We need to get dressed. I need to make sure Portia is all right," I stated glumly.

Ian looked about as happy as I was about that, but he knew the veracity of it. That was why he kissed me, then pulled me with him off the bed.

He zipped me up this time, which was good. Getting that zipper done the first go was a contortionist's nightmare. He put on a gray suit. We both fixed our hair.

And then we went to dinner.

~

WE WERE BACK in Ian's room, against the wall right beside the door, we hadn't even made it fully into the room.

And he was fucking me.

My skirt was bunched at my waist, the bodice of the dress pulled down, and he was driving inside me, slamming me into the wall, with his eyes tipped down, watching my breasts bounce in my bra to his thrusts.

"Ian," I moaned.

His gaze shot to mine and darkened in a way I spasmed around his driving cock.

He wrapped his fingers around my jaw and dragged his thumb hard across my lips before he forced it between them.

I sucked.

Hard.

He watched, eyes heated, and growled, his other hand clenching my ass and lifting up so I was no longer standing with a leg wrapped around his thigh. He was holding me up with the aid of the wall and my arms around his shoulders, pounding inside, his gaze not leaving my mouth.

He slid his thumb out, swiped it across my cheek, drove his fingers into my hair and clenched so it tugged at my scalp.

I whimpered.

"You were goddamn made to be fucked by me," he announced, his voice thick, gruff, amazing.

"Yes," I breathed, holding tighter with my legs wrapped around his ass, tensing and relaxing the walls of my sex to his rhythm.

He dropped his forehead to mine and groaned, "Christ, your cunt, darling. Bloody beautiful."

"Keep fucking me, Ian," I begged.

His eyes so close, we could give butterfly kisses, he said low, "Never going to stop."

"Never," I whispered.

"Never," he vowed.

We stared into each other's eyes, feeling those words, both of us. I knew it. Feeling it deep into our hearts and guts and the marrow of our bones.

We did this until, abruptly, he ordered a commanding, "Come."

To my shock, instantly, I came, pushing my face in his throat and gasping.

He sunk his teeth into my shoulder, causing a further ripple in my climax as he snarled his own.

Needless to say, it was after dinner.

Everyone loved my orange cake, even Richard, who took his first bite and couldn't hide his pleasure.

Naturally, Daniel had a hefty stock of condoms, and both brothers slipping out while we had after dinner drinks in the Wine Room, he gave Ian and I a full box.

And dinner had been a disaster, but we all pretended it wasn't.

Ian waited until our breathing had slowed before he lifted me off his dick and set me to the floor, but still kept me pressed into the wall, which was good. My legs were happy stands of jelly.

I still had my arms around him, and I slid one hand into his thick, soft, luscious hair and said, "I must say, milord, you're one seriously great fuck."

His head twitched, and then he pressed me into the wall and roared with laughter.

~

I LAY on his bed on my belly, naked.

Ian slid a hand up the back of my thigh to my ass as he slid his lips up my spine.

Then at my ear, he noted, "You're upset she forgave him."

Earlier, when Ian and I left our room to belatedly go to cocktails, we ran into Portia and Daniel coming out onto the landing from the northeast hall.

Portia looked like me, swollen lips, hazy gaze, in happy la-la land of a recent orgasm.

Daniel looked relieved and chuffed with himself.

I'd claimed my sister by hooking my arm in hers and walking down the stairs with her in front of Ian and Daniel.

"All right?" I whispered.

"We talked it out," she whispered back and then gave me a radiant smile.

Daniel might be an idiot, but he was good at one thing, I could see.

But...*damn*.

We hit the Wine Room to Richard's hypercritical glance that we were all twenty minutes late.

And one could say that Portia and Daniel might be over it, but I wasn't, nor were Richard and especially Lady Jane. She was so cool to her youngest son, it could have frosted the windows. And Daniel might not be the brightest bulb in the box, but it was so obvious, even in his bad-boy-forgiven mood, he didn't miss it.

The night went to shit from there, alternating between awkward silence, stilted conversation, and Lady Jane doting (in her own inimitable way) on Ian, me as well as Portia, to the obvious exclusion of Daniel.

But at least we'd scored a box of condoms from the affair, of which we'd already used two.

I turned my head to look at him. "I don't want to talk about Portia and Daniel."

"Just assure me you're okay and I'll drop it."

God, I liked this guy.

"I'm okay, baby," I told him softly.

He kissed me.

I turned so he could do it pressed up against me.

When he released my mouth, he said, "So about these dreams," while skimming his hand down my side, then up, and curling it to trail his knuckles along the side of my breast.

I shivered and replied, "Well, Augustus might have been frolicking with his children, but Adelaide was reminiscing about him going down on her that morning, fucking her on the dining table, eating her out in a dark parlor at some ball, and fucking her ass bent over his desk in the study in their room."

He grinned and rubbed his thumb over my nipple.

I trembled and pressed tighter to him.

"You have quite the imagination," he remarked. "But I can confirm he went there. How he referenced it was 'your darkest secret, my dearest, that I treasure and only I can invade.'"

Sounded like it.

"Have you memorized their letters?"

"Pretty much. I discovered them when I was fifteen."

"Randy, teenage soon-to-be earl, I can see it," I quipped.

He smoothed his hand down my belly and curled it in at his destination.

I gasped.

"Randy, indeed," he murmured.

I rocked into his fingers.

"Leg over my hip, sweetheart," he ordered.

I did as told.

"I want you in my mouth," I requested.

He put his lips to mine and said, "Later."

"You can do this while I do that."

"I wouldn't be able to concentrate."

"Ian—"

He kissed me, effectively silencing me.

He then concentrated.

And I was glad.

∾

WITH A LOW GRUNT, Ian came in my mouth.

I swallowed it down.

I licked and sucked him until the tension left his body, and I looked up at him sprawled on his bed, head and shoulders to the headboard, gaze hooded and on me.

Lord of his manor.

Lord of me.

I was powerless to his pull, and I didn't care.

I went up, kissed his furry belly, then he moved down as I kept crawling up.

He wrapped an arm around my waist, rolled us both to turn off the only light we'd turned on, then he yanked the covers over us.

I snuggled into him, half on, half off, cheek to his pec.

"If you dream, I want you to wake me, sweetheart," he murmured.

"Okay," I mumbled in return, kinda hoping to go back to Augustus and Adelaide, if only for ideas.

He gathered my hair and started twisting it in a coil between my shoulder blades.

"You give great head," he noted.

I smiled a sleepy smile into his shadowed chest. "Every girl's dream compliment."

"Every guy's dream girl."

He didn't just mean enjoying me going down on him.

Again with saying the right thing.

"I want you again," he said quietly. "Does that frighten you?"

I tipped my head back even if I couldn't see his face in the extreme dark of the room.

"Are you up for that?" I asked with no small surprise.

Truth, I didn't know if I was. I was fucked out.

But with how Ian fucked, I could find it in myself to rally.

"No. I just think it interesting I've come four times tonight, I'm no longer eighteen, I'm shattered, but I still want more."

"You like me," I reminded him.

"I do. I already did. Though, I had no idea how talented you were with your mouth and pussy, so one could say I like you quite a bit more now."

I laughed softly, righted my head on his chest and hugged him closer.

His hand tightened in my hair, and I tensed.

"You're extraordinary, Daphne."

The words were low and fierce, and I felt them in my womb and heart.

"Ian—"

"If you didn't know that, you do now. And it's my job to make sure you never forget."

Oh my God. He was killing me.

"Shut up," I demanded, voice husky with feeling.

"All right, darling. Sleep."

I turned my head to kiss his chest and closed my eyes.

But I could feel my lips were smiling.

Though I didn't see, as both Ian and I drifted into sleep cuddled together under his duvet in his bed, the time on his tablet said it was three oh three.

Thirty-One

THE CONVERSATION

We were seated in black velvet wingback chairs in a void. No walls. No color.

Just black.

And she was wearing a spangled, black sheath, her legs crossed, her T-strap shoes with the arched heel were covered in jet beads, and a black beaded band was tied around her forehead.

Her platinum hair and the alabaster skin of her bare arm, therefore, shone stark against the abyss we were occupying, and she was examining me, like she needed to decide whether to deem me fit or not, for what I did not know.

"I wouldn't let a little nothing like Rose be the end of me," Dorothy Clifton informed me.

"I know. It was David," I told her.

She made a scoffing noise. "I wouldn't allow a man to be the end of me either."

"Then what happened? Why were you up there? Did you fall?"

"I can hold my drink, girl. I did not fall."

I was losing patience.

"Okay, then *what happened*?"

"Why do you care?" she demanded.

"Why wouldn't I?"

"I'm not what's important that's happening in that house."

"You *were* important," I returned.

She rolled her eyes then again focused on me. "I know *that*."

"So, tell me, what's important in the house?"

"Him. You."

It was my turn to roll my eyes, and I returned. "I know *that*."

One side of her lips curled.

"I think I like you," she decided.

When I said nothing, she went on.

"There's more going on in that house."

"Tell me something I don't know."

"Okay then, the flute. You don't know about the flute."

I was confused. "The flute? The one in the Music Room?"

She nodded. "Tell Ian about it."

"No, *you* tell *me* about it."

"It has to be Ian."

Whatever.

I wasn't playing this game anymore, not even in my dreams.

But while I had her...

"Why'd you do it?" I pressed. "To Virginia. To Rose. You're a sister. Why did you sleep with both their husbands right here, in this house?"

"Virginia didn't care I fucked David. Virginia herself had no interest in fucking David and so, when she could avoid it, she didn't. And William didn't care about Rose's feelings."

"He should have. She might not have been the love of his life. But she was his wife."

"Tell that to him." She made a mock-horrified face. "Oh no! You can't! He's dead. Like me."

"Stop it and tell me," I demanded.

She suddenly looked forlorn. "I was in love with him, you know."

"Which one?"

Now, she made a face of distaste. "Well, not David."

"William?"

Back to the forlorn when she shared, "It wasn't true. What I said. He did care about Rose. It hurt him every day, knowing she'd wake up to such pain, having to live in that house with her husband and the woman he loved."

"So if you loved him, why did you make things worse for him and Rose? For Virginia?"

"The heart wants what the heart wants," she said softly.

"And David?"

"A grave mistake. I thought William would wish to let her go. Force her to divorce him. I could make him forget Virginia. I could make it so he could leave that house. He could see his patients, and I'd see to paying our bills. Divorce wasn't done in our time, not often, but he would have taken care of her. That was the man he was. She would have been seen to. And she'd have had a far better chance at finding someone to make her happy. But his pesky scruples were always at the fore."

"Not enough he didn't fuck around on his wife."

"Darling," she drawled, sweeping a be-ringed hand down her body, the diamonds on her wrist twinkling in light that came from nowhere. "Not many men could say no to me."

Ian would.

"Yes, he would," she whispered, reading my thoughts. "But he's not many men."

"True," I muttered.

"To answer your question, most men, not yours, though there's an element to it with him as well, it's inescapable for them, are ruled by a certain appendage, just one of them, the one they think is so important. And when they want to bury it into something someone else is enjoying, they do the most delightful things."

"So it was all a game," I remarked.

"I lost," she said.

She sure did.

And I was sad about it because, even if the games she was playing were far from cool, she was kind of a kick.

She then looked beyond me, into nothing.

"Our time is done. She's calling," she told me.

I turned to peer where she was looking.

There was nothing.

I turned back to Dorothy.

She and her chair were gone.

I looked again the other way, and suddenly I was standing.

She was twisted to me, another woman, wearing a long, heavy cream dress with light-blue silk lining the wide, voluminous bell sleeves. It was edged at the hem with an embroidered ribbon of blue and gold. The close-fitting sleeves of her underdress were pale yellow. The belt hanging around her waist was a cord of light blue.

Her hair was unfettered, but blue ribbons had been woven through it around her crown and they trailed in the abundance of the golden-honey blonde hair tumbling to her waist at the back.

She held a hand to me, and her lovely face was filled with excitement.

"Come." She rounded her hand impatiently. "Come! He's arriving."

She didn't wait for me.

She started running, through the arched gate made of thick stone and connected to walls spanning the area.

I ran after her.

A group of horses rode over the moors.

Gaily, she turned back to me, laughing and still running.

"He's arriving!" she cried.

A horse broke from the pack, kicked into a gallop, heading straight to her.

"Watch out!" I yelled.

I thought horse and rider would hit her, but with the chainmail of his armor clinking, the big, fair-haired warrior on its back just scooped her up and planted her in front of him.

The horse trundled to a stop and then started sniffing at the brush and heather as the two on its back went at it, full embrace, straight-up make-out session, mouths fused, hands roaming all over each other. He even cupped her breast over her dress and squeezed.

He broke the kiss and told her, "We've a guest."

"She's me," the woman replied.

He peered down at me with a severe expression.

He looked back to his love.

"So she is," he agreed.

She cupped his face in her hands. "You came back to me."

"I always will." He looked down at me. "I always will." Then to her, his expression shifting to something infinitely loving, he said one last time, "I always will."

She smiled at him.

Then she turned to me.

"Welcome home."

❧

I OPENED MY EYES, feeling like I had the night before, content and sated.

The Dorothy thing I got.

But, whatever.

The second part, who knew?

It was a dream, but it wasn't a bad dream or a weird dream.

It was kinda sweet.

So I snuggled back into Ian, who was now again spooning me, and I returned to sleep.

❧

IT WAS LESS me bouncing and a whole lot more of Ian fucking himself with my pussy as he pulled me up and down on his dick, and I stared down at him lying on his expensive, pristine, white sheets, looking hot and delicious.

With that vision a feast for my eyes, feeling him impale me, those were all I needed.

My head fell back as my climax threatened.

"No, you don't," he growled, pulling me off him.

I cried out in protest as he positioned me on my hands and knees, facing his sitting room. He got behind me and powered back in.

I instantly genuflected, but he twisted a hand in my hair and tugged, grunting, "Up, Daphne."

I got back up to my hands, feeling my breasts swaying, my body rocking to the violence of his thrusts.

"Ian," I warned.

"Don't come."

"Ian!" I exclaimed.

He spanked my ass and demanded, "Don't fucking come, Daphne."

The sting of that spank, his cock.

I couldn't hack it.

"Oh God," I moaned.

He let my hair go and grabbed my hips, slamming me back, the pads of his fingers digging in so hard, I knew they'd leave bruises, and I gave zero shits.

"Baby," I begged.

"No," he denied.

"*Baby*," I whimpered.

He shoved his thumb up my ass and ordered, "Now."

Splintering before him, I came apart and was surprised there was something left for him to keep fucking as I came, and he fucked my ass and cunt, and I kept coming.

Finally, pressing into me, he pushed me off my hands and knees to my belly, pulled out of my ass, planted both of his hands on my cheeks there, immobilizing me. He then fucked me even harder as I gasped and clenched, and took it happily before he gritted his release, buried deep but pushing like he could get deeper.

He collapsed on top of me.

When I had the capacity of speech, I noted, altogether breathlessly, "You're a damned bossy lay."

He nuzzled my neck. "Like you don't love it."

"Just observing."

He chuckled, the noise slithering over my skin in a satisfying way, then I gasped as he abruptly not only pulled out of me, but me out of bed.

His hand in mine dragging me toward the bathroom, he said, "Shower."

I smiled and replied.

"Okeydokey."

"After we do that, I have to return something I've stolen."

Now at *that*, I entered the bathroom grinning.

Thirty-Two

THE CONSERVATORY

I sat in the Conservatory with one of Aunt Louisa's diaries in my hand, my legs crossed, my foot bouncing.

Update.

Clearly Portia and Daniel were in the throes of an epic make-up fuck session. They hadn't been seen all day, and to my text to ask her how she was, Portia replied, *Talk later, Daph. We're busy.* She ended that with five kissy face emojis, and if I didn't get the gist, an eggplant and a peach.

No.

My sister would never grow up.

I found that heartening and worrying at the same time.

Ian and I would be doing much the same thing, however, if he hadn't set a late morning meeting with his dad to talk about the title handover.

So, although I'd read a bit of what Louisa wrote about Lord Walter and Lady Anne (and yes, they seemed a true love match), mostly my mind was on what was happening with Ian and his dad.

It seemed he'd been gone forever, and I was worried.

When he emerged from the plants about two minutes after I had that thought, I was no less worried.

"Looking at your face, I don't really have to ask how it went, but still, I'm going to ask. How'd it go?"

"For shit," he bit off, going directly to the drinks cabinet and pouring himself a stiff whisky, not bothering with ice.

He came to me with glass in hand, folded onto the couch beside me and immediately turned to his cigarettes.

"Since nothing is going to change, except a title, I don't know how it could go poorly," I noted carefully.

He lit his smoke, blew out a plume, sucked back some whisky even though it was barely noon, and said, "I didn't say things weren't going to change."

"Uh-oh," I mumbled.

He turned to me. "As this event began to loom, I pulled the covenants and read them. So did my solicitor. I had ideas. Obviously, I would carry them out after Mum and Dad were no longer with us, but I had ideas."

"Like what?" I asked.

"Like the days of house parties and hundreds of people attending a ball are long gone. Mum entertains. Small dinner parties. Huge bashes for all our birthdays. Her annual Christmas party. They host a Bonfire Night out on the front lawn every November for the village. And she and Dad throw a massive event every five years for their wedding anniversary."

That would seem sweet if they were a happily married couple who were truly celebrating their love through the years.

As it was, it was more than a little sad that Lady Jane would go through that motion.

"Okay," I prompted when Ian said no more.

"But I'm sure you've noticed on the first two floors alone, three wings of eight go entirely unused. The whole second floor is constantly deserted. It's a waste."

I couldn't disagree.

"So, I thought a veteran's convalescent home," he continued. "Or an orphanage. Or a psych hospital. There aren't enough good mental healthcare facilities in this country."

I was staggered.

And more than a little alarmed.

"You're going to turn Duncroft into...something not a home?"

"Daphne, for the most part, only two people live here. The trust that runs this place is embarrassingly enormous. It'd have to be to use the interest to run this house and provide for the staff and family in it. But the years of something like Duncroft existing for the purpose it was built, to lord, quite literally, over the location where it was erected, are long past. This is a relic of another time. But it could be useful."

I couldn't disagree about that either, even though it gave me a funny feeling it wasn't mine to have.

And this explained how things went awry with his dad.

"I can imagine your father definitely wasn't thrilled with that news."

"I didn't share it. The covenants are ironclad. As long as the Alcott trust can support this house, it's to be used only as the home of the earl. It cannot be deeded or gifted, not even to someone inside the family, should I, say, want to give it to Danny. It can be used for no commercial enterprise. It is for the earl's personal use only."

"Okay," I repeated slowly.

"So I had another idea. And *that* is what Dad got pissed as shit about."

"What is that?"

"I told him, he and Mum are secure. I had no plans to take over, move home from London, change anything, even their allowances, unless inflation or the market forces me to. That went over fine. He seemed relieved."

He took a drag of his cigarette, another sip of whisky, but didn't immediately return to talking.

So I pushed, "And?"

"Then I told him Duncroft was a part of the British legacy. That it wasn't just the earls who made it great. The people who built it, the people who staffed it and took care of it, the things collected along the way that are in it, were a testimony to this country. And as such, it should be enjoyed. And although I assured him it wouldn't be through the National Trust or English Heritage, both of which he respects, in a manner, since they safeguard and maintain some of Britain's greatest structural, historical and natural locations, he still looks down on those who own their properties and allow visitors through those organizations. Nevertheless, I told him I'm opening the house for two weekends a month to ticketed tours to show people this legacy."

Another sip and puff and he continued.

"I went on to share the monies received from ticket sales would pay for the tours, and anything left over would be invested in the village. The school or the ambulance service, or no-interest loans to farmers or businesses who might fall on hard times."

"That doesn't sound so bad."

And it didn't.

It sounded like a great idea.

"Dad doesn't agree. He was livid. His face got so red, I thought he'd have a stroke. He told me, over his dead body would Duncroft be open 'to just anybody.' Regrettably for him, he has no choice. I told him he could absent himself for two Saturdays and Sundays a month from ten to the last tour ending at four, or hide in his room, which would be part of the house not opened to the tour, obviously. Alternatively, he could move out and live somewhere else."

I stretched out my lips in a non-verbal *Eek!*

"This isn't Buckingham Palace, darling," Ian replied to my expression. "We don't have an army of staff and host heads of state. Even at Christmas, when Dad's brothers and sister and my cousins come and stay for a week, only twelve bedrooms are occupied, outside direct family. We have forty-three bedrooms in this house."

"Yowza."

"Indeed."

"So, he lost it," I deduced.

"He did," Ian confirmed. "We have three Turners, one Gainsborough, and Persephone was sculpted by fucking Bernini."

I knew those were Turners and Gainsborough!

And Bernini?

Whoa.

"There's a magnificent piece by Ansdell in the Hunt Room in the northwest wing. That room's never used because we no longer hunt, so no one even sees it, for fuck's sake," he groused.

I reached out and curled my hand on his knee.

299

"You don't have to convince me, honey," I said soothingly.

It was like I didn't say anything.

"Houses like this are museums and they should be treated as such. History is fascinating, rich and full of beauty and tragedy. What's left of that in this house is just beauty. And it should be shared."

"You won't get an argument from me."

He seemed to realize he was no longer stating his case to his father and fully focused on me.

"I'm sorry, sweetheart. I'm annoyed."

"I can tell."

He watched me closely. "Do you think it's a good idea?"

"Yes," I said readily.

Ian grew silent, but he did it still watching me.

"You love this house," I said quietly. "You want other people to enjoy it. You want it to be useful. I think that's beautiful." I gave his knee a squeeze. "He'll come around."

"He won't. He'll hate it every weekend there are tours. He'll never change his mind. He'll bitch and hand me shit about it, and he'll never forgive me for doing it. But I'm doing it."

At that, I fell silent.

After another sip and drag, he suggested, "Let's stop talking about it."

"If that's what you want."

His eyes fell to the diary. "What are you reading?"

"About Walter and Anne. The derring-dos of Duncroft's only pirate and the damsel who waited breathlessly in their home for him to return from his adventures on the high seas. I think I dreamt about them last night. Though, their outfits were wrong. They were all medieval."

"You dreamt again last night?"

I nodded.

"Why didn't you wake me?"

"It wasn't a bad dream. It started with me having a conversation with Dorothy, however. She was kind of a hoot."

It appeared he didn't like that. "A conversation with Dorothy?"

"Yes. We were sitting in a void, and she told me Rose didn't kill her, neither did David." I grinned. "I think she liked me. At least she told me so. Then again, as you well know, I'm highly likeable."

Ian didn't shift with my mood.

He demanded, "What else did she tell you?"

I sobered and shared, "That she was in love with William. That he hurt for Rose. It all faded away and I was in the bailey of a castle, just inside the gate. Some woman, presumably Anne, ran out to meet her husband when he came home from somewhere."

"The castle was gone before Walter's time. Dismantled. Some of the stone was used to build Duncroft. He and Anne lived in this house."

"I know. The dream got it wrong."

His gaze coasted to the drinks cabinet, down to the whisky in his hand, and he muttered, "I don't like these dreams."

"A lot is happening in my days. It stands to reason my mind would process it at night."

He looked back to me. "Who did the Dorothy in your dream say killed her?"

I shrugged. "She didn't. She said it was more important for me to worry about what's happening in this house. I didn't disagree. Oh, and she told me to tell you about the flute."

He grew very still, and his words were vibrating strangely when he asked, "The flute?"

I didn't like his affect or his tone, so it was hesitant when I said, "The flute up in the Music Room, on the second floor."

He remained perfectly still for a long, tense moment.

Then he surged forward and crushed out his cigarette, his glass went down with a crash, and he was up and moving.

Heart already racing, I got up and followed him.

Thirty-Three

THE MUSIC ROOM

I had to run.

Ian took the stairs two at a time.

To keep up with him (which I didn't, entirely), I was winded when we hit the second floor and he took off at a jog to the end of the northeast corridor.

He threw open the door to the Music Room and prowled in.

He stopped and looked around.

I turned to the table where the flute had been.

But now it was gone.

My stomach twisted.

"Where's the flute, Daphne?" he asked.

I pointed. "It was there. On that table. It's not there anymore. But I swear, Ian, it was there."

He moved to the table, bent at the waist, inspected it closely.

Then, without a word, he took off, and I again followed.

He entered another room, this one, the furniture was covered with big sheets.

He pushed on a wall by the door, I heard a click, a panel came away, and he pulled it open. He reached in and yanked on a string, and a single, stark hanging lightbulb inside turned on.

False wall.

Hidden passageway.

Shit.

Okay, it seemed like he was going to enter the belly of the beast, and I was not one with the idea.

Before I could share that, he pulled out his phone, engaged the flashlight and went in.

I didn't want to, but with the way he was acting, I also didn't want to be alone. So I followed him.

It was dark in there, musty, the stair treads covered in a well-used, faded runner and dust. There was a small landing, it was a very narrow flight of stairs, up and down.

He went up.

Expelling a breath, I went after him.

We came out on the top floor, in the hallway. I'd never been up there. The ceilings were lower, and the décor was nice, but a whole lot more utilitarian.

He walked down two doors and across the hall where there was a keypad next to the door.

He punched in a six-digit code, I heard a click, and he opened the door.

He walked in, switching on the lights.

I went in after him.

The air was very fresh in there, and it was cool.

It was a big room, lots of old-fashioned filing cabinets. There were some paintings stacked against the wall. A table holding crates with photographs, cardboard tabs sticking out, the numbers of years scrawled on the tops. Carefully stacked and labeled boxes. There was an old pair of riding boots in a glass case on a table. A mounted saber. Both with tabs stuck to them with a lot of writing on them.

And there were two humming units that looked expensive sitting in the corners, I knew, filtering the air.

Boy, Ian wasn't wrong. Louisa did put in a lot of work, and it was meticulous.

Ian was staring at the line of filing cabinets across the room between the two windows that had their curtains carefully shut to hold back any rays of sun that might fade anything.

On top of them was the flute case, currently shut.

A now familiar shiver snaked down my spine.

He pointed at it. "That was open in the Music Room downstairs?"

I nodded. "A couple of days ago. I saw it. The velvet inside is blue." I took in an unsteady breath and asked, "What's going on, Ian?"

Ian moved to the filing cabinets and carefully inspected the flute case and its surrounds.

"Ian?" I pressed.

He straightened and looked at me.

"This is my great-grandfather's flute," he said.

"Okay," I replied.

"Joan and David's son."

I started trembling.

Ian kept talking.

"He stopped playing it as a child. It's said he stopped playing it the day after Dorothy Clifton died. He'd loved it and was good at it, some even contend he was a prodigy. He practiced all the time. But the day after she died, he never touched it again. He put it in here himself when Louisa was doing her work and confiscated this space for cataloguing. And that flute never leaves this room."

Fucking.

Hell.

~

WE WERE all gathered in the Music Room, including Lady Jane, and a fucked-out looking Daniel and Portia.

We were waiting for Richard.

This, an audience demanded by Ian, who I'd trailed after when he went down to the Robin Room, pounded on the door and ordered them to get their asses up to the Music Room, then he texted his mother and father.

Ian had returned to prowling, this time back and forth across the room like a lion in a cage.

Understandably, this didn't give me glad tidings.

Lady Jane was watching him carefully, and her concern was evident. Daniel and Portia appeared foggy and confused.

I was silently freaking out.

Richard arrived, demanding, "Why in bloody hell have I been commanded to the second floor?"

"Close the door," Ian ordered tersely.

Even Richard had nothing to say in the face of his son's mood. He shut the door and fully entered the room.

"The maids, they clean up here...what? Once a month? Every other month?" Ian asked his mother.

"I don't know. Christine makes the schedule," she answered.

"Text her. Ask her. Now," Ian demanded. "I want to know when someone was last in this room cleaning."

She pulled her phone out of her cardigan pocket.

Ian waited until she was done, and we all waited with him.

After she put her phone hand down, he said, "Over on that table, it's faint, but you can see the dust pattern is disturbed. Something was lying there. Now it isn't."

I was too far away to see from where I was, but since I'd seen the flute, there and gone, I didn't need to look.

Daniel went over to look.

"Don't touch anything," Ian warned.

Portia asked, "Oh my God. Has something been stolen?"

"Moved," Ian told her. "Out of the History Room and into here, then back out again. I don't know when it was moved in, but it was moved out sometime in the last..." He looked to me.

"I don't...it's all cobbling together, but I think three days?" I told him.

"Three days," Ian said.

Portia turned accusing eyes to Daniel. His face got red.

"It wasn't Brittany," Ian decreed. "It was taken from a locked room. She doesn't have the code. No one does, but Stevenson, Christine and members of this family."

"Stevenson would never," Richard proclaimed.

"Christine neither," Lady Jane said.

"Someone's been in this house and they're moving shit around," Ian told them. "A photograph that was also housed in the History Room was put in the safe in Brandy."

Lady Jane went white as a sheet.

Richard's face got splotchy.

As they would. I didn't see much else but what looked like more historical papers in that safe, but if someone was availing themselves of secured spaces, it'd cause anyone alarm.

"Why would someone do that?" Daniel asked.

"That's what I'd like to know," Ian replied. "And I'm going to find out. So, before I embark on that, if anyone in this room has anything to say..."

He trailed off but didn't take his attention from Daniel when he said those words.

Daniel morphed straight to fury. "You think it's me!"

"You and Portia started this week at home with games," Ian pointed out.

"I don't know anything about any History Room!" Portia exclaimed.

Ian didn't even look at her.

He raised his brows to Daniel.

Daniel exploded.

"Fuck you, Ian! I may have fucked about and screwed up, but I'm not stealing things from my own damned house."

"Nothing has been stolen, at least not that we know. And I'll be doing an inventory with Stevenson as well," Ian told him. "They've been moved."

"And why would someone do that?" Lady Jane repeated after her son, still looking more than mildly troubled.

"I don't know that either, but the photograph was the one of everyone at the party where Dorothy Clifton died, standing in front of the house. And the thing that was in here, but is now not, that Daphne saw, was great-grandfather's flute," Ian explained.

"That's just odd," Lady Jane murmured.

"It's more than odd. It's what Brittany tried to do, attempting to frighten us, playing on the ghost stories. Except whoever this is, is not only doing it under our noses. They have the codes to secure rooms and safes."

"We're changing all the codes," Richard said instantly.

"Yes, we are," Ian agreed.

And then he carried on.

"And until we figure this out, I don't want any of the women in this house alone and always carry your phone. Mum, take the women somewhere then text me where you are. Dad. Danny. You're with me."

And on that, he marched out.

Thirty-Four

THE PORT ROOM

Lady Jane, Portia and I were in the Port Room.

Portia and I were watching mindless TV. Lady Jane was playing solitaire on her phone.

It had been hours since I told Ian about the flute. Lady Jane had asked for lunch to be served up there, and then she'd ordered up popcorn, which Portia and I had decimated.

Now, it was getting late, and my relief was extreme when, finally, the door opened and Ian, Daniel and Richard walked into the room.

"I've talked to Bonnie," Richard said immediately to his wife. "We're going to have an informal dinner in the Viognier Room this evening."

"Good idea," Lady Jane replied, putting her hands to the arms of her chair and pushing up to her feet. "When?"

"Same time. Seven fifteen," Richard told her.

I looked to my phone.

It was six forty-four.

"I'm going to freshen up," Lady Jane murmured, and swept from the room, Richard following.

"Me too," Portia said, hopping up. "See you at dinner," she bid, and she, too, left, Daniel trailing.

308

Ian came in and folded beside me.

I grabbed the remote, turned off the TV, then shifted my attention to him.

He raked his hand through his hair, which made some of it fall to his forehead in a way that made him appear boyish and cute, a new look to be listed among many I considered my favorites.

I had no time to enjoy how adorable he looked.

I demanded, "Talk to me."

"We found things," he told the coffee table. He turned to me. "A lot of things."

My blood ran cold.

"What things?"

He settled deeper into the couch and twisted my way.

"To preface this, quite a bit of the top floor is storage. If we didn't have so much room to put things, the Alcott family as a whole over the generations would be considered hoarders. Aunt Louisa's work could be so thorough because she had generations of Alcott debris to sift through. Over the years, very little was discarded."

"All right," I said.

"Therefore, we found a pair of velvet slippers sitting beside the bed in the Jacaranda Room. They're monogrammed. WAA. William Albert Alcott."

"Oh shit," I mumbled. "Was that his room?"

"It was," he confirmed. "And in the wardrobe of the Dahlia Room, Rose's orange dress, the one she was wearing the night Dorothy died, was hanging there."

Good Lord.

I shivered at learning that and asked, "Was that Rose's room?"

He nodded. "Yes." Then he carried on, "In the Smoking Room in the northwest wing, we found a pipe that isn't usually there, next to a silver Cartier pen. I don't know about the pipe, though I've seen pictures, and he did smoke one, but the pen is David's. It's also mono-grammed. It's usually kept in the Whisky Room, and it's still used. However, Dad didn't notice it missing."

Ulk.

"Okay," I prompted.

"There was also a framed picture of Joan, holding a baby, who would be George, my great-grandfather, set in the nursery."

How disturbing!

"God," I breathed.

"And an old-fashioned lady's hat, presumably Virginia's, was sitting on a sofa in the Morning Room in the northeast wing. To my under-standing, that being where she spent a lot of her time, it being situated all the way across the house from the Smoking Room, where David normally spent his time."

"Fuck," I said.

"Indeed," he agreed. "We've made the decision to leave everything where it is. In order not to raise suspicion, we only alerted Stevenson to help us search. He's going to discreetly inventory the house. He'll recruit Christine to help. The rest of the staff won't be told what's happening. I've forwarded staff records to my investigators in London so they can be thoroughly researched, and one is coming up tomorrow to have a look at things. I'm afraid I'm going to have to find a way to sneak her in. I don't want any of the staff to know what she's doing."

"So you think it's an inside job."

Another nod. "We also inspected the staff corridors and stairwells. They don't clean those and some of them, which should not be in use at all, those being the ones to the storage areas, have had the dust on the treads unsettled. Only those who live or work here know how to navi-gate that network of passages through the house. At the very least, no one would have access to them unless they were in the house, specifically the primary entry points, those being belowstairs. It has to be someone who has access and understanding that they're there to be found...and used."

"But how do you explain them knowing the code to the History Room and the combination to the safe?"

"All the safes have been checked. Nothing moved into them, nothing missing, except what you found in the Brandy Room. We've changed the code to the door to the History Room. There are several safes that have been switched to electric. Those codes have been changed too. The ones that require combinations will be more difficult. But to answer your question, I can only deduce that someone was around to watch someone else entering the codes or combination. That's the only explanation because, in working with them to search the house, it's apparent Dad, Daniel nor Stevenson are behind this."

I asked the million-dollar question, even if I knew he had no answer.

"And why would someone be doing this?"

"Your guess is as good as mine," he told me what I already knew on a sigh, then pushed up slightly in the sofa. "It doesn't add up. All of these areas are not used by family. Only staff would find these things. Also, why lay out the flute, then put it away? I discovered from Stevenson that those rooms aren't cleaned except once every four months. No one has been in them for ages, except you."

"I wandered the house on my own on the tour. And Brittany saw me up there, maybe she mentioned it to someone else. It would have been easy for someone to see me. Perhaps they knew I saw it, and then moved it, the better to freak us out that it was there, then gone."

"Perhaps," he allowed, then asked, "Did you see any of these other things?"

I shook my head. "I can't say my perusal of those rooms was thorough, though. And I didn't look into many rooms on the southeast wing. It was clear from seeing a few those were family quarters, and I didn't know whose was whose. I didn't want to pry."

He nodded yet again, slumped back into the couch, rested his head on the back and did the pinching of the bridge of his nose thing.

Watching him—and being pissed on his behalf that this was happening in his home, a blatant mindfuck, a violation—it suddenly hit me.

"I saw a girl coming out of the Whisky Room. I haven't seen her before or since."

He turned his head to me. "A girl?"

"She was wearing what Jack and Sam wear during the day."

"Ah," he murmured. "One of the cleaning girls."

"Cleaning girls? Don't Harriet and Rebecca and Laura do the cleaning?"

"They do," he affirmed. "It's beside the point, but it's my feeling we're grossly overstaffed. I've often seen people idle. Something I've since discussed with Stevenson, and he agrees. Therefore, Brittany will not be replaced, and it's likely, when one of the others leaves, they won't either. A cost-cutting measure that won't affect the running of the house but will allow me to increase Mum and Dad's allowances, which might assist me in making them more amenable to the other changes I intend to make."

I thought of Harriet hanging in the kitchen, eating toast, and nodded, but outside noting how very much Ian paid attention, and cared about his house and his parents, I said nothing.

Ian continued, "But those women's responsibilities tend more toward the personal. Making beds. Tidying bathrooms. Doing laundry and otherwise seeing to our clothes. All in the spaces that we use. They clean other areas as well and serve. But this is a big house. We own a great many things. And it's our responsibility to see that it's all cared for and maintained. We don't need a leak in the roof and water damage that we don't know is happening. Wood will get dry and crack if it isn't oiled. Chandeliers collect dust. There's silver that needs polishing and china to be fetched, depending on which room it's being called for."

I cut in to have my suspicions confirmed. "So each room has its own set of china?"

"Not exactly, but some of them do. Pearl. Rose. Which makes sense, Rose being the room of the lady of the house, Pearl being the room where we most entertain outsiders. But for the most part, the service selected matches the room it's being taken to. I've seen it all, though there's so much of it, I don't have a register of it in my head. However, masculine rooms have masculine services, and vice versa. I suspect favored rooms of members of the family over the years had services purchased for when they used those rooms. It stands to reason. We've had centuries to collect it and money to burn on those kinds of things."

"Hmm," I hummed.

"Tell me about this girl," he ordered.

"There's not much to say. Slender. Brown hair. She avoided my eyes. I thought she was shy. Now I wonder if she was somewhere she wasn't supposed to be."

"If you've seen her, she was. The cleaning girls use the staff passage-ways almost exclusively. They're also not full-time and, it's my under-standing, they have the greatest turnover. Usually, they're young women who go to the college in town. When they earn their degrees or certificates, they move on."

If they used the staff passageways exclusively, then they'd have healthy knowledge of them.

"Do you know them?" I asked.

"Not the current ones, no." Another heavy breath from Ian and then, "I'll make a call. Set my investigators into diving into those two first."

"Do they live here?"

"I don't know. Some of them have, as a benefit of their employment. No skin off our noses. We have the room. Some don't. I don't tend to pay attention to the intricacies of the running of the house, and not only because I don't actually live here."

He did pay attention, but perhaps not to that level.

And...

Okay, time to get into the creepiest part.

Or, the second creepiest part.

"Tell me about these passageways."

His expression grew understanding, and he assured, "There isn't an entry into my room."

At least there was that.

"Okay, but tell me about them anyway."

"Honestly, if someone had the time and energy, it wouldn't be hard to know about them, though, it'd take quite some effort. In past times, they were used often, and not just by staff. It was a running joke that a husband could run into his wife, both of them on their way to an illicit liaison."

"Members of the family?"

"Yes, most definitely, but also guests. If they wrote about them in letters or diaries or told others who did the same, anyone who was looking into Duncroft House could piece them together and use that information to move around this house, in large part, sight unseen."

Not...

Good.

"Is there an entry into the Whisky Room?"

He shook his head. "No."

"This is fiendish, Ian," I remarked.

"I know, darling. But it'll also be figured out. My investigator can lift fingerprints, evaluate the footprints in the dust, thoroughly check the house, including the staff rooms. Stevenson already has a plan to keep the staff occupied so she can do so without being seen."

Although he'd mentioned her before, that time it struck me.

"Your investigator is a woman?"

"The one coming is. I have two. The other one will remain in London and look into the staff and assess outside motives for someone to pull this shit." His aura changed, and he said, "Don't drink anymore Amaretto unless Stevenson gives it to you himself."

I felt gooseflesh glide over my skin when I asked, "Why?"

"I've been feeling sluggish the last few days, including right now, and it isn't just having half a whisky at midday. Daniel and I had a talk about how this started, you mentioning the flute from your dream, and he told me Portia has been dreaming too, and she seems more highly-strung when she's here, sometimes even erratic. I grew concerned, mentioned it to Dad. He's a G and T man. After dinner, he goes for port or brandy. Mum is G and T too, and after dinner brandy or sherry. He says they're not experiencing any changes, though he's noted that Mum seems more vague than normal."

"So what are you saying?"

"I asked Daniel, and Portia likes to unwind at the end of an evening with an Amaretto too. She's been drinking it from the decanter in the Wine Room. Daniel also isn't experiencing this, but outside lager, he's a vodka man."

"Are you saying...?"

I couldn't bring myself to finish it.

"I'm saying I've noticed a marked change in your affect when we finish the night with a drink. You seem you, but hazier, and you yourself have told me you've felt off. Then there are your dreams, and the things that happened to you are frightening, your responses natural to them. But Daniel mentioned in passing that Portia was very upset by how scared you were with what Brittany did. She said, you might not enjoy horror movies and scary things, but she's never seen you like that." He gave me a ghost of a smile. "She said you're always together."

It was nice Portia thought that of me.

But he still wasn't saying outright what I thought he was saying.

So I asked after it. "Do you think someone put something in the alcohol?"

"I think I told Stevenson to carefully switch all of it out but keep what's been decanted so my investigator can take samples of it. The new will still be out for anyone to slip something into it, so Stevenson knows if we call for a drink, he'll have bottles locked away and will serve us directly from them."

One could say there was no way to express how I really, *really* didn't like this.

Which was why I tried, perhaps hopelessly, to offer, "They're just dreams, honey, and some woman touched my face in the pitch dark wearing a dead woman costume in the middle of the night. My response to that wasn't unwarranted."

"I don't disagree," he returned quietly. "But I'm a busy man, Daphne. A lot on the go all the time, and people who depend on me. I enjoy it greatly, but it can get hectic and consuming, so I work out daily to clear my head and have time to narrow focus on one thing so I can be fresh when I see to the rest. Bottom line, I stay fit. Occasionally, I can go at it hard, and that can be exhausting. But this is something else. For instance, I don't sleep heavily. You leaving me in my bed is something I'd normally notice. I had no idea you'd gone. Didn't feel a thing."

More indication of why that had tweaked him so much.

Oh, and the reason he had such a fantastic body.

"Stevenson won't mind," he continued.

"It's not that. It's just...in all this, the idea that someone may be drugging us..." I shook my head. "The rest of it is not cool. It's freaky and weird and scary as hell. But that's something else entirely."

"Well, if my intention was to terrify the occupants of a house, drugging them so their reactions to what was found were more pronounced would make sense."

"And again," my voice was high-pitched, "why would someone do that?"

Ian reached out and cupped my jaw. "And again, it's in hand. We know it's being done. We're looking into it. It has to be an inside job, so it isn't as if the cast of characters is infinite. We'll sort it, put a stop to it and deal with them when we discover who they are."

I drew in a shaky breath to calm myself, then let it out.

Ian watched me do that and then, taking his hand from my face, he said irately, "I wish I could take you to London now. But regrettably, if we leave, the jig might be up and the person doing this might make their escape."

"Ugh," I grunted, and it was me sagging into the couch.

Ian gave me a few moments to get over it, before he queried, "Do you need to freshen up for dinner?"

"Probably," I mumbled, though I had no idea what that meant.

That said, I'd only done the basics after our shower. Our thwarted plans were to spend the day in bed after he had his chat with his dad. Ian had returned my vibrator, which boiled down to him showing me where it was. It was still charged up and waiting.

I could slap on more makeup.

Ian pushed out of the couch and held his hand to me. "Up."

I took his hand, he pulled me out of the couch, and we left the room.

IAN NUZZLED me after we both finished, his big body covering mine in his bed.

Eventually, he rolled off, taking me with him.

He dealt with the condom, we both put our pajamas on, and we headed back to bed with me saying, "I'll duck out and buy some more protection tomorrow. No one will care if I do it."

He agreed by saying, "It'll get you out of the house. And I need to go meet the investigator in town."

He moved to the bed, but I went to the windows.

"Darling?" he asked after what I was doing.

I was opening the curtains at the two windows that were in his bedroom area.

I turned to him. "I just...I don't usually have a problem with it, but I don't want the dark. Will you have a problem sleeping with the moon shining in?"

"Not if it'll mean you'll sleep easier."

He was the best.

I opened the curtains and met him in bed.

Ian turned out the lights and tucked me close.

Even after very nice orgasms, neither of us found sleep quickly.

But when I finally slept, for the first time in Duncroft, I did not dream.

Thirty-Five

THE BRANDY ROOM

Late the next afternoon, Portia and I returned from our outing.

We'd gone into the village for lunch at the tearoom, and Portia also stocked up at the chemist when we popped in there.

We then took off to the ruins of a local castle, which were not exactly close. They were on the coast. They were magnificent, the view even better, and it felt good to breathe the sea air and tramp around outside.

It had been a nice day, but when we were nearing the house, she said, "I love Duncroft. It's stately and beautiful. But even though I know why Daniel asked me to stay, I don't want to go back there."

I understood what she was saying.

"Daniel wouldn't let anything happen to you," I assured.

At the same time I said this, what I didn't say was I *hoped* that was true.

"I know," she mumbled.

"You two seem to have worked it out," I noted.

"He's very sorry, and he promised he was going to sort himself out. The way he did, I believe him."

And I hoped yet again, this time there was something to believe in.

But I said nothing. She seemed content, and we'd had a good day together, getting along the entire time.

I didn't want to rock that boat.

"It's nice Ian offered to help Daniel with the money," she ventured. "I probably shouldn't have done it. Or at least not offered it myself, then quit my job."

No, she shouldn't have done that.

"Well, it's handled now," I remarked.

"Ian to the rescue again," she mumbled, but in glancing at her, she didn't seem downhearted about it. Just like she was noting the truth.

Even so, I told her, "He loves his brother, Portia."

"Daniel worships him, you know. Part of that whole app thing is about making Ian proud of him that he did something smart. Made a load of money."

"Yes, but Ian has mentioned Daniel is competitive."

"He is, but it isn't about that. I don't think he thinks he can become a billionaire from an app. He just wants to make his own way. Especially with Ian soon to inherit everything. And I'm not making a thing of it, just stating fact, but I know how it is to depend on a sibling for money. He's a man. It's worse for them."

Right or wrong (read: *wrong*), that last part was the truth.

However, until then, it hadn't occurred to me to what extent Daniel might be concerned about the state of play with the title change.

I'd have to give Ian the heads up about that, though I didn't relish it.

It seemed to all fall on him to make everyone feel okay about things he had no power over, and they'd all lived their lives knowing it would happen.

But then, in the end, he got the title and Duncroft.

It just proved nothing came without a price.

"Is Daniel upset that he had to rely on Ian to swoop in and save the day?" I inquired.

"Not at all. I thought he would be, but he's excited about Ian being involved. Knowing what's going on. This is probably because Ian was impressed with the project. He told me Ian seemed pleased, and that meant a lot to him. He was ticked at first Ian thought he was behind what's going on at the house. But then, with what we pulled at the beginning, it wasn't surprising. Daniel saw that. And then Ian involved Daniel in searching and keeps asking him what his thoughts are and stuff like that. I can tell, it makes Daniel feel important that Ian seems to be taking him seriously."

Well then.

Good.

That said, since she brought it up.

"Why *did* you pull that shit with me?" I asked.

"You hate scary movies, and Duncroft is famous for its supposed ghosts. I know you. I knew you'd look into it before you came. I was messing with your head. I thought it would be funny." She took a breath and said, "It wasn't funny, and I feel like a total bitch I pulled that on you. Daniel was angry with me. He wasn't thrilled with the idea in the first place. He thought it was immature. He said you'd never like him now."

I didn't say anything to that.

She turned to me. "I hope you know I truly am sorry. And I know you're not sure about him, but Daniel really wants you to like him because he really likes me."

Gah!

"I'll give him a chance, honey," I allowed.

"Yay!" she cried happily.

"I'm trusting him to take care of you during all this," I warned.

"Oh, he will," she promised.

Yes.

Gah!

Shortly after that, we rounded the drive and parked at the foot of the steps.

Stevenson met us at the door.

"Welcome home, ladies," he greeted.

Home.

Portia and I exchanged glances.

She looked excited.

I was mildly freaked that he didn't have to say it.

It felt like home already.

"Daniel is in the Bordeaux Room. Ian is in Brandy," he went on to tell us in a genteel way where we were ordered to go next.

We loaded him up with our bags, scarves, gloves and coats, and we headed down the southeastern hall.

It was sweet when Portia stopped outside the Bordeaux Room to give me a hug.

She'd enjoyed our day too.

She then ducked in, and I walked to the end of the hall.

The door was open, so I went in.

"Hey."

Ian was sitting on a sofa, surrounded by papers and a laptop.

He looked up, his face grew soft, then he ordered, "Here. Kiss."

Lord of the manor, indeed.

I moved to him, bent to give him a kiss, and with his hand sliding in my hair, he changed my intention of a quick peck to a lot of tongue.

When we were done, while I recovered from the kiss, he shuffled his papers around so I could sit next to him.

"Do you want me to order you something?" he asked. "Some tea?"

"No. I'm good, honey."

"So what did you two get up to today?" he asked.

I wanted to know more about what he did, but I told him, "The village. Lunch at the tearoom." I grinned. "Provisions."

He grinned back.

"And we went to the ruins."

"Ah. Lovely," he murmured.

"It was. Now, your turn."

"I met Kathleen, my investigator, in town. She's come and gone. I worked out upstairs. And now I'm here."

I'd seen the rather large, very equipped workout room that had been installed on the first floor in the northwest wing, which was more bedrooms, mostly children's rooms, and that workout room, so I asked after it. "Do you work out on the first floor?"

"Yes."

"Did you put that room in?"

"Yes."

Another grin from me, which Ian returned.

"Did Kathleen find anything?"

"She lifted a great many fingerprints. Took some pictures. She can compare what she lifted in staff rooms to what was found in storage rooms. It might come to nothing. This has all been very clever, carefully planned out, it would be an uncharacteristic mistake for whoever is doing it not to wear gloves."

For certain.

"Did she take the samples of alcohol?"

He nodded.

Good.

"What did you think about the ruins?" he asked.

"Amazing. Beautiful location. A castle there would have been stunning. It's too bad it's mostly fallen down."

"It went into disrepair after Alice married Wolf, which is understandable. She was the last of that line, and she came here."

She came...

Here.

"Pardon?" I asked.

"Alice was the only child and daughter to Eustace, the last lord of the castle that is now the ruins. Eustace had an ongoing feud with Torsten, who was the liege lord of the fortress he built here. And as they did in those times, they settled their feud by marrying their children to each other, Alice to Wolf."

"His name was Wolf?"

"Mm-hmm," he said. "It was a common name back then, but apropos. He was reputedly a fierce warrior and a favorite of King Stephen, often called upon to fight England's wars, not only the civil ones of that time, but also with David of Scotland. The earldom didn't exist back then, but essentially the beginning of it was Torsten, however mostly Wolf. For his efforts, Stephen awarded him with great lands and wealth. It was the beginning of the endowment of Duncroft. Loyalty, bravery and smart allegiances in the ensuing centuries increased our wealth and lands, earned us an earldom, and here we are."

I couldn't stop staring at him.

So he asked, "What?

"I told you I dreamed of a man and woman from medieval times, and you haven't mentioned them yet. All of my dreams have been permutations of stuff we've discussed. But not them," I said shakily.

And not Rose, or David's wife, Joan, now that I was thinking about it.

However, I could have run into both those names in researching, and I just didn't pay attention to them, even though I thought that was thin.

That said, I'd never heard word of Alice and Wolf.

"Darling," he soothed, "there are perhaps a dozen paintings and tapestries depicting Alice and Wolf all over this house. There's one where she's standing, wearing an ivory gown, reaching up to him wearing armor while he's astride his horse in the Wine Room. They're in the tapestry hanging in the Turquoise Room. Though small, they're in the top, left corner with a castle behind them. She's again in an ivory dress, he's in armor, and they're surveying all they owned, which is the rest of the twelve-foot tapestry depicting the moors."

I was almost certain I hadn't noticed them in that tapestry, but maybe I had.

I'd naturally seen the picture in the Wine Room. However, I didn't put it together because I didn't know it was a picture of Alcott ancestors. I just thought it was simply a picture someone liked along the way.

It certainly was pretty, and I'd had a good look at it.

"It's what you've seen, what you've heard, how your brain is sifting through it," Ian stated firmly. "It's nothing else. Enough is happening, don't frighten your own self."

"Yes," I agreed. Then I queried, "What's their story?"

He gave a slight shrug, but said, "Apparently, she hated him on sight. He thought her a shrew. But they married anyway and had five children, only three of whom survived. Though, this was in the twelfth century, so there isn't much left of them now to know what their lives together were like. But back then, it wasn't unusual in arranged marriages for the spouses to live relatively separate of each other, but still find the means to procreate."

I thought of the picture in Wine.

Admittedly, I also thought of my dream and how the woman seemed so happy he was home.

So I asked, "They didn't get along?"

"Again. I don't know. In what I've read, it's more about Wolf's talents on the battlefield, his single-minded brutality there, the fear he engendered because of it, his unwavering loyalty to the king and the rewards he collected from that, than about his marriage. He also had a reputation for being a brute off the battlefield. His courtly manners were famously seriously lacking, but Stephen didn't mind, as long as he kept winning conflicts."

And again, I remembered the picture in the Wine Room.

"If they didn't like each other, then why were they painted like they were great loves?"

"Because people romanticize the past," he explained. "That painting was commissioned hundreds of years after they were gone. It wouldn't do for the two people who essentially started our legacy to be portrayed as shouting at each other."

True.

"I can't see many medieval maidens waiting breathlessly for their brutish husbands to come home, and she was no shrew in my dream," I muttered.

"Daphne, it's all manifestations of what you've seen and heard in this house. They're simply dreams, nothing more," he chided. "There's enough to be worked up about. You don't need to create things."

"You're right," I allowed. "I'm just on edge."

"We all are. But Stevenson has made a large dent in his inventory. He's noted nothing else has been moved and nothing is missing. The storage rooms aren't locked. If someone was paying attention, it'd be easy to watch when someone else entered the code. The safe in this room is a concern. It isn't often accessed, and it'd be hard to see which numbers were selected on the dial unless you were very close and watching closer. But everything will be explained. And soon. My investigators don't fuck around."

"Okay, baby," I whispered.

But I'd noticed he'd been getting pissed as he talked, and he stayed that way.

Therefore, I asked, "Have I made you angry?"

He shook his head. "This situation makes me angry. Mum's good at keeping her emotions hidden, but she's failing. She's distressed. And she's a mum. That's worse because she's distressed we're all distressed. Dad is taking it like a declaration of war. His personal property has been violated. He's furious. Danny is not thrilled with keeping Portia here if there might be danger. I'm the same with you. And we don't like what it's doing to Mum and Dad. I truly hope it's sorted and soon. I want to know who's done it, but more, I want to know why. You called it fiendish. It's that and morbid and cruel. Dad can be an ass, but outside this house, he's the courteous, if haughty, country gentleman. Mum's never harmed a soul in her life. Brittany notwithstanding, Danny's the kind of guy who's everyone's best friend. It doesn't make sense."

"When people do things like this, it never does," I reminded him. "If you don't have it in you to harm someone, you can never understand why someone could do it."

"Mm," he agreed.

"Is dinner in the Turquoise Room tonight?"

"Yes. Dad wants everything to go back to normal, and Danny and I agreed. It also makes sense. If we suddenly start huddling together in the Viognier Room or elsewhere, it'll give it away."

"So, do we have time to fuck before dinner? Or do you have to work?"

That alleviated his mood.

"We absolutely have time to fuck before dinner."

"I bought three boxes of condoms."

Surprising me, he frowned.

"I made sure they were your size," I teased.

"I'm scrupulous about protection, Daphne."

"I've noticed."

"And I'm healthy."

I got what he was saying.

"Oh," was all I could think to reply.

His voice lowered. "If it's too soon for you, I understand. But if you're taking something—"

I cut him off, stating, "I'm on the pill."

"Your choice. No pressure. I just want that on the table."

I knew men got more out of the experience when they went in ungloved.

But this was something different.

Ian Alcott, soon-to-be-earl of Duncroft couldn't go around taking chances at being baby daddy to all his lovers. He was rich, but there was a lot at stake. Not just his legacy, and his money, but his reputation and the reputation of soon-to-be Earl Alcott.

That he would trust me to protect both of us said a lot.

"Oh shit. I'm going to get all weepy because you want to fuck me and trust me to take care of us."

He smiled. "Darling."

I jumped up and offered him my hand. "Let's go fuck. We'll see how we roll. I'm positive I'll get over it when we're in bed."

He took my hand only after he rose from the couch, and said on a wicked grin, "I'm positive too."

Thirty-Six

THE PICTURE

The next morning, I was in the bathroom and all was right in the world, because Ian had woken me by going down on me.

I loved what he could do with his cock, but he was a master with his tongue.

I'd blow-dried my hair and was sitting on the little bench covered in chocolate silk, putting makeup on at the wide and handy built-in makeup vanity, when I heard it.

A crash in the other room.

For a second, I froze.

Then I got up and raced into the other room.

Ian was standing in the sitting room, phone to his ear, head bent, hand at the back of his neck, and I saw one of the glasses from his personal drinks cabinet in shards on the floor.

"Yes, yes. I'm all right. Just find out who the fuck did this shit," he snarled into the phone.

He then beeped it off, tossed it on the couch and scowled at the shards of glass.

"What's happened?" I asked.

He turned to me. "I've paid for expedited tests. And my suspicions have been confirmed. The whisky had traces of Valium. The Amaretto, psilocybin."

"Psilocybin?"

"It's a psychedelic. Did you dream last night?"

I hadn't.

I shook my head.

"Then it's also highly likely that's been assisting you in having such vivid, imaginative dreams."

Dear God.

Someone had been drugging me.

Us.

"Holy crap," I breathed.

He stared at me.

"What?" I asked.

"I hesitate to share this, but none of the other liquor was tainted. Just what I drink and what you and Portia drink."

"What's that mean?" I breathed.

"It means whoever this is seems to be targeting me and you two."

I didn't ask why. He wouldn't know.

"Kathleen told me it wasn't much," he shared. "Less than a micro-dose when drunk one glass at a time. But prolonged exposure might have a layering on of effects. Specifically for the psilocybin."

I didn't know how to feel, or at least not how to process all I was feeling, when I noted, "That seems to be a definite possibility with me."

"Yes." Then he exploded, "*Fuck!*"

I started to get closer to him. "Ian."

He lifted a hand to me. "I need a second, Daphne."

I stopped.

"I ran into Jack yesterday," he began. "I've known him since he was a lad in the village. And I couldn't stop my mind from exploring every possible slight me or one of my family might have delivered to make him do something like this."

That had to seriously suck.

"Oh, honey," I whispered.

"Rebecca brought my lunch to the Brandy Room yesterday, and I watched her like a hawk to see if she'd give anything away. She didn't miss it, and now she probably thinks I'm some kind of lech."

"This is a lot for you," I noted.

"It's a lot for all of us."

"Like you said, you're on it and we'll have answers soon."

"Not soon enough."

"Yes, but soon," I stated firmly. "Can I come to you now?"

He did the chin lift again, it was a little less warm, a lot jerkier, but it was still affectionate.

I went to him and put my arms around him. He returned the gesture.

"I'm sorry someone drugged you in my home, sweetheart," he murmured.

I gave him a shake. "It isn't your fault, Ian. I'm angry the orgasm I gave you has worn off so soon."

He blinked, then finally he gave me a smile.

"Shall I remind you?" I offered.

"I'm not about to say no."

He seemed to be shifting us to the bed.

But I stopped him when I dropped to my knees.

"Daphne," he whispered.

I looked up at him. "Hold on, baby. I'm about to rock your world."

That got me a big grin and him threading his fingers in my hair.

Then I set about rocking his world.

"Why are we doing this again?" Portia asked.

"Just humor me," I muttered, staring intently at painting number seven we'd found in my dogged attempts to track down all that showed Alice and Wolf.

Don't ask me why, but I was faintly obsessed.

On the other hand, with Ian holed up with Richard and Daniel, it was something to do.

This one was in the hallway of the southwest wing. I'd walked by it multiple times when I was in the Carnation and Rose Rooms. And, yes, I had noted it when I did.

It was much like all the rest, but with two big differences.

In the others, Wolf was always in armor, most of the time wearing a helmet. But if he wasn't in armor, his hair was dark.

In this one, he was like my dream. Fair-haired with the stamp on his features of arrogance and pride.

In fact, this picture must have been what struck my subconscious because he looked a lot like the man in my dreams.

As did she (it was the flowing blonde tresses that hit her waist, in many of the other portraits, she was veiled).

The other thing was that, in all the others, he'd been in Proud Warrior (not yoga) Pose or Lord of the Manor Pose. Straight. Tall. Mighty. His face carrying the expression of superiority.

But this looked like a romance novel cover.

They were standing on a moor. Alice was at his side, her hand on his chest, head tipped back, gazing up at him adoringly. He had his arm wrapped possessively around her waist, his other hand covering hers on his chest, head tilted down toward her, matching her look.

"This is kinda...gorgeous," Portia said, and I turned to her to see her examining the picture. "It makes me feel...happy."

Yes.

And not just happy because we were girls and prone to respond to romantic images like that.

There was something more.

Before I could put my finger on it, we heard, "There you are."

We turned to see Lady Jane leaving the landing and coming to us.

"I thought a walk would be the thing," she suggested.

I could see she definitely did, currently wearing outdoors gear that would keep any countess warm in style as she strolled her country estate.

"I thought you two might want to join me, but I love you found Alice and Wolf," she finished.

She stopped at us and gazed contentedly at the picture.

And then she shared, "Adelaide had this commissioned. It's one of my favorites in the house."

It felt like a bolt hit me at learning this news.

Which was why I sounded strangled when I asked, "Adelaide?"

She made no note of the tone of my voice when she turned my way and nodded. "Yes. Adelaide. There are those who say this is less Alice and Wolf and more her and Augustus. She was indeed blonde, but he dark. But it's more than just his hair color. It doesn't look a thing like them."

It didn't, though there was a bit of Augustus in Wolf, which would not be right in reality, since Augustus would be the descendent of Cuthbert, not Wolf.

"Do you know much about Alice and Wolf?" I asked.

The penetrating look she turned on me had my heart skipping a beat.

"Every countess knows of Alice and Wolf."

"What do you know?" I pushed.

She tipped her head to the side in that way of hers. "Has Ian spoken of them?"

"He said they didn't get along."

She turned back to the picture. "Yes, that *is* the story."

Though she said it like it *wasn't* the story.

"They look pretty happy here," I noted leadingly.

"Yes," she agreed.

But she said no more.

"I—" I began to coax further out of her.

However, I got nothing more out because we all went still when we heard a scuttling in the wall.

"Where are the men?" I whispered.

"With Richard in the Whisky Room," Lady Jane whispered back.

"You're sure?"

"I just popped in to tell them I was going to find you and go out."

I turned to her. "Where's the entry into this wall?"

She'd never looked motherly at all.

She did when she started, "Daphne—"

I grabbed her arm urgently. "Where's the entry into this wall?"

"Narcissus."

"Get Ian," I said.
"I don't think—" she tried.
I didn't listen.
I took off.

Thirty-Seven

THE PASSAGEWAYS

I found the hidden panel easily in the cheery yellow and white bedroom, and as I had seen Ian had done, I pressed against it.

It came unlatched immediately, springing away from the wall about half an inch.

I opened it more and wondered at my sanity when I peered into the gloom.

Then I heard a creak down the way...above me.

There was nothing for it. I engaged the flashlight on my phone and headed in.

This wasn't a stairway, this was a passageway, but it did lead to a stairway, one that only went up inside the wall which on the other side would be the grand stairwell.

That was where the sound came from, so I went up and there was nowhere else to go. There was also no one there. It was a landing.

Except it had a door. I could see the ring that could be used to pull it closed.

I pushed it open.

And found myself in a bedroom on the second floor.

This one, the furniture was again covered in sheets.

But unlike how they kept the house, the door was open.

I moved that way, out of it, and looked left.

I couldn't be certain, but I thought I saw someone going into a room down the hall, beyond the stairwell, in the southeastern wing.

I ran that direction, entered the room, and yes, you guessed it, a quick perusal exposed a hidden door.

Worse, I heard someone in the wall.

My heart beating madly, I opened the door, went in and shined my flashlight.

Well down the dark hall, I saw shadowed movement going up.

I raced down the hall, my feet in my booties pounding on the threadbare carpet under them.

Not exactly stealth, but they were far ahead of me, and this was a big place, easy for them to lose me.

I heard a slam above me.

I chased up the stairs.

Another landing, I pushed through the door.

And stopped dead when I saw the twenties style, black evening shoe on the floor. The T-strap was silver leather.

I shook myself out of it and raced out of the room.

And thus commenced chasing a shadow through the house.

But it was definitely not a shadow. It was somebody. I heard their footfalls and followed them.

Into rooms.

Down passageways.

Up and down stairs.

They were just always out of reach.

And worse, sight.

We were heading down to the ground level, but right when I exited the passage—the door left open in their haste, I thought—some kind of blanket or rug was thrown over my head and I felt a hand in my chest, shoving me back.

I threw my arms out to stop myself and the back of my forearm slammed against the doorway to the passage. Wood crashing against bone, the pain registered, which was most unfortunate.

I curled it in instinctively to cradle it, when I should have used it to help find my footing. I crashed into a wall, teetering and trying to pull the thing off my head.

That was when I went flying.

Down the stairs. The thing on me sailed off (though, it felt more like it was *pulled* off), and thank God, I somehow managed to grab a railing. It was this which stopped me from falling down the entire flight of stairs.

I'd had my breath knocked out of me, though, and the tumble hadn't felt good. I had to take a moment to get my wind back.

I looked around, and no one was there. Not a soul to help me by grabbing that blanket.

Another shiver snaked along my spine.

I was sitting on a tread when I heard a crashing of footsteps above me, looked up, and was blinded by a phone's light.

I put my hand out to guard against it when I heard, "Bloody hell, are you hurt?"

Richard.

"Go," I told him then pointed to the still-opened door I'd been shoved through. "He went that way."

"He? Who?"

"He. She. I don't know. I just know I saw them, I heard them, and they went that way."

He hesitated. "I don't want to leave—"

"Richard!" I yelled. "*Go!*"

His back shot straight. "Assure me you're all right."

"I'm fine. Go."

He wasted another ten valuable seconds.

Then he went.

WE WERE all in the Pearl Room.

Portia sat on the sofa across from me, giving me big eyes anytime I caught hers.

Like right now.

My attention shifted, and I watched Lady Jane pinch some invisible lint off her wool trousers from where she sat, legs crossed, next to Portia. Cool as a cucumber, even though I questioned its existence, she flicked the lint away.

The men were standing: Richard and Daniel scowling at me, Ian prowling the room.

Newsflash, whoever it was got away.

And whoever it was, was not a member of staff, unless they'd returned on the sly.

All others were accounted for and had been busy doing their duties when all this was going on.

I couldn't take this silence, of which there had been about fifteen minutes of it after Ian gathered us here.

So I started, "Ian—"

"*Quiet!*" he bellowed.

I fell silent.

Not because he told me to.

Because he'd never shouted at me.

I didn't like it.

He immediately went back on his command when he then asked, "Have you bloody *gone mad*?"

"I—" I started.

"Chased after some deranged lunatic who's trying to terrify us in our own *fucking house*," he finished for me.

"It's just—"

"Incredibly foolish?" he suggested.

I crossed my arms on my chest. "Since you're intent to carry on this conversation by yourself, I'll let you do it," I stated crossly.

"You fell down the fucking stairs, Daphne."

"Only a few."

"Only a few?" His tone was incredulous. He leaned my way. "*Are you insane?*" he roared.

I remembered I was going to be silent while he worked his shit out, thus, I went back to that.

"So, do I have this straight, darling?" he asked sarcastically. "You heard someone in the wall. You, by yourself, with no weapon or training to say, do a bloody fucking thing if you caught this person, chased after him through the staff passageways, of which you have experience traversing only one in *fucking dozens*. And you ended up falling down *only a few* stairs when you could have tumbled down the whole fucking lot and *broken your goddamned neck!*"

He ended that shouting again, so I kept silent.

"I'll repeat," he said dangerously, "have you gone bloody mad?"

I changed my mind about silence. "If I caught them, or at least saw them, we'd know who was behind this."

"I'm finding out who's behind this," he hissed. "I don't need you racing through the walls in assistance."

I glared at him.

He scowled at me.

Daniel entered the conversation at this point.

"It *was* bloody stupid," he groused.

"Daniel!" Portia cried.

"Lovely, it was," he spat.

"She was trying to help," Portia defended me.

"She should have found one of us men," Daniel proclaimed.

Portia's face instantly went red, and she lost it. "One of you *men*? So a little ole woman can't take down the bad guy?"

"She fell down the stairs," Daniel shot back.

"I know. And I don't like that either. But is she now to be tarred and feathered because she was trying to do the right thing?" Portia retorted.

"What's in question is if it *was* the right thing," Daniel returned.

"Oh my God," Portia snapped then looked at me. "Men!"

At this point, Lady Jane rose.

"All right, children. What's done is done. We can't undo it." She looked down at me. "Although I applaud your bravery, I can't commend it, because it was indeed not exactly intelligent to chase after the villain in that manner, and you could have hurt yourself badly." She turned to Ian. "And I understand this frightens you, and being male, fear is expressed through anger. But, my boy, you need to get a handle on it before you say something you regret." Onward to Daniel. "You need to stay out of it." Then to Portia, "Your support of your sister is lovely, dear."

Delivering all that, she looked to Richard.

"Dearest, we need to let the young ones sort themselves out. I feel like Indian for lunch. I'm going to the village. Would you care to join me?"

"Gladly," Richard replied.

He collected her and they walked out of the room arm in arm like they were promenading beside the Serpentine.

"Good luck," Daniel said to Ian, then to Portia. "Let's go."

She got up but warned, "I'm only going with you because I don't want to be alone in this house, but Ian needs us to leave so he can *apologize* for being a *meanie*."

A *meanie*.

I almost laughed.

I was way too pissed to laugh.

They took off too, with Daniel trying to grab her hand, but she pulled it away from him.

Which left me with Ian.

I returned my glare to him.

He walked to me, and I sat very still in umbrage as he reached toward me.

He didn't touch me, exactly.

He pulled something from my hair, and when he came away, I saw the nuance of the gossamer of a cobweb.

Ulk.

He brushed it off his fingers and moved to recline, legs crossed, in the corner of my couch, arm stretched across the back.

I scooched away from him.

But I found his deathly calm unnerving.

"Promise me you'll never do something like that again," he demanded in a voice much like his current attitude.

"What would you have done?" I asked.

"Chased after him. But I have several pounds on you, several inches, and I know those passages like the back of my hand, playing hide and seek with Danny, cousins and friends, and other fuckwittery kids get into when they're young."

"Did you find the shoe?"

"Yes."

"Is it Dorothy's?"

"From the pictures of her that night, it appears to be."

"Was that shoe, to your knowledge, housed in storage here in this house?"

"Not to my knowledge, no."

"So this is our bad guy, or girl, and they're escalating in the creepiest way imaginable."

"Daphne—"

"I don't need my boyfriend dressing me down in front of his parents, brother and my sister."

"Then don't do anything else that's stupid."

Oh.

My.

God.

I moved to stand up.

He caught my hand and pulled me back down, much closer to him. I was almost on his lap.

"Ian, I wish to leave."

"I know you do, but we're making a deal right now that when we have an argument, we sort it. One doesn't leave the other and stew, which invariably makes it worse. We *communicate* and move on. We're communicating."

It was tough to find the high road when someone was hogging it.

And now, woefully, I was understanding Daniel's actions of the day before.

I went back to glaring.

"Do we have a deal?" he asked softly.

"You can't fight fire with maturity, it's annoying."

His lips twitched.

I narrowed my eyes on them.

"You said the other day, that when a woman doesn't want to talk, you wait until she's ready," I reminded him.

"I meant Danny and Portia. Not you and me."

Ugh!

"You're infuriating."

"I've seen my marks on you," he whispered. "I like them. I'm proud of them. I love leaving them because I love fucking you. Hard. You've made no attempt to hide you love it too. What bruises will I find on you tonight, love? Hmm?"

Okay, maybe it was a *little* foolish I went racing through the dark corridors with nothing but a phone flashlight and adrenalin to aid my pursuit.

And yes, if I'd fallen all the way down those stairs, shit could have been real.

And finally, yes, I'd likely have been powerless to do anything if I caught him (or her). And in order *not* to get caught, who knew what they might have done with me? What was known was that they effectively shoved me down some stairs.

But I wasn't ready to admit to any of that out loud.

Ian, in my *fucking brain*, read my thoughts and tugged on me to pull me into the curve of his arm, murmuring, "Come here."

"I'm mad at you," I said, even as I slouched into him.

He curled me closer. "You're mad at what's happening. And you're scared. You aren't mad at me, outside of knowing I'm right, and that wounds your pride."

Argh!

"So do I have your promise?" he pushed. "You'll let me figure out what's going on?"

"It's not right that Dorothy's shoe was up there, Ian."

"No, it isn't. But it's another clue, and we'll use it to figure out who's doing this."

I grew silent.

"You haven't promised," he prompted quietly.

"Okay. Okay. I promise not to go chasing bad guys in scary-as-shit, dark walls."

He gave me a squeeze, let me get over it then said, "Mum's right. It was brave."

"Whatever," I muttered mutinously.

"Though also right it wasn't commendable."

I tipped my head to glare at him again. "You've made your point."

"Good," he murmured, his eyes moving over my face like he was belatedly trying to figure out if I was unscathed, though, when he'd gotten to me earlier, he'd done an all-over body scan with eyes and hands.

Or he was memorizing it should I do something idiotic again and break my neck.

"Was she right about you using anger to cover you being frightened?" I asked snottily.

"When Mum and Portia told us you took off after a noise in the wall, I was terrified out of my brain."

I sat motionless, staring at him.

"Whoever is doing this isn't right in the head, and you were chasing after them."

"Ian—"

"When Dad told me you'd taken a tumble down the stairs, it felt like my heart stopped."

I pressed my lips together.

"In other words, yes. Mum was right about me too."

Okay.

Damn.

"I'm sorry," I whispered.

Another squeeze and, "You're not going to do it again. It's over. You're fine. We're fine."

"I'm also set to leave on Sunday," I pointed out.

"Me as well. And you're correct, we should move on from this and talk about that. Are we landing at your place or mine when we get to London?"

I blinked.

He made a decision. "I have to drop off papers at my office. I'll go to my place and pack a bag. Next weekend, though, you're all mine *at* mine."

"So we're going to continue with this kind of intensity?" I hazarded.

His brows ascended. "I see no reason not to. I enjoy being with you. I very much enjoy fucking you. I enjoy more getting to know you. And now, I'd rather not change the habit of sleeping with you at my side. Do you have reservations?"

I smiled. "Not a one."

His eyes fell to my mouth. "Then it's sorted."

It totally was.

"In retrospect, you're hot when you're pissed off," I told him.

"When it comes to you, I'm hot all the time."

I rolled my eyes.

Taking my chin in his fingers, he pulled me to him and kissed me.

Then he proved how hot he was for me as we made out on the couch in the Pearl Room.

Thirty-Eight

3:03

Our Saturday had been blissfully peaceful.

And Duncroft, when I wasn't chasing anyone through the walls or being drugged, was heaven.

Ian and I had started it with a lazy morning in bed (and that was also heaven...in a bed). We'd gotten up to take a long walk on the moors with Danny and Portia. Ian and I then spent the afternoon in the kitchen. Bonnie and I made a *fraisier* to be served with dinner while Ian chatted with us and made me fall a little bit further for him as he watched me work like I was sculpting David.

He also demanded to lick all the bowls.

The first was sweet, watching him taste my work was hot.

Now, it was our final night, and I'd packed as Portia instructed me.

In other words, I'd saved the best for last.

Walking into the sitting room at six forty-seven that night, I came out wearing a black evening gown with mesh panels at the sides and all of the racer back, except along the zipper. It had a cut at the neckline, a slit up the side, fit my upper body like a dream, and fell in graceful folds to the floor with a small train at the back.

Ian, wearing an impeccably cut three-piece black suit and white shirt opened at the collar, took one look at me and whispered in a silken voice I heard across two rooms, "I'll never tire of you."

I stopped and swished my hips, replying, "Well, thank you, milord."

"The paparazzi won't be a problem. But they will feed on you. You're dazzling."

I stopped swishing and stood stock-still.

He held a hand out to me. "I'll fuck you in that dress later and enjoy thinking about it all night. Now come here, we're already late."

Mutely, still overwhelmed by what he said, I went there and took his hand.

When he had purchase of it, he reached for the other and twisted it gently so he could see my outer forearm.

The bruise (one of many, but the only one visible in that dress) where I'd slammed my arm on the doorjamb had risen in brownish-purple relief.

I then watched with absolute fascination as he raised that bruise to his lips and touched them there tenderly.

And yes. After that, I fell for him even further.

Finally, arm in arm, of course, like we were strolling the Serpentine, he led me down to the Wine Room.

IAN STOOD BY THE BED, his suit still on, only his trousers open, and he fucked me while I lay on my back, fully clothed.

Yes, he'd tossed my skirt up.

I watched the savagery of his expression, felt it driving into my body, and I came for him with just that.

While I did, I heard my dress tear as he wrenched it at the bodice before he tugged my nipple.

I cried out and came harder.

When I came down, I watched with captivation and awe as he worked for, then found his.

He bent over me when it left him.

He kissed me tenderly and then promised, "I'll have your dress mended."

"I'm never wearing it again, but I'm keeping it, and I want it to stay torn as a memory of just how awesome that was."

His eyes heated, and he kissed me again, but not tenderly.

I stroked his cheek when he finished and whispered, "You're dazzling too, you know."

Ian smiled at me.

~

I SLEPT but did not dream.

Even so, I opened my eyes, and I knew why.

I looked to the time on the tablet.

It was three oh three.

I slid away from Ian, and in the moonlight, walked through his bedroom, his bathroom, to his closet.

We'd carried on with our activities, fallen asleep naked in our exhaustion, so I put on my pajamas, shrugged on Ian's big, navy velour dressing gown that was on a hook, but I'd never seen him wear it, and walked out.

I stopped this time to see through the moonlight he'd turned to his back, covers up to his pecs, and he was asleep.

He was still lord of the manor in his slumber.

Sheer beauty.

He was no longer secretly being dosed with Valium, but I knew why he slept now, and since I didn't want to be gone from him long, I walked out.

I found her in the Sherry Room, a light lit by her side where she sat in the corner of the sofa, another one lit on the table between the two chairs facing it.

"There you are," Lady Jane said, setting her phone aside and smiling beatifically at me. She floated an arm before her. "Sit with me."

I went in and sat.

She had a tall stack of leatherbound books at her side on the couch. She picked them up and I knew their heft with how she did it. She put them on the low table sitting between us.

"I believe these are yours now," she said.

"Is the house talking to me?" I asked.

She did that head tipping thing and replied, "I believe it knows. I also believe that's fanciful. But you did arrive on your first day with us at three oh three."

Oh God.

Here we go.

"What does that mean?"

She sat back. "It is true that Wolf was not pleased he was going to be saddled with their sworn enemy's daughter as a wife. It's also true that Alice felt the exact same thing. Wolf and his father went to the castle on the cliff for the betrothal meeting fully expecting to be slaughtered when they reached the bailey. They weren't. They were treated to a generous banquet. Alice was presented to her future husband, and it wasn't that they hated each other on sight. It was they hated each other before they saw each other. This meeting, Daphne, did *not* go well."

"How do you know this?"

"Women were often discounted in history, but the women of this place,"—she reached forward and laid her hand on the books—"told their own stories."

I looked to the books.

I looked back to her when she spoke again, and she'd returned to being ensconced in the corner of the couch. The better to be comfortable while she answered all the lurking questions I had about Duncroft House.

"Wolf may not have wanted his bride, but that didn't mean she wasn't beautiful. So he would find to his frustration that he wanted something else from her. Unfortunately for him, she wasn't keen on giving it. Furthermore, she had a radiant smile and a gentle soul she showed not to him, but to others, thus his servants and vassals quickly fell in love with her, and he quickly became enraged they had from her what he did not. They clashed. Arguments and miscommunications and misunderstandings. Wolf, too, was a fine specimen. Alice didn't want to be taken with him, but she was. She found his honesty and disdain for courtly gestures refreshing. His men adored him, and she discovered it was his hearty sense of humor, generosity and loyalty that made it so."

She hesitated.

I nodded to tell her I was listening, though she couldn't miss it, since I was listening avidly.

She went on.

"One night, during a rather passionate argument, they both discovered why they fought so much. And for the first time in their marriage, they made love. This was such a momentous occasion. She couldn't know, because there were no clocks at the time, but it's understood by countesses since, from her retelling of her recollections of that night, this event put a lasting mark on this place. And it occurred very early in the morning. At three oh three."

I felt a whoosh as my breath left me.

Lady Jane kept talking.

"From then, every earl and countess has been married at three oh three. Because, and this was lost from record, except for what the countesses knew, but back then, Alice and Wolf's love was known as unrivaled, even by Paris and Helen, Antony and Cleopatra. It's the fate of the time and lack of resources that the minstrels' favored story of Wolf and Alice wasn't written down for all to know."

She took in a breath, and then continued.

"She despaired every time he went to war. She rejoiced when he came home. She gave him five children. They mourned the loss of two. The bones of a pretender are not buried under the foyer of this house, Daphne. Forever entwined, the bones of Wolf and his Alice are there. He died, at what was an old age back then of seventy-three. The next day, she simply didn't wake up. Everyone said she loved him, and her body understood she couldn't live in a world without him. So it coaxed her spirit to join his."

"You have to know, as beautiful of a story as that is, this is freaking me out, Jane," I informed her.

"I know. And I'm afraid I'm not done."

Great.

"Dorothy Clifton's death was an accident."

Oh my God!

It was breathless this time when I asked, "How do you know?"

"Because Virginia had no love for her husband, but she adored his son. And George adored his stepmother. Thus, he hated Dorothy and how she behaved, openly hurting the only mother he ever knew or would ever know. People were very taken with him playing his flute. All except Dorothy. She teased him about it. Told him it was unmanly. That night, in a child's tantrum, he snuck from his bed, and while William was consoling his wife in a session in Jacaranda, and David was imploring Virginia to thaw to him in an argument on the moors, Dorothy, her playthings not available to her, was in a foul mood. Drinking alone, George found her and tormented her with his flute. Playing it, even as she told him to stop. She chased after him. They made it to the top floor, and she tried to wrest it from him. Somehow in the struggle, she fell over the balustrade to her death."

And there it was.

"And George never played again," I whispered.

She shook her head. "Never again. It was a loss. He was extremely talented. But he went on to do wonderful things regardless."

"And you know this because he confessed it to Virginia," I deduced.

"Yes." She tipped her head to the books. "She protected him like any mother would and kept her silence. She even endured years of others thinking she was a possible murderess. But she wrote it down in these journals, like every countess has done. Our history is faithfully shared among each other, from Alice. Secret, but shared, to help the next, and warn others. At some point in modern times, the sheets of rolled parchment were painstakingly copied to the books. We all keep account of our time here at Duncroft."

"But both William and David were having an affair with Dorothy?" I queried.

She nodded. "This would have no effect on Virginia, except relief. It gave her a reprieve from David's desperate machinations to make her fall in love with him. The only lasting tragedy for her was George's upset that he felt responsible for Dorothy's death. For William's part, it had the unusual result of making him see how deeply Rose hurt because of his love for Virginia, and his dalliance with Dorothy. It also made him realize he'd somewhere along the way fallen in love with his wife. He worked for it and earned it. She forgave him, and they eventually moved from here to a small home in town where his practice flourished, and they did too."

Well, at least there was a happy ending for Rose.

"Did Dorothy die at three oh three?" I asked.

Her brows ticked together. "Why, no. It was around midnight."

"Things are happening to me at three oh three, Jane. Is it the house?"

"I feel the house knows its mistress. But no, dear, outside of that, it doesn't talk to us. It doesn't involve itself in our lives. It's just a house."

"Then that's one serious coincidence. Just tonight, it's three oh three when I woke up."

"That's because you are you," she said softly, "and I am me."

"What does that mean?"

"You got a Wolf. You got an Augustus. A Walter. And I got a David."

My heart broke for her, and you could hear it in my, "Jane."

She waved a hand in front of her and said, "My lot. I love him regardless of his flaws. He's given me two loving and handsome sons. We've managed to have happy times, once I learned to live with his penchants. He loves me, as David truly loved Virginia. He just thought he could do what he pleased. Just as David thought."

"It doesn't have to be that way," I pointed out.

"Did you forgive Ian for his high-handedness this morning?"

I did.

Damn.

"Some of us have bigger things to forgive. Ian was out of order in how he spoke to you. Perhaps understandably, but out of order. Daniel was out of order in how he handled Portia. But if we care for them, we find a way to forgive. I'm not perfect either. Richard is social. I'm an introvert. He loves to travel. I prefer to stay home. He finds his way to happy with me, even if, in several important respects, we don't share the same interests. It's no excuse, but I do sometimes wonder if I spent more time with him doing the things he enjoyed, if he wouldn't have strayed." She gave me a small smile. "But then I remember it's no excuse, and he knew who I was when he married me, so that's simply his lot, as I have mine. He did try to change me, but I'm me. Unchangeable. And the same with him."

I didn't have a response to that because she was right, and her choices weren't mine, they were hers, and for my part, I had no choice but to respect them.

"I'm sorry about Lou," I murmured.

"Don't be," she said forcefully. "You're not supposed to have favorites, but you gel with certain people. Ian and I get along splendidly. He butts heads with his father. Daniel can sometimes frustrate me. Richard adores him. Daniel wanted me to like Portia, Richard wants to give his son everything. The writing was on the wall with a meeting of the family. And Louella is family. It was inescapable. Awkward, but inescapable. Now,"—she kept her eyes steady on me—"even more so."

Well, as to *that*.

I looked down at the books. "I'm not the countess."

"Oh, my dear, I think we both know you will be."

I felt a lump in my throat.

"I despaired," she said quietly. "He so worried he'd turn out to be like his father, he let many suitable women slip through his fingers. He's a gambler. In a way, he made his fortune gambling. But he wouldn't gamble on love. Until you."

Until me.

I crossed my arms and rubbed them with my hands, like I was hugging that thought to me.

"It's only been a week, and I know I'm falling for him," I admitted.

"I know that too," she pointed out the obvious.

"But he's not Wolf or Augustus," I said carefully.

She smiled a knowing smile. "Ah. The tragic Cuthbert. Yes, he did give Joan children, but not her first. Her first was a true Alcott, Thomas's son. I know, I know," she said when I opened my mouth. "You wonder how *she* could know. Women of that time were careful to provide heirs, it gave them power. She was careful to provide Thomas an heir, a true one, in hopes of gaining some power. But the Alcott men have had a thing for blondes. Joan wasn't blonde. She was dark with blue eyes the color of sapphires. You can see this in her portrait upstairs."

TOO GOOD TO BE TRUE

I didn't have to, I'd been up there, and she was indeed dark.

So this meant it was not only Joan who gave the Alcott line their royal ancestry, but also their coloring.

I loved that she took over that way and enriched her line even if Thomas didn't deserve it.

Duncroft did.

"All this doesn't explain..." I took a hand from my arm and flipped it out. "You and me here, right now. It's eerie."

"Of course it's not. You leave tomorrow. With what's going on with my son, this conversation had to happen. I've been waiting for you here since ten thirty."

"Oh," I mumbled.

"You can't know how glad I am with how taken he is with you. You're a lovely woman with a kind heart. But I hope you never have to sit and wait until your son is done with his love so she can have a conversation with his mother."

I scrunched my nose.

"Exactly," she decreed.

"But I came right to you."

"This is my space. Where else would I be?"

"Your bedroom," I suggested, not adding *or about a hundred and fifty other rooms in this house.*

"I would hope you wouldn't disturb a woman in the middle of the night in her bedroom," she sniffed.

No matter what she said, or how she explained it, it didn't change the fact this was weird.

And I didn't buy the three oh three thing. There was no way to cypher three oh three was exactly when Alice and Wolf first made love. Or me dreaming about Alice and Wolf at all. I might have seen the painting, but dreaming about them like I did made my noting in passing of it a stretch.

Most of all, the numerous uncanny things that happened at three oh three.

Not to mention, Dorothy giving me the fatal clue as to what killed her. Or my dreams telling me about Rose and Joan before I even knew they existed.

Oh, and one couldn't forget that *something* pulled that throw off my head so I didn't tumble all the way down the stairs.

It sounded crazy, but even so. It didn't just fly off.

This house was looking after me. I felt it. I *knew* it.

But...whatever.

Coincidence or supernatural, I had no argument with the results.

"One last question. What happened to Joan, George's mother?"

"This is still a mystery, perhaps solved by what Joan wrote in the journals herself, and what Virginia discovered later. This being the butler at the time, a prim and proper man by the name of Johnson, found himself in the most unfortunate of circumstances. He fell in love with a maid. After some time of longing glances, eventually unable to resist her pull, they began an affair. Joan discovered it and had him sacked, without references, the maid too. They couldn't find employment without references, fell on hard times, and Johnson and Joan were seen later, arguing in the village. That very night, she was hung in the buttery. Johnson, nor the maid he'd taken as his wife, were seen again."

"So...the butler did it."

Her lips quirked. "It would seem so."

"A lot sure has gone on is this house."

Her gaze slid to the books momentarily and then she gave me a small smile and said, "You can't imagine." She stood. "Now let's get to bed. If you'd like to read some tomorrow before you leave, I'll run interference for you. In the meantime, I'll keep these safe for you."

I still wasn't sure they'd be mine because I wasn't sure Ian would remain mine.

But I hoped he would, so I grinned at her and said, "Thanks."

We turned out the lights and headed together into the hall, yes, you guessed it, arm in arm.

We made it to the foyer.

And as we did, sensing movement, we both looked up.

And at the body in the black dress plummeting down, I let out a blood-curdling scream.

Thirty-Nine

THE CULPRIT

The body careened off Persephone, and with a deafening crash, fell to the floor and flew apart on impact.

Jumping back, I screamed again.

My heart in my throat, Lady Jane and I clutching each other, I stared in shock, and it took a long moment for me to realize it was a mannequin dressed in a black flapper dress. The platinum wig on her head having flown off on landing, was resting several feet away.

I heard running steps, a commotion upstairs, a man's grunt, and I turned to Jane and ordered, "Stay here, I'm getting Ian."

I was halfway around the first flight when the lights came on, blinding me.

I then heard a man shout, "Stay right there!"

I looked up, my eyes adjusting to the light, and saw Sam leaning over the balustrade on the first floor, pointing at me.

When I stood still, he took off running.

Not away.

Up the stairs.

There were more noises on the top floor.

A struggle.

I started when someone touched me, looked and saw Lady Jane had joined me.

She took my hand.

I held it tight.

And then, at the landing at the top of the steps, I saw Ian in jeans and one of his long-sleeved T-shirts, and Daniel, wearing the same, shoving a man I'd never seen in my life toward the stairs.

They wound their way down, keeping him moving by pushing him, and Stevenson came out of the hall on the second floor.

Down farther, and more people emerged from the shadows. Richard. Christine. Bonnie. Jack. Rebecca, Harriett. And Laura.

"What on earth?" Lady Jane breathed.

"Go. To the Diamond Room," Ian ordered us.

I didn't quibble. Neither did Lady Jane.

We took off down the steps, and turning lights on along the way, we dashed to the Diamond Room.

Soon after, they all came in, *sans* Daniel, and Ian shoved the man to sitting on a couch.

He seemed to make a movement to get up, but stopped when Ian snarled, "Give me a reason."

He sat back.

"We'll wait until Daniel fetches Portia," Ian announced. "I believe everyone in this house deserves your explanation."

The man opened his mouth.

But when he did, Ian lost control, lunged at him and growled a ferocious, "*Shut it!*"

The man shut his mouth.

And boy, my guy was definitely hot when he got pissed. So much so, I had no idea what was going on, and I still didn't miss it.

It seemed an interminable wait, but finally, Portia, wearing one of Daniel's sweaters over her short nightie and some slippers, came in, her gaze darting around and landing on the man.

Ian started it immediately.

"As we're all gathered here, in Dorothy's favorite room, let's begin. You saw the light on in the Sherry Room, and since we were all leaving tomorrow, you decided tonight's the night, hmm?"

"I don't have to answer your questions," the man sniped.

"You don't have to, but you're going to," Ian said in his dangerous voice.

The man swallowed.

But he didn't say anything.

"Allow me to start," Ian said expansively. "You bribed one of our cleaning girls to pay attention to things, like what I drank, and what Portia drank. Something she couldn't see herself, but she could ask the others. This she did. Also to fetch things you couldn't get your hands on because the staff corridors didn't lead to them, and you couldn't risk being seen in the main house. Like David's pen. By the way, she's being arrested right now. It's frowned on by the police when someone is drugged without their knowledge."

I gasped, even though I knew this, I just didn't know who did it.

Portia and Lady Jane gasped with me.

And again, the man's throat convulsed with his swallow.

This meant Ian's deductions were correct.

"She also let you in," Ian continued, "Giving you access to the corridors, and probably keeping a lookout, or placing the items herself in rooms that have no access, like the Smoking Room and the Jacaranda Room."

He stared at Ian and kept his silence.

More proof, in my estimation, what Ian was saying was true.

"It wasn't meant to be Daphne you drugged. It was meant to be Portia. And me. Why me?"

"You're bloody perceptive," the man spat.

Indeed he was, for he was proving that right now.

"Ah," Ian replied. "So you wanted me fuzzy so I wouldn't notice your shit."

"It didn't bloody work," he muttered. "I told her to put more in. With your size, you'd metabolize it too easily. She didn't like doing it in the first place. She refused to do it again."

"That might serve her well now," Ian drawled. "As for the psilocybin?"

The man glanced at Portia.

355

I moved protectively toward my sister just as Daniel circled her with both arms, his glower on the man outright vicious.

I turned again to the man on the couch to catch him looking back to Ian. "She was the one who was supposed to leave here and tell others the story. You bloody lot keep your secrets. You would never do it."

"And Dorothy haunting the manor would sell more books, wouldn't it, Mr. Clifton?" Ian surmised.

I gasped again.

So did Portia.

Lady Jane obviously knew him, so she did not.

"You watched Dad enter the code when he let you in all those times to do your research," Ian said. "The combination to the safe, when he took you to the Brandy Room. So when you maneuvered your way back in, you could get what you wanted. Your mouse in the house told you about Portia and Daniel, how Portia was coming to visit. And you hatched your plan."

The man slumped into the couch, crossing his arms like an angry child, and said, "You've figured it all out. So I don't have to say anything."

"Yes. My investigators are thorough with bank records and ferreting out royalty statements and tracking prescriptions. It seems I'm not the only one who thinks your book is absolute rot."

The man's face flushed with anger.

"Dorothy was loved by her family, she takes care of you all to this day in a manner, does she not?" Ian asked.

The man looked away.

She did.

"The dedications in your book, both of them were sarcastic. Your private joke. You didn't think Dorothy had talent. You scorned her because you thought she slept her way to the top. And your parents didn't support you. They thought you were the piece of shit you are and disinherited you. So you used the only thing you had, and it was still Dorothy's, to make money off her very dead back. Going so far as to take her things from your family's archives, should you need to use those too. Like her shoes from that night. Her dress. One way or another, you were going to use all you had of Dorothy to line your pockets, and you did."

Boy, Ian's investigators didn't mess around.

And microdoses of Valium did nothing to affect Ian's perception.

Not at all.

"Now, let me tell you why you're here right now," Ian offered. "Stevenson has been losing sleep to keep an eye on the staff entrance, which has an entry close to it that leads to the corridors. We could have set up a camera, but Stevenson wouldn't hear of it. This house means something to him, as do the people in it. You didn't just violate the Alcotts with your devilries, Mr. Clifton, you violated our whole family."

Ian swung out an arm to encompass everyone in the room.

And yes, that right there was when my fall was complete, and I knew I was in love with him.

I looked to Stevenson who was standing, back straight, staring down his nose at Steve Clifton.

"Nevertheless, he didn't need to. My investigator was following you and saw you approaching the house. She phoned me. But Stevenson saw you come in," Ian went on, "and he roused the staff to creep around and find you. I'd already roused Dad and Daniel. Daniel and I were the ones who first saw you. Daniel used the corridors to round to the other side. And I watched you myself carry that mannequin to the landing. Then I watched you lie in wait. This was a big play. Were we taking too long to be terrified, Mr. Clifton? Or, at the end of our week together, was this your grand finale?"

"The girl told me what was happening. That the sister was having tricks played on her," he mumbled sullenly.

"So you thought you could ride those coattails," Ian surmised.

Clifton lost it but phrased it in an attempt to find the moral high ground.

"You lot think you can get away with bloody murder!" he yelled.

I looked to Lady Jane.

She glanced at me with an expression of *lips zipped.*

Not that I would say anything, but I didn't say anything.

"First, that was a hundred years ago. Everyone who was there is dead," Ian retorted. "More importantly, second, you don't care who killed Dorothy. You might be covetous of what we have and wanted to fuck with our heads because we have it, and you're a shit writer, apparently a shit son, and definitely a shit individual. But that's an aside. Mostly, you needed renewed interest in your dead aunt so it would sell books because you're broke, and your millionaire family doesn't give a flying fuck."

Clifton said nothing.

Thus, again, Ian hit the nail on the head.

"You weren't expecting to be caught. Just toss the mannequin, terrify Portia, or members of staff who found the things you left for them to find, or whoever would tell the story, covering as many bases as possible, and make a clean getaway, reaping your reward. You were there when Daniel and I tackled you, and now we're all here," Ian concluded. "Have I missed anything?"

"Go fuck yourself," Clifton sneered.

"No. Though I'll rather enjoy watching what becomes of you doing it to yourself," Ian returned.

On that stellar comeback, no one said anything for a long time.

Then, the police sirens could be heard coming from outside.

"This house and the one before it have been protecting our family for a thousand years," Ian said quietly. "Did you honestly think it would fall down on that job to the likes of you?"

"I'll be wanting to call my solicitor," Clifton replied.

"Good luck with that," Ian said, before he informed him, "None of this is good, but it also isn't that bad. But what you did when you shoved Daphne and she fell down the stairs will be considered assault."

Clifton blanched.

Casually, Ian turned, nodded to his father, and then Richard moved, herding the women out.

Epilogue

THE CONSERVATORY

It was necessary for me to share my story with the police, so I did.

After that, I was hustled with brusque, maternal clucking by Christine to the Conservatory, where I joined Portia and Lady Jane and was bundled in a fluffy, soft, woolen throw and given a mug of hot cocoa by Laura.

After some time, Richard came in to collect Lady Jane, but she didn't leave without giving a cheek kiss to me and Portia.

I thought that was sweet.

Daniel came next to claim Portia. She and I hugged for a long time before I let go, and Daniel stunned me by taking me in his arms and holding me tight for a moment before he too released me, and they went to bed.

As they left, Stevenson came in to announce that Ian was finishing up with "the local constabulary" (his words) and would be joining me shortly.

I accepted this news with a nod, and he turned to leave, but I called out to him, and he stopped.

"Thank you, Stevenson," I said quietly.

To my surprise, he executed a very formal bow, and when he

straightened, looked me right in the eye and said, "It was my pleasure, my lady."

And after delivering that, leaving me breathless and tingling, the butler of Duncroft vanished into the greenery.

It wasn't long after when Ian joined me, the sun kissing the horizon as a herald to dawn.

I waited until he'd collapsed beside me and lit his smoke before I asked, "Is it done?"

He nodded. "They've arrested Clifton. Taken all the statements. Dad and Daniel and I walked them around the house and showed them the evidence. They've taken pictures, their own fingerprints, collected samples of the liquor and the mannequin, and Kathleen is meeting them at the station to lay out what we found."

He took a drag, blew the smoke away from me, then turned back to me.

"The cleaning girl, her name is Trudy, was taken in for questioning. She's talking. Admitting everything. Apparently, she was getting cold feet. As such, she returned the flute but hadn't had time to collect the other things, some of which she didn't know Clifton had positioned."

Another mystery solved.

"Did something else happen to you in the Rose Room?" he asked.

"I don't know what you mean," I replied.

"They told me Trudy said something about your tablet. Clifton told her to download his book or something?"

And another mystery solved.

"Yes. I thought it was me. But someone opened it to that picture."

Ian nodded, took another drag from his cigarette, and blew it out.

"Alas, my darling, although things don't look good for Mr. Clifton," he carried on, "it's unlikely he'll be drawn and quartered for his shenanigans. He'll probably spend some time in jail, but not much of it. And when this hits the media, it's a sure bet he'll get what he wanted,

and his book sales will skyrocket."

I knew that was the sad truth.

But we'd endure it, we'd already endured worse.

And now, mercifully, that last was all over.

He took another drag from his cigarette, blew out the smoke, and turned more fully to me.

"Daniel took me aside," he announced.

"Oh boy," I mumbled.

After seeing the protective gestures Daniel treated my sister to while Ian was laying out the case, I was expecting him to tell me Daniel had shared he was going to ask for Portia's hand.

"He wanted to come clean."

That was a surprise.

"About what?" I asked warily.

"With what happened tonight, he wants it all out, and he's told me he's right now sharing this with Portia too, but he lied about not being out that first morning you were here."

I felt my lips purse.

"You were correct in your deductions," he informed me. "Brittany was furious Daniel was perfectly fine allowing her to serve his family and see to his new girlfriend. She was making more threats and demands. Alas, he had nothing more to give, so she told him she was going to tell Portia about them. He went out that morning to meet her away from the house to try to reason with her. His efforts, as we know, failed. And this, my love, is the real reason why he packed Portia up to escape later that day. He wanted to get her away from Brittany."

This was annoying.

However, now, everything was explained.

Except.

"Did you have suspicions it was Clifton?"

He took another pull from his cigarette and nodded. "Yes. He's the only stranger in recent memory who had been shown to the areas of the house he utilized. Including the Brandy Room. Dad showed him some papers there, and shared that Clifton was with him when he opened the safe. Although I suspected, I didn't want to entertain it. The fact someone on staff was letting an outsider into the house to wander at will unseen while we went about living our lives none the wiser was unsettling."

He could say that again.

I shivered.

He noticed and murmured, "We should go up. You've had a trying night."

"We all have. Finish your cigarette," I replied.

Ian being Ian acquiesced by taking another pull and wrapping his arm around me.

"It all came together when you saw him," I guessed.

"Yes, and no. When Kathleen called to warn me he was approaching the property before it culminated, she'd already told me they'd tracked him to a grubby flat in town. So he was staying close, which made him the prime suspect, and therefore she was keeping an eye on him. Sadly, they discovered this after his earlier visit and mad dash from you. But yes, after she shared that, I realized his intent was to terrify anyone who might happen upon some scene he created, and from what was already reported to me, his motive was clear. I know these types of maneuvers well. He was hedging his bets."

"Mm," I hummed.

His attention on me changed, and I knew why when he asked, "Did you have a nice chat with Mum?"

Nice wasn't how I'd describe it...exactly.

"Yes," I said.

"Care to tell me what you two discussed at three in the morning?" he requested.

I put my head on his shoulder and replied, "Perhaps someday I will."

"All right," he gave in gallantly. But then, his tone changed, it was very quiet, when he queried, "She knows, doesn't she? And now you do too."

"About?" I inquired cagily.

"Everything."

I sighed.

Then I turned and kissed his neck.

I settled in again and answered, "Yes, honey. She knows everything. Though, I suspect, the lady of the house always does."

Ian didn't reply.

He smoked his cigarette, and I sat cuddled into him while he did.

And when he was done, arm still around me taking me with him, he leaned forward and crushed it out.

"I'll ask Stevenson to dispose of the rest of these in the morning," he murmured, indicating his cigarette box.

It wasn't right, and I didn't have the energy in that moment to protest, but I was going to request he didn't. It wasn't healthy, but he could at least finish them. They had to be expensive, and it would be a waste.

Mostly, though, it was about memories of me and Ian in the Conservatory, and I didn't want to lose any part of our time there.

However, I supposed I'd get used to it.

He pulled the throw off me and helped me to my feet.

He went to the tablet and extinguished the lights.

Then, holding each other, Ian's arm around my shoulders, mine around his waist, we walked through the shadowed paths lit faintly with the coming day, into the deserted foyer, turning lights off along the way.

And we returned to the Hawthorn Suite.

~

TO TIE IT ALL UP...

DANIEL AND PORTIA didn't make it.

They gave it a go, but in retrospect, I believed everyone knew they were doomed to fail.

Daniel's expanded app launch was a resounding success, however. He and his mates dreamed up another one, and it, too, performed swimmingly (Ian invested in that one as well).

Nonetheless, all of this meant he was very busy and didn't have time to give my sister the attention she thought she deserved.

A mutual decision, they broke it off.

Though mutual, Portia was Portia, so it was also dramatic.

Daniel then turned his attention to launching a new social media platform, which was highly successful (Ian invested in that too).

Not long after the breakup with Portia, Daniel found a no-nonsense woman named Jenny, who took absolute zero shit. They married in a tiny chapel on the coast with only very close relatives and friends in attendance (Jenny's idea).

Daniel went on to make his own millions, and as such, Jenny could turn her attention from being a nurse to managing him, their home and their brood of four children (the number of children also Jenny's idea).

They bought a farm that had a big, rambling, stately house close to the coast and not near, but not far from Duncroft.

They were happy.

Portia found a position at Liberty.

She then invested her time, and her money, in opening her own boutique.

It was very stylish, and with her taste, offered beautiful things, but she wasn't a natural businesswoman. Even if she often asked Ian his opinion on how to run things, it stayed afloat on a wing and a prayer.

She eventually met a professor at Cambridge named Colin. He was tall, handsome, quiet, studious, whip smart, had piles of patience and worshipped the ground Portia walked on.

They married in a registry office with Portia wearing an antique forties, ivory satin, to-the-knee dress and a pretty fascinator. Lou wept. I signed their marriage certificate as a witness.

I often marveled at Colin's profound fortitude in the face of Portia's persistent antics (no, she never really grew up). And I credited him and him alone with keeping their two children's feet on the ground when she put great effort into spoiling them rotten.

But it worked with them.

Beautifully.

LOU'S SURGERY WAS A SUCCESS. Her migraines went away, and she found cute hairstyles to wear while she was growing back what they had to shave. She eventually fell in love with an old-money MP who was fifteen years her senior, married him, and along with their townhouse in London, she had her own manor to oversee in Kent.

But I had her beat; hers only had eighty rooms.

. . .

EVENTUALLY, I told Ian about Lou and his father. I didn't think it was fair, when things remained awkward between Lou, Richard and Jane, that he didn't understand why.

I also didn't like keeping things from him.

He, of course, knew. He'd just been doing the same thing I had, and thinking I didn't know, he was shielding it from me.

If he ever thought less of Lou, I didn't know.

More importantly, she didn't either.

STEVE CLIFTON, and Trudy, both did jailtime.

Though, as Ian suspected, not much.

I didn't keep track of Trudy, but Ian was also correct that the hullabaloo piqued interest in his book, and it sold scads of copies.

His family, however, was terribly embarrassed about what he'd done and wrote Richard and Lady Jane a formal apology on his behalf.

When Clifton was released, emboldened by the sales of the book about his aunt, and buoyed by his infamy, he quickly researched and wrote another one about an unsolved murder mystery at an aristocratic estate.

The reviews of his writing were scathing. Historians and investigators alike were quick to point out the shoddiness of his research, and as such, his findings. His continued bent toward misogyny was called out contemptuously and broadly on all social media platforms, and the book flopped.

None of this played well with publishers, and he couldn't find another contract.

His personal grand finale came not long after, when he drank himself to death in a drafty, dilapidated cottage on the Isle of Wight.

JUST TO BE THOROUGH, even though Michael and Mary were invited, Chelsea was not, this being to Ian's birthday party.

However, this was reversed at the Christmas bash.

She never said, but I suspected Lady Jane did that specifically because, by that time, I had an enormous, heirloom diamond-surrounded-by-rubies ring on my left ring finger.

Given to me by Ian.

As PLANNED, Ian showed at my place in London that Sunday evening with a bag in hand.

Then he took one look around my cramped Kensington flat, and, being the arrogant viscount-very-soon-to-be earl he was, he bundled me up and took me to his massive, modern, penthouse apartment with a view of the Thames.

Within a month, I put my flat on the market, because after that night, except to get my things, I never went back.

We started with a dog, a chocolate Labrador puppy I named Charlie.

Ian made threats that we'd never have children, considering how much trouble and oversight a rambunctious puppy brought to our lives. And he still grumbled, even if he took Charlie to his office with him every day, and when we were photographed walking him on the street or in the park, it was Ian who was always holding his lead.

Considering he effectively stole our dog, I came home one day to an adorable ragdoll kitten he presented me.

I named her Moxie.

She liked me.

But she adored her daddy.

I DALLIED in the vestibule past the allotted time on the invitations, so I walked down the aisle at precisely three minutes after three when Ian and I were wed in a sanctuary stuffed full of friends, family and villagers.

The pews packed, it was standing room only in the pretty church on the knoll in Dunmorton.

I'll never forget the look on Ian's handsome face when he first saw me, nor his bark of laughter that shocked everybody as it rang through the space.

But I *was* about to be a countess.

The bodice of my gown was lace and pearls with a low vee and pretty, all lace cap sleeves.

But the skirt was an enormous poof of countless layers of tulle that trailed behind me a good four feet. It was so huge, Mom and I barely fit as we walked down the aisle.

What could I say?

I wasn't about to let Alice and Adelaide and Anne down.

But most especially, Ian.

As for his part, he surprised me, and as we dashed out under floating, baby-pink rose petals on a warm summer day, a shining, open-topped carriage awaited us at the end of the path.

It was a long journey, and slow going, but I didn't notice it or anything else because Ian and I made out the entire way. And the driver was occupied, Ian was stealthy, and his mouth kept me quiet as my new husband's hand found its way under my skirts.

OUR RECEPTION WAS a garden party outside the back doors of the Conservatory at Duncroft.

It, too, was packed and alive with laughter.

Happy.

THE TITLE WAS TRANSFERRED, and the tours began, but to our surprise, Richard loved them.

Perhaps it was the awe he saw in the tour-goers' faces when they took in his family's legacy. Perhaps it was because he was indeed social, as Lady Jane said he was. Perhaps it was a bit of both.

But it wasn't unheard of for the deposed earl, to the irritation of the guides, to suddenly appear in order to confiscate a group and take them on his own private tour of his home so he could brag unashamedly and show them all his favorite places.

And then it was Richard's idea to open the house for free to student tours a couple of weekdays a month. Kids from all over the United Kingdom took field trips to see Duncroft House and learn about it and its part in England's history.

For those, only Richard played guide.

LONG BEFORE THIS, though, Ian, Richard, Daniel and Stevenson put their heads together, and although Duncroft had a security system (first floor windows and all the doors), a new, far more extensive system was installed.

Cameras and a room that was dedicated to video monitors and sensors.

Sam was promoted to head of security.

Along with that, all the panels were nailed shut, except those that opened to the Turquoise and Viognier Rooms. Those solely because the passageways made it easier to serve.

This was done to prevent any further high jinks, and possibly mishaps, from happening in the walls of Duncroft.

But also, and mostly, it was because the staff was part of our family, and we wanted them to feel that way as they went about their duties of looking after us and our home.

IAN and I remained in London after the birth of our first child, Alice, and our second, Gus (Augustus, obviously) as well as our last, Walter (though, he eventually earned the nickname Wolf).

But then city life became too much for us. Ian and his holdings, me and the patisserie, three kids, a cat and a dog, it was too busy and there wasn't enough time for the important things.

So I trained up my assistant chef, transferred my responsibilities to her, Ian cut back on work, and we moved to Duncroft.

Ian still worked, and I opened a patisserie school I mostly oversaw, but sometimes taught at, in some converted stables in the village.

Ian got Alice another cat. I got Gus another dog. We both presented Walt with his own pup.

Lady Jane and I, together, planned all the birthday parties, the Christmas party, the Bonfire Night, and we added funding a big fireworks display in the village for New Year's and an annual open house for the villagers on May Day.

Duncroft was no longer a great hall shrouded in mystery.

The tours were sold out months in advance, the ambulance service in the village was fully funded, and a small charity was created to look after the local elderly so they could remain in their own homes.

And again, due to Duncroft, money poured into the village, as two weekends a month, the tourists arrived.

The Bernini was ooed over, the Ansdell was ahed, and thousands of feet shuffled over the spot where Dorothy Clifton lost her life.

Under which the bones of Alice and Wolf were entwined for eternity, the foundation of a sweeping legacy.

YES, I read the words of the countesses who came before me.

Every last one.

More than once.

And some of it wasn't easy, for more than obvious reasons. Alice's entries were reminiscent of *Beowulf*, others were akin to trying to decipher Shakespeare.

But I got the gist.

Joan might have given the line her coloring, but it was Wolf who gave Ian (and others) his hotness.

Shoowie.

I scribbled my own lines at the end of the last journal.

And there were a lot of them.

I couldn't help it and didn't try. I didn't want future countesses to miss anything.

And I wanted our love story to be known.

So it would be.

TOUR VISITORS, students, dogs and cats, kids, staff, and Daniel and Jenny and their brood, Lou and her man, Portia and hers, also their children, my mom, visits from friends and further family, brought the house back to life.

And there was no denying, the house loved it.

It was what it was built for, naturally.

Say what you will, but I believe the house spoke, at least to me, and I believe it took care of us all, and not just providing a roof over our heads.

Then again, that might just be fanciful.

BUT EVENTUALLY, those sad days would come, and they did.

We lost Richard, then Lady Jane.

However, it wasn't simply our mourning that made it so Ian and I didn't move.

We never left the Hawthorn Suite.

Tradition be damned.

AND LAST, on the second floor, in the gallery, a new portrait was hung.

Very tall and proudly large, it showed me seated, wearing an edgy red gown that Portia selected for me. Ian was standing next to me, wearing a handsome, perfectly-fitting charcoal suit.

The collar of his shirt was open.

I had a two-year-old Walt in my lap. Ian had our four-year-old Gus on his hip, seated at his side was a chocolate lab, and standing next to him with her hand on Charlie's head, was Alice. Curled at my feet, was a ragdoll cat, at Ian's, a Himalayan, and seated panting at one outer edge was our English bulldog (Walt's) and lounging at the other one was Gus's springer spaniel.

We were placed directly across from the portrait of Adelaide and Augustus.

The perfect spot.

Ian, Alice, Gus and I were smiling.

Walt was giggling.

It was painted in the Conservatory.

The End

PS:
Oh!

It's important to note, I had my mind on other things, so I was in no state to check. But while her Grandpapa and Grandmama were in the city for one of their many visits (yes, it would take grandchildren to wrest Lady Jane from Duncroft, and they did, often), out and about entertaining baby Alice, her mummy and daddy were utilizing this much needed alone time in bed, making her brother.

And when that conception occurred, I couldn't be certain, but I was pretty sure it was three oh three.

Walt, as Walt became wont to do, made his own times.

However, I knew, because they kept track of these things, that on a very early stormy morning just two days before her father's birthday, after too damned much labor, Alice was born.

And I would never know what it meant, truly, but it gave credence to the legend.

Because that joyous event definitely occurred at three oh three.

The End

Author's Note

Daphne's assertion that the transfer of Richard's peerage to Ian being "weird" is correct.

I've taken liberties with British law for the purposes of this plotline in this story.

In actuality, hereditary peerages cannot be transferred until death. In other words, there could be no covenant that forces one earl to relinquish his title to his heir while the earl is still living. He can 'disclaim' the peerage for his lifetime under very specific laws, but no one can take it up while he's still alive.

Fortunately, I have a fabulous editor who shared this with me. On reflection, I liked what it meant for the story and the characters, so I took the decision to keep it in.

However, I feel readers should know, in real life, it's incorrect.

Acknowledgments

I can't express enough thanks to my editor and proofer, Kelly Brown and Stacey Tardif for diving into this book and turning it around so quickly. I get many wild hairs I don't hesitate to act on, and I drag my people with me. Their support in helping my stories come to life means the moon and the stars and beyond.

I don't mention my agent, Emily Sylvan Kim of the Prospect Agency, near enough in the work I do. She's been with me since the start, over ten years of working together, and she's tireless in putting my best face forward and helping advance my books in a very competitive industry. It's been an amazing relationship, and I'm privileged she's a part of my life.

As ever, a huge shout out to my reading cheerleaders, Liz Berry and Donna Perry. Like everyone, I need encouragement, especially in creating my babies. And their excitement feeds the process in such beautiful ways.

Last, forever and always, thank you to my readers for going along on many, many different rides with me. I hope you enjoyed this one!

Try More
Kristen Ashley Suspense

Ghosts and Reincarnation Series

Haunted houses, past lives and ghosts galore factor into this series. But fear not! I dislike horror or scary things, so it's not that. It's just that some things go bump in the night, though all of them aren't bad!

This series is really a gaggle of standalone books, but there are some lovable characters in *Penmort Castle* that appear in *Lucky Stars*. And may appear again somewhere...

Lacybourne Manor
Ghosts and Reincarnation Book Two

In 1522, the very night they were wed, Royce Morgan and his new bride, Beatrice Godwin, were murdered on their way home to Lacybourne Manor. After the cruel deed was done, a local witch came across their bodies, witnessing firsthand the tragedy of star-crossed lovers. Vowing that Royce and Beatrice would someday uncross those stars, using magic mixed with murder as well as true love, she linked their spirits together with hers (because someone had to protect them) forever...or until their reincarnated souls find happily ever after.

Now arrogant forbidding Colin Morgan lives at Lacybourne. He knows from lore (as well as the portraits of Royce and Beatrice that hang in Lacybourne's hall and the small fact that he looks exactly like Royce Morgan) that he's the reincarnated soul of his ancestor.

One stormy night, flighty, free-spirited, scarily-kind-hearted Sibyl Godwin comes to Lacybourne and it doesn't escape Colin's notice that Sibyl is the spitting image of Beatrice.

However, murder, magic, a warrior's heart beating in a modern man's chest, a woman bent on doing good deeds even if they get her into loads of trouble, a good witch whose family has vowed throughout the centuries to protect true love, distrust and revenge make a volatile cocktail.

This means the path to happily ever after is paved with tranquilizer darts, pensioners on a rampage, Sibyl's bad morning moods, heart-breaking misunderstandings and all kinds of magic, good...and bad.

Continue on to read an excerpt of *Lacybourne Manor*.

Lacybourne Manor

GHOSTS AND REINCARNATION BOOK TWO

Prologue

People try to explain magic in a variety of different ways.

They use the excuse of science, miracle, divine intervention, luck, fate and coincidence.

It's all just magic in one form or another.

~

And the purest magic is love.

And the purest, *purest* magic is *true* love.

~

Everyone has magical powers.

Some know they do.

Some would never believe.

Some are greater than others.
Some are good and kind and true.
Some are evil and wicked and violent.
And sometimes they all get tangled together.

~

This is the story of the purest, *purest* form of magic, *true love*.
It is a story about all kinds of magic, mixed up in a crazy, mystical mess.

~

Esmeralda Crane was there when Royce Morgan first laid eyes on Beatrice Godwin.

It was the Year of our Lord, 1522, and even though Esmeralda had already lived a goodly number of years in two centuries, she had never been blessed to witness true love.

He was handsome, a rich, land-owning knight wearing shining spurs. He had thick hair the unusual color of sunshine mixed with honey and eyes the color of the richest, most fertile clay.

She was dark of hair and fair of skin, her hair so dark it was only a shade lighter than black, and her skin so fair it was without blemish except for the freckles that danced across her nose. She had extraordinary hazel eyes. Eyes that could be more green then brown on occasion (with ire, which was a good deal of the time, considering her fiery nature), more brown than green on other occasions (with love or happiness, which was also a good deal of the time, considering her kind heart).

Esmeralda watched their stormy courtship with fascination.

There were times that his personality (which was mostly autocratic, reserved and often cynical) would grate roughly against her personality (which was buoyant, free-spirited and often explosive).

Esmeralda feared both these stubborn souls would never see the magnificent stars in each other's eyes and understand what kind of precious gift they had been given.

As ever, the magic of true love was victorious. Esmeralda should never have doubted it.

Even though Esmeralda wasn't invited, she created a glamor for herself so she could attend Royce and Beatrice's wedding.

One rarely had the honor of witnessing true love in the giddy hours right before its consummation.

But she felt the black soul there that day, dark as midnight. The soul was sitting in the church, as bold as can be, even though lightning should have struck it dead the minute its foot crossed the sacred threshold.

As Royce and Beatrice stood in the front of the church, Esmeralda saw the stars in the lovers' eyes.

Alas, Esmeralda knew those stars were now crossed with darkness.

She hurried from the church before the ceremony was finished, jumped on her sweet-spirited, but not very swift, nag so she could quickly get to her larder. There, she pulled out herbs, incense and oils, all the while muttering to herself. She put all of her efforts, all of her energy, all of her (considerable) power and all of her (even more considerable) magic into a protection charm that would keep the lovers safe.

Once done, exhausted with her efforts, she shrugged off her fatigue and scurried to Lacybourne Manor, frightened that she would be too late.

Nearly to the doors of the grand house, Esmeralda found that she *was* too late.

She came upon the newly-wedded pair outside the house, lying entwined under a copse of trees, the blood from their slit throats now fertilizing the soil around them.

Esmeralda wanted to cry, to scream, to keen into the night all of her despair that their love had not been consummated. The glorious consummation of true love, the like of the love between Royce and Beatrice Morgan, would have protected them like a powerful shield.

The old witch, no matter how tired, was not yet done with magic that night.

She picked up the delicate hand of the fallen Beatrice and saw the flesh and blood beneath the girl's fingernails. The same could be found under the nails of the once mighty knight.

Taking her dagger, she gouged the human particles from beneath the lovers' nails and also collected a dagger blade full of the soil that had absorbed the couple's mingled life blood. Lastly, she pierced the point of the dagger into her finger and squeezed her own blood into her powerful brew.

Working swiftly, the witch mixed the protection charm with a fierce shake. More of her conjuring was muttered, she opened her charm and sprinkled her potion around them.

Forever linking them.

Forever, through eternity, binding them together.

Until one day, many, many years in the future, the stars in the lovers' eyes would uncross.

Esmeralda knew the black soul would hunt them but she prayed that her protection charm and the added power of violence, death and true love would protect them.

The witch knew one day, they would find each other again.

And that day, they would need her.

~

Chapter One
Reincarnated

Marian Byrne stood at the door of Lacybourne Manor smiling at the last tourists that left through the grand entry.

At seventy years old, she'd been a volunteer for The National Trust working at Lacybourne for seven years. She had no idea how long she would be able to continue, her feet were killing her.

Marian was tall, straight, thin as a rail and had the energy of a fifty-year-old (or at the most, a fifty-five-year-old). Her hair was cut short, its curls dyed a peachy red that was *not* old lady peach but a color she, personally, found very becoming.

She was under strict instructions to have all the tourists and their cars and the other flotsam and jetsam cleared from the area before the man of the house came home.

Colin Morgan had inherited Lacybourne just over a year before. His aunt and uncle left no heirs, so upon their untimely death (he of cancer, she of a broken heart, the latter Marian believed although the doctors said differently) the man from London became owner of the grand house with its medieval core.

The old owners were not nearly as demanding as Mr. Colin Morgan. They would often mingle with the tourists and even open some of the private chambers.

Not Colin.

He closed the house all days except Mondays and Tuesdays and allowed it open only one Saturday a month. It was available solely from February through June, which was quite a muddle for The National Trust as that cut out the height of the tourist season and school holidays. And he expected all of the tourists and The National Trust pamphlets and laminated leaflets that lay about the rooms to be locked out of sight by the time he came home.

This would have vastly annoyed Marian, if she hadn't met Colin Morgan.

He was near as the spitting image of the man in the portrait that hung in the Great Hall.

For that reason alone, Marian knew she'd do whatever he required.

The day had turned gusty, the sky already dark with encroaching night. The clouds, long since rolled in, had begun to leak rain.

Marian began to push the heavy front doors closed when she heard a feminine voice in an American accent call, "Oh no! Am I too late?"

Marian peeked out the door just as thunder rent the air and lightning lit the sky, illuminating the woman who stood on the threshold.

Marian couldn't stop herself. She gasped at the sight.

The woman was wearing a scarlet trench coat belted at the waist and her long, thick hair, the color of sunshine liberally dosed with honey, was whipping about her face. She had lifted a hand to hold the tresses back but she wasn't succeeding. The tendrils flew around her face wildly.

"It's so hard to find time to fit Lacybourne in the schedule, it's rarely open," the woman continued as she smiled at Marian.

It was then that Marian realized she'd been holding her breath and she let it out in a gush.

The woman standing before her was the image of the *other* portrait that hung in the Great Hall.

She was not, however, dark-haired, like the lady in the portrait, but rather blonde.

Marian thought that interesting, considering Colin Morgan had the exact visage of the long since murdered owner of this house, except Colin's hair was dark, nearly black, rather than fair.

"I'm afraid you are late, my dear. We close at four thirty, on the dot," Marian informed her lamentably.

The disappointment was evident on her face, Marian could see it by the light shining from the entry. She was pleased at this. She hadn't been volunteering at Lacybourne for seven years without having some pride in the house. It was nice to know this woman on the threshold so desperately wanted inside.

There were other reasons as well that Marian was pleased the woman wanted desperately to be inside.

"Why don't you come back tomorrow?" Marian asked, her voice kind, her face smiling but her mind working.

She was wondering how she could finagle a meeting between the American woman and the man of the house.

For she *had* to find a way to arrange a meeting.

It was, quite simply, Marian Byrne's destiny.

"I can't, I'm working. I couldn't be here until well after it closes. I've been trying to find time to get here since last year."

"What time could you arrive? I know the owner of this house, perhaps, if I explain—"

"No...no, please, don't do that. I'll just try to get here next Monday," she offered politely then lifted her hand in a gesture of farewell.

Giving one last, longing look at the house, she started to leave.

Marian rushed her next words in an effort to stall the woman and then she fibbed (for, she knew, a *very* good cause), "He's a lovely man, he won't mind. I'll stay personally to give you a private tour. Or he might like to do so himself, considering how much you wish to see the house."

She'd turned back, hesitating. "I couldn't."

"Oh, you could," Marian moved forward and encouragingly placed her hand on the woman's forearm. "Truly, he won't mind."

That was an outright lie, Colin Morgan would very much mind. But what could she do? She could see the indecision on the other woman's face, Marian *had* to do something.

She forged ahead. "We'll set it at six o'clock, shall we? You can give me your telephone number and I'll phone you if there's a problem. What's your name, my dear?"

"Sibyl," she said, smiling her gratitude so sensationally Marian felt her heart seize at the sight. "Sibyl Godwin."

It was with that announcement that Marian's hand clutched the woman's arm with vigor far beyond her seventy years.

"I'm sorry, what did you say your surname was again?"

The woman was studying her with curiosity and Marian watched the spectacular sight as the hazel in the other woman's eyes melted to the color of sherry as curiosity became concern. Her hand, Marian noted distractedly, had moved to cover the older woman's hand protectively.

"Godwin."

At her single word, Marian couldn't help herself.

She whispered, "Oh my."

Lacybourne Manor is available everywhere.

About the Author

Kristen Ashley is the *New York Times* bestselling author of over eighty romance novels including the *Rock Chick, Colorado Mountain, Dream Man, Chaos, Unfinished Heroes, The 'Burg, Magdalene, Fantasyland, The Three, Ghost and Reincarnation, The Rising, Dream Team, Moonlight and Motor Oil, River Rain, Wild West MC, Misted Pines* and *Honey* series along with several standalone novels. She's a hybrid author, publishing titles both independently and traditionally, her books have been translated in fourteen languages and she's sold over five million books.

Kristen's novel, *Law Man*, won the *RT Book Reviews* Reviewer's Choice Award for best Romantic Suspense, her independently published title *Hold On* was nominated for *RT Book Reviews* best Independent Contemporary Romance and her traditionally published title *Breathe* was nominated for best Contemporary Romance. Kristen's titles *Motorcycle Man, The Will,* and *Ride Steady* (which won the Reader's Choice award from *Romance Reviews*) all made the final rounds for Goodreads Choice Awards in the Romance category.

Kristen, born in Gary and raised in Brownsburg, Indiana, is a fourth-generation graduate of Purdue University. Since, she's lived in Denver, the West Country of England, and she now resides in Phoenix. She worked as a charity executive for eighteen years prior to beginning her independent publishing career. She now writes full-time.

Although romance is her genre, the prevailing themes running through all of Kristen's novels are friendship, family and a strong sister-hood. To this end, and as a way to thank her readers for their support, Kristen has created the Rock Chick Nation, a series of programs that are designed to give back to her readers and promote a strong female community.

The mission of the Rock Chick Nation is to live your best life, be true to your true self, recognize your beauty, and take your sister's back whether they're at your side as friends and family or if they're thousands of miles away and you don't know who they are.

The programs of the RC Nation include Rock Chick Rendezvous, weekends Kristen organizes full of parties and get-togethers to bring the sisterhood together, Rock Chick Recharges, evenings Kristen arranges for women who have been nominated to receive a special night, and Rock Chick Rewards, an ongoing program that raises funds for nonprofit women's organizations Kristen's readers nominate. Kristen's Rock Chick Rewards have donated hundreds of thousands of dollars to charity and this number continues to rise.

You can read more about Kristen, her titles and the Rock Chick Nation at KristenAshley.net.

facebook.com/kristenashleybooks

instagram.com/kristenashleybooks

pinterest.com/KristenAshleyBooks

goodreads.com/kristenashleybooks

bookbub.com/authors/kristen-ashley

tiktok.com/@kristenashleybooks

Also by Kristen Ashley

Rock Chick Series:

Rock Chick

Rock Chick Rescue

Rock Chick Redemption

Rock Chick Renegade

Rock Chick Revenge

Rock Chick Reckoning

Rock Chick Regret

Rock Chick Revolution

Rock Chick Reawakening

Rock Chick Reborn

Rock Chick Rematch (Coming January 2024)

The 'Burg Series:

For You

At Peace

Golden Trail

Games of the Heart

The Promise

Hold On

The Chaos Series:

Own the Wind

Fire Inside

Ride Steady

Walk Through Fire

A Christmas to Remember

Rough Ride

Wild Like the Wind

Free

Wild Fire

Wild Wind

The Colorado Mountain Series:

The Gamble

Sweet Dreams

Lady Luck

Breathe

Jagged

Kaleidoscope

Bounty

Dream Man Series:

Mystery Man

Wild Man

Law Man

Motorcycle Man

Quiet Man

Dream Team Series:

Dream Maker

Dream Chaser

Dream Bites Cookbook

Dream Spinner

Dream Keeper

Moonlight and Motor Oil Series:

The Hookup

The Slow Burn

The Rising Series:

The Beginning of Everything

The Plan Commences

The Dawn of the End

The Rising

The River Rain Series:

After the Climb

After the Climb Special Edition

Chasing Serenity

Taking the Leap

Making the Match

Fighting the Pull

The Three Series:

Until the Sun Falls from the Sky

With Everything I Am

Wild and Free

The Unfinished Hero Series:

Knight

Creed

Raid

Deacon

Sebring

Wild West MC Series:

Still Standing

Smoke and Steel

Other Titles by Kristen Ashley:

Heaven and Hell

Play It Safe

Three Wishes

Complicated

Loose Ends

Fast Lane

Perfect Together

Too Good To Be True

Printed in the USA
CPSIA information can be obtained
at www.ICGtesting.com
LVHW040531131123
763725LV00001B/58

9 781954 6804